ALLY

BOOK SIXTEEN OF
THE GUILD WARS

Kacey Ezell & Marisa Wolf

Seventh Seal Press
Coinjock, NC

Chris Kennedy/Seventh Seal Press
1097 Waterlily Rd.
Coinjock, NC 27923
https://chriskennedypublishing.com/

Publisher's Note: This is a work of fiction. Names, characters, places, and incidents are a product of the author's imagination. Locales and public names are sometimes used for atmospheric purposes. Any resemblance to actual people, living or dead, or to businesses, companies, events, institutions, or locales is completely coincidental.

Cover Design by Brenda Mihalko.
Original Art by Ricky Ryan.

Ordering Information:
Quantity sales. Special discounts are available on quantity purchases by corporations, associations, and others. For details, contact the "Special Sales Department" at the address above.

Ally/Kacey Ezell & Marisa Wolf -- 1st ed.
ISBN: 978-1648552571

For all the Companions to all the Hunters. We honor you.

Prologue

The Hunter ignored the voices.

She'd been doing so for endless cycles. Since she'd driven away her clan. Since she'd gone into the city one last time to have her pinplants removed. Since she'd chosen the jungle for her death, whenever it managed to get the best of her.

You are the last, the voices said, even as she twisted her ears to focus on the rustle of iveri in the branches below her. *Come to me.*

She very well might be the last, from what the assorted beings she'd collected over the previous months had said. Perhaps other hunters stalked the jungles, far from clan and the broader world, though it seemed unlikely.

More likely, other hunters still roved out in the stars, though without clan, they would do what she had done—survive for a time, but fade. They would refuse to die easily, of course, so it would take time to come to the end of their lives.

Did they hear the voices too?

Why should they? The whispers wound through her skull, and she stared unblinking through the vines. *They didn't fail, not as you did. They weren't here. Come to me.*

The Hunter breathed through her nose, taking in the twined scents of bloodvines and treegore. She listened closely to the sounds of prey and predator making their way wide around her presence.

You are the last, and you are here. What will you do?

Her tail lashed, bones rattling, and she breathed deeper, again, until her lungs creaked in protest. She snapped to her feet, padded to the end of her chosen perch, and tilted her head.

"You do not climb well," she said, fur shivering as the voices receded.

"And yet, I climb." The voice was deeper than hers, not as rough. A voice more often used than her own. The formerly sigiled beings talked too much. Like the voices that followed her, they were unrelenting. Their words grated, unwelcome. She was meant to be alone.

She'd made a *choice* to be alone, as was proper, as was needed, so long ago.

Yet they'd come, and despite herself, she had chosen not to force them away.

"Why do you climb?" she asked, though she'd meant to ignore this too, as she ignored anything beyond the fight they'd taken up together.

"We have plans to make, Hunter, and we need you for them."

"You plan well enough." The Hunter sat and curled her tail close around her with a dry rattle of bones. This sigiled being was the worst of those who had gathered. The most dangerous.

This one had been well-loved by her Dama, and the Hunter could see why, but she hated it, the draw of this one. Zuul. Fighting race but not a fighter. Even hunters who chose not to hunt off-world still… *hunted.* They hunted hurts, energy, mechanical issues, and a myriad of other things that needed hunting.

But this Zuul, fighter who didn't fight, fought now and fought well. She watched the Hunter. Anticipated. Protected.

The Hunter snarled to herself. She did not need protection. Nor companionship. Nor beings to keep alive as she stalked the jungle, and yet…

She twisted her ears, rattled the bones she'd long ago pierced through her tail, and refocused on the Zuul. Aryo.

"Well?"

"We believe more ships have arrived. Traffic from the station has picked up."

They'd stolen assorted technology from the parties they'd destroyed, and Fip and Zia had been clever, tinkered, and created several ways to monitor the space above them. The Veetanho had learned quickly the safest way to navigate the jungle was to fly well above and never land inside. They flew above constantly, as though they had any chance of seeing inside, seeing *her*.

Though they weren't looking for her, specifically. Only for whatever haunted the sprawling jungles and brought death to their people over and over again.

"More Veetanho?"

"That we can't tell. Perhaps they've brought reinforcements from the Mercenary Guild to secure their grip on Khatash." Aryo finished pulling herself up to the Hunter's broad branch and crouched, not bringing herself too close.

The Hunter began to relax, then hissed. *Do not anticipate me, Zuul.* She'd meant to say it aloud, but the words snagged in her throat.

"Fip is wondering why they'd bother with Khatash at all." Aryo turned her long muzzle up and regarded the solid mass of the middle canopy above them. "Without the Hunters, it provides little for them, strategically." Her voice roughened over the last words, and the Hunter flared her claws.

"It provides plenty else that will kill," she replied, twisting her ears back, "provided they can live long enough to control any of it."

"Truth." Aryo dropped her head and briefly met the Hunter's eyes. "His theory is that they have no choice. The Hunters proved too much of a setback for the Veetanho here, and they lost influence in the Guild, or more has gone wrong, and this is serving as a retreat of some kind."

"A retreat that will be their end," the Hunter murmured, digging her claws into the wood under her. The vines woven through the branch shivered in protest, and the scent of treegore sharpened, bright and biting in the night air. "If more have come to join them, they are readying for a push into the jungle, or they have no choice."

"So it seems."

"Either way," she continued as though Aryo hadn't spoken, violence writhing through her words like bloodvines through tree bark, "they are desperate. Desperate prey can be more dangerous because they become unpredictable."

"The desperate also make mistakes."

"Indeed, sigiled Zuul." The Hunter rolled her head on her neck, then swept her hand through the curls of wood she'd peeled away from her perch. "Let them be dangerous. Let them be unpredictable. Let them thrash their dying protest and scream their last breaths to the stars."

"We have plans to make, Hunter," Aryo said again. "Will you join us?"

The Hunter cocked her head and lashed her tail, listening closely to the shiver of old bones clacking with the motion. The voices did not return.

"I will, Aryo."

The Zuul straightened, the breath she took in audible. The Hunter supposed she'd never used the Zuul's name before. Well enough.

"Perhaps it is time to bring the jungle to the city."

The Veetanho could bring all the reinforcements they could imagine. None of them would leave Khatash whole.

* * * * *

Part One

Chapter One

Fssik lifted his head and inhaled death, fear, and warm ocean wind.

"Are you nervous, my Human?" he asked, pressing his long, furred body next to his companion's legs as they walked down the ramp from the planet-side shuttle.

"A little," Ziva said. She dodged to the side to avoid plowing into another Human walking more slowly, and Fssik took the opportunity to leap into the air, twist his body around, and land squarely on her shoulder.

"I would tell you not to worry, but I try not to waste my breath," Fssik said, trying to inject some humor into his tone. "You know I will be with you every second."

"I know, my Hunter." Ziva reached up to run her hand along his furred side, and she continued to navigate the crowd as they made their way out of the arrival terminal and into the blindingly bright Azure afternoon.

With a thought, Fssik used his pinplants to engage the dark protective lenses that came from the slim, almost unnoticeable harness he wore around his ears and the back of his skull. The harsh light dimmed to a less-painful level, and he blinked rapidly then used his vantage point atop Ziva's shoulder to take a look around.

"This is a hospital?" Ziva asked, incredulity in her voice as she, too, stepped out of the flow of foot traffic so she could look around. They stood on an elevated terrace, with gracefully spiraling ramps

13

curving away from them on either side. Ahead of them, lushly mani-
cured green lawns stretched out for about three hundred meters,
where they abruptly ended in a hedge of brightly flowered green foliage. The hedge, Fssik realized, was more than decorative, for it kept
the patients and guests of the Cerulean Clinic and Spa well back
from the face of a cliff that fell to the turquoise waters below.

"Not hard to see where this place gets its name," Fssik murmured in Ziva's ear. "Between the sky, the ocean, and those three…
artificial ponds? I've never seen so much clear blue in one view."

"They look like ponds," Ziva said, pointing, "but they're swimming pools. Look, see that pile there that looks like porous lava
rock? It's got a slide worked into it—and someone's enjoying the
ride!"

Fssik turned and couldn't help slow blinking as a milk-kit-aged
Human slid, shrieking and splashing, down into the water where her
adult waited with raised arms and a wide-mouthed Human smile.
Like the cliff face, these swimming pools were wreathed in a colorful
riot of local flora. He felt Ziva's shoulders relax bit by bit as they
stood there, taking it all in.

"Ziva! You made it!"

Fssik wrapped his tail around Ziva's neck for balance when she
turned at the sound of her name.

"Alinore!" Ziva called out, hurrying forward with outstretched
arms. Fssik braced himself on Ziva's shoulder as Alinore and his
companion shared a hug. "I didn't know you'd be here already!"

"We're all here," the older Merc said, and she let Ziva go after a
good, long squeeze. "Can you blame us? Isn't this place something?"

"Beautiful," Ziva said, taking a deep breath. Fssik knew, with her
Human senses, Ziva wouldn't pick up the hospital scents he'd no-

ticed right away. That was a good thing, he decided, since she seemed to relax another degree. He looked around and noticed most of the people on the shuttle had already gone past. They were relatively alone.

"I greet you, Merc and clan-sister," he said, dropping his quintessence field. To her credit, Alinore didn't jump, but she did look up at him with her Human smile.

"Shoulda known you were lurking about, Flyboy," Alinore said, using her unique nickname for Fssik. "Are you ready to let your Human go under the knife?"

"Since it will be Esthik's knife, if I understand your Human expression correctly, I have no objections. Where is our Healer? You said everyone was here."

"He's down at the pool," Alinore said, "with Ward and Lara. It will be Ward's knife, technically, but Esthik will be there."

"Then I am satisfied."

"You guys know I can hear you, right?" Ziva asked, humor threading through her words.

"We weren't sure since you haven't gotten your Hunter upgrades yet," Fssik said without missing a beat, his voice dry as ever. He did, however, rub his cheekbone against hers in an unspoken apology for his joke. She lifted her hand and rubbed the spot he liked under his chin, and he knew he was forgiven.

"Well, let's go down to the pool if they're there," Ziva said. "I could use a swim to work off the travel restlessness before bed. Early start tomorrow."

"The procedure takes most of the day." Alinore nodded her agreement with Ziva's plan and turned to lead them down the long, curving ramp toward the lower level and the multiple swimming areas. They followed a black concrete path stamped to look like it was made out of individual rocks mortared together. It wound through the lush blue-green lawn and the brighter pops of flowers and shrubs. They passed by the three pools Fssik had seen from the landing and continued around the corner to a more secluded area.

"We've got this entire building and area reserved for our process," Alinore said, waving a hand at a long, low-slung building framed with more trees and flowers. Every ten lengths, a covered alcove held seating cushions and reclining apparatuses suitable for most species. Each of these alcoves had quite a few plants in pots around them. Overall, it was a lush, lovely setting.

"So, we have our own pool?" Ziva asked. Alinore turned and smiled over her shoulder and nodded. Fssik looked just past the building and saw that, indeed, another jewel-blue pool of water lay nestled in the grass and flowers situated just on the edge of the cliff, overlooking the ocean below.

"I think it's the best one in the resort," Alinore said, her voice smug. "I don't know what strings Ward and Auntie Tamir pulled to reserve this place, but I am *not* complaining!" She lifted her hand in a wave, and one of the figures in the water waved back. The breeze shifted, and Fssik lifted his nose to the air and caught the scent of three other members of his clan.

Strange, he thought as they continued toward the water and greeted Lara, Ward, and the Healer Esthik. *Not so long ago, I would have argued this group could never be a true clan, but here we are, working toward the same goals, and I feel just as much love for the Humans and the Wrogul as I did for my sister kitas when I was a tiny kit.*

"What are you contemplating so deeply, Hunter?"

Fssik slow blinked behind his protective goggles and focused on the face of the only other member of his species in evidence.

"Healer," Fssik said and leaped down from Ziva's shoulder to rub against Esthik's side. "I greet you. I was just thinking this is a strange kind of clan we have here."

"I've chased that scent myself," Esthik replied, returning the warm caress of his clan-brother. "But I cannot think to call it anything else, not after everything we've done and are about to do. Your Ziva, for example. She is willing to change her DNA just to be with you."

"I know," Fssik said. "It is not a small thing, and though we went through our own adjustments to compartmentalize our nervous systems… this seems bigger somehow."

"Perhaps because Humans are bigger," Esthik said with a shrug. "Who knows? But she is here, as are you, and it is good. Just as the water is good! You should swim. I think you will enjoy it. If you are relaxed, it will help Ziva relax before her surgery."

"Spoken like a sneaky Healer," Fssik said, twitching his ears in amusement. Up ahead, Ziva let out a war cry and jumped into the water like a half-grown kit.

"Why sneaky?"

"Because you know that I will do anything for her, so if you want me to do something, you make it benefit her."

"Ah. Well, yes. But that's just the way of things," Esthik said, with the philosophical air of one who deals with life, death, and difficult patients.

"Apparently so," Fssik said. Then he sighed and reached for the catch on his harness. "Well, then, Healer," he went on as he dropped the harness from around his body and continued toward the beckoning blue of the water. "Let us swim and relax so our Humans may do the same."

* * *

Fssik watched as Ziva's eyes drifted closed, and her breath evened out into the rhythm of sleep. He lay curled on the pillow by her head, content to soak up the time together before being separated for her surgery.

Esthik had been right. Healers were often annoyingly right, but Fssik couldn't deny the swim had helped him relax and stretch after being confined to the small spaces inherent in interstellar travel. Ziva had enjoyed the exercise as well, and Fssik felt a deep satisfaction in both her joy and the satisfied repose that followed.

After a while, though, his restlessness came creeping back. He trusted Esthik and Ward without question, but what they were doing was no minor undertaking. Ziva would be in recovery for some time, learning to use her enhanced senses and adjusting to the changes the protocol would create in her brain and body.

His ears perked up as a thought occurred to him. They *would* be there for some time, and he didn't know how soon it would be safe for Ziva to leave her recovery room. The time would go much faster if they had some basic supplies and comforts—things she liked, like the fat-encased wicks with the strong scents and soft soaps for her body and hair. This was a tourist destination as well as a medical facility… surely he could find that kind of stuff somewhere.

Fssik rose to all four feet and stretched his back, then he leaned forward and rubbed his face against Ziva's cheekbone. She'd settled quickly into a deep sleep, so she didn't twitch, but he whispered that he loved her, and he would return shortly. Then he turned and leaped for the door of their room.

A quarter-hour later, he wrapped his quintessence around him and walked out the resort's front door. Esthik had still been awake, so Fssik had told the Healer where he was going and asked him to look in on Ziva. Esthik had given him a look that said he would have done so anyway and then slow blinked as he left.

The night on Azure was as warm and pleasant as the day had been. The ocean kept the air comfortably humid, and Fssik felt a sort of *frisson* of energy as he walked into the streets outside the resort complex. It wasn't terribly crowded, but there were plenty of beings in vehicles or using their own locomotion to move along the street in both directions. He picked one group of Cochkala to follow and slipped into the flow of traffic, trusting that eventually, he'd find a store of some kind.

He found the bar first.

The Red Eye was the kind of place Fssik pegged as a merc bar right away. Either it was a popular place, or there was some kind of event going on, because the music and the crowd spilled out through the front door into the open area between the bar and the street. Fssik stayed cloaked in his quintessence and wound his way through the lower extremities of Humans, Oogar, Lumar, and even a growling Besquith Alpha who looked around as if she were searching for someone to eat.

Once inside the door, Fssik followed the scent of liquor through the roughhousing, dancing crowd to the bar, where a big Human stood pouring an amber-colored liquid from a tap into a mug. He hummed a strange, catchy little melody as he worked. Fssik jumped up onto the bar, let his quintessence drop, and then slow blinked when the Human didn't flinch.

"I greet you, Hunter," the bartender said, still humming in the pauses between words. "What can I get you?"

"I greet you, Human," Fssik said. "Welcome to our negotiation. I'm interested in information rather than beverages."

"Information comes at a range of prices, Hunter. What do you want to know?"

"Where can I find—"

"Just a second, please, Hunter," the bartender said. He put down the half-full glass and looked past Fssik, his eyes narrowing. Then he shook his head, flipped up a nearby section of the bar, and headed into the crowd. Fssik blinked, then pulled his quintessence around him and followed.

"Oy!" the bartender yelled as he approached a group of mostly Human mercs tussling on the dance floor. He waded into the fray and grabbed one of the combatants in a kit-hold, then flung him to the side. The merc stumbled backward, reeling into the crowd, arms flailing. The crowd shifted and shoved him back toward the fight. He reached into his vest and came out with a knife that glinted in the flashing lights from overhead.

Fssik leaped and twisted in midair to strike the merc's wrist with his back feet. He knocked the arm aside and dug in with his digits, sheathing his claws so as not to draw blood but clamping on hard enough to grind tendon against bone. The merc howled and dropped the knife, and Fssik let go and landed on his hands before flipping back up to his feet.

"I suggest you leave, now," he said, speaking from within his cloak of quintessence. The merc flinched, looked wildly around, then cradled his wrist to his chest and turned to wade out through the milling crowd.

Fssik turned back and saw the bartender had sorted out the situation. Or mostly so, anyway. He held two more mercs by the backs of their necks in the strong kit-hold and stared down at a younger Human male who was sitting up and wiping the blood from his nose.

"Where's your buddy?" the bartender asked, his voice gruff and low. Fssik dropped his quintessence and slow blinked up at him.

"I crushed his wrist and sent him away." He sat down in the middle of the dance floor and began washing his face. A murmured gasp rippled through the crowd, and Fssik saw several beings edge back from his position. "He pulled out a knife. Bad manners in a bar fight."

"Very bad," the bartender agreed. "My thanks, Hunter. I'm going to toss this trash out, and I'll meet you at the bar. Your information is on me."

"I accept the terms of your negotiation," Fssik said, and slow blinked. The bartender cracked a tiny smile before resuming his lilting hum. He turned to haul the other two toward the front door, and, for the first time, Fssik got a look at the side of the Human's head. Several pins glittered in a blue pattern just behind the man's left ear. Fssik blinked, curious, but resolved not to waste his free information on questions that weren't going to get him what he needed for Ziva.

"I greet you, Hunter."

The voice was rough and threaded through with a little bit of pain. Fssik looked away from the departing bartender with his mysterious pins and focused on the young Human male who had been the object of the thugs' ministrations. He, too, was a merc, Fssik realized as he pushed slowly up to his feet, groaning as he straightened.

"That's right, isn't it? I don't want to be rude. I've never actually met one of your kind before."

"Close enough," Fssik said, borrowing an expression he'd heard from Ziva. "I am Fssik, of Clan Tamir. I greet you, young Human. Welcome to our negotiation."

"Negotiation? Do I have something you want?"

"Start with your name," Fssik said. He slow blinked and then followed up with a Human-style grin for good measure. "Want some help getting through the crowd?"

"What? Sure," the young man said. Fssik stood and leaped, twisting his body around in a showy somersault so he could land on his back feet on the young man's shoulders. The crowd gasped again, and a path back to the bar slowly opened across the dancefloor.

"Wow!" the young man said. "That's awesome! How do you do that?"

"Reputation," Fssik said, allowing his voice to go dry and laconic. "Your name?" he prompted again.

"Oh! Right. Um. I'm Lucky."

"Is that a name or a description? Because you didn't look terribly lucky back there."

"You and Ginz showed up before I died, didn't you?" the kid answered with a grin. "But no, it's my nickname. "Lucky" Coonradt because somehow I always make it through without getting too badly banged up."

"That is lucky," Fssik said and then shifted his weight to steady himself on the kid's shoulders as he walked. "Do you know a Human merc named Tom Coonradt?"

"Hmmm… maybe? I think I have an uncle… maybe a second cousin? He retired, though, a while back. Why?"

"I think I know him," Fssik said. Then, because he wasn't sure how much information Memory's companion wanted to get back to his former family, he twisted to look at the front door. Sure enough, the bartender was coming back through the doors, and the crowd shifted to create a path just as they'd done for the kid.

"What did you say the bartender's name is?" Fssik asked.

"Ginz. Mikhail Ginzberg. Used to be a Mk 6 driver. He doesn't allow fights in his bar."

"Wise policy. What's the story with his pinplants?"

"Ohhh…" Lucky dropped his voice so low, Fssik was sure no one standing nearby could hear. "No one really knows. There's all kinds of stories. He won't talk about it."

Fssik's fur rippled as he shrugged. "A being is entitled to his privacy."

"Wait," the kid said, improbably craning his neck to try and look at Fssik. "You're not here to… you're not going to hurt Ginz, are you?"

"I'm not presently on contract, no," Fssik said, hoping the kid couldn't hear the humor in his voice. "If I were, you would not know I was here."

"Oh… I guess so. Hey, thanks, Ginz!"

"You need to keep yourself out of trouble in my bar, Lucky." The bartender flipped up the section of the counter and returned to his post by the beverage taps. Fssik watched with approval as the Human washed his hands before returning to his earlier task. "What, did you two make friends or something?"

"Something like that," Fssik said.

"Well, I appreciate the help, Hunter. And like I said, I will give you what info I can, but I can't let you conduct your business in my bar."

"It's okay, Ginz," Lucky piped up. "Fssik's not presently on contract, are you Fssik?"

"I am not," Fssik said and leaped from the young man's shoulder to the pristine surface of the bar. "I am just looking for directions to a store where I can buy some supplies for my companion."

"What kinda supplies do Depik need?" Ginz asked, his tone skeptical. Fssik dropped his jaw in a laugh.

"The same as most beings, I imagine, but my companion is Human. I am shopping for her. I need the smelly, wax-dipped strings and things for her to wash with… that kind of thing."

Ginz's face lit up with understanding, and a ripple of light flashed across his pin grid. "Oh! You're buying girlie stuff for your… companion?"

"Yes," Fssik said. "That's exactly it. I thought a resort town like this would have something suitable."

"Yeah, there's a place. It's an all-night convenience store, so they've got other stuff too, but they have the smelly candles and the bath salts and stuff. You know the spot, Lucky? Miana's place?"

"Yep! Want me to take you, Fssik?"

Fssik looked up at Ginz's sly smile and slow blinked to acknowledge his deft handling of the situation. In a rough bar like this, a young kid like Lucky was going to get hassled repeatedly. Far better to send him on an errand with a deadly escort. It was well played.

"I would like nothing better, Lucky. After you finish the drink Ginz is going to pour for you, you may lead the way."

* * *

Fssik had given up on not pacing and was prowling through the flora surrounding the swimming pool when Alinore found him.

"She's going to be fine," Alinore said. Fssik froze, dropped his quintessence, and pushed through the plants to emerge on the pool's deck. His clan-sister looked down at him with a tiny smile and opened her arms in invitation. Guilt and gratitude surged through Fssik in equal measure, but he leaped into her offered embrace anyway.

"She'll be fine," Alinore said again. "Ward and Esthik and Lara know what they're doing. Hell, they worked on *you*, and you were fine!"

"I know," Fssik murmured, hating that he sounded like a tiny kit, lost and mewling for his dama. "I just… I don't know why I feel like this, but it's almost like I can't breathe because I know she's at risk, and I can't do anything about it!"

Alinore laughed and stroked him between his ears and down the length of his back to his haunches.

"That's love, dear one," she said. "Love makes you crazy, and you Hunters were already most of the way there. I sometimes wonder if upping your bonding instinct was the right call."

"What do you mean?" Fssik asked.

"You didn't know?" Alinore asked. She held him close, still stroking his back, and began walking slowly around the perimeter of the pool. "It was part of the protocol when Ward separated your nervous systems. I don't remember all of it, but Lara talked it through with Esthik and me. Hunters already have incredibly developed bonding drives. That's why you're born so devoted to your clans. But Ward increased the drive, just a little, to encourage you all to take companions who could help watch your backs. Now that the Hunters aren't hiding in the shadows anymore, having a few friends seemed like a solid call."

"So, what I feel isn't real?"

She snorted in derision. "Does it feel real?"

"It feels... overwhelming. All-consuming."

"Seems pretty real to me. Just as your immunity to the freeze ray is now real. Just as Ziva's bond to you will be even more real after she's done."

"They're increasing her bonding instinct as well?"

"Didn't you listen to any of the briefs, Fssik?"

He shifted in her arms and pressed against her instead of answering. Her resulting laugh rumbled against the side of his face.

"Yes," she said. "Ziva will have her bonding instinct increased for the same reason you did. If she and the other companions are going to live on Khatash, they're going to need to stick closely to their Hunters to survive."

"So, she will love me more?"

"I don't know if it's possible for her to love you more than she already does, dear one." Alinore scratched deliciously under his chin, coaxing him to stretch his neck in pleasure. "Maybe it's fair to say she will love you harder. She will love anyone she chooses to love harder than she otherwise would have."

"Do you mean Cartwright?"

"Possibly. Is that still going on?" Alinore's fingers stilled, and Fssik let out a tiny mewl of protest. She chuckled and started scratching again.

"I am not certain, but I believe she still cares for him. She left rather suddenly to come here, so she may have some things to work out with him, but I suspect she really does care."

"You know... that might not be a terrible thing for us," Alinore said slowly. "Not that I would condone trying to manipulate Ziva or anyone, but... well... there could be worse things for the clan than to have a tie with Cartwright's Cavaliers."

"He does make her happy. I will talk with her afterward."

"If it seems right," Alinore cautioned him. "Ziva may be your companion, Hunter, but she's lived for almost two of your lifetimes. She can make her own decisions."

"As long as the decisions are good for her," Fssik muttered, and Alinore laughed again.

* * *

"Fssik..." Ziva's voice, weak and thready though it was, shot through Fssik like electrified joy. He rose to all fours from where he'd lain curled on her chest and pushed his face up under her chin.

"I am here, my Human," he murmured, letting out a long, low rumble as he did. As soon as Ziva had been wheeled back to her resort room for recovery, Fssik had installed himself and begun to purr a low steady hum. He didn't know why, but his instincts told him she needed it. He was still purring when Ward came in several hours later.

"Oh! Have you begun your vibrational therapy, then? That is excellent, Fssik. Excellent!"

"What are you talking about, Healer?" Fssik asked. His tone was sharper than he intended, but Ward had that effect sometimes. The

Wrogul was a valued member of the clan, but he had a tendency to skip such things as polite greetings and jump right to whatever was on his mind. Fssik didn't mind, per se, but it was always jarring to have someone act in such a blatantly rude manner, no matter how they intended it.

"Your purr! Vibrations between 25 and 150 Hertz are extremely beneficial to healing tissue, particularly bone tissue. Though I didn't make any skeletal adjustments on Ziva… but the soft tissue will be positively affected, I am sure of it! And it certainly won't hurt your bond to be close right now." The Wrogul Healer wheeled forward on his chair and began to hum a harmonic counterpoint to Fssik's sounds. It reminded Fssik of the bartender from the night before.

"Hmmm… yes, this is pleasing, very pleasing," Ward said, breaking off his hum. Fssik could talk through his purr, but he wasn't surprised the Wrogul could not, especially since his voice had to be electronically translated through his water-filled bubble.

"Don't keep secrets, Healer," Fssik warned when Ward didn't immediately go on. The Wrogul lifted two of his unoccupied arms in a shrug.

"No secret, Hunter. Your Ziva is an excellent physical specimen. She is not, perhaps, as young as we would like for these adjustments, but her fitness level and excellent nutrition have kept her metabolism and physiological processes working at peak efficiency."

"So, what does that mean?"

"It means she is doing very well, Hunter," Ward said, turning away from the portable displays that showed graphs and numbers Fssik didn't understand. He reached into the pocket of his white lab coat with one of his tentacled arms and pulled out a skinny, bright light. He used the tip of another tentacle to lift Ziva's eyelids and shine the light into her pupils.

"What does that do?" Fssik asked. He wasn't suspicious, exactly; it was just that... well, this was his Ziva.

"It confirms what the scans have shown me. We adjusted the composition of her retinal tissue and the shape of her iris. The scans say her dilation and contraction response falls within target parameters. In other words," Ward added, swiveling his chair slightly so he could look at Fssik, "she can now see in the dark as well as most Hunters."

"That's good," Fssik said.

"Hmm. Yes. It is very good. Enhanced vision was one of the stated objectives of the protocol. Let us hope we were equally successful with all the other tweaks we made to her genetic code."

Ward continued his examination, and Fssik didn't bother asking any more questions. He simply watched as his Wrogul clan-brother poked and prodded the sleeping Ziva.

"Well," Ward said eventually, wheeling away from Ziva's bed with a satisfied air. "I am very pleased. These protocols appear to have delivered our best result yet. Of course, that could be because of the subject's fitness, as I mentioned, but either way, she is really doing superbly!" He rubbed the tips of two tentacles together and leaned forward in his chair as he spoke. Fssik slow blinked at Ward's obvious glee.

"Congratulations," Fssik said, making sure to keep his tone light. His tail twitched slightly every time Ward referred to Ziva as a "subject," but Fssik knew that was as much his own anxiety about his Human as it was irritation with Ward's word choice. In Fssik's experience, healers and scientists all talked like that.

"Thank you," Ward said, wheeling his chair around the bed to look inside Ziva's ear with an instrument. "Yes, this looks very nice. Her inner ear balance organs are not as refined as yours, but we were able to tweak them to give her a better sense of her body's positioning in space. She will never be able to do some of the wild flipping stuff you Hunters can do, but she will be one of the fastest and most well-balanced Homo sapiens..." Ward's patter trailed off with a hum of discontent.

"What?" Fssik asked, his ears instantly alert, his fur quivering along his spine. "What is it? Something wrong?"

"What?" Ward asked, then shook himself and refocused his eyes on Fssik. "Oh! No! No, her inner ear is beautiful. No, I was just thinking about her name."

"Ziva?"

"Her species name. Humans are technically Homo sapiens sapiens, but it occurs to me she—and the other companions, now that I think about it—have become something else. If she breeds, her offspring will carry these changes in their genetic code. She is no longer simply Human. She is, in effect, a different subspecies."

"A Hunter subspecies," Fssik said, without really realizing he had.

"Yes! That's exactly it. Not Homo sapiens, but Homo... venatores! From the Earth Latin for hunter! Ziva and the other companions will be Homo venatores. I must add that to the paper Lara and I are putting together. Yes." He continued to mutter as he moved quickly down her body, glancing from her prone form to the monitor and back. Fssik continued to watch the Wrogul work, but a soft sound from the head of the bed brought him to all four feet as he whirled and saw Ziva slowly blink her eyes open.

"F-fssik?" she whispered, her voice cracked and gravelly.

"I am here, my Human," Fssik said, stepping carefully up to rub his head gently under her chin. She let out a sigh and leaned her cheek into his caress. He let his eyes drift closed and breathed in the scent of her skin.

"Welcome back, Ziva," Ward said, rolling his chair back toward her head. "How are you feeling?"

"Groggy," she said. "And... my eyes hurt."

"Ah! Excellent. Not that they hurt, but that they are sensitive to the light. Let me just..." Fssik opened his eyes and saw Ward fiddling with something on his chair. The lights in the room dimmed. He hadn't been uncomfortable before, but he had to admit the dimness was soothing.

"Is that better?" Ward asked.

"Yes," Ziva said. "Thank you. May I have some water?" Her voice was strengthening, and as Fssik closed his eyes again, he felt her hand come up to rest on his back. She scratched him just behind his skull, in that spot he liked best.

"Yes! Of course!"

Fssik tuned out their conversation when he felt the whirr of the bed's motor and the tilting sensation that meant Ziva was elevating the head of the hospital bed. Instead, Fssik focused on his purr. He pushed the vibrations forth, willing them to move through the air and into her tissues, to speed her healing, to give her ease.

"Fssik. Fssik! My Hunter, are you awake?"

Fssik pulled himself back to the present and opened his eyes. He lifted his head and slow blinked up into the face of his person.

"Naturally," he said, pushing down the thickness of emotion in his throat. She stretched her mouth in a Human smile, and he inhaled sharply. Her beautiful eyes echoed his in the shape of their pupils, and they contracted down to slits of pleasure as he returned her joy back to her.

"Ward says I should try to stand up. Want to stay with me?"

"Where else would I go?" he asked. He ignored the slight crack in his voice that betrayed his usual cloak of insouciance. Ziva slow blinked at him and gathered him into her arms as she swung her feet to the floor.

As he'd known she would, she stood easily enough. The blankets that covered her fell to the floor behind her, and she picked her way through them in an effortless, light-toed way that made Ward flush blue in delight.

"Excellent!" the Wrogul crowed through his translator. "Your balance and grace are *exactly* what we hoped for, and so soon after the procedure... your neural pathways are already well established! Catch!"

With no more warning than that, Ward picked up a small toy—Fssik thought it looked like a stuffed version of a flightless, aquatic Earth avian—and hurled it at Ziva. She let go of Fssik with one hand and caught it mere pad-tips from her face. Fssik blinked again, this time half in surprise; she'd been nearly Hunter-fast!

"That is really, really excellent!" Ward said, his blue tint rippling with purples and greens of exultation. "This is the best result we've seen yet! How do you feel? Are you tired?"

"No," Ziva said. "In fact, I feel like I could go for a run or a swim... only I don't want to leave Fssik."

"No," Ward said. "Nor should you. We've reinforced the strength of your companion bond. You now need his company as much as he needs yours. It will be interesting to see if you can still pair-bond with another Human enough to breed. I suppose you could come to an arrangement with another Hunter companion if need be. I know there are some males. It will be fun to watch how this plays out."

"Happy to be of such entertainment value," Ziva said, and Fssik twitched his whiskers in appreciation of her dry tone. "I'll be sure to let you know if I'm still able to fall in love."

"We have no reason to suspect you will not. It was just a thought I had—"

"Don't worry about it, Ward," Ziva said, smiling at him again. "You did great. I'm mostly just teasing. Besides, I've always thought love is more than a zero-sum game."

"Zero-sum... ah! Yes! Interesting concept. Though, given the relative amounts of oxytocin in a system..." Ward's voice faded as he turned and rolled out through the door, still muttering to himself. Fssik curled in Ziva's arms and watched him go, amusement threading through his continuous low purr.

* * *

Fssik darted from under the broad-leaved plant that edged the walking path and flipped into the air. As he flipped, and his feet extended to land on Ziva's shoulder, she flinched and looked his way a heartbeat before he landed.

"Oof!" she let out. "Damnit! How did I miss you that time?"

"I don't think you did," he said as he dropped his cloak of quintessence. He rubbed his cheekbone against her ear in reassurance and then leaped to the ground. "You felt something because you turned to look in my direction."

"You still would have slit my throat before I could do anything."

"Well, yes, but you have only been able to sense quintessence for a day and a half, my Human. You are still like a milk-eyed kita. You *did* feel something."

"Yeah," Ziva said, continuing down the path. "Maybe."

"Describe it."

"It was like... I don't know... like... did you ever play a game when you were little where you jumped on a trampoline?"

"Perhaps. What is a 'trampoline?'"

Ziva let out an annoyed huff then shoved her long black hair away from her face. With short, staccato motions, she twisted it into a knot at the base of her skull. Fssik watched her do so as she walked. Ward was right. Ziva had always been graceful, but now, her body flowed like liquid.

"A trampoline. Like a big blanket stretched between a bunch of springs, so when you jump on it, it bounces you back into the air."

"We played a game with my molly and her friends where they would put us on a blanket and toss us up to see who could best land on their feet. Is that what you mean?"

Ziva turned and looked at him with a tiny frown, then shook her head and turned her attention back to her path. "Whatever. Close enough. Do you remember how, when the blanket was taut, you could feel the other kits moving on it?"

"I suppose I could."

"It feels something like that. Like I'm on this vast trampoline, and there's a ripple of movement coming from where you are."

Fssik slow blinked and even allowed his tail to twitch in joy.

"So," he said, careful to keep his voice even. "Feel that trampoline now, yes? How does it change when I do this?" He pulled his quintessence field around him, bending the light so it wouldn't reflect off of his form.

"Oh!" Ziva's eyes widened. "Oh! I felt that! It felt like... like a ripple or a pulse through the fabric!"

"Excellent," Fssik said. He began to stalk slowly around her, and though she closed her eyes, she pivoted to continue facing him as he moved.

"And now, it's like there's something under the trampoline, pushing it up... not large, but... but larger than before, I think. And it's moving. Is that you?"

"It is," Fssik said, dropping his cloak. He stepped toward her and pressed his furred length against her calves. "Can you feel anyone else?"

"N-no... wait. Maybe there's something... no."

"You need to trust your instincts," Esthik said as he stepped out of his cloak on the path beside them. "They will keep you alive on Khatash."

Ziva jumped and put her hand to her chest as she laughed. "Stars above, Healer, how long have you been there?"

"Since we started walking," Fssik answered. "It is interesting that you can feel me, but not Esthik. I am much more skilled with quintessence than he."

"That is likely the effect of the companion bond," Esthik said. "There is a lot of neurological entanglement between the emotional bonding centers of the Human brain and the quintessential sensing nodes we built. It was the only way we could see to increase what needed increasing for the companions. The connections are similar in our own brains. Have you never noticed it is harder to hide from your clan-siblings than from anyone else?"

"Of course," Fssik said.

"It is because you have emotional bonds with them, too. Nothing as strong as the companion bond, but it is there. Emotional closeness will always make a being easier to sense."

"That's true even without quintessence," Ziva said, her eyes crinkling a little as she smiled. "My mother could always tell when my father was close."

Esthik's jaw dropped in a laugh.

"That wasn't without quintessence," he said.

"What do you mean?" Ziva asked, narrowing her eyes. "My mother can't sense quintessence."

"Maybe not as you now can, or as we do, but it exists everywhere, just as baryonic matter exists everywhere. The baryonic signals in the emotion centers of the brain have always interacted with quintessence. They do in every being everywhere. It's not outside the realm of possibility that your mother began to sense that interaction with her baryonic nervous system. It would have been unconscious, of course, and more instinct than anything, but it's not illogical. In fact, I hypothesize that *all* beings who emote have the potential to sense quintessential interactions. They just don't have the infrastructure in their nervous systems. You now do."

Fssik looked from Esthik to Ziva and then back to the Healer. Fssik might have been on to something, but he didn't want to think too hard about it, so he leaped up to Ziva's shoulder.

"That's enough for this evening," he said, looking at the stars and satellites overhead. "I don't want you tiring yourself out, my Human. Let's get you some food and then, maybe, a swim?"

"I'm not tired," Ziva said, reaching up to stroke the fur behind Fssik's ears. He leaned into her touch and let out a low rumble as she continued, "Though I am hungry."

"I will see you both later," Esthik said. "I've eaten, and I want to confer with Ward and Lara about a few things."

"If you see Alinore, please tell her she's welcome to join us," Ziva said. Esthik slow blinked in her direction and then leaped into the air, pulling quintessence at the top of the leap, so it looked as if he had simply vanished.

"Show off," Fssik rumbled. "He's in a good mood. It must be because you're such a perfect patient."

"Perfect?" Ziva laughed and moved her fingers to scratch under his chin. Fssik stretched his neck and let his eyes close in bliss.

"Mmmhmm."

"I complain too much and push too hard. I've never been a good patient."

"The Healer hasn't once had to threaten to gut you to keep you from reinjuring yourself. Trust me, my Human, you are a much better patient than those Esthik is used to." He slow blinked and continued, "These scratches are lovely, but let us move toward food, yes?"

Ziva let out a long, rippling laugh and obliged. Fssik opened his eyes as she walked, his ears twitching as he inhaled the scent of the lovely night. As ever, he caught the underlying tang of hospital, but the flowers on the night breeze were lovely, and the quiet rushing sound of the waves behind them filled him with a deep sense of calm.

They made their way up to the main lodge and into the all-night restaurant. Ziva took a seat at the bar, and Fssik pulled his quintessence around him and hopped down to explore the long, highly polished surface. He saw her order and then excuse herself to go to the restroom, so he headed back to her spot so it wouldn't be taken by anyone while she was gone.

Anyone, for example, like the Sidar who approached and looked around.

Fssik sat on the bar in front of Ziva's stool and dropped his cloak. He kept one eye on the Sidar and began washing his face as if he hadn't a care in the world.

The Sidar—a male, judging by the size of his crest—saw him and shivered, his wings rustling under the long coat his species habitually wore, then he stepped forward and gave a small half bow.

"I greet you, Hunter. My name is Frieloch."

"I greet you, Frieloch," Fssik said, intrigued by the Sidar's manners. He quit washing his face and rose to his feet. "I am Fssik of Clan Tamir. Welcome to our negotiation."

"So... I did say that correctly, yes? I have not given you offense?"

Fssik slow blinked. "No. Not yet. Do you intend to?"

"Offend you? Not at all! The opposite. It's just that I was taught that Depi—Hunters are very particular about the courtesies."

"We appreciate courtesy, yes," Fssik said, slow blinking again. The Sidar were a long-lived race, but he'd bet a red diamond the one in front of him was barely out of adolescence.

"Well, please do let me know if I step wrong. I've not had the pleasure of speaking with one of your race before."

"You'll know," Fssik said and smiled in the Human way, so his fangs gleamed from the lights behind the bar. Frieloch shivered again and nodded, his crest bobbing up and down.

"Yes. Well. You mentioned a negotiation. I... that is, *we* would like to offer you a contract for your services."

Fssik perked up his ears. He hadn't taken any contracts since he'd last left Khatash. Like most active Hunters, he wasn't exactly short of funds, and Ziva had her job with the Cavaliers, but an infusion of cash—especially if they could truly afford him—would be welcome. Staying on Azure wasn't cheap, and, while the Clan covered the expenses, he would vastly prefer to contribute his share.

"Can you afford me?" he asked.

"Personally? Not at all. But I represent a group called Theela Financial, and it is they who wish to retain your services. A certain individual on Earth has been engaging in illegal activity that is interfering with our business interests there."

"If the activity is illegal, why not turn the individual in?"

"To whom?" Frieloch asked. "Humanity is slowly rebuilding stability on Earth, but we do not really have time to wait for their law enforcement to be up to task. We need this individual neutralized soon."

"How soon? I am not planning on leaving Azure for another ninenight or so."

"That will be soon enough."

"Who is the individual? What race, and are they of adult age?"

Frieloch nodded and shifted his wings under his cloak. "He is a Human named Cooper Hatfield, and he is past the Human age of majority. My mentor told me you would not accept a contract on a being who was not fully grown."

"Your mentor seems to know a lot about us."

"Hmm, yes. Well, I am authorized to offer you a sum of three hundred million credits. Half as a deposit now, half upon completion of the contract."

"Any stipulations? Must it look accidental?"

"No. In fact, we want it to be obvious that it was a Depi… Hunter hit, though obviously not traceable back to Theela Financial."

"Obviously." Fssik used his pinplants to do a cursory GalNet search on the target's name. He wasn't anyone Fssik knew, but neither was he on the list of beings for whom a contract would be inconvenient to the Clan, and the money was enticing.

"Very well," Fssik said. He rose on his back feet and held out his hand in the Human gesture of greeting and deal making. He rather liked the symbolism of it. "I accept the contract and your terms. You can remit payment to your room account here, on Azure, and it will funnel back to me via untraceable means."

"That's convenient," Frieloch said.

"We have ins everywhere," Fssik said with a smile. And while it was true, he was playing just a little fast and loose. The truth was, he'd hacked the Azure resort's payment system when they'd arrived, just for something to do. The resort would never know the payment had been made. He'd funnel the extra funds through the backdoor he'd created and then permanently close it when he left. It would be, as he said, untraceable.

"Excellent. Once you have completed the contract, place a secure call to the Law Offices of Ben Smith in Houston to inquire about a refund for your retainer. They will ask you to provide proof of some kind. They will not be picky, as long as it is clear the contract was successfully fulfilled."

"I can provide proof," Fssik said, letting his voice go dry. Frieloch shivered again and then nodded quickly.

"I am certain. Well, thank you, Hunter. This has been a fascinating... um... negotiation."

"Good night, Frieloch," Fssik said, slow blinking again as the young Sidar turned and left through the door.

"What was that about?" Ziva asked as she approached and slid back onto her stool. The bartender sauntered over and placed the food she'd ordered in front of her, and she smiled at him in thanks.

"Nothing," Fssik said. "Just meeting a new friend. Eat up. Let's get you healthy."

* * * * *

Chapter Two

Tsan paced on silent feet. She kept an ear turned toward Tamir and Esthik's conversation, but, as she was in her quintessence field, and neither knew she'd arrived, she had no need to contribute to it.

They spoke of important things—new kits, the need for more worthy companions, Fssik and his Human—but the words skipped off the edge of her thoughts, like ships missing their insertion points.

The blood beating through her called to a different concern, and she had yet to smooth it into a proper series of actions.

One moon and a series of ships are not enough. Tsan's tail lashed, and she rose to two legs to better flex her front claws. *Khatash was not enough, and this asteroid has even less of its own protections.*

Except so few knew it existed. Though, as the raid on the Science Guild had demonstrated, few locations remained secret forever when one had determined enemies.

Events had intensified across the galaxy. They would have more enemies before long.

The register of Tamir's voice changed, and Esthik left with a warm word for his Human Dama. Tsan tilted her head toward him, but he was not her priority now. She preened the fur on her cheeks, smoothing her outward appearance, as her thoughts circulated with repetitive frustration.

"If you're here to see me, we might as well begin," Tamir announced. She turned her chair away from the door and back toward her bank of screens. "I don't have endless time left."

"You have enough." Tsan released her field and slow blinked at the ancient Human facing her. "Tell me, Dama, do you sometimes make announcements in empty rooms on the assumption one of us is here?"

Tamir's smile, brilliant enough to ease some tension in Tsan's claws, displayed the wrinkles that spoke of a well-aged Human.

"You'd ask me to give away such a deep secret, Dama?" Laughter threaded through her voice, and hearing it settled the fur along Tsan's back.

"I'll withdraw my request—" she arched her tail high and pointed her ears politely ahead, "—and take that as my answer."

Tamir laughed fully. She drove her chair forward and dropped her arm into her lap as she passed Tsan. The Hunter accepted the invitation and leaped onto the thin armrest.

"What work keeps you from rest this evening?" Tsan asked, with a brief touch of her forehead to Tamir's nearer cheek.

"The usual. Logistics. Moving credits and trade routes ahead of conflicts."

"Ahead?"

"Allow an old woman some optimism, my dear one." Tamir sighed. "Moving things reactively as we learn of them and proactively as best we can. It's a mess out there."

"It is always a mess out there—" Tsan uncurled her tail and brushed Tamir's folded arm as Tamir parked the chair at the table full of screens, "—though of a stronger flavor these days, I admit."

She cocked her head as Tamir opened a star map, and she studied her fellow Dama's notations.

Several gates had changed color since she'd last been in Tamir's study, and one section had been newly added. Tsan studied the system the Science Guild had occupied, and her pupils narrowed.

Tamir frowned at the sprawling holo in front of them. "The Horsemen cleaning up the Mercenary Guild has helped in some parts and worsened things in others. Nature abhors a vacuum, and so it goes with intelligent beings and power—where this is a gap, there are many who will try and fill it."

"There are fewer and fewer Veetanho leading obvious actions against the Guild." Tsan heard the dissatisfaction in her voice and shifted to lean against Tamir's shoulder. Not heavily—the Human became more fragile each time Tsan returned, though Tamir made no concessions to such things—but enough to reassure them both.

"The more allies they secure for the new configuration of the Guild, the harder it is for them to justify direct attacks, but the Veetanho have plenty of brilliant commanders left, despite our best efforts." Tamir smiled briefly at Tsan, who dipped her head at the acknowledgment. "They don't have the grace to slink away and lick their wounds."

"A wounded enemy is twice as dangerous." Tsan's tail flicked, and scorn coated her words. Throughout generations of memory, Hunters did not have enemies. They had prey and clan. So much had changed. "I will not underestimate them. If they retreat, it is strategic."

Tamir nodded. She pressed keys, and seven sections of the map shifted to yellow.

"They are here?" Tsan asked, her eyes fixed on the large highlighted space.

"These are our best guesses of where they're going to ground." Tamir traced the air around one section, and Tsan steadily regarded her home system. "My gut says they'll go to Khatash or somewhere over on the edge of Cresht, but we'll need more than one Human's intestines to tell us what to do."

"We know what to do." Tsan slow blinked and stretched out all ten of her front claws, one after the other. "We will take Khatash back, whether some, or all, Veetanho wait for us there." A purr built in her chest, and she let it coat her words. "I hope they do attempt to tame the jungles; it will bring me joy to see their organs strung through the canopies." She resettled herself and deliberately looked away from the map.

"Do you think we're ready?" Tamir asked, and Tsan recognized the tone. She lashed her tail, then dipped her head in acknowledgment at the leading question. She was no kit to ignore a prompt or let her pride argue that she had more to think about.

"Of course, information is key to a successful hunt. It will determine the when." Tsan's fur shivered down her sides, and she placed a hand on Tamir's shoulder. "We know there are more threats moving through the galaxy—Peepo had much to say about what she was protecting us from." Her ears flattened, but she kept her claws sheathed.

"She would have said anything in those moments," Tamir offered.

"Yes." Tsan shrugged and swiveled her ears forward again. "But I doubt she was lying. That her being all that could save us, of course, was a lie, but that there are looming powers out there, lying in wait?"

"Someone is always out there waiting for their moment to strike."

"Exactly. And if what we learned at the Science Guild is any indication, there is even more than Peepo knew." They let the silence hold for a span of breaths as they studied the map, then Tsan continued.

"We can only do what we can do and hunt the prey in front of us."

"So, we ready for Khatash."

"Then we have that battle behind us when the next comes. The what and the when. As for the who…"

"Esthik, Ward, and Lara continue to exceed—the mothers and litters of kits are thriving better than our projections. As for companions for the kits, when they're ready…"

Tsan envisioned her path to Tamir's quarters. The corridors, never teeming, echoed hollowly. So many companions were Azure-bound—receiving their upgrades, recovering from same, or traveling there or home. As their Healers exceeded projections in producing healthy kits—a marvel that warmed Tsan every time she considered it—their pool of worthy companions shrunk.

"Our fighting force, all told, is enough to put up a worthy fight, especially as kits mature."

"But?" Tamir prompted and lifted her hand. Tsan leaned her cheek against it for a breath, then straightened.

"We need more. Khatash is ours, and we will take it back, but it will never again be our only home." Finally, the twisting circles of her thoughts settled, and her path unfolded before her.

"More companions?"

"Of course, that." Tsan nodded, her mind racing ahead. "Humans, as there are many who are worthy." She slow blinked and rumbled at Tamir's answering gesture. "I heard your discussion with Esthik, that younger Humans take to Ward's procedure better." While Tsan had not been paying attention, she had registered their conversation word for word, and she trusted their judgment. "I leave it to you to determine where to find more Humans." The matter required no further thought from her, given their strengths. "Yet that will not be enough."

"Hunters are fighters beyond peer," Tamir said, her eyes steady on Tsan, "and Humans hold their own. But to take back a planet…"

"We are shadows," Tsan agreed. "We stalk. We watch, then we find a way. We do not, as a rule, invade planets."

"You want other companions."

"Humans, yes. Zuul." She thought about Aryo, her sigiled Zuul. Not a trained warrior, but ferocious enough to have saved Tsan, herself, long ago. "Others who can fight, who would value their kits. Others the Wrogul could modify to better suit our needs."

"That will provide a ready force, when it is time to take back your home."

Which would not be now, no matter how that itched against Tsan's spine. *Watch, then find a way.*

"It will." She leaned briefly against Tamir, then forced herself to stillness when she longed to leap into battle. "But Khatash will be *our* home, not only for Hunters. And *a* home, not our only one."

"You don't mean Land's End." Tamir proved her understanding of Hunter minds was as exceptional as ever. Tsan slow blinked and flicked her ears toward the Human.

"Of course, here as well, Dama. And Azure. And perhaps Earth and other worlds of the allies we make. We will seed our kits across the galaxy, where no enemy can threaten the entirety of our clan." The Dama, once of Whispering Fear, and now, alongside this extraordinary Human, Dama of the entirety of her kind, turned her sharp gaze back to the star map in front of them.

"I have learned many things, my Tamir." The purr wrapped itself through her words, and her pupils widened until they covered most of her irises. "More beings than the Veetanho move against us, but we are not alone any longer on one planet at the edge of space." She stretched, luxuriating in the shifting of her vertebrae. "Our enemies have enemies of their own."

"Allies," Tamir murmured, and the ferocity that suffused her voice belied her age. "The Horsemen."

"And the Wrogul. They are fierce when they choose to be. Zuul. Lumar. Tortantulas. Those the Veetanho have subjugated, but who fight regardless." Tsan leaped from Tamir's chair and turned her back to the map with a twist of her tail. "I will tie the best warriors in the galaxy to us, and we will fight until the stars bleed."

The time to take back Khatash was not now. Assassins were not made for wholesale, head-on attacks. Sansar and Nigel were brilliant in their own way and had led assaults on planets and systems. The Wrogul leashed violence in their tentacles, no matter how cheerfully Ward burbled through Land's End's domes. The Lumar destroyed any target they aimed for. Tortantulas were nearly unstoppable in direct battle. The Zuul knew war like Tsan knew hunting.

Unseen enemies swam in the space between civilizations. A pressure built throughout the systems. Tsan had yet to identify all the components, but she'd seen the impact of the thing that ran the Science Guild. *You don't have to see the teeth of the keran to know its swirl in the water.*

"We have enough traffic with Azure to make that an easy first step toward a conversation," Tamir said, her expression rapt. "What do you need from me?"

"Numbers. Logistics." Tsan laughed at the echo of Tamir's earlier response to her. "Those you think would do well on Azure, or 'Tlor, or Earth. I am not here often enough to see how they have grown."

"I have files and reports from everyone," Tamir answered with a laugh of her own. "Ward and Lara, Alinore and Ref, my own notes. Even Pura and Hrava have begun sending me their thoughts on the younger kits, those they—" the chuckle nearly broke into a cough, but Tamir continued after a moment, "—believe need more seasoning."

"Wisdom," Tsan murmured, and they smiled at each other. "Send me all of it, but who leaps immediately to mind?"

"Ziva and Fssik are warriors and can take contracts as needed. They remain a vital link to Earth and, in the meantime, can strengthen our bonds with Cartwright's and find more Human companions." Tamir mentioned several of the older pairings quickly. Tsan was well acquainted with Aryss and her Meredith, Esthik and his cluster of Humans, Azho and Jessica.

"Memory and Coonie can go to Azure, where they will spread their knowledge of our culture and stories and determine whether any Wrogul would be fitting companions."

"I will bring some of the mothers there as well," Tsan added, considering. "As Ward, Lara, and Esthik travel, it may be better to spread the breeding to new, safe corners." Few places would be safer than Azure for any medical intervention needed.

"Justice has yet to choose a companion, though his other siblings are content with theirs. He has declared he must have a proper Hunt across the stars before he can know who he is."

Tsan slow blinked, hearing both the kit's youth and the rightness of the sentiment in his statement.

They spoke for some time of kits—a promise of a future they both had bled for. Tsan asked few questions, as Tamir knew exactly what she needed to know and volunteered the information. Her fellow Dama also knew what questions to ask her when the subject changed.

"How will you approach the Lumar?"

"I have some ideas from the work the Golden Horde has done in securing the Mercenary Guild. An ancestor of mine once owned Proud Fist; he left interesting stories of things he learned long ago."

Tamir's chin snapped up. "Del, you mean." She laughed and shook her head, murmuring, "Long ago, indeed."

Tsan laughed, as she remembered that generations of her clan had passed in Tamir's single lifetime. It rarely bothered her, only, there was so much work yet to do.

She would simply have to be efficient with the time she had, like any being.

"As with any of the allies we need, I'll do what I always do." She paused, the very tip of her tail twitching with humor, then Tamir spoke the words along with her. "Watch, then find a way."

They would plan, and they would build alliances, and they would be ready. They would not retake Khatash now, nor strike the final blow at the Veetanho who remained. Soon, though. Soon enough, they would bring entropy to their enemies, and Tsan would use whatever time she had left to ensure safety for her people. All of them.

* * *

Tsan had travel plans to arrange, which meant she had a stop to make before preparations began. She sent an invitation to some of the beings she wanted to see before leaving, then made her way to the edge of Land's End.

The play den had been a loading bay at one point. Now, it was filled with all manner of creations—an ever-evolving assortment of toys, traps, and all-around exercise equipment.

Which meant that, more often than not, any combination of kits ran, laid siege, and generally clawed their way up and through it all.

It was very like a den, if any den on Khatash had ever boasted tens of kits at once.

Her fur settled into sleek smoothness the moment she crossed into the room, and she let her quintessence field flicker for a bare moment in invitation.

"Dama!" a small voice cried, but Tsan had known too many kits who were drawn in by the audible joy. Indeed, a moment later, three indeterminately visible figures rushed her from various angles. She slid to the side and let two collide, then rolled to her back and caught the last, pulling the wriggling figure close against her belly.

"I caught you, Dama!" the little one declared, all brown stripes and big eyes.

"Very nearly," Tsan replied, touching her nose to the kit's before rolling them both over. "You should have worked with your siblings instead of trying to go alone."

"They never listen," he harumphed, rubbing his head under her chin. "I greet you, Dama," he added, chirruping.

"And I you, my little one. Go teach your siblings about teamwork."

"Dama," Fssik said from behind the gaggle of kits. He hopped over one of the play pedestals and walked toward Tsan, his tail held high in respect and affection. "I greet you as well. How lucky to find you here. Ziva should be along any moment. She has missed you."

"Fssik." Tsan slow blinked as she returned his greeting. "I am glad our paths have crossed. You and your Ziva are away nearly as often as I am."

A ripple of stripes and spots stalked closer as they spoke, blue-green eyes intent on the tip of Fssik's tail. Tsan ignored the movement, though she flickered an ear in its direction.

Fssik's tail began to wave back and forth in lazy arcs as he stretched, then looked over as one of the ground-level doors irised open.

"Hunting has been good," he said, content in this moment. "My recent contract from a new client, Theela, should prove profitable on our next trip."

"How convenient," Tsan replied with a slow blink.

"Dama," Ziva said as she walked through the door, her gait easy, a smile on her face. She moved well, Tsan noted. Better than most Humans. Better than Ziva, herself, usually moved.

"Rrrow!" a tiny striped ball of fury and aggression launched itself at the group, small claws extended as it swiped at Fssik's tail. The male Hunter threw his body to the side, rolled, and caught the attacking kita in both hands, pinning the little one's arms to her sides, rendering her foreclaws useless. Her back feet clawed at the air as she reached down to try and get his vulnerable underbelly, but Fssik was far too strong and fast to let that happen. He continued the roll and pinned her under his forepaws as he rose easily to his feet.

"You announced your attack with noise, Sessi," Fssik said, his voice patient. "You would have done better to hold your silence and let the strike do the talking."

"I wanted to get you!"

"Someday you will, if you listen and keep working hard, kita. Now, greet Dama Tsan and then go play with the others."

The tiny striped kita rolled her eyes and arched her back so she was looking at Tsan, who carefully composed her ears and whiskers in a solemn, not-at-all amused expression.

"I greet you, Dama."

"I greet you, Sessi. Was this a good lesson or will you need to learn it again like a foolish kita?"

"I learned it. It was good."

"Then thank the Hunter and do as he said."

The little one squirmed under Fssik's paws until she could look up at his face. "Thank you, Hunter Fssik."

"You are welcome, Kita Sessi." He bent down and touched his nose to hers, and she arched up to rub her cheek against his in return. Then Fssik lifted his forepaws and held them high. The little one wriggled back onto all four of her feet and dashed away, shouting for her siblings to come so she could teach them what she had learned.

"That one, at least, has a sense of teamwork," Fssik said.

"Sometimes," Tsan agreed. "She enjoys being in charge a little too much."

"Future Dama material?" Ziva asked with a Human-style smile.

"Perhaps. I greet you, Human… or perhaps not totally Human anymore?" Tsan shifted her attention to the dark-haired woman who lowered herself to sit on the ground beside them. Ziva's features echoed Tamir's in their shape and configuration, and Tsan felt the sudden urge to rub against her arm and share scents as she sometimes did with her fellow Dama.

"Not entirely," Ziva said. "Ward is calling us *Homo venatores*. It means 'hunter human' in an archaic Earth language."

"Why use a dead language?"

Ziva shrugged. "Tradition? Humanity has used Latin to name species for as long as anyone has cared to name species."

Tsan twitched her tail in a shrug. "Tradition has its place."

"As long as it doesn't get in the way," Ziva finished for her. Tsan slow blinked at her perception, and Ziva returned the gesture, her enhanced retinas glinting in reflected light from above. The Dama leaned close and tilted her head to the side to better examine Ziva's slit pupils.

"I see they've altered your eyes, as we discussed," Tsan said. "How has it affected your vision?"

"I can see much deeper into shadows, Dama, though not quite as well as Fssik. I've retained most of my bright light and color vision as well; I just need sunglasses religiously instead of once in a while."

"Fascinating. And the other enhancements?"

"Balance and somatosensory factors," Fssik put in. "She moves more like a Hunter and could feasibly take a route through the trees if needed, though the lack of claws would still be a problem."

"One that can be mitigated with the proper equipment," Ziva said. From her tone, it was clear to Tsan that this was an ongoing debate between the two. She found herself slow blinking at their tones; they sounded like a long-bonded Dama and Deo, arguing over their kits.

"Possibly," Fssik allowed. "She's also got an enhanced immune response to all the catalogued toxins and venoms found on Khatash. It doesn't protect her from everything, of course, because we haven't catalogued everything—"

"For good reason," Tsan said.

"Yes, but unlike sigiled beings, she at least has *some* protection against the dangers in the jungle, which is useful and comforting to know."

"And her nervous system?" Tsan asked, her voice quiet and intense.

"It's been... reinforced. I don't know how else to put it. She cannot pull quintessence but—"

"I can *feel* it, Dama," Ziva said, shifting forward slightly as she spoke. She lifted a hand toward Tsan, palm up, as if she were offering some invisible gift. "When I think about it, when I... pay attention, it feels like I'm sitting on a vast trampoline—"

"Like the bouncing blanket over there," Fssik put in, pointing to the apparatus in question, where four laughing, shrieking kits practiced bounding high into the air.

"Yes, it feels like that, and when Fssik moves, or when you move, if I try really hard, I can feel your movements across that bouncing blanket." Ziva closed her eyes and furrowed her brow in concentration.

Tsan said nothing. She merely rose to her feet and pulled her quintessence cloak around her, then began walking slowly around behind Ziva. Fssik's companion sat straighter and then, slowly, haltingly, she began to turn toward the dama until she again faced her directly.

"That is excellent," Tsan said, allowing a purr of satisfaction into her voice. "This appears to be a much greater level of adaptation than our previous companions had."

"That's what Ward said." Fssik's pride in his Ziva resonated through his words. "He said she's the most complete success they've had in any of the older companions. He said it's much easier to make the adjustments to younger beings because they aren't fully developed yet."

"That logic smells sound," Tsan said. "You two have given me much to think about. I am very glad I spoke with you before I left."

"We knew we would find you here, Dama. You often come to play and teach the little ones. We all do. I think… I think it's something we need."

Ziva looked at her Hunter and reached out a hand to stroke his spine. Tsan watched the way Fssik leaned into her touch and made a mental note. This pair was almost perfectly matched, the love between them clear for all to see. Ward's *other* changes to Hunter and Human had obviously created a synergy that made this companion bond something significant… and, perhaps, something to watch?

* * * * *

Chapter Three

"Can we talk for a minute?"

Fssik looked over his shoulder at his Human and narrowed his eyes.

"I will always talk to you."

"I know," Ziva said, blowing out a puff of air. "I mean, can we talk through something that's been bothering me?"

"Yes," Fssik agreed. He turned and jumped onto the shuttle seat beside Ziva. "As we get closer to Earth, your heartrate is up, and you smell of... not fear exactly—"

"Stress," Ziva supplied. "Thanks. Now, I'm going to need to shower as soon as we land."

"You would want one anyway. You always do after we travel."

"Fair point. No, I just... do you remember when we last left Houston?"

"Yes."

"Did you think our departure was a little... abrupt?"

"No."

"Really?" Ziva's eyebrows shot up toward her hairline. "Are you sure? I didn't really give Jim time to say goodbye or tell him where I was going..."

"You told him you were going home and then to Azure."

"Okay, maybe I did, but I didn't tell him what I was going to do."

Fssik tilted his head to the side. "Why would you have told him that?"

"Well, we were kinda… seeing each other. What if…" she broke off.

"What if what?"

"What if he doesn't like me now?"

"Why wouldn't he like you now? He liked you before."

"Yes, but Fssik, I'm not exactly… Human anymore."

"No, you're better than Human. You are MY Human." Fssik watched as Ziva's worried expression faded into a wide smile that lit up her face from within.

"I love you too, my Hunter," Ziva said. "I don't know why this is bothering me so much. It's just…"

"Do you regret your enhancements?"

"No!" Ziva shook her head. "No, not at all. I feel… I don't know how to describe it… like a veil has been lifted. Like I can see better, hear better…"

"Because you can."

"Yes, and it's wonderful. It's exactly what I hoped for, and if it means we get to stay together, it was totally worth it, but I… I don't know. I feel this strong need to get back and talk to Jim, and I really hope he doesn't reject me because I chose to do these things."

"Ziva, you are the most beautiful of Humans. Even if you were not mine, I can tell others of your race find you physically appealing. I cannot, for the life of me, imagine why you are worried about the opinion of one particular man… even if he is the commander of Cartwright's Cavaliers."

"Because he's Jim," Ziva replied in a small voice. She shrugged one shoulder. "I like him."

Fssik shook his whole body from nose to tail, then began to wash his face. This entire conversation was far too introspective for his taste, and he was growing rapidly bored.

"Nothing more to say, my Hunter?"

"Only that you Humans make your relationships more complicated than they need to be."

Ziva threw her head back and laughed. Fssik abandoned his face-washing, stepped into her lap, and pushed his head up under her hand. She obediently began to stroke him behind his ears.

"All passengers, please secure yourselves for atmospheric reentry."

The computer-generated voice issued from speakers overhead, speaking the English dialect Fssik had begun to learn from Ziva and several other companions. It never ceased to amaze him how the Humans had so many language variants. His translator repeated the message almost instantly via the integrated link with his pinplants.

"Let me hook you in," Ziva said, reaching for the connection points on the strap of his harness. Fssik let her lift him and clip him in, then he relaxed against her chest as the shuttle's drive pulsed through the frame of the ship.

"When we land, I will leave you for a bit," Fssik said. "So, if you want to go talk to your Jim and try to uncomplicate your relationship, be my guest."

"What do you mean, you'll leave me?" Ziva scratched under his chin, making pleasure ripple under his fur.

"I will never *leave* you, but I have taken a contract in Houston, so you must look after yourself for a little while. If you return to Cartwright's compound, you should be as safe there as anywhere."

"I *can* take care of myself, Hunter. I did for quite a while before you showed up, you know."

"I know. It's one reason why I love you. Now that I'm here, though, you don't need to watch your back ever again."

Ziva smiled down at him, wrapped her hand around the side of his jaw and skull, and scratched him the way he loved. Fssik leaned into the steady touch and strength of her hands. She didn't need to watch her own back, per se, but it was a source of endless comfort to him to know that she always *would*.

And his, as well, if it came to that.

The engines continued their pulsing throb as the shuttle decelerated through the atmosphere of Earth. Fssik felt the press of additional Gs on his body and cast about for something to distract himself. He *hated* letting someone else fly.

"What do you call your atmosphere?" he asked, trying not to gasp as he fought to push the words out against the increased pressure.

"What do you mean?" Ziva asked. She, too, sounded a little breathless from the Gs.

"I mean, is it the Earthen atmosphere? Earthling? What do you call things that belong to Earth?"

"Terran."

Fssik craned his neck upward to look into her eyes, despite the effort it took to move.

"That doesn't make any sense," he said. "If it's from Earth—"

"It should be Earthen," Ziva said with a tiny smile. "But 'Earthen' means it's made of dirt, which some things are. Terran means 'of Terra,' which is the Latin name for Earth."

"What under the nine moons is Latin?"

"An old Earth language." She grunted softly, straining to keep the blood in her brain. Fssik supposed it was harder for her, since she was so much bigger than he. He'd never really thought about it before.

"I've never heard it."

"It's a dead language... no one actually uses it... for everyday speech anymore. It's just for... religions and medical stuff... and... things like that. Ward used it when he named me *Homo venatores*. You remember."

"If it is dead, why use it at all?"

"I don't... know. They've always... used it?"

"That's a terrible reason to do anything," Fssik grumped. He pushed closer under her chin as she closed her eyes to fight off the worst of the reentry discomfort. He felt her chest rising and falling underneath his belly, as well as the weight of her head as she tilted her chin to press back into him.

This pilot sucks, Fssik thought. *We should have brought my ship.*

* * *

Once they'd landed and disembarked, Fssik said goodbye to Ziva and watched her wind through the crowd of Humans and other beings thronging the Houston starport. He followed her for a little way, hanging back in his quintessence, watching to see how well her stealth skills were developing.

He saw her get into a cab and give the driver directions, then he deliberately turned away. He could *feel* her through the cloak of his quintessence. Despite the clan-instinct that screamed at him to go back to her, Fssik forced his mind to focus on the here and now. He had a job to do and a contract to fulfill. Ziva would be fine.

His target, on the other hand...

Fssik flowed through the crowd to a side corridor. About midway along the hallway, a small seam indicated the presence of a door with a primitive locking system. Fssik used his picks to slip the lock and let himself inside a tiny room that held buckets and tools and bottles of acrid-smelling chemicals.

Cleaning closet. What a novelty! I didn't realize Humans cared so much about their spaces, Fssik thought, then he shook his head to clear the fumes from his nose. He closed the door silently behind him and pulled up the file he'd gotten from the client in his pinplants.

The target's name was Cooper Hatfield. He lived in a residence in a nearby suburb of Houston. He had apparently tangled with Human law enforcement enough to have a record of criminal activity, mostly for selling stolen goods and avoiding import taxes. Fssik didn't care much about either—he'd done his fair share of smuggling—but the last item in the file caught his attention. This guy had pled guilty to charges of trafficking in Human minors.

Trafficking… to whom? Fssik felt his lip curl up over his teeth as he considered this information. If Cooper Hatfield was selling young Humans into galactic slavery, it could be a large complication. Not that it mattered one way or the other. He'd accepted the contract, so the job must be done. It appeared Hatfield was not, as Ziva would say, "a good guy," which was a good thing because it meant Fssik could let himself play.

He slipped out of the cleaning closet and made his way out into the close, stinking air of Houston. It wasn't his first time in the Human city, but Fssik never failed to be amazed at how so many of their species could live so packed together in a place so dirty and reeking of pollution and unhappiness. He allowed himself a moment to desensitize his nose to the stench before joining a ragged line of Humans who waited for one of the large public transport vehicles.

He could have taken a cab, or better yet, hired his own vehicle, but either of those would have left more of a trail than he felt like clearing up. It was just as easy to follow some hapless bipeds as they mounted the rubberized steps of the big vehicle with the belching engine and the creaking, hydraulically assisted door.

Luck smiles on me, Fssik realized as he stepped to the side to avoid the center aisle of the vehicle. It wasn't particularly full, and only four or five Humans and an elSha boarded with him. So, rather than crouching under the cracked plastic seats as he'd planned, Fssik leaped onto the back of one of the seats, happy to have a better view.

In fact, he realized as he looked around, *I could jump to that rack above the seats. There's an egress port just above it where that ventilation cover is cracked open.*

He waited until the vehicle lurched to a stop to move. Before long, he lay curled atop a shapeless bag half-filled with one of the passenger's belongings. The air from the vent cover was humid, but at least it was moving, and Fssik found himself more comfortable than not. Always a good thing in his mind.

He watched the route of twists and turns the driver took and noticed two things. One, they were headed roughly in the right direction, per the map of Houston he'd studied while in transit, and two, they were not taking to the air like the cabs Ziva favored. The vehicle rumbled and roared but kept its wheels firmly on the ground, except for jolting bumps every few minutes. Either they were cutting a path through the piles of trash and debris he frequently noticed on the streets of Human cities, or the streets were in total disrepair.

Both were believable. Both were probably true.

The better part of two Human hours rolled by, punctuated by occasional stops as passengers got on and off the behemoth of a ground vehicle. Eventually, they reached a cross street Fssik recognized from his map, and he leaped down from the luggage rack when they lurched to a hissing stop.

Fssik focused on the driver's electronic UACC terminal and used the vehicle's spotty net to connect via his pinplants. Then he sent a fraction of a credit, roughly double the posted fare. The driver had done a good job, and they hadn't been shot once, despite the distant pops of gunfire he'd heard along the way.

After descending from the vehicle, Fssik looked around to get his bearings. Like a lot of neighborhoods he'd encountered in Houston's suburbs, this one had seen better days. Unlike most of those places, however, he saw scaffolding and construction debris, and one of the buildings on the corner had fresh paint on its brick facade. The industrial building across the street had a large sign advertising loft apartments for sale. It swayed slowly in the tiny, hot breeze.

The map in his memory told him to follow the main street for two blocks and then turn right. Fssik walked quickly, feeling the heat of the sun-soaked concrete beneath the pads of his feet. He began to see increasing evidence of someone pouring money into this neighborhood. A cafe on the next corner had banners proclaiming its grand reopening, and there were more than a few Humans moving in and out.

Interestingly, there were several other species as well. He counted more than one elSha, and he thought he caught sight of a Zuul in the shade of a large potted tree near the corner of the outside awning.

Stay on task, Fssik reminded himself as he flowed past the unseeing eyes of the cafe's clientele. *You can tell Ziva all about it later. She'd probably like to know that Houston is becoming more cosmopolitan.*

When he turned right off the main road, however, the thin veneer of revitalization fell away, and the general miasma of hopelessness and despair settled firmly back into place. Weeds sprouted from cracks in the concrete path, and piles of trash filled the street and the walkway.

He walked to the address his Sidar client had given him and looked up at the tall, skinny brick building. Four rows of boarded up windows, four Human-sized floors. A glance down showed him the tiny half-windows Humans used when they dug out a floor below ground level. These weren't boarded over, but they were covered with dirt and not reflective. He moved closer to one and sniffed, inhaling the scents of plastic and fear along with the much cleaner smells of dirt and glass.

If his time with Ziva and the other companions was any indication, Humans tended to go to ground. Someone had been in that basement relatively recently. Someone who was afraid.

Cooper Hatfield had a Hunter contract on his life. If he wasn't afraid, he was a fool.

Of course, he might not know about the contract, but Fssik figured it didn't really matter. It was a good enough reason for him to investigate the basement. Besides, he was curious.

He looked up at the side of the building. He hated to be predictable, but sometimes, the obvious answers were obvious for a reason. The pile of garbage and broken cargo pallets provided the perfect base for Fssik to start his ascent.

Using the crumbling windowsills, rusted sections of drainpipe, and toeholds in the bricks, Fssik made his way to the top of the building. When he reached the roof, he took a deep breath and looked around.

He spotted two security cameras right away. They weren't particularly sophisticated models, just basic streaming cameras that continuously uploaded to a private network. Since the Sidar had specified they were more interested in style than stealth, Fssik stopped the feeds by cutting the electronics out of the cameras. He allowed the second one to record his hand, claws extended, for a single frame before excising the lens and pulling the camera's innards out.

There, Frieloch, Fssik thought as he slow blinked. *That should make it obvious, don't you think?*

The cameras weren't the only bits of electronic gear on the roof. In the center, a small shed with a single door housed what Fssik figured was the terminus of the roof-access stairs. Several antennas rose from the top of the shed, and as Fssik studied them, he realized two were of quite good quality. They were certainly powerful enough to transmit and receive anywhere within line of sight, including low orbit. Who was this Human talking to? Was that part of the reason he'd annoyed Theela Financial?

The lock on the door was a simple mechanical deadbolt. Fssik had it open in three seconds, then he slipped inside with a sigh of relief as he left the punishing lightscape outside. Even after sundown, Houston had so many lights, it never really got dark.

It was certainly dark enough inside. Fssik retracted his goggles back into the harness he wore around his head and loosened his grip on his quintessence field. In the near-total lack of light, he would scent or hear anything well before it saw him. He took a deep breath and inhaled traces of dust and old gunpowder, but no Humans. Not in quite a while.

Fssik followed the stairs downward, enjoying the feeling of his body stretching and moving through the darkness. He stepped lightly, stopping often to scent the air and listen to the building's sounds. A faint, muffled scurrying came from inside the wall next to his right shoulder. He didn't hear an accompanying electronic whine, however, so he figured it had to be a native animal of some type, probably scrambling to get away from him.

That was one thing about small prey animals the galaxy over— they always recognized a predator when it entered the premises.

Based on the change in pitch and direction of the traffic noise filtering in from outside, he realized he had reached the ground floor. Every floor above had been empty, abandoned for over a season if he had to guess. The ground floor was no different, except for a single room near the back. As he stepped out of the stairwell, he pulled his quintessence around him, then followed the high, electronic whine coming from that direction.

He walked down a narrow hallway that twisted awkwardly through some spaces Fssik was certain weren't part of the building's original structure. After one last turn to the left, he came face-to-face with a hinged door that leaked cold, sickly light around all four sides. He eased up to the door and listened. When he heard nothing and smelled no one behind the door, he pushed it experimentally.

It swung gently inward and then back into the hallway. He stepped out of its path, and when it next swung into the space beyond, he slipped in behind it.

Ah! A kitchen! Fssik thought. He jumped up on the roughly meter-high counter and looked around.

The room was filthy, with a single dim light mounted high in the center of the ceiling. Like many of the rooms upstairs, the kitchen had windows that had been boarded over, then covered with paper from the inside. The electronic whine he'd heard came from a refrigeration unit that didn't match the dingy surroundings. Its stainless steel panels gleamed in the dismal light.

On silent feet, he padded over to the ancient stove and felt residual heat coming off one of the decrepit electric coils. He could hear the distant gurgle of water in the pipes leading to the nearby sink. The scent of lightly preserved meat and dairy hung in the air.

Someone is using this room to prepare food. That's a good sign, Fssik thought as he continued exploring. The cracked, dirty counter ended above a stinking garbage receptacle. Beyond that was a closed door with one of the round knobs Humans favored.

"Shut the hell up! You'll eat when I say you can eat, you fucking brat!"

The shouted words sounded as if they came from below, but they were loud enough to be only slightly muffled by the closed door. Fssik felt a pulse of anticipation which he tempered when he realized the voice was female and was, therefore, probably not his target. Humans had been known to change sexes occasionally, but as he understood it, it was a rather lengthy undertaking, and his contract wasn't *that* old.

Stomping followed the words, and the round knob turned as he watched, secure in his cloak of quintessence. The door opened, and he heard crying drifting up the stairs beyond. A female Human, with lanky, light brown hair hanging in her face, emerged, her expression sour.

"Damn kids," she said, grinding the words out between clenched teeth. Fssik could see a sheen of sweat on her forehead, and her dilated pupils indicated she was likely enjoying one chemical cocktail or another. Underneath her muttering and stomping, Fssik heard a muffled whimper, like someone very young crying behind a hand held over their mouth.

A slam echoed through the space, as if someone had opened and closed the front door of the building very quickly. The greasy-haired woman looked up, fear flashing in her drug-addled eyes.

"What the fuck happened to the security cameras?"

This voice was male and just as loud. Heavy footsteps echoed down the hallway Fssik had already explored. The swinging door exploded inward, making the woman jump back against the sink, as a large Human male stalked into the room. Anger twisted his bearded face as he charged the woman. He grabbed her by the throat with one hand and cracked her across her cheekbone with the back of the other.

"Baby!" she cried out. "I don't—"

"Shut your whore mouth! You're supposed to be watching the security feed, but I just checked my slate, and it's been down for the last fifteen fucking minutes. What've you been doin'? Lazing around like the fat-ass cow you are and getting fucking high?"

"No—" she gasped. Fssik could see her eyes starting to bulge. "No! I… fed… kids…"

The man leaned his face close to hers and snarled so viciously that flecks of spittle flew from his mouth and landed on her pale, blue-tinged face.

"Are you fucking lying to me, cunt?"

"Yes, she is," Fssik said, dropping his cloak of quintessence. The man was Cooper Hatfield. Fssik had authenticated the man's vocal print the moment he pushed through the kitchen door. Hatfield started at Fssik's sudden appearance on his kitchen counter and staggered backward, dropping his grip on the woman's throat. She doubled over and folded to her knees, gasping for air. Hatfield pulled a projectile weapon from the small of his back and pointed it at Fssik.

"You're not going to shoot me with that," Fssik said, curling his lips in an approximation of a Human smile.

"The fuck is this, a talking cat?"

Fssik snorted. "You must not get out much. I am Fssik, a Hunter. Your people call us Depik. Welcome to our negotiation."

The woman on the floor looked up with wide, terrified eyes and let out a breathy scream. Hatfield's lips curled in disgust, and he kicked her unprotected ribs with his booted foot. Fssik heard the crunch of breaking bone, and the woman screamed again in pain.

"Shut. Up," Hatfield demanded, punctuating his words with more kicks. Fssik launched himself up into a twisting leap. At the top of his arc, he drew his dart gun from the holster on his harness and fired three darts into the unprotected side of Hatfield's neck.

If Fssik remembered what Lara and Ward had taught him about Human anatomy—and he did, just as he remembered everything— the psychotropic cocktail in those darts should have started to work right... about... now.

Fssik's paws touched down on the counter next to Hatfield's elbow just as the man shuddered and began to convulse. He slumped slowly to the ground and melted into a puddle of tangled limbs next to the woman he'd beaten into near-unconsciousness.

The woman let out a groan and reached out, her bony hands scrabbling weakly at the dirty linoleum floor. Fssik ignored her for a moment and watched Hatfield as his eyelids began to flutter, and a thin pink froth sputtered forth from his lips.

"What you're experiencing is a potent paralytic from the planet Hrulgia in the Cresht Arm of the galaxy." Fssik sat down on his haunches and quickly reloaded his dart gun before putting it away. "I'm told it's not totally uncomfortable, but it is one hundred percent effective in severing your nervous system from your control. It is also one hundred percent fatal, but not quickly, so we have a moment. You won't be able to talk, but I'm told you can listen and understand, and you appear to be fully conscious. So, that's the good news." Fssik looked over at the woman again. Blood ran in a thin stream from her mouth, down her chin, and left thin red streaks on the floor. He turned back to Hatfield and considered him.

"I'm not really here to judge your morality," Fssik said. "I'm a Hunter. I take lives in exchange for money. In your case, I was contracted by Theela Financial to take your life because your illegal activity is interfering with their business interests. Their interests might also be completely illegal for all I know or care. The point is this: I'm here not because of right or wrong, but because you made someone very rich very angry. I would tell you not to do that in the future, but your future is only going to last a few more minutes."

Fssik jumped down from the counter and walked to the door the woman had come in earlier. He stretched until he could grasp the knob, then he turned it and used his body weight to pull the door open. The woman moaned.

The crying had stopped, and Fssik couldn't hear anything from the darkness that waited below. He inhaled and caught the mingled scents of Human sweat and waste. He looked up and saw Hatfield and the woman looking generally in his direction. Terror swept the woman's features. Hatfield just kept twitching.

"Cooper Hatfield, you don't know anything about my people, but the female companion you so brutally damaged appears better informed. Regardless, let me tell you both something about me and those of my species. We are not typically prolific when it comes to reproduction. This is something we have mourned and fought against for centuries, and even now, the members of my clan are doing heroic work to correct this problem. We do not often conceive litters of kits, but when we do, the little ones often do not survive."

Fssik stepped away from the door and casually pulled a thin, leaf shaped blade from one of the sheaths that crossed the chest strap of his harness. He started playing with the blade, letting it glint in the sickly light from the overhead fixture.

"I wonder if you Humans will ever be able to imagine just how sickening and infuriating it is, then, for me and other Hunters to witness how some of your race can be so careless, so neglectful, so *abusive* to your young?"

As he spoke, he crouched, until he was looking at the woman dead in the eyes. Her mouth worked, and more blood streamed from the corners of her lips.

"I'm… sorry…" she whispered in a broken exhalation.

"Who am I going to find downstairs?" he purred, letting her see the wickedly sharp points of his canine teeth.

"M-my kids. D-daughter… s-son."

"And?"

"T-two more."

"And what are they doing in that basement?"

"K-kept th-them. T-till the b-buyer came."

Fssik felt disgust curl through his entire being. Slavery was a reality throughout the galaxy, and he never really thought one way or another about it. But to look upon a—he couldn't associate the term "mother" with this creature—person who would sell any child, let alone her own offspring, into that wretched state made his rising fury flare into an inferno.

Without another thought, Fssik lashed out with claws extended and ripped the woman's throat open from ear to ear. Blood fountained forth, the hot saltiness of it spraying all over him and pattering on the linoleum and the warped particle board of the nearby cabinets.

Fssik stepped out of the spray and wiped his face and hands clean on the scrap of towel hanging from the shiny new refrigerator's handle.

That was a kit's move, Hunter, he chastised himself. *She was terrible and needed to die, but that's no excuse for sloppy work.*

Still, the Sidar *had* said they wanted it to look like a Hunter kill. It wouldn't take much forensic analysis of the dead woman's throat to show that it had been ripped open by claws, rather than an edged weapon of some kind. And, in the end, it didn't really matter too much anyway. She needed to die.

Now she was dead.

On to the contract.

"Are you still with us, Hatfield?" Fssik asked. Hatfield didn't move, but then, Fssik didn't expect him to. He swiped the bloodstained towel over his face one more time and dropped it on the floor, then walked over to Hatfield.

"She was a terrible person," Fssik said. "And, again, I'm not here to judge morals, but no one who squanders the gift of motherhood like that deserves to keep breathing. So, I stopped her from breathing ever again. On the house." He slow blinked at his joke. Ziva had told him about that expression, and he found he rather liked it.

"As for you," Fssik went on as he crouched next to Hatfield's paralyzed face, "I've killed you too. Your body just doesn't know it yet. As I said, that chemical is 100% fatal to oxygen-breathing species. Problem is, the client wants proof, and when you're paid as much as I charge, the client gets what the client wants. So, let's see..." Fssik licked his lips and flashed his teeth again. It wasn't a natural gesture, but he'd seen it in enough Human vids to know their species found it to be particularly unsettling. Hatfield's general stink intensified as his brain pumped more fear and adrenaline into his system.

"I know," Fssik said. "How about a retinal scan? Those are exceedingly difficult to fake, I hear. I'll just take your eyes!"

The fear-stink doubled, then tripled as Fssik pulled a small container out of one of his vest pockets.

"I would tell you to hold still, but I suppose that would be redundant," he said, slow blinking again at his own joke. "I have a scalpel, but honestly, I'm better with my own claws. It might hurt more, but then, you're just as terrible as she was, if you knew about the kids in the basement, and it seems eminently clear you did. So here goes, Cooper Hatfield!"

With that, Fssik extended his forefinger claw and pierced the skin in the outer corner of Cooper Hatfield's eye. With his pilot's steady hand, Fssik slowly dug and cut the connective tissue around the inside of the Human's eye socket. He carefully severed the optic nerve and gently pulled the round globule from its seat. He put it in the case.

"Well done, Hatfield!" Fssik said. "One down, one to go."

By the time Fssik was finished with the second eye, Hatfield's breath had gone thin, quick, and reedy, but he still hadn't moved.

Fssik snapped the case closed on the proof of his contract completion and patted his target on the shoulder.

"All done, Cooper. You did great. I imagine that hurt quite a bit. Don't worry, it won't be too long now. You're already short of breath. Your heart should stop in… oh, about thirty minutes or so. Goodbye, Cooper Hatfield."

Fssik tucked the case back into its pouch on his harness, then he turned to the shiny new refrigerator and pulled it open. A warmer light flooded the dimly lit room, making him squint. He snapped his goggles back into place and peered inside. Rows of canned beverages filled the bottom two shelves, but he found a package of sliced meat and some cheese in a drawer near the top. It took some doing, but he eventually got the drawer open and removed the two packages, then jumped back onto the counter, letting the heavy refrigerator door close behind him.

Fssik walked along the counter above the carnage he'd left on the floor. He leaped over the trash receptacle and landed in front of the door he'd opened earlier. Beyond the open door, a set of stairs stretched down into the darkness. He pulled his quintessence around himself, retracted his goggles, and started down the stairs.

The stairs emptied onto a concrete floored hallway stretching straight ahead. On either side of the hallway, thin wooden walls stretched down from the ceiling, broken every few lengths by a door. He heard the distant sound of sniffling and the soft murmur of someone singing.

Fssik padded through the darkness, following the sound of the song. It led him to a locked door at the far end. He pulled out his picks, and within minutes, the door swung open.

The song abruptly stopped. Fssik leaned around the doorframe and peered in.

It was a small room, no more than two lengths deep and just barely wider than that. A thin mattress lay on the floor, pushed up against the far wall. A young woman—girl, really—crouched on the mattress and leaned against the wooden wall that ran perpendicular to the door.

"Who's there?" she called out. Her voice sounded both terrified and angry, as if she cloaked herself in fury for protection. Her wide-pupiled eyes blinked in the dim light, and she curled further into herself.

"I am Fssik, a Hunter. I greet you, Human kita. I will not hurt you."

"You better show your face, or I'll hurt you!"

She likely couldn't see him in the darkness, but Fssik dropped his quintessence and slow blinked at her. This girl had fire, even under these wretched circumstances.

"I will not let you hurt me," Fssik said, "but you can see my face if you wish." He pulled a tab, and a small LED on his harness lit up under his chin. It wasn't bright enough to hurt his eyes, but it was enough to let her see him. Her eyes grew even wider, and she recoiled backward.

"You're... a cat?"

"I am a Hunter. You Humans call us Depik. We're from the planet Khatash, which is quite far away."

"You're an alien."

"I suppose so, since we're on your home planet."

"What happened to Beza and that asshole boyfriend of hers?"

"Was Beza your mother?"

"*Was?* What happened?"

"Please answer the question. Was she your mother, and does her death cause you pain?"

The girl sniffled, her lips trembling. She shook her head violently, and Fssik could see that her long hair was also lank and greasy. The entire room smelled as if she hadn't been bathed in… far too long.

"She's dead?"

"Yes."

"How?"

"I killed her out of anger when I realized she was neglecting you. You and the others."

She drew in a shaky breath and closed her eyes. Fssik felt a pit open inside him, and he stepped into the room. He didn't know this girl, but her pain cut him like an accusation, and he wanted to curl up next to her and rumble her fears away.

"Thank you," she breathed, and he froze.

"You… you are not sad?"

"Of course, I'm *sad!* Beza was my mother. I loved her when I was little, but the last few years… it's been all about the drugs and the shitty boyfriends. This last asshole was the worst. He…" She broke off and closed her mouth with a snap.

"I killed him too," Fssik said, taking another step closer to the girl. "He is dying slowly upstairs. He watched the woman's quick death and then felt me pull his eyes out of his skull while he couldn't move. Couldn't even scream."

The girl lifted her head and met Fssik's eyes with a rage and a savagery that burned brighter than a star gone nova.

"Good," she said.

"How old are you?" Fssik asked the girl.

"I'm eleven. Why?"

"Is that close to being an adult for a Human? I can't remember."

The girl let out a bitter laugh. "Close enough for some, I guess, but not really."

"That is what I feared. Where are the others?"

"In the rooms down here. Beza and the asshole kept us separated because it made it easier for them to… sometimes they had to drug us and whatever."

"Listen to me, Human kita," Fssik said. He gave in to the instinct that had been pounding inside his skull since he opened the door to her filthy little cell and walked up to her. A deep, healing rumble started within him as he wound around the thin, bony sticks of her legs. This close, he could feel the scent of the abuses she'd suffered, and he suddenly wished he'd made Hatfield's death last even longer.

"Wh-what?" she asked, her voice suddenly small and fitting for the child she still very much was.

"This is the end of this, I promise you. This will not happen to you ever again, nor to the others down here. I am very rich and one of the deadliest beings in the galaxy, and I promise you this nightmare is over. You don't have to think about it, and you don't have to talk about it unless you want to. Unless that will help you heal. Because you *will* heal. I promise you that, too. You and your brother and the two others that woman mentioned. You have survived, and it will make you stronger."

"Okay," the girl whispered, and Fssik felt her trembling hand slide softly down the length of his back.

"Now, please tell me the name you'd like to use and take me to get the others. You may have to help me convince them I mean no harm."

"I'm Diya, and they'll listen to me. I take care of them… when I can."

* * *

Fssik led Diya and the other three children—all boys, ages eight, five, and two—through a door leading from the basement. They may have hated Beza and Hatfield, but no child needed to see the aftermath of a Hunter kill, especially when their mother was one of the dead.

Outside the building, Fssik had Diya keep the boys together, hiding behind the pile of debris he'd used to get to the roof, while he moved to where he could access the local 'net with his pinplants. Though he usually preferred to travel in a less conspicuous manner, he put out a call to Beloro, which was commonly known as the best of the locally available armed transport companies. The fee was significantly higher than the bus fare he'd paid on the way in, but Beloro was fast and had a good reputation.

And the kids would be safe in transit.

A few minutes later, a sleek Beloro vehicle hovered down to the street in front of them with surprisingly little noise or exhaust. Fssik helped Diya and the boys board, then followed them into the plush leather interior of the backseat. The driver glanced back at him through the mirror.

"I greet you, Hunter," the driver said. "And your... uh... friends."

"I greet you, driver," Fssik said. "My friends have been through a lot, so please take us directly to the Law Offices of Ben Smith. I will pay a premium for speed and discretion."

"No premium fee required," the driver said, though Fssik knew very well that there ordinarily would have been. "If your friends are interested, I believe there are snacks in the center console."

A panel in the middle of the leather seat popped open, revealing rolls of what smelled like fresh Earth fish surrounded by a white, soft grain. Fssik realized that in his haste to get the kids out, he'd forgotten to give them the food he'd grabbed from the refrigerator. He produced the packages of meat and cheese from inside his carrying pouch and handed them to Diya.

"We can eat this?" she asked, her eyes going wide.

"Yes," Fssik said.

"It's all included," the driver added. Fssik heard an odd note underneath the man's professional tone and looked up to meet his eyes in the mirror again. There he saw compassion and rage for the state of these children. Fssik slow blinked and sent the man a generous tip through his pinplants. The man didn't give any indication that he'd noticed or received it… but then, he wouldn't. Beloro insisted its drivers always be professional. In fact, the driver didn't react or engage further until after they stopped at a landing platform halfway up one of Houston's shiny glass skyscrapers inhabited by the very rich.

"The Law Office of Ben Smith, Esquire," the driver said, toggling a switch to open the gull-wing door on the left side of the cab. Diya took the youngest boy by the hand and helped him out then shepherded the other two along while Fssik watched. He wanted to be sure they didn't trip on the platform. Just before he stepped out, the driver spoke up again.

"Hunter," he said quietly, "the ones who did that to them—"

"Are dead," Fssik said. "At least, the ones who held them captive are. I suspect there were others, perhaps many others, who paid money to contribute to their abuse. I do not have the luxury of time to track them all down at present, nor do I have the connections to do so, here, on Earth."

"I do," the driver said and met Fssik's eyes again. "Especially with the generous tip you just provided."

"Good hunting to you then, Driver."

"And to you, Hunter. Keep them safe."

Fssik slow blinked at the reflection of the driver's eyes, then bounded out of the vehicle. The double doors leading off the platform were already open, and a woman waited with a welcoming smile, gesturing for them to proceed in.

"My name is Nathalyia. I greet you Hunter… and children. Please come this way."

Diya looked over at Fssik with something like fear in her eyes, but Fssik slow blinked at her and stepped forward.

"I greet you, Nathalyia, associate. I have the proof of the completed contract for Mr. Smith, but these children have been through a lot. Is there somewhere they can rest while we talk?"

"Of course," she said smoothly. "We have a witness waiting room that has several comfortable recliners. Do you like Tri-V? I have a few kids' vids I can put on to keep the little ones occupied," she said, looking at Diya.

"That would work," Diya said, straightening her shoulders.

"I will do that, and if you'd like, I can stay in the room with you and help entertain them. Or not. Your choice, miss."

"I… why my choice?"

"Because you are the closest thing these boys have to a Dama now," Fssik answered. "You have taken care of them and are continuing to do so. It is not fair, perhaps, because you are so young, but then, what about this life is fair? You are the only stability these boys know."

"Are you gonna leave us?" Diya asked. She lifted her chin as she spoke, her eyes hard, but her voice trembled.

"Eventually, yes, I must. I cannot take you with me where I am going, but I do not have to leave you alone before you know whom you can trust," Fssik said.

"Of course," Nathalyia said. "I will let Mr. Smith know that we will all be meeting in the waiting room."

The waiting room was quite large. As promised, it had four or five comfortable recliners arranged in a conversational grouping around a huge Tri-V screen. Diya sat down in one, and the three boys piled in next to and on top of her while Nathalyia put on a kids' show. Fssik watched them settle, then bounded over to the small, round table at the other end of the room. Just as he reached the table, a door opened, and a male Human of medium height with dark hair walked in.

"Greetings, Hunter," he said, inclining his head. "I'm Ben Smith."

"I greet you, Lawyer Smith," Fssik said. "Welcome to our negotiation."

The man threw his head back and laughed. "That's fitting, all things considered. We lawyers are known for our negotiating skills."

"We Hunters are, too," Fssik said and smiled in the Human style, flashing a little fang.

Smith laughed again. "So, I hear. I'm told you have completed a contract you entered into with my client on the planet Azure?"

"I have," Fssik said. He reached into his pouch and pulled out the case that contained Cooper Hatfield's eyes. "A simple retinal scan will verify the identity of the target, or you can always spring for DNA analysis if you're unsure."

"Retina's hard to fake," Smith said, inclining his head. "That was smart of you. The target is fully terminated?"

"By now, yes. I left his body at the scene. The Sidar said they wanted it to look like a Hunter contract. It does. I wasn't subtle." He put the case on the table and slid it toward Smith. The lawyer reached out and caught it.

"Fair enough," he said, opening the case. He looked at Hatfield's irises, frozen in their wide, dilated state, and then snapped the case closed. "Nathalyia will take this for analysis. Once the retinal scan is done, we will forward the rest of your fee to the appropriate account."

"Excellent," Fssik said, cocking his head to watch as the woman approached and collected the case, then let herself silently out of the room. She moved like a Hunter, he noticed. He'd bet his very best set of lockpicks she was armed to the teeth.

"Does this conclude our negotiation, Hunter?"

"Not quite," Fssik said. He turned his attention to Ben Smith, then looked over his shoulder at the children sitting in the recliner. The youngest two had fallen asleep on Diya's lap, and the eight-year-old was leaning heavily against her shoulder. "I need to figure out what to do with them."

"Ah, yes." Smith frowned slightly. "I assume you found them at Hatfield's residence?"

"Yes. He and his woman had them captive there. From the state of things at the residence and what Diya said… and didn't say… I suspect they were systematically neglected and abused, physically and sexually. Diya and the older boy were the woman's offspring. I don't know if the other two have families that want them."

"Perhaps we can start there," Smith said. "I will put one of my investigators on it. In the meantime, I can set the four of them up in an apartment, with a caregiver trained in dealing with traumatized children. Unfortunately, we have to do that from time to time."

"I will never understand how carelessly Humans treat their offspring."

"Some Humans, Hunter. Not all of us."

"Fair point, Lawyer Smith. I apologize for any offense."

"No offense taken." Smith curled his lips in a tight smile. "Just clarifying. This kind of thing infuriates me and is part of the reason I do what I do."

"I suppose I am hiring you, then," Fssik said. "I know such things cannot be inexpensive."

"They are not," Smith said, with a little smile, "but we would have managed. I am happy to take your credits, though, especially since Nathalyia informs me that the late Mr. Hatfield's identity has been verified, and therefore, a rather large sum is being transferred to the account specified by the client."

"That makes things easy. You can use that account for the apartment and caregiver."

"As you like. I'll see it done. Welcome to the family of Ben Smith, Esq, and Associates, Hunter."

"Your clients are family?"

"In a manner of speaking."

"Fair enough. I must speak with Diya now, my lawyer."

"Of course. I will leave you the room."

"Come with me first," Fssik said. "She should know who you are."

"Good idea."

Smith stood, and Fssik leaped from the table to the floor, then back up to land on the headrest of the recliner the kids were sitting in. Diya craned her neck to look up at him.

"Diya," Fssik said, feeling the warm curl of affection and pride in the resilient girl before him. "I want to introduce you to Ben Smith, lawyer. I have hired him to see to whatever you and your brother—brothers if you like—need."

Suspicion creased her face, but the young Human girl shifted her gaze to Smith, who walked around and crouched in front of the recliner to speak to her.

"I understand you've been through a lot," Smith said, speaking softly, but not condescendingly, "and it's clear you care for these boys. My staff knows a woman who is trained to help kids like you. We're going to set you up in an apartment where you can live together unless and until we find the little boys' parents."

"Their parents are dead," Diya said. "I heard Beza talking about it. She said no one was looking for them… or us."

"That will never be true from this moment on," Fssik said. "I will always come looking for you—all four of you. And Lawyer Smith—"

"Ben. Please," Smith put in with a smile.

"Ben will do the same because I am paying him quite well, and he knows what will happen if he does not. I told you I cannot stay for long, but I promise you that *I will come back* and make sure you and the boys are well. I don't know what the future holds for you, but I keep my promises. No one will ever hurt you again."

Diya swallowed so hard, Fssik could see her larynx bobbing up and down. She stared at him for a long moment and then nodded. Fssik slow blinked at her and then turned to look at Smith.

"I must speak with her alone now."

"Of course. Diya, it's my honor to meet you. I hope you will think of me as *your* lawyer, and in time, come to trust me." When Diya didn't say anything, Smith gave her a small smile and then stood. "Use the room as long as you like. The caretaker is on her way, but it will be a little while before she gets here."

Fssik slow blinked at him, and Smith left the room. When the door clicked closed behind him, Fssik turned back to the girl.

"You are worried."

"He could do anything to us," she said, her voice small.

"Perhaps, but my instinct says he will not. Still, just in case, you must take this." He held out a small metal disc. On one side, a design of a Human hand with a Hunter paw atop it had been stamped into it. It was a new symbol; one the clan had recently adopted.

"This is a new version of a very old thing. Once upon a time, my people used discs like these to indicate that we owed someone a favor. A being had to present the disc to one of our retainers or connections to call the favor in. This one is different." Fssik turned the disc, so the raised edges of the design caught the light.

"This metal is actually a type of antenna. If you activate it, it will signal every Hunter in the galaxy, though the signal can only travel at the speed of quintessence, which is close to the speed of light. That should be enough for a Hunter to feel it and respond. If anyone, including Ben, ever tries to hurt you again, or separate you from your brothers, or in any way abuse you, you merely need to activate this token, and I or another member of my clan will come."

"How do I activate it?" she whispered.

"With blood. Yours or someone else's. Just a drop will do. But you must keep it hidden on you. Can you do this?"

Diya nodded and took the token. She tucked it inside her pocket and then reached out with her arms to Fssik. He leaped into them and nuzzled up against her as she pulled him close, clinging to her rescuer above the heads of her sleeping brothers.

"Thank you," Diya breathed into his fur. He felt her shudder slightly, and her arms trembled.

"You don't have to thank me, kita," Fssik said. "I'm sorry I didn't know sooner, but I promise you, no one will ever hurt you like that again."

"I know," Diya said. "You won't let them, and more importantly, *I* won't let them. I know I'm just a kid, but I'm gonna learn. I'm gonna learn to protect myself and the boys."

"That is wise," Fssik said. "If you tell Lawyer Smith what you wish to know, I am certain he will find those who can teach you, but you must also take time to heal. Promise me."

"I will," she said. "And you will come back? Eventually?"

"Eventually," Fssik said. "I cannot say when. But I will come back to check on you, tough kita. You are strong. You have it in you to heal from this."

Diya sniffled and nodded and rubbed her tear-wet cheek against Fssik's fur. Then she loosened her grip, and he stepped from her shoulder to the back of the chair, then jumped down. As he started toward the door, it opened.

"Hunter, this is Jennifer Wolffe. She is the caregiver I mentioned," Smith said as he walked into the room. A woman followed behind him. She had long, dark hair, worn loose, and she wore glasses over her large, blue eyes. She smiled at him and inclined her head.

"I greet you, Hunter."

"And I, you, Caregiver Jennifer Wolffe."

"Call me Karen," she said. "It's my middle name." She was dressed in a skirt suit of the kind favored by wealthy female Humans, but she moved like someone who was familiar with violence. *Merc*, Fssik decided, *or former merc, at least.*

"As you like, Karen," Fssik said. "I believe Lawyer Smith has explained the situation to you?"

"He has," Karen said, and though her professionally pleasant mask never slipped, Fssik saw the flicker of rage in her eyes. He slow blinked in approval. "Unfortunately, I have experience dealing with trafficking survivors from pretty much this same scenario. I understand you've taken financial responsibility for the children?"

"I have... and personal responsibility."

She smiled. "That's the correct answer," she said. "Ben informs me you cannot stay with the children, but that you'll be back."

"I will. Eventually."

"I see. It's not optimal, Hunter. These children need stability to heal. They need someone in their lives who will not leave them. If that can't be you, we need to find that person."

"I understand, Karen, and I am happy to assist in such a search, but I won't just hand over their care to anyone."

Her smile grew. "Another correct answer, Hunter. Well done. Good enough. Ben, would you like to introduce me?"

"Yes, right this way. Hunter, we'll be in touch."

"I expect so," Fssik said as he watched them walk over to greet the children, then he slipped out into the darkness of the hallway beyond.

He pulled his quintessence around him and walked back to the law office's landing pad, his mind in a whirl. What Karen had said about the children needing stability had struck home. They *did* need someone who could focus on them and only them. He couldn't be that person for them because he had to keep Ziva alive and help her accomplish their missions of furthering the Clan's interests. But how was he to find someone who could—

This is not your closest target, Hunter, Fssik admonished himself as he stepped out into the dawnlit air. *More pressing matters await.* His business had taken him through the night, and fatigue pulled at the edges of his mind as he wearily snapped his goggles into place. He used his pinplants to call an aircab that would take him back to his Ziva.

* * *

When Fssik initially found Ziva, he was pleased to discover she had finally consummated her fantasy and had sex with Jim. He revised that opinion shortly after, when Human insecurities caused the two of them to fight, then revised it again when they made up.

Now, here he was, surrounded by burning cars, with mortars falling from the sky, and he was seriously considering changing his mind yet again. Ziva definitely cared for him, but it was official: Jim Cartwright was a giant pain in Fssik's tail.

"Ziva!" Fssik shouted, but it was lost in the sound of another mortar exploding overhead. He watched helplessly as his Human took off running toward the building where they'd just seen Jim Cartwright's CASPer stagger and fall.

"Child, what is your name?" Fssik demanded of the kid he and Ziva had found hiding in the park in this chaos-ridden city.

"Antonio."

"Antonio, stay close to me. I will go slowly."

"All right."

The boy didn't do too badly for one so young, Fssik reflected. He wasn't particularly good at guessing in Human years, but he would put the child's age somewhere between the other two young males. Despite his age, Antonio did as he was bid—stayed close, kept his head down, and followed as quickly behind Fssik as he could manage. Still, he was only Human and a child, so by the time they caught up to Ziva, she was kneeling atop a half-open CASPer, tears streaking down her face as she pleaded with an unconscious Jim not to die.

Fssik pressed against her, and little Antonio reached out a hand to awkwardly pat her shoulder. Fssik was just about to suggest they try to move somewhere more secure, when an atmospheric ship bearing the insignia of Cartwright's Cavaliers hovered into place overhead. It seemed the cavalry had arrived.

* * *

"Thank you for staying with me," Ziva said quietly as they sat in a hospital waiting room some hours later. Fssik looked up at her in disgust.

"Where else would I be?" he asked.

"Somewhere? Anywhere? I don't know. Jim isn't—"

"Jim is yours. You are mine. Therefore, I am here. Do not waste time being stupid about it, my Human."

Ziva let out a short, startled laugh that made little Antonio stir. In the absence of a better solution, he and Ziva had elected to keep the boy with them for the time being. While they waited for the doctors to do all they could to repair Jim Cartwright's shattered body, the boy fell asleep with his head in Ziva's lap. She reached down and ran her fingers through the short, black strands of his hair.

"What are we going to do with this one?" she asked softly.

"Maybe if we think about that, it'll take my mind off Jim."

"What do you want to do with him?" Fssik asked, keeping his tone carefully neutral. He had yet to tell Ziva about the children he supported in an apartment in Houston. Quite a bit of time had passed since he'd rescued Diya and her brothers, and he'd visited them twice, but he wasn't exactly sure how Ziva would feel about him "adopting" four human children.

"Keep him," she sighed. "I want to cuddle him close and assure him that nothing will ever harm him again. But I can't do that, can I? It's hardly fair, when I don't even know what planet I will be on next."

"Still," Fssik said. "It's a good instinct. Children should be protected as kits are. You have Hunter instincts on this matter."

"Yeah, but he's not a Hunter kit, is he? Does he have a family? Someone who is missing him?"

"We can ask him," Fssik said. "If he does not know, I may have someone who can find out."

"Yeah," Ziva sighed, stroking the boy's hair back from his face. It was ragged and dirty, but she couldn't keep herself from petting him. "That's probably our first step—"

"I greet you, clanmates."

Fssik looked up from the sleeping child, gladness pouring through his body as a familiar form leaped through the door of the hospital waiting room.

"Esthik!" Ziva cried out, making little Antonio shift in his sleep again. "What are you—"

"Fssik called my ship. I happened to be close by, checking on something for Dama when I got the message. Is Jim Cartwright alive?"

"He was when we saw him last," Fssik said as Ziva pressed her lips together and blinked rapidly. "He is in there, with the Human doctors and his Dusman. I told her you were coming. If you go in, I don't think they will make you leave. She will see to it."

"Excellent," Esthik said, turning to head through the double doors into the operating area. "I will return when I have news."

* * *

"The news is not as good as it could be, but Jim Cartwright will live."

Fssik looked over at Ziva where she sat in the orange plastic hospital chair, her hands clasped together in her lap. Her knuckles shone white in the fluorescent lights from the ceiling. She exhaled slowly and closed her eyes.

"I will return," Fssik whispered to Antonio, who had awakened and was sitting with Fssik in his small lap. The child tended to be calmer when the Hunter was nearby. Ziva had been jumpy and fidgety while she waited for news.

The news had come. Antonio looked down at Fssik and nodded, and Fssik leaped from his seat to Ziva's in a single bound. Without opening her eyes, she lifted her arms to gather him close and pressed her cheek against the top of his head.

"How 'not good' is it, Healer?" Fssik asked for her.

"His spine is damaged. We don't know the full extent yet, but it is possible he will never walk unassisted again. He is strong for a Human, and, as I said, he lives. Where there is life, there is hope."

Ziva nodded and opened her eyes. Fssik didn't miss the sheen of wetness in her gaze.

"Thank you, Healer," she said softly. "Can we go in?"

"Not yet," Esthik said. "The Human doctors are finishing up and then they will wake him from the medical coma. You may see him then. It will not be long. In the meantime…"

Fssik turned away from the pain in his Human's face to study his clan-brother. Esthik slow blinked at him and then looked, very deliberately, at Antonio.

"Antonio," Ziva said. "The Cavaliers should hear this news. I think they're in the room just beyond this one. Would you mind going to check?"

"Sure," the kid said, hopping to his feet. "How long do you guys want to talk about me, so I know when I should come back?"

Fssik dropped his jaw in a grin. Much like his kids in Houston, Antonio was young, but he'd seen things no child should ever have to see, so he possessed a worldly maturity and intelligence far beyond his years.

"Just a few minutes, kit," Esthik said, also slow blinking. "It's good you're so perceptive. You may listen at the door if you like."

"I was gonna, anyway," Antonio said with a small, savage grin, before walking toward the hallway that led to the larger room where the members of Jim's Cavaliers waited.

"He's very smart," Esthik said, speaking in the Hunters' native language. Esthik must have deactivated his translator via his pin-plants because no English translation followed. Ziva frowned slightly in concentration, but she and Fssik had been practicing before they went to Austin, so Fssik was confident she'd get the gist of things.

"He is," Fssik said. "He is a survivor, that kit."

"That is excellent, and exactly what I want to speak with you both about. I told you I was nearby on an errand for Dama, but I didn't tell you what it was. To be honest, I came to Earth looking for the two of you. I have an assignment for you from the clan."

"A contract?"

"Not exactly," Esthik said, "but similar. As you know, the surrogacy program is working better than we could have hoped. Kits grow quickly, and the first generation are starting to bond already. However, therein lies the problem. We will soon run out of useful companion candidates."

"And you want… but Antonio is just a kit!"

"Yes, he's too young to bond just yet, but he will be perfect in a few years. He's not the closest target, perhaps, but Dama feels—and I agree—that we must play the long hunt when it comes to preserving our species."

Fssik nodded. "You couldn't have known we found a likely child," he said. "So, what is this assignment?"

"Dama thinks you two are perfectly suited to find more candidates, particularly among the Humans. We are looking at other races as well, by the way, but your situation here puts you in a good position to find the Humans we need. In fact, you already have."

"You… want… kids?" Ziva asked, her words halting in the Hunter tongue. Fssik slow blinked up at her, even though she spoke with an incredible lisp.

"To an extent, yes. Slightly older than Antonio, if possible, perhaps teenagers. But more important than the age is the personality. These young ones will be presented to bond to a Hunter kit or kita, so they must be strong. As you put it, survivors, and they must not have family who will conflict."

"Unwanted," Ziva said.

"Exactly. We want the Humans humanity does not want or fears to have."

"I have some for you," Fssik said. He deliberately didn't look up at Ziva, but he felt her head swivel to stare at him, nonetheless. "In Houston. Four kids, around Antonio's age. They're survivors, too. I rescued them on my last contract. I've been paying for them to live and be... healed, as best they can. I think they would thrive as companions. They each need someone who is theirs alone."

"That is excellent," Esthik said. "When we are done here, perhaps you can take me to these children and introduce me."

"Me too," Ziva said in a small voice. Fssik stood up on his hind legs and rubbed his skull under her chin.

"I am sorry I didn't tell you," he whispered in English. "It never seemed to be the right time."

"It's all right," she said. "We can talk about it later. I'm glad you rescued them."

"So am I," Fssik said.

"So are we all," Esthik finished.

* * * * *

Chapter Four

Tsan did not pilot the ship. This chafed down the insides of her limbs, but she remained sleek coated and unperturbed while in the common area with the kits.

A party of fourteen accompanied her to Azure, a mixture of ages and races, but predominately kits. The pilot was perfectly acceptable, or Dama Tamir would not have employed him. Tsan had no reason to upset her fellow passengers.

Passenger. Even the word grated. She did not pilot when she slipped onto a ship to move between gates unnoticed and untracked, but that was different. Here, she could just as easily be piloting as she could be fastened into the long bench-like seating of the circular space in the middle of the ship.

Instead, she was charged with the kits—those too young to have bonded, but old enough to travel, those paired with Humans going to Azure for their upgraded genetics, and those who were grown and should have known better than to act as kits—evaluating them, preparing them, considering them, and soothing them.

Soothing them, not herself. She kept her traitorous limbs tucked underneath her and slow blinked with calm appraisal as the kits burbled and played in zero G all around her. She did not pilot. She watched. And waited.

The fur down her back shuddered, and she smoothed it again, knowing none were close enough to her to notice.

"Hrava!" one of the younger kits pronounced and somersaulted through the open center of the room with abandon. "Come and play with us!"

The striking kita, near-grown and only a little older than the first batch of kits born on Land's End, waved her tail from her perch halfway up the wall across from Tsan.

"I am reading, Devsi. Perhaps it would benefit you to learn about Azure before we get there."

"Why?" the speckled kit demanded, twisting his body to regain momentum. His action moved him from the path of two attacking kits, but he pretended not to notice them. "We'll see it when we get there. Plenty of time to learn about it with our own eyes!"

"Dama Tsan would tell us if there were something we should know first!" Nsiya declared, spinning away from her failed attempt on Devsi.

"Would she?" Hrava sat up on her perch and curled her feet around it to hold herself in place. "Or would she expect that if you are old enough to leave the den, you are old enough to learn for yourself?"

This question stilled quite a bit of the movement from the five kits frolicking in zero G. Momentum continued to move them about, but, for a moment, they paused in their fine acrobatics as they considered Hrava's point.

"*I'm* reading about everything they're going to do to Sid," Zemsta declared from her position on a bench to Tsan's left. "Ward gave us a *lot* of information."

"I'm going to be ok, Zem," Sid said, his young Human voice cracking the way it apparently did when Humans changed scents.

'Matured' the Humans called it, but facts were what they were. "He's already done a few, and Meredith is doing great."

"Well." Zemsta flexed her unusually long claws and flicked her ears. "*I* want to be very sure you're safe. Seems like the responsible thing to do."

"We have a hundred more hours to be responsible, kita." Will, Zemsta's littermate, rolled off his perch and used his Human companion, Twilight, as a launching pad to throw himself into the muddle of younger kits floating about. "Fighting in zero G is a skill. Maybe you should try it."

Tsan laughed at the clear challenge, which was instantly met by Zemsta, who shoved her slate against Sid and angled herself perfectly to intersect her brother's path.

The spreading knot of kits abruptly began to reshape, as several began flipping and twisting to get closer, and others did the same to get out of the way.

Kits, Tsan thought with a slow blink. *Always the same.*

It was comforting to see them, see how entirely kit-like they were, even though they were born of Earth cats and raised in the tunnels and domes of Land's End, rather than the dens and jungles of Khatash.

That was likely why Dama Tamir had chosen to employ a different pilot and charge Tsan with the messy, inexhaustible, squabbling, precious, perfection of them.

Damas, she said to herself, her tail twisting behind her. *Always the same.*

* * *

A zure had an appropriate amount of moisture in the air—closer to Khatash's jungles than Tamir's domes—but far less trees than she'd expected. Though she had never been to a planet with quite the same… magnitude of trees as her home.

The ocean, a stretch of water that extended as far out as her eyes could process and as far down as the core of the planet, as far as she could tell, had a familiar weight. Though it plummeted down rather than scraped the upper atmosphere, it was as dominant here as the jungle was on Khatash. The fur along her spine twitched, not entirely uncomfortably.

If kits stay here to grow, will they swim? Will Ward tweak them to dive alongside their Wrogul companions?

It made her wonder if the Wrogul had turned their tinkering nature on their Human compatriots on Azure. Ward considered himself Human, but he did not speak as though that were a unique point of view among his people here. After he stretched his tentacles and finished with *Homo venatores*, would he have an interest in *Homo Azurus* perhaps? *Aquaticus?*

A vision of Humans and Hunters, skills and adaptations guided by the Wrogul, made her chuff deep in her throat and twist her ears in something that wasn't quite worry.

A consideration for another time.

She sat at door of the disembarking bay and waited for the various members of her party to arrive. The cheetahs would stay on board until she confirmed the location of the place where they would have a long stretch to run.

Sepnil and Treeves had already borne three litters each and were willing to bear more. Both had grown increasingly restless in Land's

End, however, and, at the very least, they deserved a break on a planet with room to run and stretch. Perhaps, if Tsan and Azure's leaders came to an acceptable agreement in their negotiation, the spotted Earth felines could stay, with occasional trips back to Land's End to bear a litter or two.

Or perhaps they would retire from their breeding. The tigers and lions comfortably carried seven to nine kits per litter, while the cheetahs were safest with four. Trips to Earth no longer needed to be clandestine, and Land's End had acquired more than a few big cats willing to trade their lives in a small refuge—or, in one odd case, a Human garage—for one with many kits and a chance to walk among the stars.

It reminded Tsan of a story her molly had told, but before she could fall too far into old thoughts, Hrava dropped her quintessence field. Faint sounds indicated her Human followed close behind.

"Dama, I greet you," the young Hunter said, dipping her head.

"Hrava." Tsan leaned forward and brushed her cheek against the white and black swirls along the top of the near-grown kita's head. "You are early."

"Not as early as you." She slow blinked at Tsan, her pupils dilated in pleasure at the greeting.

"Ah, did you think to be here first, little one? Or—" Tsan glanced back, toward the closed airlock, "—were you thinking you might slip outside and see what could be seen before we disembark?"

Hrava groomed herself and called out a greeting to her approaching companion in lieu of answering. Tsan rumbled a laugh deep in her chest. *Kits.*

"Dama, I greet you," Ayamani said, dipping her head far more deeply than Hrava had. She glanced behind herself and twisted her long, human hair into a fastened knot. "Sid is on his way, so my credits are on everyone getting here early." She shot a glance at Hrava, who tilted her head as though she didn't notice.

Out of politeness, Tsan did not laugh a second time in front of Hrava's companion, but she did flick an ear toward the younger Hunter.

Ayamani was not the sort of Human who chattered nervously during a comfortable silence, which Tsan appreciated, so they stood together quietly for a few moments before a commotion heralded the other kits and Humans.

"I already tagged you, Nsiya!" Devsi announced, skidding around the corner, her tail puffed to three times its usual size. "You're supposed to fall to the back."

"I was in the back!" a disgruntled voice replied from a spot to the left and not quite behind the striped kit. "*You* were just too slow."

"Pirri got in my way!"

"Nsiya's right, you were slow." Pirri bounded up to Tsan, dropping her field mid leap. "Dama! I'm so glad you're here early. It was a long trip." She chirruped and twined around Tsan briefly before jumping back and belatedly making a proper greeting.

"I think we're all ready to stretch our legs," Ayamani interjected, allowing the young Pirri a moment to groom herself back to appropriate behavior.

"Not as much as Sepnil and Treeves, maybe." Will appeared at a more sedate pace, though his cheeks quivered with his excitement.

This would be the first outside planet for most of the kits, Tsan reminded herself, wishing she'd thought to ask Tamir to send a molly. Minding one or at most three kits was all very well, but keeping up with seven of them…

"Everyone is to report to their assigned location *first*," she said, making narrow-pupiled eye contact with each of them. "I will not find you underfoot in places you are not meant to be."

At the chorus of 'Yes, Dama,' and 'No, Dama' in their appropriate windows, she slow blinked. Hrava, at least, had caught both the warning and the permission. Tsan was not to find them. It didn't mean they couldn't be wherever they felt like being.

They'd done much to keep the Hunter species alive up to this point. But they hadn't, would never, fundamentally change kit behavior, or Hunter behavior, for that matter.

Tsan flicked her tail and pulled quintessence.

Ward had squirmed and flashed a series of colors while discussing the Governor of Azure. There had been quite a bit of action on the far-flung planet, which had led to a recent leadership change. While events had settled for the time being, he thought it likely they'd be open to negotiation.

"Keep in mind, though, they're only newly... read in? Yes, read in, to the Hunter situation." Ward had twisted his tentacles and studied his slate rather than making eye contact with her.

"Our situation?" she'd asked mildly, her voice velvety soft.

"That you exist. That you have allied with some Humans. That I... we... there are Homo venatores *now. I needed access to the clinic at Azure for some of the more fragile cases. Tamir cleared it."*

She'd had to acknowledge the wisdom in the situation, and it had given her decision a clearer path.

Still, though many of Azure's denizens involved in the clinic knew of the "Hunter situation," Tsan saw no need to parade herself through the colony en route to her meeting. Let herself and her purpose remain opaque.

The kits were entrusted to their companions or to the older Hunters with them, and they knew when they were to check in and how. Letting them loose on a strange planet was no more dangerous than the critical time in any kit's life when they left the den for the jungle.

Indeed, she thought, leaping to take the high route through the passageways, *while danger exists here, it will likely be less than what they'd find on Khatash.*

It gave her a pang, as it always did. As precious as kits were, they were still thrown into the jungle with minimal protection. They had to survive Khatash to mature, and clans lost many to that necessary rite of passage.

These kits had much to survive and master, but if…

When…

When they returned to Khatash, more than their enemies would be ready to bleed them.

It would be their home as well, taking its delayed due. The jungle was not a forgiving place.

Tsan flicked her ears to dismiss the thought and increased her pace. She had plenty of time before her appointed meeting, but she would hardly wait until the designated time to scout the location. She had much to see before she met with the Governors.

* * *

Many of the Humans wore gloves with photosensors. From inside her quintessence field, Tsan studied them each time she saw them being used. They echoed the colors of the Wrogul, and she decided translators didn't make the most of the Wrogul language. Did Ward wish they had such things?

She considered their usefulness in sending coded messages through the trees, when pinplants couldn't be trusted, then released the thought with a hint of regret. Pretty, but not practical, with quintessence and the light-swallowing triple canopies of Khatash. Still, she filed the idea away to ask Ward about later. Their Wrogul had done quite enough to earn such consideration if he would like it. Perhaps, too, it would fill in some of those odd starts and stops of his half-thoughts and incomplete sentences.

She directed her steps back toward the governors' office, which neither Governor seemed to spend much time in. They both, Human and Wrogul, spent a great deal of their day out and about with other members of the colony.

She rather liked Gamboa, the Human, who had a way of speaking that indicated he was well used to getting his way.

Perseus, the Wrogul, seemed less comfortable in his position, but competent all the same.

Tsan was pleased with what she saw of them and the interactions between species, in general, so she chose to arrive only a few minutes before the meeting, still cloaked in her field.

"Ward didn't say what they were going to ask for," Perseus said, flashing colors Tsan tentatively designated as 'curious,' "only that they are pleased with his work so far."

"Octavius doesn't have, or won't give, details," Gamboa replied, his elbows comfortably resting on the table in front of him. "He seems pleased with Ward's work as well. Says it's giving him some ideas for Azure."

"That…" Perseus paused, though this struck Tsan as thoughtful, unlike Ward's constant interjections. "I can't decide if that's promising or not."

"Better than the evil penguins having ideas for Human physiology," Gamboa replied.

Tsan knew more than enough Wrogul body language to translate Perseus' wordless reply as "*Is* it?" and she huffed a silent laugh to herself.

"I suppose we'll know what the Depik want soon enough. Do you think they'll announce themselves?"

"For all we know, they're here now," Gamboa muttered, his eyes moving steadily across the room. He did not smell nervous, only alert, and Tsan dropped her field accordingly.

"So I am, Governors of Azure. I am Tsan of Clan Tamir, and I greet you."

She slow blinked at his careful posture, which betrayed none of the surprise his scent indicated. The Wrogul controlled himself quite well, only his smaller tentacles curled at her appearance. Tsan allowed a small measure of warmth into her tone as she continued.

"Welcome to our negotiation."

"Depik, we greet you," Gamboa said, his posture straightening. "We look forward to learning what we're negotiating for."

"I will not leave you in suspense, Human Governor of Azure, nor you, Wrogul Governor. Ward has shared some of what you have defended against, recently."

"Not the pineapples," Perseus murmured, his translator much better at volume regulation than Ward's.

"Ward shared less of what you have been doing," Gamboa said, his tone dry. Tsan flicked her ears in acknowledgment.

"He did not go into great detail, I assure you." This was entirely true. It didn't mean Tsan hadn't gone and *found* more detail, but that was hardly the point. "It was enough to know you acquitted yourselves very well from a disadvantage and made excellent use of allies of various species."

"That's a neat enough summary."

"And that is what I am here to negotiate. An alliance."

Whatever they'd expected, that clearly wasn't it. Both stared at her for a long moment.

"Our troubles—" Perseus began.

"Are hardly at an end. I know. Nor are ours. There is a great deal moving across the systems, Governors. Guilds collapsing. Power shifting. We Hunters survive to this day, thanks, in large part, to our alliances, Human and Wrogul." It did not pain her to say such words, though once it might have. Truth cut, but it did not tear. "We intend to survive all that comes next, and for that, we are interested in expanding our alliances."

"Why us?" Gamboa asked, his voice changing in some subtle way she could not quite place. An accent, perhaps? Several of Tamir's Humans had different accents, depending on where in the galaxy they'd begun their lives.

"You strike us as survivors, as well. Resourceful. Full of surprises." She slow blinked and spread her hands wide, claws mostly sheathed, in emphasis, not threat. "Valuing the lives of those you work with, not only your own species'."

"We believe in treating others the way we want to be treated. It's a key component of life here. What would this alliance entail?" Perseus asked, his flashing colors indicating 'pleased' to her understanding.

"A home for some of our Hunters and their companions. A home, and perhaps companions, for some of our young."

"Not resources? Trade goods?" Gamboa's voice remained sharp, but his shoulders had eased at her response.

"No." Tsan lashed her tail, now understanding more about their recent conflict. "We lack nothing credits can buy. The Hunters I propose to leave here will consider Azure their home. They will add to its defense."

"Bodies, then, that you can throw at your own conflict?"

"There will be fights enough ahead for all of us," Tsan replied, the truth of it a weight against the base of her spine, "and you are not the only allies I propose to have."

Gamboa had already softened, but his voice remained firm. If she hadn't spent so long with Humans, she would have missed the signs. As it was, his stubbornness made her like him more.

"You would fight with us, if needed?" Perseus asked, colors muted. Tsan turned her attention to him and slow blinked again.

"Allies shed blood as needed." She warmed to him as well, as he flashed 'pleased' again, then she held up a hand. "I will not lie. Our forces, as of now, remain small, and we have a large fight ahead of us, but it's not one you need to be overly involved in, should we ally."

"What is it?"

"We are taking back our home." She'd considered leaving it vague, but they knew few details that could leak back to the Veetanho and harm her people. Besides, if this went as she expected it to, before she left, these too would be her people. "Hunters have been... more than decimated, in response to actions from the previous leadership of the Mercenary Guild. I will not commit all of us to the battle, but the battle will be had."

"You want to leave some here, so your people will survive." Perseus grasped it instantly, confirming her understanding that he was as brilliant as Ward, and then he made a leap she didn't expect. "You… one of your kind… destabilized the Mercenary Guild."

She inclined her head. Her fingerpads twitched, but she would do nothing different if she had Peepo in her claws again, though doing it all over would be satisfying.

"We are allied with its current leadership," she said, which was all the information that was necessary to share now.

"And the other Guilds?"

"That is not of our doing." That was not entirely true, but now was absolutely not the moment to speak of Minerva, or what she suspected to be true of many, if not all, of the Guilds.

"We understand defending your home," Perseus said after a moment, his tentacles curling. "I wish we had the resources to help you retake it, but—"

"That is not the purpose of our alliance," she finished, with a nod to show she understood.

"I believe we are aligned in outcomes then," Gamboa said, tapping his fingers on the table. "So, our negotiation becomes the process."

Tsan nodded, jumped to the table between Gamboa and Perseus, and wrapped her tail comfortably around her body. She slow blinked once more before she spoke.

"Let us begin."

* * * * *

Chapter Five

Tsan did not, technically, exist on the transport ship *Hestial*. Secure in her quintessence field, she curled into a corner of a duct that had been left intact when retrofitting routed the coolant system in another direction. It was her third such out of the way nest in as many ships, and she had two more to go before reaching 'Tlor. She could have brought one of the smaller Hunter ships and tucked it under a merchant's craggy hull or created a false trail to cover her movements or simply paid for passage.

Each of those risked leaving evidence of her path, however, so she'd taken a route simpler in some ways and trickier in others, to keep any enemy or too interested party from tracking her.

Which made it concerning when a message pinged her as they approached the next gate.

She didn't worry immediately—messages were left at gates to be carried further by ships all the time. The code on this one, however, was addressed to her, at this gate, meaning it was likely someone had known she would pass this way.

Her fur lifted down her spine, and her tail lashed in her field. Someone.

Or something.

She did not flex her claws, nor did she say the name *Minerva*, even silently to herself in the quiet of her own protected thoughts.

Before she opened the message, she ran her fingerpads over each weapon on her person. Small throwing knives studded along harness, check. Gun holstered on the left, check. Longer knife sheathed on the right, check. Blast rifle disassembled but easy to reach in pack, check. Fragmentary grenades, check. Twenty perfectly sharpened claws, check. Additional knives, charges, and slate for programming delayed charges, check all.

It was unlikely to be Minerva, or anything like it, that had sent the message to her. It was therefore even more unlikely that her opening the message would cause the beings on the transport to become puppets of Minerva, or something like it, and made to charge this unused corner of the transport.

Unlikely was certainly not the equal of impossible, and she felt better after taking stock of her options.

She opened the message and blinked. Her ears flattened against her skull.

Transport Hestial *has 79% chance of being attacked on way to Suroma Station or back to gate after the station.* Vessels Kichan, Naroovet, *and* Sipside *have greater than 85% chance of attack upon departure from Suroma Station. Recommend* Tinsey *or* Craddleben *for next leg.—Theela.*

What under the canopy-eaten stars was a Theela? The name plucked at her memory, but without context, she couldn't place it. Tsan's tail lashed, and she growled low in her throat before forcing herself back to silence.

She forced her ears upright and swiveled them, stilling even her breath until she confirmed there were no approaching sounds in answer to either her noise or the message she'd opened.

Entropy would eat the entirety of the universe before she'd entrust her safety to the recommendation of a mysterious contact.

Suroma was a large enough station that she could slip off the transport and find plenty of corners to wait. What, if anything, happened to the ships named in this Theela's message would tell her... something. It was more than worth a delay for her trip to 'Tlor.

* * *

Suroma was a straightforward station—three large, round sections connected to each other and their common central spike. Tsan left the transport for one of its small tending ships to board the station. She tucked herself under a secondary console and ignored the bumpy docking procedure. Security was far too lax for her to so much as blink at it, and she took the long way to the top of the station, rather than expend the energy to move around other beings in the air lifts.

Tsan prowled each level of the station, paying special attention to the security offices, both public and tucked away. She found no unfamiliar technology that could pierce her quintessence field and no alerts or alarms outside the obvious.

Deep in the guts of the third level, she found a security closet with a clear view of the screens, one Goka with a neutral odor, and a perfectly comfortable ledge on top of the storage cabinet facing the screens. This closet—office—tracked incoming and outgoing traffic rather than in-station movement, and, while ideally she'd like to keep an eye on both, the priority was confirming the message's contents.

In the hours she'd taken to survey Suroma, check departure and arrival logs, and eat some of the dehydrated food in her pack, the *Hestial* had completed its business. She watched as the tender dropped off the station and accelerated to catch up to the transport's wide run through the system.

Noting three ships other than the "suggested" *Tinsey* and *Craddleben* that would take her closer to 'Tlor, if not all the way to the Lumar home world, Tsan settled in for a long, hopefully boring, watch.

Three hours in, the Goka grunted, stood, and did a careful dance around the incoming Goka who arrived to relieve them. The new one smelled more strongly of a recent meal, which twisted Tsan's stomach.

She'd taken longer trips than this one and stayed thoroughly hidden, and, of those, her only complaint was the lack of good food from a proper hunt. Though, usually, on any trip where she chose to be this far off the radar, she had a far more solid plan, far fewer questions, and a different sort of hunt to keep her occupied.

Since she'd received Theela's message, she'd had a squirming feeling under the fur of her neck, as though a larger predator were about to bite down and carry her off. It was unlikely that she was being hunted, but…

She flexed her claws and slowly slid further down on her side to keep her harness from catching on anything, then she wriggled to get comfortable.

Hestial continued toward the gate, its path unchecked and unchallenged. Tsan mentally sighed—seventy-nine percent was not one hundred, and the transport wasn't safe yet, but it did seem as though Theela had warned her off nothing. At this point in its trajectory, the transport was close enough to gate transit that an attack would very likely draw the attention and ire of the Cartography Guild for threatening the safety of the gate.

Tsan did such a solid job of convincing herself there was nothing in the Theela message that the Goka noticed trouble before she did.

A very quiet alarm—a pattern repeating three long and two short tones—sounded on his console, and he began chattering through his comms. Her translator fed about half of it into her pinplants, which was enough to catch the gist.

The *Kichan* and the *Sipside* had dramatically changed course, the smaller *Sipside* sending readings that indicated it was doing a number on its inhabitants as it juked and jerked off its initial parabola.

The station didn't yet have readings on what they were avoiding, but they'd either had some sort of near simultaneous navigation failure, or they were both under attack.

There were no obvious reports on the *Naroovet*, and she'd still need to see if the *Tinsey* and *Craddleben* left the system untouched, but she'd seen more than enough to tell her Theela knew a few things.

Like when ships were in someone's target sights. Or where a Dama might be, even though she'd employed effort in ensuring no one knew where she was.

All in all, Tsan did not approve.

'Tlor would wait.

She had hunting to do. And that meant going to Karma.

* * *

Tsan did not like Karma. It was convenient since it provided a pass through to just about anywhere. If one were ever bored, there were plenty of contracts and clients to entertain. Nearly every species one would hope to meet wandered through at one point or another.

She had expected to love it the first time her Dama sent her offworld to meet a repeat client. Adventure, intrigue, new beings to learn about!

What she'd found had been too bright lights, stale smells of old fights, and only the boring sort of bodily fluids.

You can find danger anywhere, if you close your eyes and poke at it, her Dama had said, so long ago. *But you, my fierce one, will always have one eye open.*

She hadn't understood her Dama, not quite, not then. She hadn't thought about those words in nearly as long as she'd been Dama herself. Now, walking Karma's well-trod corridors, goggles dialed against the strobing signs and advertisements, she heard them again.

She'd thought her Dama meant something simple—anywhere in the great, wide galaxy was dangerous to someone foolish, someone who didn't pay attention. Observe, prepare, and any danger could be mitigated.

She considered the memory, her steps light as she moved through a crowd that couldn't see her, and she realized her Dama had been praising and warning her both. Anything could be dangerous; it was as true in the jungle as in a random station in the Tolo arm. Never take your skills for granted.

Perhaps if she'd paid more attention…

She made a noise deep in her throat that was lost among the babble of translators and posturing groups of mercenaries around her. Guilt served no purpose and was not hers to carry.

It had all been cause and effect. Peepo had closed her eyes and poked, Cahli had set a course of action in response, and Tsan had stripped the Veetanho to her smallest parts in answer.

The weight Tsan now carried was in ensuring the future safety of her kind, not in trying to undo that which was done. Very well.

She smoothed her fur, tensed her legs, and leaped to ricochet from the overstuffed pack of a nearby Jivool to the head of a Cochkala to the ledge of a sign across the hall.

The Cochkala swiveled around, grunting, then muttered to itself and ruffled its head fur before shoving through a pair of elSha and moving off down a side passage.

She wasn't here to keep herself amused.

Someone had known she, or the ship she'd meant to take to 'Tlor, was about to be attacked. That meant a host of causes and effects she needed to check before they conglomerated into a real threat to her clan.

Tsan made herself comfortable over the sign, keeping her eyes steady, but not particularly focused, on the part of the crowd that moved below her.

She considered what she knew. Facts first:

Tsan had not entirely made a secret of her survival. A great deal of traffic had picked up between Land's End and Azure. Minerva had known a great deal it shouldn't have known.

Potential truths and implications next:

Peepo had raved about other, older threats. The Veetanho's motivation in enslaving fighting races was, allegedly, to fend off these threats. Minerva was unlikely to be unique in the galaxy. The organized survival of Hunters was likely to have been noticed, between the travel to and from Azure and the slight uptick in contracts taken. Perhaps not to a casual observer, but to something like Minerva, with its wires in every informational hub…

But why would something like Minerva want Tsan warned? Why not let her fight her way out of an unexpected attack?

Karma was a font of contacts, beings moving through the galaxy, and knowledge. She'd come here to learn more, but now that she had arrived, she only wanted to be gone again. Karma stank of Peepo and her plots, and there was nothing left for Tsan to sink her claws into in response to that lingering memory. Yet threats remained, hanging around her, undefined. The discomfort of it roiled the fur down her spine.

Deliberate movement snagged her focus, and she sat up, sweeping her attention over the milling crowd again. There.

Two Pushstal, craning their necks, as though trying to keep something in sight.

Two more—no, three—trailing behind, staggered through the crowd, ears swiveling in a way that caught Tsan's instincts.

Pushtal were not known for stealth, but they were trying to maintain it in the long corridor below her. None visibly spoke into communications devices, and they did not signal to each other, but she noted their efforts to keep eyes on each other.

Perhaps they were separated in the crowd, Tsan considered. As one lagged, slowing to let a small group of Goka pass in front of him, she dismissed the thought with an ear flick. *No. They're hunting.*

She had missed what or who they might be following, but this was her best potential for a fight. A little quick violence often cleared her thoughts, and, given that she could no longer step out into the jungles of Khatash and cheer herself up by hunting something nearly as deadly as she, she pushed off, landed in a small clear spot, and stalked the stalkers to see what they had found.

* * *

Before long, she had narrowed their target to a small Oogar, a female Zuul, or a chattering group of Goka. They turned, and it became evident they were trailing the Zuul. Tsan wrinkled her nose. The female mercenary had the twisting ears and downturned muzzle of a Zuul lost in thought, if Tsan's knowledge of Aryo was representative of the race.

I never had a contract to kill a Zuul, Tsan thought, realizing she'd never truly studied any other members of the race. Odd. Zuul had enemies, like anyone else. *Empty night, we were offered a contract to kill a Phidae once.*

Tsan lashed her tail, dropped to four feet, and increased her pace to close the distance. Aryo. Tsan had sigiled the Zuul cycles ago, before Tsan had become Dama of Whispering Fear.

She'd been a young Hunter offworld for the first time, disappointed in the reality of Karma, in the ease of her contract. Bored, overly self-assured, she'd stumbled into a trap laid for someone else and been so excited about the violence, she'd nearly had her spine severed by an enemy she thought she'd downed.

Aryo, chasing the scents of her gods, had helped. Aryo, not even a fighter, though of a fighting race, had done well enough to ensure Tsan's survival.

Aryo, lost to her, on Khatash, with the rest of their sigiled clan. The rest of everything and everyone that had once meant home.

The memory of it coiled hot in her stomach, and she continued to follow the Pushtal following the Zuul.

When the corridor around them was empty, save for the six figures and Tsan in her quintessence field, the Zuul turned to face those that followed her. Tsan approved of the directness, though she didn't pay much attention to the words exchanged as she scouted the long hallway for perches, cameras, and other access points.

Until one of the Pushtal growled something about getting a mysterious message. Her fur shivered, and her focus lasered onto the lead pirate as she replayed the words. She hadn't been concerned with the words, but her sharp mind had recorded them nonetheless.

"We got a little note that told us to watch out for them. Said they had new friends with big accounts," he'd said.

Got a little note. Like Tsan had gotten a little note? She flexed her claws and decided to incapacitate at least one of the Pushtal and drag him away to learn more. Perhaps it was nothing, but she'd rather drag her claws through skin and find nothing than potentially miss a scent trail entirely.

Things moved quickly after that.

The Zuul shot the speaking Pushtal. Two others rushed her. The one closest to Tsan stepped back and touched the side of his head.

"Check with the speaker," her translator sent to her pinplants. *"Does it need her alive? We might need backup."*

Backup? Tsan huffed a breath. She considered the part of the conversation she'd initially disregarded. It told her enough to find their ship; she could learn more there if needed. Also… this Zuul had an alliance with… other Pushtal?

Interesting. She didn't know many beings who would consider an alliance with the Pushtal. In fact, they hadn't been on her list—she considered them grossly overlarge, grossly overconfident for their level of skill, an uncanny and unworthy simulacrum of Hunter elegance.

But, watching them fight… perhaps they were not so unworthy after all. Not these, who may have already been corrupted by something like Minerva, but this Zuul had an alliance with others?

Hmm. Backup wouldn't do if she wanted to learn more from the Zuul. Fair enough. Tsan launched at the trailing Pushtal's back. She didn't know what fight she was interrupting, nor did she know this Zuul. Four against one seemed far more manageable for a lone Zuul, and this one was currently out of the melee, and so this one became her clear target.

As any Hunter knows, death is remarkably easy when the target has no reason to expect it. Tsan slid out her longest knife mid leap, and as she dug her back claws into the larger Pushtal's shoulders, she reached around with her knife and a front claw to tear out his throat.

Silent. She twisted hard as he began to fall and sprang clear. There was nothing on his back that would clatter, unlike the rings of metal on his front, and she cocked her head to see if the others had noticed.

They had not.

The Zuul was in the process of handling two others, messily but effectively. Tsan approved.

The last Pushtal hung back, and Tsan padded closer to him. He was snarling something too quietly for her translator to pick up but was silent by the time she reached him. She moved slightly to his side to better watch the Zuul's progress and ensure that he didn't shoot.

As the Zuul stood, clear of the last dead Pushtal, her long ears turned slightly back.

Is she thinking of running? Tsan weighed her knife and considered throwing it at one target or another. The surviving Pushtal in front of her raised his gun, but the lean in his shoulders said he wouldn't fire, not yet.

He spoke and proved her right.

* * *

"**Y**ou get me on *Venging Claw*, peaceful-like, I'll let you go." He gestured with his non-gun hand, pointing upward. "I have friends too, and they're going to pay real well for whatever you have on that ship." His tufted ears twitched as he spoke, and the Zuul steadied, her ears pointed back toward him.

Zuul don't run, Tsan thought, hearing Aryo's voice, and she loosened her grip on her knife.

"*Valiant Revenge* has nothing on their ship for you," the Zuul said, lifting her knives. "Shoot or fight."

"Nah. Note was clear. We get what's on the ship, we get a million credits." He waggled his gun, and Tsan blinked in pain at the lack of professionalism. "Get me on the ship."

"The day calls, and I see its light." The Zuul crouched and dropped her jaw in a grin. "The night calls, and I sing its song." She waved her larger knife, and blood dripped from her torn forearm through her fingers. "Space opens, and I embrace the void." She flicked her ears toward him and away, dismissing his threat, welcoming his shot. "I am a child of Zuul, and I have no fear."

Sparks shot from the base of Tsan's spine to the tips of her fingers. Aryo's scent touched her nose, the memory blindingly clear in the forefront of her mind.

Aryo throwing herself into a crowd of attackers for a Hunter she did not know. *The day calls, and I see its light.*

Aryo throwing herself in front of a kit as a blade lashed out. *The night calls, and I sing its song.*

Aryo laughing in the clan den, the words bright from her muzzle. *Space opens, and I embrace the void.*

Tsan leaped without a running start, rage and grief powering her. She didn't need silence from her target, so she started the cut from behind him. A space between vertebrae. The full force of her strength to shove the knife through.

"All right then, bi—" The words started from the Pushtal but had no chance of finishing. She severed his vocal cords, then the rest of his neck.

His head bowed forward. It slid away.

Tsan dropped her quintessence field and rode the much larger body almost fully down to the deck.

"Warrior, I greet you," she said, steadying her voice and leaping free of the separated body. "Apologies if I interrupted a death you were welcoming."

The Zuul's jaw snapped shut, and she took a step back before she stilled herself. Her eyes showed no recognition, and Tsan preened the blood off her own face without concern. Not all Zuul would have had cause to meet a Hunter, though Aryo had known what she was from the first.

"Welcoming death is not the same as wanting it." The Zuul straightened, her tail very still behind her. "Thank you for your assistance."

"Hmm." After smoothing her perfectly smooth gray fur, Tsan rose back to two legs and adjusted her harness. "Well said. I sigiled a Zuul, years ago, who once provided me similar assistance."

"I… do not know that term." The Zuul's ears swiveled, then pointed back toward her.

"No." Tsan tilted her head and twitched her tail. "I suppose you wouldn't. I don't know if more are coming, but I imagine someone will be this way before long. We should be on our way." That was fully accurate—she'd only heard the last Pushtal say backup might be needed, but it didn't change the reality of their situation.

"Why…" The Zuul shook herself and straightened, her tail raising slightly. "Why did you help me?"

"The prayer, I suppose. I miss my Zuul and hearing her words…" Tsan shrugged and tucked away the memories of Aryo. Her Zuul was alive on Khatash, bringing vengeance where she could. Tsan believed that to her bones. She spread her claws and sauntered closer. "Let us walk, warrior. I believe we both have places to be that are not here, and I also believe I have a way you can repay my assistance."

The Zuul cleared blood from her eyes and nodded, then she fell into step with Tsan as they walked, returning the way they'd come.

"I am Tsan, Dama of Clan Tamir." Tsan kept her eyes on the path ahead but watched the Zuul's movements. "Many call our kind Depik."

"I find myself disappointed that I don't know of your kind, Dama Tsan. I am Veska Insho'Ze in service to Krif'Hosh. I swore to return alive to my Kal'Shin—I am grateful to you for allowing me to uphold that oath."

"These Pushstal are your enemy?"

"No…" The Zuul—Veska—waved her tail as they stepped over the first Pushtal Tsan had killed. "I was considering the same thing. Many Pushtal attack where directed, for profit."

"Is that not all mercenaries?" Tsan asked, amused. Technically, such things could apply to Hunters, as well, though she wouldn't consider herself in quite the same category.

"Not all," Veska said, her muzzle lifting and her ears suddenly very, very upright. Tsan swallowed her laugh and nodded. "We have not made any specific enemies of the Pushtal, and in fact, we recently allied with a… clan." Even the translator staggered over the word as though conveying her hesitation in using it. "Very few should know that, and we took great care that none would know I was here." Veska's pace began to slow, and Tsan wondered if the Zuul were about to suspect her new Hunter companion, but then her pace recovered.

Either way, she knows well enough we need to distance ourselves from the bodies.

A thrill of connection spiked Tsan's nerves. Very few should have known about the Zuul, but someone had found her. Very few should have known about Tsan, and yet that message had found her.

Coincidence is not enough to direct a hunt, but it is enough to point to a direction to investigate. Tsan nodded and made an affirming noise the translator carried.

"One of the attacking Pushtal spoke of a note from someone else, directing them to me and to something on our ship," Veska continued after some moments. "That is my enemy."

"It is possible, Veska, we have a similar, or perhaps the same, enemy." Tsan frowned, considering what might have happened if she had drawn out Peepo's death a hair more. Perhaps she would know more. Or perhaps she would have simply had more Veetanho pelt to slowly clean from under her claws.

"You've had mysterious messages directing attackers to you?" Veska asked, dropping her jaw in humor.

Tsan tilted her head so the Zuul could see her slow blink, then followed it with a shrug.

"Something like. I know it is not much to go on, but that is the definition of mysterious, is it not?"

Veska barked a laugh, and Tsan huffed in reply.

"You said there was something more, Hunter… Dama Tsan?" The taller warrior was polite, and though she looked nothing like Aryo, there was something familiar in her scent. Tsan moved steadily forward, not letting herself slide over to rub against this stranger. For she was a stranger.

"Zuul allying with Pushtal is not… common, is it? I know one Zuul very well, but unfortunately not many of your kind."

"We are a well-settled race." Veska pointed to a left junction ahead, and Tsan nodded. They would continue together for now. "There are many Zuul across many planets, and just as many different ways of living as far as I have seen. But," she added, lifting her tail, "no, I would not say it is common. Neither is my Kal'shin."

"Veska, of clan Insho'Ze and Krif'Hosh, I have a favor to ask of you." Tsan had no need to welcome Veska to their negotiation; she knew the honor of the Zuul. No matter how spread out or how different, Aryo swore that sense of honor was ingrained in every Zuul, and Aryo would never say such words lightly.

"You saved my life and allowed me to keep my word to my Kal'shin. Ask, and if it is in my power, I will turn my focus upon it."

"Take a message to your Kal'shin for me, Veska. I will give you coordinates where his reply can reach me."

"Do you wish to record the message? Then I will—"

"No." The fur along her spine prickled. "I do not trust these mysterious enemies of ours. My people have always been few. The GalNet will tell you that and some little about us—that we are assassins, that we are the best, that there is no target that can escape our claws for long."

Tsan flexed her claws. Dim sounds ahead told her they didn't have long before they rejoined the crowds of Karma.

"We are fewer now, as the Veetanho attempted to use the weight of the Mercenary Guild to enslave us, and we refused."

The Zuul next to her drew in a heavy breath, and Tsan supposed Veska had either accessed information through her pinplants or matched Tsan's words with some rumors or stories she had heard before. Either way, it was enough for the moment.

"We are not the sort who wait to be finished. We will retake our place and more. We have a planet to retake, we have enemies to destroy, and we have kits to settle in new colonies."

Veska's steps slowed, and one hand rose in a checked movement toward her midsection. Tsan pretended not to notice, but she marked the reaction with interest and a rising protectiveness that had no place in the moment.

"We have near endless credits and a desire for allies. Warriors with a history of honor and choosing unusual allies themselves seem an ideal choice."

"Allies to… fight?" Veska's ready posture spoke of interest, not hesitation, but Tsan couldn't rest easily on such an assumption.

"Allies who do not want to be controlled by mysterious enemies. Allies who choose freedom, who choose to fight against those who think we can be owned, directed by another hand."

"I think my Kal'shin will be very interested in your message, Tsan," Veska said, the words slow but delivered with confidence.

Tsan stopped, turned fully to Veska, and slow blinked up at the Zuul fighter. She slid a data chip out of one of her harness pockets. "Here is how he can reach me with his reply." As Veska took the chip, Tsan pulled quintessence and stepped back. "I will see you again, Veska of Clan Insho'Ze, in service to Krif'Hosh."

Veska's ears flicked with surprise, but she did no more than snap her jaw.

"And I you, Tsan," she murmured, with what might have been a laugh.

* * * * *

Chapter Six

Tsan stilled, the world around her fuzzy and out of focus. She held the message steadily in front of her, but her lip curled back from her teeth.

Khatash system traffic increased 205%. Veetanho moving from all systems, converging on Khatash system. 75% probability they stripped weapons and resources from previous postings. Attached: gate logs, estimated numbers, inventory irregularities. Unknown: additional forces, scale of offensive weapons, full number of ships available. —Theela.

Theela again.

The straightforward neutrality of it carried a weight of its own. A claw, curving in half light, barely seen between leaves. A threat? A welcome?

Tsan did not trust blindly, nor did she jump at shadows. Three times, Theela had interjected, unbidden. Contracting Fssik. Warning her of a possible attack. Sending her details on Veetanho movements from nine and more different systems.

Gate logs were not impossible to get; she had lifted more than a few herself. But the scale of the information…

Why?

A Veetanho trap? They were stealthy, her enemy, and widely known for their strategy.

For long days, she dug through records and sifted veritable tons of data bytes.

Theela, in the end, was no more a mystery than anything in the Merchant's Guild. It was a bank, which existed to move credits into different parts of the galaxy to make more credits.

Tsan understood the concept, if not the need. Whispering Fear's main den had entire rooms full of credits, red diamonds, silverfifths from the asteroid belt outside of Khatash's orbit, and what passed for currency on hundreds of planets. Her clan had plenty of electronic accounts for any who hunted offworld, which had turned out for the best when her clan den became... unreachable.

She lashed her tail and considered the information as she tapped her claws.

Theela was Theela Financial, but what did a bank have to do with her? Whispering Fear had never contracted with one, nor had Tamir linked them to anything like this. Why would a bank know of a pending pirate attack?

A bank might very well request a Hunter's contract, as Theela had with Fssik, to remove someone interfering with their business. That was sensible, as far as it went. But a bank having information on Veetanho movements to Khatash and choosing to share that with her for no discernible reason...

And knowing she existed, how to find her, in order to share that with her?

Was the Merchant's Guild, like the Science Guild, moved by the predator in the pinplants? The intelligence that moved through pinplants and ether? How many of them moved throughout the galaxy, hunting without consequence, because no one knew they were there?

Banks were not in the habit of revealing their clients, but she found enough of them to verify that Theela was what it appeared to be. The GalNet had told her all it was going to, and her next steps had led her from Karma to this city of towering buildings.

A mix of beings went about their business, mostly from races she had encountered before. Feathered Buma, stout Cochkala, Lumar guards, winged Sidar, and non-mercenary Humans were nearly all involved in conversations through their pinplants or with a visible companion.

No one blocked the side passages, and traffic moved freely. She appreciated the efficiency, though it bored her.

She reclined on the thin perch provided by an ornate door frame of a building across the corner from Theela Financial's sky-reaching headquarters. Her tail swung in the air, but even the tallest of the Sidar who passed cleared it by a head, and her quintessence kept her unnoticeable in every other way.

Perfectly normal beings walked in and out of Theela, none moving in the oddly jerky way of the commandeered beings at the Science Guild. She made a noise in her throat, knowing that proved nothing. The creature—the SI—had only taken over its puppets in extremis, and if she had approached correctly, this one would have no idea she was so close.

If it existed.

She flexed her claws and smoothed her fur with effort. Theela had found a way to deliver information to her before, when she was hunting and should have been undetectable. She had been beyond humbled, not so long ago, when she was reminded that she did not know all the tactics and technology their enemies might have devised.

Theela was not the Mercenary Guild, nor the Science Guild, but banks were a part of the Merchant Guild system. It would be foolish to assume that any guild was harmless.

She could not wait and observe any longer. It was time to invade Theela's den and see what there was to be seen.

* * *

She had expected them to have more security than a Sidar at a desk and a handful of wiring, but that would be enough for one who could not be invisible to deal with. There was enough traffic in and out of the building that she did not have to wait for either doors or lift, so she spent a remarkable amount of time exploring and encountering only the unremarkable. Dissatisfied, she leaped to the top of an oversized desk, curled her tail around herself, and considered the option of killing beings until someone in charge presented themselves.

Perhaps, only perhaps, that was a bit of an overreaction. Tsan looked over the desk again, saw a thin drawer slightly askew, and slid a claw into it to work it open. She assumed from the electrical buzz in the corner there were cameras, and she rather hoped someone watched the drawer open by itself.

The contents of the drawer were two small metal fasteners and, right above, an unlocked slate. She slid further over the desk and angled her harness bag close enough in her field so the camera would only catch a flicker of motion and, hopefully, be unable to discern that a slate had moved from drawer to Hunter in a blink.

Of course, if the resident of the office were to return or see the recording, they would know their slate was missing. They would also know it was their own fault, as they had such a blatant disregard for security. It didn't matter that their office was behind at least three layers of locks and guards, leaving a slate unlocked and unwatched was an invitation to someone in the galaxy to come and look at it.

Far be it from her to ignore such an open invitation.

She slid the drawer closed again, leaped from the desk, and found a quiet, camera-less corner two floors down, where she could read at her leisure.

With access to internal files, it was much easier to learn about the leadership of Theela Financial and their clients.

One, a Sidar well into a long lifetime, had a robust portfolio, but much of it was tucked behind access walls this slate, unfortunately, did not connect to. According to communications she skimmed through, a great deal of this Sidar's credits—amounts that dwarfed many other members of the bank combined—were a mystery to many other people in the bank.

She sighed and skimmed further. From the size of the desk, she'd hoped the slate belonged to someone more important to Theela, but they appeared to be mid-level, without access to a great deal of information.

Except...

A note, added not so long ago, that one of this Sidar's clients had gone dark. The date coincided with that of the mass death of her people on Khatash. While, truly, this did not prove anything—a great deal of terrible things happened to a great number of assorted people across the Galactic Union every day—it was enough of a coincidence to give her some direction.

The preparation needed for the invasion of Khatash pressed on her, but she would not move forward with a mystery at her back, not one that could prove to be as dangerous as Minerva.

So, she did what any grown Hunter would do—she found the Sidar's office, waited in her quintessence until he gathered his belongings, then followed him home where she revealed herself, idly flipping a knife on a table in the middle of his living quarters.

He snapped his beak, but otherwise stood still, and she inclined her head gravely toward him.

"Rurranach of Theela Financial, I am Tsan. Welcome to our negotiation."

"Dama, I greet you." He inclined his head, and his wingtips shivered in a way she couldn't parse, but he did not cower. He knew not only the forms of communication, but... *her*. This Sidar, then, was at least part of what she was looking for.

"I have received several parcels of interest from your Theela Financial, and, in the interest of your life, I am curious about the motivation behind such... sharing."

"With full respect, Dama, me and mine mean you no harm, neither in motivation nor action. I propose a different negotiation—you join me for dinner, and we will discuss this freely." He lowered his beak, so she could see his eyes on her knife.

"Your proposal is not unpleasant." She tilted her head and stilled her knife, though she didn't sheathe it. "Know that there are explosives threaded throughout your quarters, should your words prove to be a lie."

"I would be surprised if it were not so." He sounded calm, and his wings didn't so much as twitch, but she noticed he glanced around regardless. After a moment, he moved to a compartment between them on the long wall of the main room. He made a point of opening it toward him, so she had a clear view of the food stored inside.

"I was planning on an ikthyoid soup, if that will suit?"

She sheathed her knife and tilted her head, studying him further.

"It will. You have worked with Hunters before."

"Extensively, Dama. I have no wish to hide anything from you. For generations, I have been engaged as the financial factor for Night Wind Clan. Indeed…" Still moving slightly, he lifted something from around his neck, which was previously hidden below his finely tailored clothing.

She lost all pretense of calm amusement and dug her claws into his polished table to keep herself from leaping across the room at him.

"You are sigiled to Night Wind? Cahli…" The faintest scent of her sister-Dama touched her nose, a passing memory that pierced her no matter how much time passed.

"Cahli never told you. I know. And yet, were something disastrous to happen to Night Wind, Whispering Fear was named beneficiary of the resources I hold."

Three different questions pushed to the front of Tsan's mind. She took a deep breath and forced her tail looser, though her rear claws would leave grooves in the Sidar's… Rurranach's… once shiny table.

"Esthik of Night Wind yet lives."

"But no Dama or damita."

She inclined her head and allowed the grief to rise through her for an eyeblink before she focused on him again.

"We are all one clan, now, regardless."

"All?" He leaned forward, intent, and she gestured dismissively with one hand and retracted her claws.

"Our negotiation was dinner and your answering my questions. Perhaps, if I am inclined, I will answer some of yours after that."

"A fair point, Dama." He reached back to the compartment, though he didn't turn his back to her, and the positioning of his head indicated he could still track her with his peripheral vision.

She had known he wasn't stupid even before she followed him home, but seeing him reinforced her assumptions. She kept track of his movements in the edge of her own vision, when she jumped from the table and sauntered through the room, as though perusing his living space.

Grief had not taken her by the throat in a season, at the least. She'd had more than enough to occupy her, and her drive had seemed to double after Ward completed the procedure to detangle her nervous systems.

He did something else to you, Lara had said, and prickles had caused Tsan's fur to rise. *Something that intensified your drive for clan, your bonding hormones. For your protection, he said, given how few of you are left.*

It was not her first hint that there was more to the Wrogul— Ward included—than there appeared, but it solidified her suspicions. Ward had hoped the bonding would be a leash, in a different way than the Veetanho had planned to use their freezing weapon. Whereas the Veetanho wanted a weapon they could control, Ward was worried about removing something that kept them in check without replacing it with something else.

She couldn't be sure that was his motivation, but it felt close enough to right for her to operate around. Only she had not responded as he'd hoped, as many of the Hunters had. The survivors were her companions, the entirety of the clan her reason for living. It had been true before the procedure, and it would be the force that moved her until the moment her life ended, whenever that might be.

Tsan lashed her tail as she walked, trying to clear her spinning thoughts. Yes, the clan was her priority, as it had been Cahli's. This echo of grief rubbed against her still-scabbed healing for the loss of her people and served as an unexpected reminder of her sister-Dama, of her friend.

Nights above, entropy take it, she spat to herself, forcing her conscious thoughts to process what the rest of her brain had been recording as she walked.

Rurranach had plenty of credits; that much was clear. His living quarters suited a flying species. Soaring ceilings and windows stretched from halfway up the wall to the roof and sparkled in a way that indicated strong security.

Pieces of what must have been art studded various columns and alcoves along the wall, so he might walk or, perhaps, fly to observe them. The main room sprawled larger than her clan common room, with clear sight lines and minimal furniture. The high windows and purposeful decoration indicated he might use his wings in here, but she reconsidered when she looked back at him.

He stood nearly as tall as three Hunters. His wings were as long as his body and were tightly furled, so she could only guess their full spread. While he might have been hollow and light, like a Basreen, she sensed he carried some weight on his frame. She estimated it would take some effort for him to get off the ground without a running start. More likely, his species preferred launching from a higher point, using the air resistance and velocity of the fall to attain height more easily.

Tsan looked over the tall walls and saw a ledge that could serve as a launching point. Though the living quarters were large compared to what she had observed in the city so far, the space would not give him much room to glide. She decided the layout was more for comfort than for attacking from above, so she dismissed her concern and returned her full attention to Rurranach.

He placed two bowls on the table, their self-heating tabs already pulled. While he could not miss the furrows she'd left in his table, he did not mention them. He gestured to the stool across from him.

She ignored him and returned to her spot on the table. She didn't intend to dig her claws into it again during their discussion, but if she did, at least it would only worsen the current damage, rather than creating anything new. She could be quite thoughtful that way.

"Generations, you said. How long have you been sigiled to Night Wind?"

"Since not long after Dama Reow founded it."

Her claws found the now familiar grooves, so she picked up the spoon he placed in front of her to distract herself. "You knew Reow?"

"Choking Deluge was my main point of contact, but yes, because of the nature of the service I provided, I did meet the Dama."

"We will return to Deluge," she said, a spike of recognition running down her spine to the tip of her tail, which twitched before she could still it. "So, you have been with Night Wind nearly as long as there has been a Night Wind."

He lowered his beak in acknowledgment before lifting his bowl.

"And Cahli… when the Mercenary Guild attempted to coerce her, you knew?"

"I had long ago been entrusted with…" He reached into a pocket, and Tsan did not so much as tense, though her eyes tracked his movement.

No surprise suffused her when she recognized the communication device, one that worked via quintessence.

"So, that's how you found me."

"I employed a very clever Hunter, once, who helped me adjust the device so I could use it to direct quintessential messages but have them appear as any normal correspondence. It has something to do with how they code to the ports."

She waved away the details but resolved to ask about this 'very clever Hunter' so she might find him if he were still alive. Time and the Mercenary Guild's attempts at enslaving the Hunter race made it exceedingly unlikely, and she didn't want to take another blow at the moment.

"Who do you receive your orders from?" she asked, her tone casual, as she sipped the soup. Rich flavor flooded her mouth, and she allowed a small sound of pleasure to let him know she approved.

"Who do I… ? Dama, with Cahli… dead, I did the best I could to locate you. I tracked several other Hunters, who made themselves more visible, for a time, but I hoped to find Night Wind or Whispering Fear before committing to any action."

"Who ordered you to do so?"

"I used my own judgment."

"Who is Theela?"

"Theela is simply the name of our organization, Dama."

"Is it? There is no… algorithm in your databases to suggest actions?"

"We use various programs to anticipate markets, trades, clients' profits and losses." He spread his wings slightly. The claw-sharp knobs on the tips lowered, then lifted in something reminiscent of a shrug. "Nothing that gives orders."

"No?" She filled her spoon, dipped it back into the bowl, then filled it again without eating. "Can you be sure it doesn't whisper directions into your pinplants?"

"Dama?"

Tsan sighed and pushed away her delicious soup.

"Is there a place you fly, Rurranach, far from any electronic listening?" She'd have him disconnect his pinplants, though she had no idea if it would be enough. If anything would be enough.

* * *

Flying with a Sidar was… bracing. She'd had to ride in a harness across his chest, like she'd carried the stolen slate earlier. This was not the smooth, directed flight of the Basreeni jets, which were level and pierced through the air. This was a glide, punctured repeatedly by a sharp fall, a buffeting rise, or a side-to-side slip that defied her awareness of ground and gravity. It was like fighting in zero G with her limbs wrapped in bloodvines.

He'd taken them out of the main reach of the city to a cliffside in a darkened plain. He murmured that it would make it easier for them to leave again, and Tsan gave herself a moment of credit for intuiting how Sidar flew. If you killed enough aliens of various builds and morphologies, the way various races worked made sense, no matter how unfamiliar.

Tsan prowled to the edge of the cliff and back, surveying the wide swathe of unpopulated land. Darkness pooled below them, and tall grass shushed in a soft wind behind them.

She gestured for him to take his pinplants offline and sat on her haunches, tail curled close.

"There are electronic creatures living in the data," she said, dissatisfied at the lack of specificity. It wasn't the *right* description, but it was the best she'd been able to put together. "Living is not the right word. None of those are the right words, but there are... 'awarenesses' that do not mean us well."

Rurranach clacked his long beak, and his head tilted rapidly from one side to the other as though he were trying to bring her into better focus.

"How many?"

She slow blinked in response, despite the pinging of the nerves along the insides of each limb. He did not waste time asking foolish questions—Are you sure? What do you mean? What could be 'aware' and yet living isn't the right word? No. He accepted and moved to the important pieces, showing Cahli's wisdom in his sigiling. Showing their ancestress' wisdom, Tsan corrected, picturing the legendary Reow much as Cahli had been.

"I do not know. Cannot know. There is only one I can be sure of, and it was recently destroyed. But the way it behaved... it was not alone. It used living beings as puppets, controlled them to do what it could not do, through data and the GalNet and communications." She flexed her claws, wishing there was something rendable in her immediate vicinity, wishing these unseen enemies, writhing in space even she could not see, had a form she could hunt in a more satisfactory manner.

"You don't think they are some sort of race, perhaps one of the rumored Dusman or Kahraman?"

"No." Her tail lashed, and she let it to keep the fur from expanding. "They are programs, not beings. I..." She glared into the darkness, her face turned exactly enough so he would not feel it aimed at him. "This is not prey I can hunt alone, Rurranach. I thought Theela was another enemy, taunting me as Minerva did the Horsemen."

"Minerva?"

"The Science Guild was directed, from the root of it, by such a program. That enemy I can be sure of. It took many of us to destroy it, if such as it can truly be destroyed."

She had done well enough at the end, but even the journey to its heart, to be in such a position... No. Much like Hunters could not retake Khatash alone, this was not an enemy they could fight with only their oldest skills. It would require something... different. An evolution.

"I am sorry, Dama. Perhaps I should have found a different way to make contact. I assumed proving my and Theela Financial's value to you first would make you more likely to—"

"No." She held up a hand, claws sheathed. "It is that careful, clever approach that tells me your skills are necessary to address this next wave of enemies. The layers of security I have seen throughout your organization only reinforce this decision."

"Next wave..." Rurranach spread his wings before drawing them back closer to his body. "First... ?"

"First, I entrust you with some additional accounts." Tsan longed to pace the bare edge of the tall cliff or bound through the tall, waving grass to chase whatever lived there. Instead, she held herself still, her eyes locked on the Sidar's.

"We have a planet to retake, and for that, we will need to spend credits without giving warning."

"We are well suited for that."

"Yes. Second, the former leader of the Mercenary Guild indicated old powers are rising, and we will hardly let ourselves be open to their attack."

"Which gives us some time to identify these other unseen enemies." Rurranach clacked his beak again, the cutting points at the top and midpoint of his wings shivered as though he were poised to attack.

"I think these enemies hope we will crush ourselves in the coming conflicts and leave them to move in on the pieces, while we struggle to recover." Tsan slow blinked and waved her tail gently behind her. "I intend for us to destroy that hope."

"Yes, Dama." Rurranach made a raspy sound that she understood to be a laugh. "I believe we will be well set up for that, indeed."

* * * * *

Chapter Seven

Choking Deluge, a young Deo of Night Wind Clan, had once found himself in possession of a Lumar mercenary unit.

He did not keep it, but sometime later, Rurranach had taken it under Theela Financial's wing.

Based on that old thread, Tsan had intended to meet with the company, then continue to follow Proud Fist's connections until she had enough of a feel for 'Tlor to entrust kits and potential companions to it. However, the bulk of Proud Fist had subcontracted to Asbaran Solutions, which would have left her more ground to cover.

With Rurranach's expertise, she'd found a shorter way. Proud Fist had spun off another company, which Theela also managed. She had a formal meeting arranged, as a representative of Theela Financial, leaving her own identity well hidden.

The Veetanho had ground the Lumar under their boots for generations. In the same way they'd wanted to bring Hunters to heel, they'd subjugated Lumar, Tortantula, and too many others. While not every species would reject the heavy hand of the Guild as... effectively as Hunters had, surely, with opportunity and allies, they would prefer freedom to servitude.

She took a roundabout way to the meeting, slipping out of her official transport at the station and sliding onto a ferry to the surface while in her field.

Thunder Fist had a proper office in the starport. Theela Financial had supplied the plans and oversight for their suite, meaning she had the layout and history of the broader building and had studied it on her trip. Her first indication something was slightly off was that the records did not entirely match the reality of the starport's wing.

She stalked through the long stretch of offices with a glare. Most were staffed by aliens, not Lumar, who were either factors or employers or otherwise involved with the Lumar. As best she could tell, not many non-natives went much further than the starport, but there were plenty here. 'Tlor was not known for beautiful sites or fanciful hospitality. The world's reputation was about the same as its ostensibly sentient species—simple, straightforward, did its job.

This hardly bothered her. Very, very few visitors ever left Khatash's central city, if for different reasons.

What itched under her fingerpads was more subtle. None of the halls of the office wing were quite right. Doors were in the wrong place, and stairways and lifts had been switched. Had it been built incorrectly? Had there been renovations?

Was there something behind the walls she wasn't supposed to know about?

Now that *is jumping at shadows. A bank's plans and a mercenary planet's execution are not likely to be the same.* There were a handful of explanations she could make up with little effort, but the logic of them didn't smooth her fur.

Something was off, and she was unlikely to figure it out before her scheduled meeting.

She narrowed her focus to Thunder Fist's office. According to Rurranach's files, it was a suite of four variously sized rooms. One mid-sized main room on the other side of the entrance for greeting. One to the left, smaller, for the commander to meet with his company members as needed. One to the right, similar in size to the commander's office, for recordkeeping. And one longer room on the far side of the entrance for company or client meetings.

There had been no other obvious exits or entrances, which had first given Tsan pause. Regardless of the Lumar reputation for intelligence or lack thereof, no mercenary worth their blood regularly put themselves into a place that did not have alternate exits.

The air conduits were cramped, even for her, and they certainly wouldn't work for Lumar. She'd considered them as a way into the office to scope out the space before the meeting, but there was only the automatic door, which only opened after an approved vocal request from the hall.

There was little traffic on this side of the starport, so it wouldn't do her any good to wait and slip in beside someone else.

Time enough to see, she thought. She dropped her field and tapped the button on the side of the door.

"Speak."

"Theela Financial representative here for my meeting with Arkak."

"Enter."

The door slid open to the left, and Tsan rose to two legs to walk through. It closed immediately behind her, and she flicked her tail in distaste. Sensible for security, perhaps, but a bit too close for welcome.

The room was painted in bright shades of yellow and green, with no pattern discernible. A long desk, covered in slates and potted plants, occupied the space directly in front of her. Behind it sat a Lumar, all arms visible, something like a smile on his face.

"Theela, welcome. Meeting this way." He stood, and she took stock of his various weapons.

There was a door to the left, but not the right, though she wished she could walk closer to see if it were simply hidden. The Lumar gestured to the left, and she had no reason to be entirely contrary. She was here for allies, not a contract.

She may have reminded herself of that fact twice during the short walk through the office.

The meeting room behind the office was longer than it was wide. It was decorated in a bright orange and purple scheme, with a wall of screens currently displaying desert landscapes that matched the paint. She touched her goggles, grateful for their dimming of the world around her.

"Sit here. Arkak coming. Drink?"

"Thank you, no." Not for the first time, she wondered how the Lumar communicated in their own language. Was their shorthand a function of the translator?

When the Lumar left, she leaped onto the chair in front of her, then onto the table. She crossed it and sat in a seat with her back to the screens. Both walls to the side of her were bare, so she kept her peripheral vision on them and was not entirely surprised when the one to her right opened.

That made it even more likely the no-door room to her left was in use.

"Am Arkak. Theela welcome. Theela has Depik?" Thunder Fist's leader was enormous, even for a Lumar.

"In a way." Tsan placed her hands flat on the table as the Lumar skirted the edge to sit across from her. He turned his chair slightly to the side. If she was correct about how Lumar peripheral vision worked, he was keeping an eye on both the door behind him and the blank wall to her left.

"I am Tsan of clan Tamir. We are part of Theela in the same way Thunder Fist is."

"Take contracts?"

"Some of my clan have, yes. They hold some of our credits and are using them to serve our interests."

One of his arms jerked but not toward a weapon. She pricked her ears forward to better listen.

"Theela same for us. Make credits into more credits. Make contracts good contracts."

"Have you had many good contracts lately?" she asked, her ears rotating a bit to the left.

"No." He shrugged, and his chair moved again. "Thought why Theela come here. With news." Each of his arms moved, and he put his upper elbows on the table. "Good news, bad news. For some change."

"Since the Mercenary Guild changed leadership?" Tsan had an idea of the tensions and changes and shifting fortunes across the galaxy. Tamir remained well informed, and Tsan studied past and current trends before determining her top choices in possible alliances. Still, she hadn't spoken directly with many mercenary companies, other than Human ones, since her time with Peepo.

"Before. Veetanho no good. Goltar as leaders?" He shrugged once more. "Will see. Some good. Contracts still…" He made another elaborate motion that indicated more of the same quite well.

Maybe Lumar were like Wrogul? Capable of communicating some part of their language through translators, but with more left out than included?

She dismissed the thought. Regardless of what did or didn't hold the Lumar back, he was making himself well enough understood in the moment.

"You were right in that I came with an offer, one that will be certified through Theela if you chose to accept it."

"Contract?"

"Something very like. Welcome to our negotiation, Arkak."

"No." He held up a hand from either side of his body. "Arkak not negotiate. Theela, or… Theela does negotiating. Arkak does…

does things. Not negotiate." He glanced to the side again, and her tail waved softly behind her.

"As I said, this can be certified by Theela." She kept one ear swiveled toward the no-door room, though nothing but her instincts indicated someone was waiting on the other side of the hidden door. *Watch.*

"Will listen." Arkak shifted his chair again but didn't tense.

"Very well. It's a protection contract, more than anything."

"Protect... Depik?"

Tsan sketched out the plan—shared space, shared fight, and shared resources. As she finished, she mentioned a den for kits, and many things happened at once.

The wall that was not a wall, leading to the no-door room, flew open. It did not slide like the others but swung out with a muffled *thwump*. In the open space it left behind stood a smaller Lumar with an enormous gun.

"Someone coming. Depik would never share kits. This is a trap."

"Depik absolutely would, as here I am." Tsan pulled her field, slipped under the table, and wound through the chairs. It wasn't a perfect cover, but it was the best she'd come up with the moment she entered the room. "Who's coming?"

"Arkak, away!" The smaller Lumar gestured abruptly and swiveled with the gun, then froze. "No. If you part of trap... Arkak be dead already."

"Depik small. Arkak fight!" he interjected. He muttered something, and the translator paused before repeating it.

"I'm not part of anything except my clan's interest, which Theela clearly knew. They wouldn't have been a part of this, otherwise." Tsan moved ahead of her voice as she spoke, and she doubled back in case this Lumar decided to get clever.

"Why Lumar?" The second Lumar's eyes tracked Tsan's movement, only a few steps behind. This one seemed to know they had a poor shot, though, as the gun didn't twitch.

"Tula, who comes?" Arkak, meanwhile, had ducked and was grasping at the space under the table with three of his four hands.

"Three companies. Maybe more." Tula jerked and blinked, her second pair of arms unclenching from behind her. She had two more guns, smaller but functional.

Lumar can be their own backup, Tsan thought to herself. She stepped softly from under the table to one of the chairs, which added more difficulty to any shot and placed her well out of Arkak's reach.

"Lumar wouldn't be here for me," she said, considering it more likely to be true than not. Rurranach had found her, in a way, and, while something like Minerva could possibly have tracked her, it was vanishingly unlikely. Whereas in a time of upheaval, mercenary companies turning on each other to lessen competition seemed... possible. It wasn't a nuance a Lumar would grasp, perhaps, but...

"Smash Fight lost last four contracts to us." Tula said, grasping the concept instantly. "Dark Hands rejected by Theela."

"And here's Theela, meeting with you." Tsan made a noise low in her throat and dropped her field. She shoved the chair back from the table and faced Tula directly. Tsan kept Arkak in her peripheral, but he was still looking for her underneath the table. "Shall we test my offer?"

"Depik fight? With us?"

"Alliances formed in blood are better than words." She waved her tail and spread her claws.

"Lumar blood," Tula said, frowning.

"*Their* Lumar blood, Tula," Tsan corrected, reaching for the weapon on her belt. "Those that attack Thunder Fist can become my enemies just as well."

Tula cocked her head, then abruptly holstered the smaller guns in her lower hands.

"Too many to face here," she said, crossing the room. "Unless more Depik?"

"Just me for this conversation—" Tsan replied, delight threading through her tone, "—but they don't know I'm the one that's here for Theela."

"Won't expect Depik." Even the translator picked up the satisfaction Tula radiated. "Alliance, Tsan. Thunder Fist and Tamir Clan." As she spoke, she fiddled with two of the screens on the back wall, and after another moment, they all slid up in a single motion.

The jumble of wires and circuits revealed sent delight spiraling down Tsan's spine, and she flexed her claws.

"You *do* have a back exit."

"Yes." Tula grinned. Tsan had never seen such a beautiful sight on a Lumar face. "Make if needed. Arkak," she added, as the larger Lumar straightened up. "Table."

Tsan leaped over the table to join Arkak on the other side of the room, then he flipped it. Tula braced herself with a lower hand and vaulted the table, then the three of them crouched behind it.

While Tsan wondered what the table was made of, it wasn't time to indulge her curiosity. She was far more intrigued by Tula and even more pleased with her decision to prioritize these Lumar for an alliance.

She flattened her ears, but the explosion still left them ringing. The wired explosives had been directional—they blew the wall out and very little debris back toward them—but sound waves lashed their way all the same.

Tula slapped something behind them, and the door to the main office slid halfway open. The Lumar who'd greeted Tsan shoved her way in and tossed a pack each to Arkak and Tula.

"Rappelling?" Tsan asked after a quick calculation. They were on the fifth level above ground. Survival was not impossible from this height, but anyone smart enough to build an explosive wall to allow a strategic retreat would have planned for that.

"Yes." Tula paused for a fraction of a second. "Want ride?"

"Oh, indeed." Tsan slow blinked, then pulled her field and bounded to the ragged hole in the wall to scout their perimeter. "Clear out here for the moment."

"Depik," Arkak said as he shrugged his pack onto his shoulders. "Good ally."

"Nice on our side," Tula agreed, and the third Lumar grunted in agreement.

Tsan flicked an ear they couldn't see and studied the stretch of land below them.

The office building was on the outside edge of the starport. At the base of the building was a strip of close-cut vegetation, then a wide road. On the other side of the road, several lines of low slung buildings clustered together.

"Barracks," Tula said, pointing to a grouping two down on the right. "Backup."

"Excellent." Tsan remained in her field while the Lumar fastened their gear with efficient motions. A great deal of excited thumping echoed from the other side of the office, either neighbors concerned about the explosion or the attackers arriving.

The latter seemed more likely, but, either way, there was no point in sticking around to figure out who. She tapped Tula's knee in warning before climbing into a comfortable position out of the way of the wire. She clamped onto the Lumar's harness with her lower claws, careful not to punch through the thick fabric, and kept her weapon trained on the window as the Lumar backed out of the building into the open air.

Given their additional set of limbs, her new allies were able to grip their ropes, steady themselves, and keep a gun—or guns—aimed above and below them.

They were halfway down when the firing started.

Tula was a crack shot. She took out the two who were foolish enough to lean over the edge even as she released the brake and plummeted faster down the building. Arkak and the other Lumar sprayed the opening consistently enough that no one else extended much more than arms and weapons without the ability to aim.

Someone above them was smart enough to throw grenades, and it got a little messier. Grenades didn't require a lot of precision.

"Go wide," Tsan said, then leaped clear as they neared the ground. She rolled until the softer ground yielded to the scrape of the road. Dirt sprayed all around, and light flared, but her goggles kept her eyesight clear, and she had a far better angle to shoot back.

Tula shoved hard off the wall and cut her tether mid-arc, sending her flying. She landed in a scatter of debris not far from Tsan. She dropped to a knee and joined her covering fire to Tsan's while the male Lumar worked clear.

Arkak made it to the far side of the road, mostly unscathed—three working arms instead of four, with the last remaining attached by slightly more than a thread.

"Marask!" Arkak shouted as he turned back. "Down!"

The third Lumar dropped immediately, and Arkak braced himself. He'd acquired a weapon larger than Tula's enormous gun, and Tsan had a moment to admire it before he fired.

THWOOM.

This was his answer to the grenades their attackers had indeterminately thrown—one purposefully aimed, large caliber—no, she corrected herself as it detonated—targeted explosive.

So much for their office. And a fair chunk of the starport's wing.

"Commed barracks. More coming."

Of course. There had only been three members of Thunder Fist in the office. An overwhelming force had been sent to send a message to the company and to the Theela representative. That had failed spectacularly, so a double punch was needed, and the next target was in sight.

"They still don't know I'm here," Tsan said, leaping onto Tula's shoulder. The Lumar stiffened but didn't startle. "I'll run ahead. What are their emblems?"

Tula described them quickly. Tsan agreed to target only those wearing such marks and offered only one piece of advice before she bounded away.

"Aim high."

They ran after her, but they were considering cover, and she had no need to worry about it. The chance of a sudden explosion or unexpected crossfire was there, but it had been too long since she'd sunk her claws into true danger. The Pushtal on Karma had been too few and focused elsewhere.

This? This would be fun.

She dropped to all fours to break well ahead of the Lumar, and she nearly beat the opposing Lumar to the Thunder Fist barracks.

The first cracks of shots sent her wide around the road to meet the flank. Some sixty Lumar charged the cluster of tents under Thunder Fist's symbol.

There seemed to be no more strategy than that.

Fair enough.

Time stuttered.

Tsan tore tendons, shot through spines, and tripped encroaching forces until they provided nearly as much barrier to each other as she had.

Thunder Fist had set up a perimeter and laid down far more effective fire.

Arkak and Tula were clearly the better commanders. No wonder Theela had acquired the company after her long ago relative had come into possession of such a gem and then stewarded the growth of an offshoot company. No wonder Theela had rejected these others. Had they previously been commanded by Veetanho?

It took both less and more time than she would have expected. Lumar did not die easily, regardless of the effort they did not put into strategy.

As time resumed its normal pace, Tsan brushed blood from her cheeks and strode toward the cluster of Lumar around Arkak and Tula.

Arkak was easy to see—even among his fellow warriors he stood nearly a full head higher. When she got close, though, it was Tula they were listening to.

"Not Theela. Depik who also use Theela. Negotiated alliance."

"Alliance." One of them spit to the side, thankfully away from Tsan in her quintessence field. It would have been a shame to kill an ally so early in their relationship. "Want Thunder Fist die for them."

"Fight good," another one argued, shoving the spitter. "Pay well?"

"Depik fight too," another added, cleaning a very long blade. Tsan hadn't known some of them fought with edged weapons, but she liked it. "Why need us?"

"Not fight," Tula said, shaking her head, "or not fight alone. Fight *with* Depik. Protect young."

"Our young?"

"Depik young?"

There was a general hubbub, but no one was truly arguing with Tula. They seemed to want to… understand.

Not surprising. She tapped two of her claws together, then resumed clearing blood off her face. *All we know about Lumar we know from when the Veetanho rode them into battle. Of course, there is more to them than the Veetanho let any see.* She paused, ears turning, as a new thought struck her.

Or more to them than they let the Veetanho *see?*

She touched Tula's leg as she came close, giving the Lumar warning before she dropped her field.

"What will you do with the wounded attackers?" she asked, paying no visible attention to the range of reactions around them.

"Kill or offer join Thunder Fist," Tula replied, her shrug saying either was a perfectly acceptable next step.

"Your enemy would join you?" Her tail waved behind her, and she tilted her head up at the smaller Lumar.

"Companies follow orders. Those orders bad. Contracts bad. Thunder Fist win. Thunder Fist good contracts." She gestured at Tsan, including her new ally in good contracts. "Other Lumar not enemy, just—" Tula twisted a hand on each side of her body, then crossed her lower set of arms, "—on different side for time. Time change. They can make Thunder Fist stronger. Or they die."

"Indeed." Tsan slow blinked, then turned her gaze on the various Lumar crowded close to them. "I believe we will learn quite a bit having you as our allies."

"Depik learn from Lumar?" Arkak said, somewhere between a question and a boast.

"Learn from each other," Tula replied, and it sounded a bit like a threat and a promise.

A pleased purr rose from Tsan's chest in answer.

This will be fun, indeed.

* * *

Tsan's visit to Planet 8190 started terribly and sank deeper into the pits from there. Tortantulas did not name their planets, and if the Flatar did, the names weren't shared. The environment of the breeding planet included a series of domes formed into habitats that were strewn across the otherwise inhospitable surface.

The moment she left the shuttle and entered the dome Theela had directed her to, her skin began to crawl, and no matter how few threats jumped out at her, the feeling did not subside. Her fur lifted in patches. As soon as she smoothed one, another rose in spiky answer to absolutely nothing.

Worst of all, her quintessence field *itched*.

She wanted to hiss and spit at everything, but she kept her pace steady even though her ears were twitching.

The matriarch she was supposed to meet with, a connection of a connection of Rurranach's, had died while Tsan was in transit. Tsan had no further details, and she had little interest in wandering the so-called streets of PN 8190, hoping to find someone to talk to. Hidden by her field, she stalked through the dome, shoulder twitching and muscles jumping in protest.

"She can't see you, but she knows you're there, Kitty."

Tsan flipped backward, her instinctive hold on her quintessence field wavering as it had not done since she was a half-sized kit. She stood back on two legs and surveyed the area, ears swiveling. After a moment, she crouched and pressed a hand where she had been walking. Her eyes were intent on the furred creature who had spoken from the shadowy recesses of a nearby alcove.

The furred creature was pointing a very large MAC pistol in Tsan's direction, despite her movements. As she watched, an enormous foreleg emerged from the alcove, followed by another, then the giant, serrated pedipalps of a Tortantula Breeding Mother. The

Flatar on her back never wavered, keeping her dead in his sights, despite the fact that Tsan *knew* he couldn't see her.

So how did he—they—know where she was?

"Killers, I greet you." She dropped her field and turned her gaze from the small set of eyes to the much larger ones facing her. The gun did not currently signify. "Welcome to our negotiation."

"You here on contract? I can't imagine who would pay for our deaths, but stranger things have happened, I guess. We won't go easily."

"I do not imagine you would," Tsan replied, inclining her head. "I am not here to test our prowess against each other, delightful as that would be. I am here to negotiate, as I said."

The Flatar stared at her for a long moment, then slowly lowered and holstered his weapon. "I'm Spalee. This is Xiyo. You can follow us to our quarters if all you want to do is talk. Piss her off, and she'll probably eat you."

"I have as little intention of being a snack as I do in killing you." Tsan nodded and stepped back, the itch of her quintessence field stinging her nerves painfully, even with its release.

She followed them silently, remaining visible, as they moved back into the shadows. The ground sloped as they went, and the shadows quickly became true darkness. Tsan slid her goggles to the top of her head and let her peripheral vision do the heavy lifting.

Eventually, they came to a turn, and then another, and then another still. Tsan counted sixteen twists and more than twenty branching tunnels before the path opened to a large cavern made of rock—though natural or synthetic she couldn't tell at first scent. The place appeared spartan, but comfortable. Containers of gear were stacked against a far curve of the wall, and a massive Tri-V terminal sat on the left, just beyond the blanketed place where Tsan imagined one or both usually slept.

Xiyo walked silently to the blanketed area and lowered herself to rest with her legs tucked underneath her. Her unblinking eyes never ceased to watch Tsan as she followed the Flatar further into the cave.

"Don't have much to sit on; I usually just sit with her. Don't recommend that for you, but otherwise, make yourself at home," he said. Now that Spalee was on his own feet, Tsan noticed a pronounced limp and stiffness in his gait. He wasn't a young Flatar, then. Not that she would have expected otherwise, not when he was paired with a Breeding Mother.

Tsan folded herself neatly on the floor far enough away to comfortably regard them but still within striking distance. She curled her tail around her body, but the tip twitched despite her best efforts to control it.

"I appreciate your hospitality, Spalee and Xiyo. I arrived here to meet with Vixah, but my timing left much to be desired. Have you been in residence on this planet long?"

Her connection to the lately deceased Vixah had been tenuous at best, but this… Tsan was not entirely sure how to delve into the conversation with complete strangers. Surely it was that lack of knowledge, not the persistent grating against the raw edges of her nerves, giving her some measure of hesitation.

"Vixah produced many fine broods," Xiyo said, her voice low and silky and surprisingly delicious to Tsan's ear, though it *did* make the uncomfortable itchiness of her quintessence worse. "Her contribution to the Great Slaughter was significant. Her flesh tasted sublime, and she died with kills beneath her feet."

"I am pleased to hear that." Tsan held her ears still and focused on the pair before her. "I had planned to speak with her about a contract of sorts, between her people and mine, so, while I am glad Vixah's end was glorious, it leaves me at something of a loss." Her tail twitched, and she curled it to her other side, attempting to still it.

"There are no Veetanho left to take contracts," Xiyo said.

"I am, indeed, very glad to hear that, for I have no wish to contract with a Veetanho. There is little I wish for them but death under my claws. I came to contract with the Tortantula, *not* the Veetanho."

Spalee laughed, the sound harsh in the echoing cavern. "You don't get it, Kitty. Without the Veetanho, there is no 'the Tortantula.' The Veet left, so it's every girl for herself."

Ah, that perhaps explained the feeling that an invisible hand had stroked the wrong way up her spine, pulling her fur apart. She'd been in the middle of more than a few conflicts, but she had never had a reaction quite like this. This was not a planet she could envision bringing kits to. The younglings would claw their skin off within a day.

Her claws twitched in their sheathes, ready to scratch until there was nothing left.

"It seems calm enough in this area," she said, letting her voice lift in a question.

Spalee chuckled, and Xiyo's pedipalps moved in something that may have been her version of a smile.

"I am very skilled," she said, "and my partner is deadly. Had you gone further into the dome, outside my territory, you would have found the ferals, and your negotiation would have been in blood. There is no order."

"I see." The understanding coiled in her gut like a cheelin, and the weight of it had claws. "You are all the order that is left on 8190."

"I am not order. I merely survive and continue the Great Slaughter."

"That will be your life now, with the Veetanho gone?"

"What else is there?"

"Slaughter in the stars, perhaps? The joy of an enemy's flesh to feast on, beyond those of the other Tortantula?" Tsan didn't know. She would want more, but how many races in the galaxy would want more than to hunt prey for endless credits? There was no judgement in her, but there was a measure of curiosity even the peeling of her nerves couldn't fully erase.

Xiyo did not answer for a long moment. Spalee got up from his seat, walked over to her, and put his hand on her cephalothorax.

"There is more," Xiyo said softly, sadness soaking her tone. "Until I know it is not here, I cannot leave."

"She's a Breeding Mother, Kitty," Spalee said, stroking his partner's exoskeleton. "Do you know what that means? Her drive is to mate, to breed. When the Veet left, there was no warning, no process, nothing. It was full-on entropy for I don't know how many days. When the dust settled, we were still breathing. Xiyo and Vixah were the only two Mothers left, and they wanted to know what happened to their mates."

"They disappeared?" Tsan tilted her head, knowing the shape of such a loss.

"Something. Maybe they all died. But until she knows, she can't stop looking for them. They're smaller, see. Easy prey for a feral, except they're smart. Real smart. So maybe they hid, figured out a way to survive. Holed up in one of the other domes. She's gonna find out because… well… she's got to, and whatever she does, I'm with her." He continued soothingly stroking Xiyo's cephalothorax, and slowly, every third eye drifted closed.

"I understand." Tsan inclined her head more deeply than she had on first meeting them. "That is not a cause I can argue against. Do you believe this to be the same on the many breeding worlds of the Tortantula?"

"As far as I can tell, yep." He shrugged. "I've reached out and contacted a few. Same story everywhere if they answer. Some don't."

"In other circumstances, I would offer to help." Tsan sat back on her haunches and forced her claws back into their sheaths. "Unfortunately, I know where many of the Veetanho have gone, and until I have taken their lives, like you, Xiyo, I am bound. Until that task is done, I cannot take on another one."

Xiyo remained silent, and eventually, Spalee again spoke up for her.

"It's okay. She didn't ask for your help. Just… maybe kill a few Veet for us, yeah?"

"I have no doubt there will be rivers of blood before long." Her tail lashed, and she breathed through the discomfort. "And perhaps when my task and yours are realized, we will talk again."

"Sure thing, Kitty. You want me to walk you out?" He glanced at her, then back down at Xiyo, who now had two-thirds of her eyes fully closed in rest.

"I appreciate the offer but tend to your partner. The path to my shuttle is clear, and if it is not—" she spread her claws wide and slow blinked, "—I will be more than happy to clear it."

* * * * *

Interlude

Aryo crouched under the spike-edged flat leaf of a sleeping bush. Their ragged, growing group had avoided the city, but it had been weeks since they'd uncovered a new clan den or found a non-Hunter sigiled being.

They were in no danger of running out of supplies, but they were running low on targets.

For some reason, the Veetanho had stopped sending fodder into the jungles.

She should be pleased about that, but Zuul knew very well how dangerous it was to trust that the future would reflect the past. The gods grew bored with sameness, and calm only heralded some larger storm to come.

Besides, it didn't take a tactical genius to know the Veetanho were up to something more than simple occupation. Orbital traffic continued to increase, and neither Aryo nor her compatriots could fool themselves into believing the occupying Veetanho were planning their retreat.

The invaders were doubling down on their possession of Khatash, though they had to have been crowding the small central city and the orbiting station to do so.

Aryo and her people had few details from which to gain a broader understanding. Zia would only let them dip into communications bands sparingly to minimize the risk of their intrusions being noticed.

Observing the city wouldn't tell them much—even overconfident Veetanho weren't foolish enough to conduct business in the open air—but Aryo had other methods.

The edges of the city bled into the jungle, and most non-Hunters avoided the outskirts. Traffic was light, but after several hours, she was rewarded by familiar movement.

Jochy, wings folded, approached with an open sack in her middle limbs. She crouched periodically, snapping a clawed upper limb into the ground, then leaping away as she tucked her foraged pickings into the bag and removed herself from reprisals.

Smart, as Jochy had always been smart. The Veetanho hadn't shut down all alien businesses upon their takeover, and Jochy's food stall remained in operation. The bleeding edge of the jungle contained many of the same dangers as the depths, so Jochy could hardly afford to pay anyone to gather supplies for her.

It had taken Aryo four separate attempts to contact Jochy—hours lost under various covers as someone else trailed Jochy, the movement of air felt wrong, or a burrowing knotwraith nearly took off Aryo's tail as she lay in wait. After the last unsuccessful attempt, their Hunter had considered moving them further away and giving up on the endeavor, but the lack of Veetanho prey had outweighed such caution.

The next time had paid off, and now they had a standing arrangement that worked more often than it didn't.

Jochy passed Aryo's location and scrubbed her bottom limb over the spiral mark in the dirt as she walked. Several steps later, she again crouched and plunged her claw into the ground, then twisted away as the ground roiled in response.

Aryo waited.

Jochy continued her path, aware of the jungle around her but unhurried, pausing here and there for collection.

After a long time, she turned, head tilted to examine her sack as she shook it. Her compound eyes sparkled, and she waved her top limbs, very slightly, in negation.

She was being followed, even though Aryo couldn't smell anyone. A drone, then, or a long-range sniper. Very well.

Aryo waited.

Jochy made her way back carefully along the path she'd walked, then crouched again near the erased spiral. She leaped away and snarled, shaking her claw hard.

Something small and wriggling flew, into the leaves.

"Rotten," she muttered, examining her limb closely, as though she were ensuring nothing had broken through her exoskeleton.

Aryo waited.

Well after Jochy disappeared again, Aryo moved, as slowly and smoothly as the heavy air around her.

She picked up the clever thing, not at all a rotten bug that Jochy had discarded, then retreated deeper into the jungle.

Before she'd moved half a klick, the Hunter appeared in her path. Aryo's nose twitched, but she kept her eyes alert to the jungle around them. The jungle was no less dangerous to her with the Hunter's presence.

"No one is following you."

Aryo's ears twitched, but she held her jaw tight to keep from grinning. Coming from the Hunter, that was very nearly a compliment. She reached for the bug she'd retrieved, but the Hunter lashed her tail once.

"When we return. You were not followed, but something moves in the jungle that would be better not to meet." She blinked, not quite a slow blink, but a deliberate gesture Aryo could not entirely parse. "There are many more we must kill before hunting that one."

Curiosity prickled, but she shoved it away. As long as Aryo had lived on Khatash, she still didn't know all the creatures in the triple canopies that could kill her. Any that gave the Hunter pause were low on her priority list to meet.

The return to their camp was silent and uneventful, though Aryo kept swiveling her head and twitching her nose, trying to detect whatever they were avoiding.

None the wiser, but thank Coshke, unbitten and whole, she climbed the striated tree that temporarily served as home. She moved slowly enough to avoid the patches of sticky sap that were occasionally harmless and occasionally digestive acid.

"I was beginning to think you wouldn't be back for dinner," Fip said as she pulled herself onto the last broad branch of camp.

"Is it a special meal?" she asked, her jaw dropping in a small smile. The cluster of assorted beings strung around the cleared wood sent a round of quiet greetings that she returned, though no one moved to gather around her.

"Ah, indeed it is. Zia and Nivedio returned with a berry the Hunter said wasn't likely to kill us, and we have the stevvings from the last clan den we…" Fip warbled cheerfully, as they were practical enough to scavenge as needed but didn't like to call it that.

"A feast," she answered, crouching comfortably across from him.

It took several breaths for the Hunter to appear. Aryo certainly hadn't out-climbed her, so the Zuul assumed the Hunter had circled a few times to scout their perimeter before joining them.

She held out her hand, and Aryo took the bug from her waist bag and handed it to her. The Hunter cocked her head, then pulled a reader out of her harness and nestled the two together.

"A kit's toy is our best intelligence asset," Fip murmured, curling his tentacles as though he were trying to keep himself from reaching for it.

"A chef is our best intelligence asset," Aryo corrected, one ear aimed at Fip, the other toward the Hunter. "But it is a clever toy."

They'd found the bugs and reader in the first outlying clan den they'd searched. Aryo had gone right past the collection, but the Hunter had paused and tilted her head. Kits learned Hunting of all kinds on Khatash, and gathering information was an arms race like any other.

This clan had perfected a technological brush pass that worked perfectly on the planet, if nowhere else. A collection of passive readers, shaped exactly like burrowing knotwraiths, could be stuck on nearly any information storage device, and could copy its information without leaving a trace behind. The device wriggled when full, and any Khatashi native who encountered one would hurl it from the den to keep the 'knotwraith' from breeding. The information could then be recovered at leisure, as it could only be downloaded by its linked reader.

The Hunter had very nearly laughed upon seeing it, declaring it all the rage among a certain cluster of clans many seasons ago. Whispering Fear must have missed the trend, and Aryo knew there was no way a Veetanho would recognize it.

So, the Zuul buried a bug along Jochy's path, Jochy copied information onto it, then released it, using her foraging for actual knotwraiths as cover.

It wasn't foolproof, but it was the best option they had to preserve Jochy's safety while gathering information to better target their attacks.

At the very least, Aryo felt like she was doing something. She hadn't been a warrior before joining Whispering Fear, but now, she itched whenever too many days passed without a proper ambush.

She chose not to think too deeply about what any of it meant. She walked the path Coshke put before her, and it would be wrong to resent it.

The Hunter made a noise low in her throat, and all the fur on Aryo's back stood in response.

"Anything helpful?" Fip asked, studying the Hunter.

"No," the Hunter said. Her eyes narrowed, and her pupils were whisper thin. "But we'll have more than enough targets soon."

A jolt stabbed through Aryo's limbs, and her lip curled in a snarl. They knew they had no chance of taking back the planet on their own, but the blood would run in rivers before they met their end.

* * * * *

Part Two

Chapter Eight

In the beginning, Fssik would make a point of leaving the room whenever Jim and Ziva had their reunions. As a rule, Hunters weren't shy about sex, and Ziva never had been, either. But Fssik knew Humans preferred to keep things private, and he typically didn't see the harm in leaving them alone.

However, he thought as he sat on Jim Cartwright's windowsill and watched the tangled bodies and twisted sheets moving one over the other on Jim's bed, *the years haven't been kind to Jim Cartwright, and thus, he has become less and less kind himself.*

Ziva could handle herself, Fssik knew that. He also knew that in his way, Jim did love her, but for a while now, his Hunter instincts had pushed him not to leave the two of them completely alone. So, he didn't. He hid in his quintessence, knowing Ziva knew he was nearby. She never said anything about it, and he didn't bring it up, so he figured all was fine.

"Holy Entropy," Jim exhaled as he rolled to his back, chest heaving. Ziva let out a throaty chuckle and rose to kiss him, then gathered her long dark hair into a tail that hung over one shoulder as she snuggled in next to him and kissed his neck.

"I missed you too," she said. Jim snorted softly through his nose and wrapped one hand around her sweat-sheened shoulder, squeezing her close for a moment before letting go.

"I should give you half of my company more often," Jim said, his tone joking. Before they'd torn each other's clothes off, he and Ziva had been negotiating. After they'd left what Fssik had decided to call the "Council of War" on Land's End, Ziva had come to Houston to request a loan of some Cavalier assets, namely an intel detachment and some assault companies, and a Fist of Raknar. Jim had readily agreed to the detachment and the CASPer companies, but he'd balked at the Raknar. Ziva hadn't pressed the issue, but if Fssik knew his Human, Jim hadn't heard the last of it.

As it so happened, however, Ziva *wasn't* the one who brought the lovers back to the subject of Raknar.

"You know," Jim said as he lay on his back, idly playing with a strand of Ziva's hair as she cuddled next to him, "I may have thought of something."

"What's that?" Ziva asked, her voice decidedly sleepy.

"I think I know how to convince Splunk and the others to let me bring Raknar to Khatash."

Ziva sat up, all her somnolence gone. "Seriously? Holy Stars, Jim! That would be—"

"Yeah." Jim grinned up at her. "I know it would work. I just need you to convince your mom to get the Depik to agree."

"They'll agree to just about anything to get their home back!"

"That's what I was thinking," Jim said, his smile growing. "I know the Dusman would be *thrilled* to welcome the Depik as a servitor race."

Tension sang through Fssik's body. He almost dropped his quintessence. Ziva put a hand on Jim's chest so quickly, it made a light slapping noise.

"Wait, what?" she asked. "Say that again?"

"All the Depik have to do is agree to be a servitor race to the Dusman," Jim said, his tone still light. He threaded the fingers of his left hand through Ziva's fingers on his chest, then he lifted her hand to his lips and kissed her knuckle.

Ziva wrenched her hand back, her motion just shy of violent. "Jim! No! They'll never agree… you can't ask—" she spluttered, shaking her head so hard her hair rippled around her sleekly muscled shoulders.

"Sweetheart, you said it yourself. They'll agree to anything to get their home back. It would be good for their survival, and maybe a way for them to give back some of what they've taken."

"What they've *taken?!*" Ziva reared back, slid away from him, and pulled the bedclothes up to cover her chest. Fssik felt the horror in her words echo throughout his body. Slowly, he got to his feet and began to stalk silently across the windowsill toward them.

"Ziva, think about it. The Depik have been killing for millennia! Think what a force they could be—you could *all* be—fighting on the side of good, instead of your own side. I know the cat in you wants to knock the bottle off the table, but please." Jim sat up, his face turning serious and intent. "Please consider this. For all our sakes."

"Jim, they literally committed wholesale suicide rather than agree to give up their free will! They'll never do this, and I will *certainly* never ask!" Ziva shook her head again, her brow pinched.

"It isn't giving up their fucking freedom," Jim said, his voice growing louder. Fssik leaped from the windowsill onto a nearby table and began to pick his way through the cast-off clothing as he moved toward the bed. "It's just agreeing to fight alongside others, with the Dusman leading."

"You and I both know that's a polite fiction," Ziva said. She took a deep breath and forced herself to calm down. Fssik knew she could feel him getting closer. He also knew she was likely trying to deescalate this situation before he acted. Because he loved her, and for no other reason, he slowed to a stop and waited.

"Hunters will be our allies," Ziva said once Fssik stopped moving. "They'll be no one's slaves. Or servitors. Or whatever pretty name you give it."

"Is that what you think we are? Is that what you *really* think we are?" Jim asked, anger threading through his rising tone. Apparently, he wasn't into deescalation. Fine. Neither was Fssik. He started moving forward again and leaped from the table to the nightstand next to Jim's side of the bed.

"Since when has humanity agreed to be a servitor race?"

"I would have agreed to it, but I wasn't the only one making the decision. We're their allies; they made an exception. I don't know why. I think it's prophecy or some shit. Ziva, there are so few Depik left. Please, think about this. Something bad is coming."

Fssik stepped silently around the lamp on the nightstand and came within striking distance of Jim's muscled, naked back.

"Okay," Jim said, looking around. Fssik froze, and Jim let out a little laugh that the predator in him gleefully interpreted as unease. "Badder. But that doesn't change the fact that, if the Depik agree to be part of this, maybe they'll come out on the other side as something more than a tiny, fragmented race, barely clinging to survival."

Ziva whipped the bedclothes back and stood up, every movement sharp with rage.

"I don't believe you," she said, her words coming out in a hiss. "I don't believe you'd subject your will to the will of another being. That's not the Jim Cartwright I love. Yes, something bad is coming, but *we can't take the easy way out!* It's not in them, and it's not in me!" She slapped a hand twice against her naked chest, then raked her hair back away from her face in frustration. "You know what I am, Jim! I'm Homo venatores. I'm proof the Hunters are *already* taking steps to ensure they're able to do more than cling to survival. I'm part of that, and you can be too, but you've got to let go of this idea of control. *You can't control a Hunter.* You have to trust them to control themselves." She paused for a moment, and when Jim didn't immediately reply, she shook her head again. "I gotta go," she said, and she began picking up her discarded clothing and pulling it on.

"Okay, Ziva," Jim said, his tone nasty and sharp. "I have to go lead my Cavaliers into battle for you and your people. Some will die; maybe I'll be one of them. I guess we're just slaves after all."

Ziva finished dressing before she responded. She walked to the door and paused with her hand on the doorknob, then she turned to look directly at Fssik. The pain and fear and rage in his companion's eyes rocked him, and his control nearly faltered again. Fssik took one more look at the temptingly exposed back of Jim's neck, then turned and leaped silently to the floor. Maybe the man deserved it, but he wouldn't be the one to make that kill. Not as long as his Ziva loved Jim so much, she could have that look in her eyes.

Ziva blinked, and Fssik watched her refocus across the room to meet the angry gaze of the man she loved. Fssik bounded out as silently as he could manage.

"Only if you choose to be, Jim," she said softly. She stepped through the door and pulled it closed behind her.

* * *

Fssik gave Ziva a ninenight before he brought it up.

"My Human," he said as she settled, with a sigh, into the Human-sized seat he'd added to the cockpit of his ship. "Is it done?"

"It is, my Hunter," she said, fatigue fraying her tone as she closed her eyes and rubbed her fingers over her face. "Jim came through as promised with the assault companies. They'll meet us at the staging area when it's time. I've got their commander plugged into our communication matrix, and they'll be in touch with Dama or whoever she designates to oversee this thing."

"And the intelligence assets?"

"All loaded up and ready to receive the coordinates from your nav computer. Jim came through with those, too. I know you don't like him much these days, Fssik, but he's delivered everything he promised."

"That is not my concern."

"You know what he asked me to do when we were… last together."

"Yes."

"But you have been suspicious of him for a long while. I thought you wanted us to have more kids."

"I want that if it's what you want, my Ziva. If you want Jim, I want you to have him. But for a while now, every time you see him, you end up unhappy. That is why I do not trust him as I once did."

Ziva said nothing. She looked away as she reached for her safety harness and buckled herself into her seat.

"My Human?" Fssik asked, his tone gentle. She looked up at him, her eyes wet. "It has been a ninenight. Do you know… were you successful in conceiving another child?"

Ziva swallowed hard and blinked rapidly, as a line of wetness spilled from the corner of her eye and rolled down her right cheek.

"I don't know," she said. "Without a scan, it's too early to tell."

"After this mission, when we return to Land's End, will you let the Healer scan you?"

"Why?"

"Because, my Human. If you are carrying kits, you know you cannot participate in the invasion mission to Khatash." Fssik held himself steady and stared at Ziva, maintaining eye contact for all he was worth. Every instinct screamed at him to go to her, to rub his furred length against her and share scents, to curl against her chest and rumble until the pain in her eyes quit twisting through him and went away.

But he couldn't. This was too important. So, he held her gaze.

Eventually, she let out a sigh and sagged in her seat restraints. Her eyelids closed as more water seeped beneath the lids, and she nodded her head. "I know," she whispered.

"So, you will get scanned?" Fssik pressed. He needed to hear her say it.

"Yes," she said. "I will. And if I'm pregnant, I'll... I don't know. I'll pass command of the intelligence piece off to someone else. It's just..."

"I know, my love," Fssik said, stealing a Human phrase he'd heard, "but that's what a Damita must do."

* * *

"**M**ama, I tired."

Ziva hitched her son up higher on her hip and reached up to gently guide her son's head down to rest on her shoulder.

"I know, buddy," she said. "It's been a long day. Don't worry, though, as soon as they open the doors of this transport, we'll be home."

"Daddy Home or Dama Home?" he asked, straightening up again with interest.

"Dama Home," Ziva clarified. "We'll see Daddy in a few weeks."

"See Memory?"

"Yes, Thad, you will probably see Memory. Hush now for a few minutes, all right? Mama's gotta process the intake point."

Four-year old Thaddeus let out a gusty sigh but obediently laid his head back down on Ziva's shoulder. From the shadows where he watched, Fssik couldn't help slow blinking at the tender softness in Ziva's face as she pressed a kiss to her son's hair.

"Welcome to Land's End. Name and business?"

The person who spoke wasn't familiar to Fssik, and that alone pulled his attention away from Ziva. Even if he *had* recognized the Human, the brusque, almost rude tone of her voice was odd. Land's End belonged to their clan's Human Dama, and Tamir usually cultivated a relaxed, polite society.

Fssik dropped his cloak of quintessence, bounded forward, and landed in front of Ziva.

"I am Fssik of Clan Tamir, and this is my companion Ziva and her son Thaddeus Cartwright. I greet you, rude Human. Welcome to our negotiation." Fssik's words were clipped, and he stared up at the functionary, whose face rapidly flushed red, then paled to a bone-white.

"Oh! Hunter! I... uh. I'm sorry. I meant no offense. It's just been busy with everyone here."

"More traffic should mean more politeness, not less, lest things escalate and someone get hurt," Fssik pressed.

"Y-yes, Hunter."

"Fssik," Ziva said as she awkwardly shifted Thaddeus' weight further onto her hip and faced the biometric scanner to let it recognize her features. "It's all right, she's learning."

"Welcome home, Ziva Alcuin," the functionary said, with even more resignation filling her tone as she realized whom, exactly, she'd just insulted. "I really am sorry."

"Don't worry about it," Ziva said, with a tiny smile as she shifted her son yet again and walked past the scanner. "But Fssik is right, it's better to be overly polite here at Land's End. You'll do fine. Good luck."

"Thank you, ma'am," the young woman said, bobbing her head as the three of them passed.

"What an idiot," Fssik murmured just loud enough for Ziva to hear.

"You're being harsh," Ziva said. "She doesn't have the easiest job."

"Still. She should know better."

"Now, she does." Ziva sighed and moved Thaddeus' almost entirely limp weight to her other hip.

"Why don't you put the kit down and make him walk?"

"Because he's half-asleep, Fssik. I'd carry *you* if you were this tired."

Fssik dropped his jaw in a silent laugh and followed in Ziva's wake as she made her way to the set of private elevators near the back of the commercial loading and unloading dock on the surface of Land's End. A large holographic sign proclaimed the lifts were private property, and that any unauthorized person used them at the risk of their own life. Most of the miners and ships' crews who frequented this out-of-the-way corner of the galaxy knew very well how serious that warning was.

Clan Tamir valued its privacy.

Ziva walked toward the door to the center lift, which irised open at her approach and then closed automatically once she and Fssik were safely inside.

"I'm worried about my mom," she said quietly over the light whirr of the lift's mechanism as they began to descend to the living quarters buried below the surface.

"Is that why you're on edge?" Fssik asked, stepping over and leaning against her calf and knee in a gesture of comfort.

"That and because this big guy is getting heavier and heavier," Ziva said, "but mostly that. I know this last year's been hard on her, and we've been so lucky to have her for so long…"

"Time ravages us all," Fssik said softly. "I know it's no comfort, but our dama at least has the knowledge that she did something truly remarkable. If she hadn't had a place for us to come to, we Hunters would have gone mad without hope. In a very real way, she saved us all."

"And now, I can't save her," Ziva said and pressed another kiss to her sleepy child's head.

They rode the rest of the way in silence. When the door irised open at the bottom level, Fssik pulled quintessence and led the way out. It wasn't because he felt he needed to scout ahead—although that was usually the reason he went first into most places—but because he disliked Ziva's pensive, morose mood. If anyone could fix Ziva's mood, it would be her mother, their beloved Dama Tamir.

He ran down the long corridor and leaped up to the Hunter entrance above the usual door, then ducked through the low tunnel and emerged on the ledge above the door. Once inside, he dropped his quintessence.

"Dama," he said, slow blinking down at the woman reclining on the pillows stacked on the bed within, "I greet you."

Tamir may have moved a little more slowly to look up at him, but her dark eyes had lost none of their sharpness as she smiled in greeting.

"Hello, Hunter. Come down from there; you're making my neck hurt. Is my daughter on the way?"

"I'm right here," Ziva said, as she pushed through the door below the ledge where Fssik stood. He waited while she entered the room and laid the sleepy toddler down on the bed beside Tamir. Thaddeus let out a gusty sigh and snuggled in close to his grandmother, who slow blinked in pure bliss.

"The journey was a bit long for your descendant, Dama," Fssik said as he jumped down from the ledge and landed on the foot of Tamir's bed. "He lasted until we disembarked on the surface and then passed out."

"He's gotten so big," Tamir said, stroking the sleeping boy's hair back from his face. "They do that, I know they do, but it's always a shock to see it."

"He *has* grown a lot," Ziva said, a softness in her words, as usual when discussing her son. "Judging by the way he's eating, I suspect he's getting ready to hit another growth spurt soon."

"Best invest in larger clothing now," Tamir said, her customary dry humor threading through her voice. "Before you know it, you won't be able to keep him clothed. You might ask around. The clan kids grow so quickly, they hardly have a chance to wear clothes out before they're too small."

"Do you think any of that is due to the change in our DNA?" Ziva asked baldly, meeting her mother's eyes. Once upon a time, their gaze had been nearly identical. Now, however, Ziva shared the cat-slit pupils of the other companions who'd taken the name *Homo venatores* for whom they'd become. Thaddeus' eyes were closed, but he, too, shared his mother's iris shape and increased night vision— proof that the genome changes wrought by the Wrogul docs were permanent.

"It's possible," Tamir said. "Though I think unlikely. Lara and Ward never said anything about tinkering with Human growth patterns. I just think he's a boy who goes hard at anything he does: playing, eating, fighting... you name it. His father isn't a small man either."

Ziva nodded, and Fssik's eyes narrowed as he watched the tiny frown crease deepen between her brows at the thought of Jim Cartwright.

"How is Jim?" Tamir asked, her voice casual, but her eyes sharp, and, not for the first time, Fssik felt a wave of love and awe for his Human dama wash over him.

"Jim is... mostly good, I think," Ziva said, her voice softening. "It's been hard to see each other, with everything that's going on. Still, I promised to bring Thaddeus home to see him for a full season as soon as we're done with this trip. I know my boy misses his Daddy."

"And you miss your man?" Tamir pressed. Ziva nodded but looked down and away. Tamir frowned. Fssik chose that moment to walk up the line of Tamir's body and thrust his head up under her chin.

"Not now, please, Dama," he whispered as he rubbed against her jaw. "Later."

Tamir frowned harder, but she stroked his back and let it go.

"But you, Mom," Ziva said, looking back up as she moved to sit in the chair next to the bed. "How are you doing?"

"I'm dying," Tamir said bluntly.

"Mom—"

"No, Ziva, my love. Don't protest. We knew it was coming, and now it's here."

"Now?" Panic crossed Ziva's face, and Fssik straightened his body, preparing to leap to her lap if she needed him. Tamir let out a chuckle.

"Well, not *now*, exactly, but soon. I'm old, sweetling. Even with all our medical advances, there's not much we can do if the cancer keeps coming back. That's part of why I asked you to come home. I want to talk to you about the future of the clan."

Ziva straightened in her seat. "Mom, I—"

Tamir held out a hand, and Ziva fell silent. Fssik watched as his companion's lovely eyes traced the wasted lines of Tamir's once-beautiful fingers.

"Do you want to be dama?" Tamir asked.

Ziva inhaled sharply and pressed her lips together. Fssik watched her swallow, then she glanced at him. That was all the invitation he needed. With a single bound, he leaped from mother to daughter with his forearms extended. Ziva caught him and pulled him in close. She closed her eyes and laid her cheek on the back of his skull, just as she did when she sometimes wept after seeing Jim. Fssik drew in a breath and started to purr, hoping the healing rumble would help her calm.

And be honest.

"No," she whispered, and he felt the wetness of her tears soaking through his fur. "I'm sorry, Mama. I don't. I can't!"

"Ziva, baby," Tamir said, her voice ragged with the anguish of a mother watching her child's pain. "Sweetheart, if you don't want it, then—"

"It's not that," Ziva said, lifting her head and sniffling mightily. "I'd be honored, but I can't fill your shoes. I don't have your vision. And with Thaddeus and Jim, I'm too entangled with the Humans to see what is best for the Clan."

It took Fssik a moment to realize just why his skin tingled under his fur as she spoke. Pride, he realized, eventually. He was *proud* of his Ziva. He knew she'd harbored these doubts for a long time. He knew she thought she'd hidden them from him, but she hadn't, and, as she spoke, Fssik realized that even though it cost her to admit it, she was exactly right.

"Baby," Tamir said again, stroking Thaddeus' hair and pressing another kiss to the sleeping boy's forehead, "you've thought about this?"

"Of course," Ziva whispered brokenly. "As you said, you're dying."

"You're not just speaking out of fear?"

"No," Ziva said. "Fear, I can handle. But if I am dama, the day may come when I'm forced to choose between the clan and my children. I can't make that choice with a clear head. It must be someone else, someone with no chance of divided loyalties."

"I… agree…" Tamir said slowly, as if she were just realizing the truth of her words as she said them. "Entropy take my wasted body, but I think you're right, baby. I didn't think about that."

"Ziva did," Fssik said, drawing his spine up straight and lifting his chin. "Ziva thinks about everything."

"Not everything," Ziva said, but she smiled tenderly down at him and scratched him under his chin. "But I do try."

Thaddeus shifted in his sleep and snuggled closer to his grand-mother, and Fssik watched as a look of pure joy crossed Tamir's face. She pulled the boy close and kissed his hair again.

"You leave a magnificent legacy behind, Dama," Fssik said, his words dropping into the silence.

"Do you think so, Hunter?" Tamir asked. "I never had any ambi-tions toward leaving a legacy. I just wanted to keep me and mine safe."

"You are the only Human dama," Ziva pointed out. "Because of you, our Hunters are not extinct."

"I didn't do it alone," Tamir said, "and you wouldn't have to, ei-ther." She looked up at Ziva as she said it.

"I can't, Mom. I was already grown when you became dama. Thaddeus is still tiny and someday…" she trailed off, and Fssik no-ticed the hand that wasn't stroking his neck dropped to her belly.

"Fair point, kiddo. I had to ask," Tamir said with a sly grin. "One last try—you know how it is. Your argument makes sense. Only now, I don't know who to name as my heir."

"Dama Tsan," Fssik said with zero hesitation. "We all follow her guidance anyway. Whereas my Ziva cannot afford to focus on the strategic future of our clan, that is *all* Tsan does."

"Do you think she would consent to cease being Dama of Whispering Fear and become Dama of all Clan Tamir instead?"

"Dama, you of all beings should know it is useless to try and predict what a dama will or won't do. I learned that lesson as a tiny kit. All I can say is that you should ask her." Fssik rolled his neck around, so the top of his skull rubbed under Ziva's fingers and then stood on his four feet to stretch.

"Tsan is due in tonight," Tamir said. "Maybe… maybe I'll leave a message for her to find me when she arrives. We should talk about other developments as well."

"Speaking of other developments—" Ziva started to say, but she broke off when Fssik leaped to the floor.

"You're going to tell her about the intel we've gathered?" Fssik asked. At Ziva's nod, he slow blinked. "I already know about that, and I'm hungry. I will leave you ladies to it, while I find out what's going on in the kitchen."

"Don't harass my cooks, Hunter," Tamir said, giving him a gimlet stare that nevertheless twinkled with good humor.

"I wouldn't dream of it, Dama," Fssik said, dropping his jaw in a cheeky Human-style grin that showed all his wickedly sharp teeth. Tamir chuckled, and Ziva rolled her eyes.

"Get the hell out of here, my Hunter, before she throws something at you," Ziva advised. "I'll meet you in our room when I'm done here. I love you."

"I love you too, my Human," he said as he jumped up to the ledge above the door to exit. Just for fun, he pulled his cloak of quintessence around himself in midair, and he heard Tamir's exasperated chuckle echo behind him as he left.

* * *

One of the best things about being home was the sensation of a full belly.

Fssik stood on all four paws and stretched, lengthening his spine until he felt several satisfying *pops*. The mass of fresh meat he'd just consumed distended his stomachs and pressed against his innards in a way that bordered on this side of uncomfortable. But he enjoyed that too. Travelling the galaxy and having adventures was all well and good, but it made being home and full that much sweeter.

He straightened up with a sigh and leaped up to the ledge above the doorway to the refectory. Dama Tamir, in her wisdom, had installed a network of Hunter tunnels that ran throughout Land's End. He didn't know the whole of the story, simply that she'd befriended a Hunter in her youth and had designed her home accordingly. He'd have to ask her someday.

Someday sooner rather than later. The melancholy thought pressed in upon him as he slipped into those tunnels and started to make his way toward Ziva's room. All in all, Dama Tamir hadn't looked terribly ill when he'd seen her earlier, but he was experienced enough to see that she had tired more easily than in the past.

Fortunately, Ziva's room wasn't far from the refectory, so he didn't have long to dwell in this somber state of mind. He pressed through the opening to her room and leaped down upon the desk where she sat, just as she looked up with a slow blink and a Human smile.

"You've gotten fat," she said, her words warm with affection.

"The kitchen staff is as skilled as ever," Fssik said as he rubbed against her arm. "I put in an order for you, too. It should be here momentarily."

"I'm not super hungry, my Hunter."

"Correction, my Human. Your body is hungry, your mind is sad. It's understandable, but you still need to eat, to care for yourself. You know that."

Ziva swallowed hard and nodded, then reached out her arms in invitation. Fssik found that he knew exactly what she needed, so he stepped into the embrace and pushed his head up under her chin, purring loudly. Maybe, if he rumbled just right, he could help Ziva's battered heart heal.

"I believe you ordered food?" Tsan's voice preceded, barely, the arrival of a cart of food. She dropped her field as the door slid closed behind the automated cart and leaped lightly away from the covered plates. "I hope you do not mind eating while we meet."

"Dama," Ziva said, turning her head toward the door. "We greet you." Fssik wormed his way up so that he, too, could slow blink at Tsan, but he stayed where he was and continued his purr. His person needed him. Dama would understand.

"I greet you, as well, Hunter and Companion." She nudged the cart back toward them and sat comfortably on a pile of cushions against the wall. "I have only recently returned to Land's End, and I hear you were not far ahead of me. How did you find your travels?"

"Our travels were interesting, Dama, on many levels," Ziva said. She laid her cheek against the top of Fssik's skull for a moment, then turned her chair toward Tsan and deliberately opened her arms. Fssik took the hint and leaped to the ground, then sauntered toward Tsan to rub against her in greeting, while Ziva retrieved her food and dismissed the robot cart back to the kitchens.

Tsan closed her eyes and leaned against Fssik for a long moment before straightening. Her tail draped casually over his back in a silent invitation to stay close or jump away as he preferred.

"I imagine they must have been. Earth and the Horsemen remain quite a nexus on which the galaxy's events turn. Is there anything of a pressing matter we should discuss before the council meeting tomorrow?"

Fssik heard Ziva inhale sharply, then hesitate. He turned to look at her and saw her incline her head toward him and lift her fingers in a "go ahead" gesture, as she sank back into her seat at the desk.

"Ziva and Jim Cartwright have quarreled," Fssik said baldly. "Jim has agreed to let us have intel and CASPer support from the Cavaliers, but no Raknar unless we Hunters swear allegiance to the Dusman, as a servitor race."

Tsan's pupils narrowed to pinpoints, and the fur along the back of her neck lifted in a sinuous ripple that echoed her hiss.

"Has he broken, your Jim?" she asked, fixing her eyes on Ziva's.

"N-no," Ziva said. "I-I don't think so. It's been very difficult for him, with his injuries and all the stress of rebuilding and… but he loves our child, and I believe he loves me. He is just… unsure."

"But," Fssik put in, as pain for his Ziva's predicament rippled through him, "he *did* agree to support us with troops and intel support. The Raknar piece is his Dusman's doing, I am sure of it."

"Love causes as many wounds as anything else," Tsan murmured. She pressed her cheek against Fssik's, then crossed the short distance to Ziva and placed a hand on the Human's knee. "None of us are operating cleanly, after all we have seen. We will take what he offers, but if he breaks…"

She blinked, not a smile, the gesture too long and her ears too stiff. Her fingerpads tightened against Ziva, claws sheathed.

"There is no shame in that, dear one. Only we must watch with clear eyes, so we may do what we must." Her tail waved slowly behind her.

Ziva swallowed hard and nodded, albeit slowly. "He is the father of my child, Dama. I love him. I... I cannot think clearly about this. As I told my mother, my loyalty is too divided for me to be... what she asked me to be."

Fssik had followed his Dama to sit beside Ziva's feet. He jumped back up into Ziva's lap. All too often lately, it seemed the only comfort he could offer his Human was his physical presence. *If that is all I can do, that is what I will do, until the universe collapses, and we all go the way of entropy.*

"We do not need another dama at this moment," Tsan replied, one of her ears flicking to the side in dismissal. "It is not your loyalties that are in question." She paused, opened her mouth to continue, then twisted both ears backward then forward again. "For this moment, we need only Hunters, and there are two before me."

Fssik felt a shock go through Ziva's body at the dama's statement. He craned his neck around to look at her face and found his Human's eyes filling with moisture.

"Dama," Ziva whispered. "You honor me."

"I do." Tsan slow blinked and turned away. "Such things come with a price, my dear ones." Her tail curled behind her. "Always."

* * *

The noise was stunning.

Fssik flicked his ears and felt tension ripple down his fur as he and Ziva walked into Land's End's largest cargo bay. Ziva's soft footsteps should have echoed on the metal grate built into the floor, but the space was packed with Humans and Hunters from wall to curving wall. The constant buzz of conversation and movement thrummed through the air, and, despite himself, Fssik pressed close to Ziva's legs for comfort.

"I had no idea we'd grown so large," Ziva muttered as she bent to run her hand down Fssik's spine.

"Nor I, though I suppose it's a good thing."

"Indeed, it is," Tsan said, dropping her field on the last word. She touched Fssik's cheek and slow blinked up at Ziva before glancing ahead. "We will be able to send the youngest to join those on Azure before we strike."

Her ears flattened briefly but flicked forward again in a breath.

"Hunters, I greet you. Are you prepared for this?"

"Dama," Fssik said, slow blinking as he leaned into Tsan's caress, "we greet you… and we think so. Is there something you're not telling us?" A tiny thread of unease pulsed through him. When a dama asked if one was ready, one could never really be sure.

"Often," Tsan replied, her tail lashing once behind her, "but it is nothing you need to know just yet." She disappeared, then reappeared moments later on the table of crates in the center of the bay. Tamir rolled closer, and Tsan lifted a hand.

In the space of a breath, the noise ebbed in the cargo bay, and Tsan inclined her head to her fellow dama.

"The time has come," Tamir said, her voice steady. "We have much of what we need to retake Khatash. Dama Tsan, will you share with the assembled council the news you brought home?"

"Warriors, allies, I greet you." She stood at ease, her tail a soft curl behind her. "As you know, the skillset of Hunters is not in the retaking of planets. We have assembled a disparate force of allies that will complement our abilities and drive our enemies before us. From one of those allies, I have collected data on the forces the Veetanho assembled around Khatash... as of a year and a half ago." She toggled something, and several packets of information dispersed through their pinplants connections.

Tsan gave them a moment to process and file the messages for later review, then gestured for them to return their attention to her.

"What we require before engaging those allies in action is current information. The Veetanho are strategists; we will not commit our resources blindly."

Fssik, who had joined Ziva on a nearby crate, sat up straight, his ears erect.

"That is where we can help, Dama," he said, and he felt more than saw Ziva nod next to him. "For the past four years, my Human and I have been working with Cartwright's Cavaliers' intelligence section. We have asked, as the damas directed us to, and the Cavaliers will provide us with an intel team, as well as CASPer support when the time comes." He paused and looked over at Ziva. It seemed best not to mention the Raknar just now.

As always, his Human understood exactly what he wanted from her and leaned forward. "Yes. Fssik and I can lead a team of operatives on a covert insertion to Khatash to gather real-time data. He's our best pilot, and the Cavalier intel team is second to none." Privately, Fssik thought Sansar Enkh and her Golden Horde would argue with that last statement, but he couldn't fault his Ziva for her loyalty to the men and women she'd worked beside.

"Excellent. The Deo and his Companion will lead their team to Khatash. We will begin staging our allies one jump away in preparation. The timing will be key—we will need to stagger arrivals in anticipation of Deo Fssik's information and to avoid undue notice from any overly interested parties at the various gates we'll be using." Tsan moved her gaze across the assembled beings, with something that might have been a pause as her eyes met Fssik's.

The room exploded in noise as everyone started talking at once. But for Fssik, it faded into the background behind the ever-changing green-amber of his dama's eyes. She lowered her eyelids in a slow smile, and he felt a rush of… gratitude? Love? Loyalty? All of these and more, all tangled up with the ever-present fear of letting her… of letting them all down.

Ziva's hand stroked down his spine, her fingers warm in his fur. Fssik returned Tsan's smile and ducked his head in acknowledgement of the honor—and responsibility—she had just bestowed upon him.

Tamir rolled forward then, toward the center of the room and raised her hands for quiet. "Obviously, we have much to discuss, but none of it will be useful if we all talk over each other. We will hear from everyone in turn. Starting with you, Aryss…"

* * * * *

Chapter Nine

It had been a long time.

Fssik felt a frisson of nervous energy skitter under his fur as they emerged from hyperspace into the Khatash system. Since they couldn't fly in openly, he'd run silent and cold, covertly attaching to one of the few merchant freighters willing to make the run to the out-of-the-way system. The Veetanho may have had significant setbacks in the past five years, but their credits still spent as well as they ever did.

And they were spending a lot of them. While there weren't many merchant freighters elsewhere bound for Khatash, once they got in-system, Fssik's display lit up like an ionization show. The system absolutely *teemed* with transports. He couldn't ping their registries without alerting someone to his presence, but his passive scans showed hulls and drive signatures consistent with designs typically used by Veetanho interests.

"I think Dama is right," Fssik said, as he keyed in the command for his ship to detach from the scow. Ziva leaned forward in her seat as far as her restraints would allow and peered at the display.

"Mother of Chaos," Ziva breathed. "Look at all of them! She must be right, the Veetanho are converging on Khatash. That's the only thing that explains this concentration. You going to be able to get us in there without being spotted?"

"I love you, so I will forgive such an insulting question, my Human," Fssik said. He twitched his tail and lightly whipped her wrist. "But do remember who I am."

Ziva laughed lightly and sat back in her seat.

"Very well, my Hunter. Amaze me."

When he was a tiny kit, Fssik's littermates had been a multi-talented bunch. His eldest sister-kita had become a Healer, a Hunter-of-Hurts. His other sister had become a beloved molly of a larger clan. Only he had never known what his Hunt would be, so he'd trained to hunt many different beings in many different ways. He'd amassed his fortune that way, but he hadn't discovered his true Hunt until after he'd purchased his first ship.

The truth was that, while hunting ran through his blood, flying infected his very soul. Fssik was a Hunter, of course… but he was born to be a Hunter of the Sky.

So, he'd returned to Khatash and taken a contract to learn to fly the Basreeni fighters that protected the skies above the city, and he'd flown his own ship as much as possible during his time off. He practiced until he could pick his way through an asteroid field without impacts, and then he disabled his assistive systems and started over again.

Fssik drew upon his experience as he kept all but his most basic, passive navigation systems powered down. His ship's fusion drive was highly customized, thanks to a friendly relationship he'd cultivated with an old Jeha mechanic, who lived a semi-retired life not far from Land's End. As the darkened hulk of the oblivious freighter started to recede in the visual display, Fssik slow blinked and smoothly poured on the power, engaging his ship's drive while keeping an eye on their EM signature.

Sure enough, silent as a corpse, Fssik thought as they accelerated toward the bright dot that was his home planet. *Well done, Garu; you're worth your exorbitant fees.*

Time flowed as Fssik worked with the navigation systems to guide his ship. With the EM signature effectively muffled, and all outward comms silenced, the only way they would be detected during the insertion was if someone spotted them or picked them up on short-range radar. But what was a Hunter who could not find a way to hide? Fssik angled his course, so they'd pierce the atmosphere on a low angle right at the duskline. The fading light from the day would scatter through the planet's ionosphere, which should take care of any optical sensors. If he was picked up by radar, well, he had countermeasures for that, too.

Eventually, they reached a point where the green orb of Khatash hung large in the viewscreen. His calculations and angling had paid off, for the duskline neatly bisected the sphere of the jewel-like planet ahead of them.

"Check on your team," he said to Ziva. He didn't look back at her, and a tiny corner of his mind noted his voice was calm and empty as he immersed himself in the tricky work of riding the line between day and night. He heard, but did not register, Ziva speaking into her intercom mic and then he felt her lean forward and run her hand down the back of his spine. She must be nervous.

"Team checks in ready," Ziva said. "All set."

"Stand by for insertion. It will get bumpy."

And it did. Because his goal was to mimic the behavior of one of the millions of tiny pieces of rock and space trash that fell out of any planetary orbit anywhere, Fssik had to keep his speed at the maximum his ship was designed to withstand. The ablative coating on his ship would keep them from getting cooked if he could keep the angle just right. It would be like dancing on a finger-thin branch above a torrent-filled ravine in gale force winds.

No problem.

Fssik lowered the nose of his craft a fraction of a degree and flicked his eyes to his relative velocity indicator. As the ship angled toward the center of the planet, Khatash's gravitational pull began to work with the fusion drive to increase the acceleration, and his speed started to rise. So did the temperature in the cockpit, but that was to be expected.

The round green orb in front of him began to grow faster and faster in his viewscreen. The ship shuddered as the thickening atmosphere created drag along the surface of the craft. Fssik lightly nudged the fusion drive control, adding just a touch more thrust to compensate for the loss of drag, then immediately cross-checked his external temperature readout. It was high, but still within the acceptable limit.

The scent of Ziva's sweat reached his nose. Fssik pushed that awareness away, as he did his own rising discomfort. He opened his mouth to let some of his body's heat escape, since he couldn't take the time to bathe and cool off.

The buffeting increased steadily as they arrowed down into the thicker layers of atmosphere. A horizon appeared ahead, and the rolling green terrain and spotty cloud layers of Khatash filled the viewscreen. Fssik pulled the ship's nose up another fraction of a degree—just the slightest backpressure on his controls—and nudged the power again to compensate. He felt the squeeze on his body as the acceleration increased. Behind him, Ziva let out the controlled, gasping grunt of a G-strain as she worked to keep the blood in her brain. His nav computer beeped, indicating he had reached the first planetary waypoint on his course, and he was right on altitude.

Naturally.

"Just a little longer," he transmitted over the ship's intercom. Again, he heard the grunt of Ziva's G-strain behind him, but he tuned her out and focused on maintaining his course, airspeed, and descent angle. They pierced a pile of billowy cumulus clouds, and his external viewport went momentarily white. Fssik blinked and refocused on his internal display, as they hurtled toward the mountains that reached up like claws to catch them.

"Rapid G onset coming," he warned Ziva and the passengers as they approached their next waypoint. Despite the obvious danger of burning in toward the high terrain, Fssik had set this course deliberately. He wanted to emulate a meteorite blasting through the upper atmosphere, but he was not all that interested in impacting the surface like a dumb piece of rock. He would have to maneuver to bleed off the incredible amount of kinetic energy his ship was carrying in the form of airspeed. But he still had to hide, particularly while maneuvering, lest he alert the enemy to his arrival. Fortunately for him, Khatash City was relatively close to one of the planet's major mountain ranges, and he was eminently capable of hiding behind mountains.

They broke through the cloud layer just in time for Fssik to see that they were roughly eye-level with the summit of the ridge ahead of them. He threw his throttles back, cutting the fusion drive to idle, and racked the ship into a hard bank to the right. The pressure of the Gs shifted, and he squeezed his body's muscles in response. He had to keep the blood in *his* brain too!

The massive amount of speed they'd built up meant their turn swung incredibly wide. Fssik fought to keep the nose down, lest he inadvertently climb and silhouette himself above the ridge line. Their ground track arced around the rolling foothills and rocketed out over the shoreline and the ocean. Fssik wrapped the bank in a little bit, allowing the craft to slice down through the air as he pulled them back toward the relative safety of the mountains. As they shot back toward the rising terrain, his altimeter chirped, indicating he'd reached his target altitude, so Fssik rolled out of the bank, let the nose track up, and finally, let the airspeed start to bleed away.

By the time he had to turn away from the slope of the highest peak on the ridge, Fssik had brought his ship within normal atmospheric controlled flight parameters, and he was running his fusion drive just above idle to keep it as stealthy as possible. He flew low, skimming over the tops of the triple-canopy jungle that blanketed ninety percent of his home. Something deep in his throat ached as he watched the heavy, flat leaves rustle when the ship soared overhead.

He was home.

Fssik toggled open the ambient air vent and let the hot, thick, sweet jungle scent of Khatash filter into the cockpit. He took a deep breath, closed his eyes for a moment, then refocused on the remainder of the course he'd set.

"I'm taking us to a place from which we should be able to access the city without being seen," he said into his intercom mic. He knew Ziva's team would hear him, which was fine. They were all in this together. "It's a tunnel cut through rock. It might be a bit tight for some of you, but you should be able to make it through."

"Ugh, I shouldn't have had those snack cakes on the transport," one of the operatives quipped. Fssik couldn't remember her name, but he could picture her short, dirty blonde hair and sweet smile. He slow blinked in appreciation of her spirit as he banked the ship to the right and arrowed toward the clearing.

He scanned the area as they approached, though he wasn't terribly worried. This landing zone was an emergency field used by Basreeni pilots, and it was hidden between two lower peaks on the ridge behind the city. Had they been looking for it, the Veetanho might have found the tunnel access from the city to the field, but he doubted they knew what to look for, and the native flora that grew on either end of the tunnel did much to deter exploration. Like everything else on Khatash, the Nyralor vines were carnivorous and perpetually hungry.

As Fssik expected, his scan showed no non-native organisms in the clearing. He started his approach, pulled his power back, and angled in to land with a soft *thump* on the moist, springy soil.

"Welcome home, my Hunter," Ziva said, as he worked through the shutdown sequence. Fssik paused for just a moment, then continued without saying anything.

It is home, he thought. *But it is not mine. Not yet.*

His Ziva seemed to understand his silence. She reached out and stroked his spine once before unfastening her restraints and heading to the back to get her team moving. They were experienced enough that Fssik trusted them to exchange the F-11 canister for one of the fresh ones in the small cargo hold if Ziva supervised. While they did that, he worked on concealing the ship from prying eyes.

He exited the ship slowly, one step at a time, then he stretched his spine out to its full length and inhaled a lungful of his native air. The thick, decay-sweet humidity wrapped around him, pressing his fur to his body, and filling his nose and mouth with the scents and tastes of home. A skittering in the nearby tree line caught his attention, and he swiveled his ears in that direction.

"Hunterrrr…"

It was barely a whisper, but it was enough to make Fssik turn and look. He never would have seen the Basreen if she hadn't wanted him to. As it was, he could barely make out the twin bright points of her retinas in the deep gloom under the tree. She lay twined about one of the lower branches, her wings tucked close to her body, her face turned toward him.

Fssik walked carefully across the clearing toward the trees. He moved slowly so he wouldn't present a threat to the deadly winged serpent who awaited him.

"I greet you, Basreen," he said politely, stopping just outside of her striking distance. "I am Fssik of Clan Tamir. Welcome to our negotiation."

"Negotiate. Talk. Not fight."

"I agree to your terms."

"Hunters return?"

"Yes, eventually," Fssik said. "Our numbers are few, and our enemies numerous. We have found friends who will help us fight, though. We plan to kill the Veetanho who have tried to take our home."

"Veetanho. In city?"

"Yes. The long-tailed creatures who live in the city. Do you know them?"

The Basreen rustled her wings against her back and let out a sound of pure derision. "Weak ones. Die in jungle. Easy kills."

"Have you made many kills, Basreen?" Fssik asked, slow blinking at her. A risk, perhaps, because the Basreen was certainly capable of striking while his eyes were closed. He found he liked her, and the thought of her killing unsuspecting Veetanho pleased him down to his claws.

"Enough," the Basreen said. She shifted backward, coiling her length tighter against the branch. "Hide ship?"

"Yes," Fssik said. "That is my crew, and we're going to cover the ship to hide it from the sky."

"Help. Kill Veeho if see ship."

Fssik felt his fur ripple in surprise. "You would do that? Thank you. That is generous."

"Like Hunters. Want Hunters back. Good for jungle. Good for young."

"Is there anything I can do for you in return?" Fssik asked.

The Basreen rattled her wings slightly and shifted her scaled body against itself so it made a raspy hissing sort of sound. "Return."

"That, I promise," Fssik said. "We will return."

"Good hunting."

"And to you, Basreen," Fssik said. He lowered his lids in another slow blink, and by the time he raised them again, she was gone. It wasn't quintessence... just her native ability to disappear into the jungles of their shared home.

Suddenly, Fssik felt longing for his old life pierce through him, followed by anger toward those who'd stolen it away. With a snarl of rage, he turned back to his ship and headed toward the cargo compartment that held his camouflage netting. It was time to get moving.

* * *

When his ship was appropriately concealed, Fssik led his crew through the tiny cleft in the rock and into the tunnel that would take them to the old Basreen launching facility. It was one of a few large buildings inside the city that were not mostly open-air, and he figured they could get some good intel on the Veetanho and their position from there.

"Wow," Ziva gasped shortly after they made the first turn in the long, spiraling path. "What is that all over the rock?"

"Gerinul. Don't touch it, it will infect your flesh. That's how they hunt."

"Is it alive?"

"Yes. Like a small plant that doesn't need light. It's bio-luminescent in the near-IR spectrum. Your team should be able to see it with their night vision devices."

"A carnivorous, bio-luminescent lichen. How perfect. Is everything on Khatash trying to kill you?"

"Yes," Fssik said, turning his head to slow blink at his companion. "That's why you have become what you are, my not-quite-Human."

Ziva chuckled softly in the darkness. "Fair enough. Team, goggle up and don't touch the walls with your bare skin."

Fssik padded ahead while the Humans donned their gear. They were making so much noise, he wanted to ensure they weren't alerting someone or something waiting farther down the tunnel.

The way sounded and smelled clear, so after a few moments, he headed back to lead the little team onward. The tunnel was designed for his kind, so the Humans had to crouch to fit. Some of them looked distinctly uncomfortable, and he could smell their nervous sweat, but he said nothing. They were intelligence operatives, trained by the best Cartwright's Cavaliers had to offer. They were professionals. They knew how to keep their nerves under control, sweat notwithstanding.

The team stayed mostly silent and didn't complain as they followed the path that pierced through the heart of the mountain and delved deep below the surface of the city. Other tunnels occasionally branched off to the left and right, but Fssik didn't feel any airflow or get any scent signatures from them, so he didn't pay them much mind.

He couldn't have said how long it took—time moved oddly when underground, at least in his experience—but it was still comfortably dark when they climbed the sloping ramp to the exit he remembered. It opened into a small space between his old Basreen squadron headquarters and a neighboring building, where the mechanics and engineers had worked.

"Stay fully back," he said to the team. "I will look outside and see what there is to see."

"I'm with you," Ziva said quickly. When he looked up at her, he noticed she'd set her jaw in a stubborn line. "I'm your companion, remember? Part of my function is to protect you. I'm going with you in case one of the rats is out there with another secret weapon."

"Fair enough," Fssik said, and he pushed away the innate fear that something bad might befall his beloved Human. "You can stay in touch with the rest of the team here."

Ziva nodded, then she turned and exchanged a few whispered words with the second-in-command of the intel team while Fssik worked the mechanism to open the mostly-hidden door.

Moonlight and fresh air rushed in as the door swung silently open. Fssik pulled his cloak of quintessence around him and slipped out, staying in the shadows so Ziva could remain close. She couldn't pull quintessence, but she could use the tricks of light and darkness to her advantage.

The alleyway appeared deserted. A rumble sounded off to the left, and soon, a bright burning trail arced overhead—another transport departing from the surface to join the veritable fleet in orbit.

Where are you going, and what are you taking from my planet? Fssik wondered for a moment before a soft scuffing behind him recalled his attention to the present. He turned and saw Ziva peering through a pair of image magnifier goggles.

"What's that building?" she asked, speaking in a low tone that wouldn't carry. Fssik bounded back to her, then hopped onto her shoulder to see where she was pointing.

"It was a broadcast studio," Fssik said as he looked through the magnifier goggles. "See the antennas on top?"

"Do you think it's still broadcasting?" Ziva asked.

"It could be, I suppose," Fssik said. "Why?"

"Look at the windows just above the ground. They're shielded, but they're leaking an awful lot of light in the IR spectrum. Whatever's in there is nice and warm."

Fssik looked at the area she indicated. Sure enough, a spill of light highlighted several basement windows of the kind his people favored when they built offices and dwellings for mixed-species use. He scanned upward with the goggles, taking in additional details of the building.

"They've connected additional cooling units to the building," he noted, "but the emergency generator on the roof is cold, so I don't think they're powering the antennas. The generator would be in standby mode if they were. I think we may be looking at a server room, Ziva."

"That was my thought," she murmured back, affectionately leaning her cheek into his side. "If we can get inside, we might be able to pull all kinds of interesting data."

"Lucky for us, we have Cartwright's best intel team waiting just behind that door," Fssik said, as he handed back the mag goggles. "Sun's coming up soon. It will be harder to hide them when we get over there."

"The Veet are nocturnal," Ziva reminded him. "If we move as the sun is coming up, we might be able to cover the distance without being seen. There will still be plenty of shadows to hide in, but the glare from the sunrise should help disorient anyone watching."

"Not bad," Fssik said, slow blinking. "Let's go tell our friends they can come out and stretch their legs."

"And backs," Ziva murmured as they turned back toward the entrance.

Thanks to his knowledge of the city's winding streets and alleyways, Fssik was able to lead the team indirectly toward the old broadcast building. Just as Ziva had said, there were plenty of shadows, and the Humans did a passable job of remaining quiet and hidden.

By the time the sun had cleared the horizon by a paw's width, they'd reached their destination. Fssik had once had to deliver a message from his Basreen squadron commander to this building, so he knew there was an entrance in the rear of the building. He led the team to a stinking alcove that held several overflowing trash receptacles but had a good view of the entrance.

"Wait here," he hissed. "Watch the doorway. When it irises open, haul your Human asses inside as fast as you can."

"Where are you going?" Ziva asked.

"To open the door," he said and gave her a teeth-flashing, Human grin.

* * *

He got in through one of the imperfectly-sealed windows.

It was almost embarrassingly easy to do, since the boards that covered the windows were made of Hrrian wood, which any Hunter could have told you warped and shrank as it aged. Because of this, most of the nails securing the boards had come loose, and Fssik only had to grip the edges and pull before the rotted Hrrian wood gave way. He froze, listening, just in case someone had heard the tiny *snap* of the boards, but he heard nothing, so he put the broken board to the side and pulled his quintessence as he slipped in through the now-open window.

Fssik stepped down and found himself on the top shelf of a storage rack shoved up against the basement wall. The shelf held several open-topped boxes of things that looked like tech components in various states of disrepair. Nothing dangerous, but certainly noisy enough if he didn't step carefully. So Fssik took his time climbing down, letting sound and scent and feel be his guides as he looked around the space.

The room was larger than it looked, with a sloping floor that angled down and away from the foundational wall on the side he'd entered. Dawnlight crept in through the windows that ringed most of the room, lighting up the space and shrinking the deep shadows every second. When his paws touched the floor, a *click* and a *whirr* made him freeze. He stood motionless, wrapped in his cloak of stealth. Heartbeats slipped by, but he smelled nothing and heard nothing but the *whoosh* of increased air movement in the ducting overhead. A breeze rippled his fur, and he realized what had startled him was nothing more than the building's ventilation system kicking on to keep the basement cool during the scorching daylight hours.

It made sense because it was unforgivably hot. It brought back uncomfortable memories of hurtling through their atmospheric reentry, and Fssik fought the urge to stop and bathe himself to stay cool. He didn't have time.

He dropped his quintessence, stepped forward, and entered the maze-like rows of floor-to-ceiling electronics racks. The heat grew more intense as he walked between the machines. They were humming, he realized as he passed. It was a low frequency, barely audible, but it sounded like his own purr. Maybe they had internal fans to keep them from overheating.

Fssik had just oriented himself and located the wall where the external door should be when he heard a padding sound overhead and off to his right. Footsteps… and voices.

"I'm telling you, it's too blasted hot! We've got to get more airflow down here, or these servers are going to slag out one by one!"

The voice was high and squeaky, and Fssik's pinplants informed him the language they automatically translated was one commonly spoken by the Veetanho on their home planet. A shiver of anticipation rippled down his spine and fluffed his fur, and he pulled quintessence around himself again.

The voice continued its tirade, interrupted occasionally by a different, slightly deeper murmur. Fssik continued down the row of servers until he found a break in the racks that would allow him to angle off to the right. He leaped up onto the rack and used the ends of the shelf to climb toward the top, careful to set his weight so he wouldn't make a sound. At the top, he looked toward the ceiling and tried to judge the location of the overhead vents by the feel of the airflow over his fur.

It wouldn't do to approach downwind like an untried kita, he thought as he lifted his nose to scent the air. The voices faded and became muffled as they moved further away from him, deeper into the room.

Fssik gave one last sniff and began to work his way toward where he guessed they'd gone. He gathered himself, then leaped across the gap between the racks, stretching his body to wrap first his fingers and then his toes silently around the vertical metal supports of his target rack. From there, he pulled himself into the space between one of the humming machines and the next shelf up, flattening his body to fit. He crawled forward, following the musk-like scent of the Veetanho.

In this manner, the Hunter stalked his prey. The light leaking in through the windows continued to brighten, and while he preferred the darkness, Fssik felt a pulse of savage gladness when he caught sight of the pair of rats crouching in front of one of their machines below him.

He moved deliberately, pulling his back feet slowly forward as he eased his head out from under the top shelf of the current rack. He reached his left front paw out first, angling downward, and gripped the rack's vertical stanchion. Then his right, balancing on the horizontal lip of the shelf below. Slowly, so slowly, his back paws followed, gripping the rack as he stalked limb by limb down toward the oblivious heads of the creatures below.

Fssik paused a half-body length above them to consider and then, as long-held rage flowed through both of his nervous systems, he decided he was done considering.

He dropped his quintessence and leaped, all twenty claws extended, mouth wide in fang-filled glee. The closest Veetanho looked up, an expression of startled surprise on her pointy face. Fssik took her un-goggled eyes in a single swipe of his left forepaw, while the claws of his feet pierced the tough skin around her throat and ripped it wide.

The Veetanho fell, and Fssik rode her soon-to-be corpse to the ground. The other Veetanho let out a scream that his pinplants didn't bother to translate and stumbled back against the rack of servers with a crash that reverberated through the heated air. Fssik ignored her for a heartbeat while he drew one of his longer, serrated knives and stabbed it into the throat wound he'd made. The body under him started to convulse. He shifted his weight to keep his balance and started sawing back and forth with his blade, while his feet continued to rake bloody furrows in his victim's face. Her arms came up, batting at him, but he simply kicked them aside and kept sawing.

Eventually, she stopped moving. Her spinal column gave way with a thick, meaty *snap*, and one more good kick sent her head rolling down the aisle between the server racks, trailing a thick, red path in its wake.

"One down," he said out loud, knowing the surviving Veetanho—who'd fled—would hear him. He'd read they'd evolved from burrowing creatures, and their hearing was even better than his own. Still, the airflow hadn't changed, and no one had left the room. He was between her and the stairwell, so she was trapped.

Just as he'd planned.

"Come out, come out, little rat," Fssik sang, using the Human slang term for the race. "I have something extra special for you."

"Aren't you going to welcome me to a negotiation?"

The voice, thin and reedy with fear, echoed over the ever-present hum of the servers and the whooshing of the ventilation. Fssik swiveled his ears to try and pinpoint—there! Was that her?

He stepped carefully forward, not bothering to draw his quintessence. He'd had it pulled for so long, he couldn't afford to tire himself out, and he was leaving bloody footprints anyway.

"I would," Fssik called out, "but I have no intention of negotiating with the likes of you." He angled toward the sound of her voice, careful to stay in the center of the aisle.

"That's fine," she called back, "because I don't intend to negotiate either!" Her head and torso appeared, leaning out from another break in the racks about four body lengths ahead. Fssik paused for just a moment and then leaped, watching as she pulled out a pistol-grip weapon and fired it at him.

Nothing emerged. No sound, no lights, no projectiles. Fssik hit the top of his arc and locked his muscles in place, bracing for the impact with the unyielding concrete floor. He felt the breath leave his lungs and fought down the panic that always produced.

"Aww… what's wrong, little *kitty?*" the Veetanho asked, the fear gone from her voice. "Did you forget we have ways of dealing with you and your cowardly tricks? Voided assassin trash!"

Fssik had landed in a heap with his head at an angle, facing away from her. He heard her words and then her steps as she came close to investigate his tangled lump of a body.

"You know what you are?" she asked softly from very close by. He felt the air move around him and pictured her crouching over him, leaning close with a malicious glint in her beady rodent's eyes. "You're a *mistake*. Neither you, nor your kind were ever meant to exist! I'm glad your entire race suicided. It was the honor of my life to stand here on your native soil and watch it happen. To watch all of those oh-so-arrogant little fuzzballs melt and dissolve because *we* figured out how to stop you from moving."

"Not entirely," Fssik said softly, and he flipped his body, so he faced her. Once more, he reached out with all twenty claws, and he grabbed hold of her head. The Veetanho let out a shriek, brought up her freeze-weapon, and pulled the trigger spasmodically. Fssik just laughed and hooked one claw into the sensitive flesh of her ear, while he reached into his carry pouch with the other. She thrashed under him, trying to bite his body, but he'd embedded his back claws firmly in the tender skin under her eyes, and she couldn't get to him. He felt her battering at him with her free hand, then with the one holding the weapon, but it didn't matter. He just had to hold on for a few moments longer…

There! His fingers closed around the cylinder he wanted. With a hiss of laughter, Fssik pulled out a single dart carrying the same paralysis fluid he'd used years ago, back in Houston, and stabbed it deep into the Veetanho's ear cavity. He felt a *crunch* as the dart stabbed through cartilage and lodged in the bone and then felt the shudder as the powerful paralytic took hold, locking her in place. Motionless.

Just as she'd thought she'd done to him.

"See," he said as her arms froze mid-swing. "I told you we had nothing to talk about. I simply came here to give you the opportunity to experience what you inflicted on the ones I cared about most.

Disconcerting, isn't it? I don't get the chance to use this poison very often, but I always find it satisfying when I do."

He leaped backward and flipped in midair, so he landed on his back feet just in time to see her topple stiffly to the floor.

"Ouch," he said as her skull hit with a dull *thud*. "That must have hurt. Not as much as what I'm going to do next, but I imagine it wasn't pleasant. Fortunately for you, I don't have a lot of time, so I will be quicker than I'd like."

She didn't respond but then he didn't expect her to. He slow blinked and then went to work. He pulled out another one of his knives and moved efficiently to disembowel her and wrap her intestines around her own neck. It only took a few minutes since the paralytic held her completely still. *Nice side benefit, that*, he thought as he wiped his knife clean on her fur and re-sheathed it.

"I will leave you now," he said, leaning down to look into her beady, pain-hazed eyes. "The paralytic is 100% fatal to oxygen-breathers, so you won't have too long to suffer. Maybe an hour, as Humans reckon such things. Good-bye."

Fssik had heard rumors of some creatures who could make themselves heard mind-to-mind. In that moment, he wasn't sure if he wished he could hear her mental screams or not.

Not that it mattered, he still had work to do.

Without wasting any more time, he bounded back past the body of his first victim and up to the exterior door. He punched the appropriate button, and the door irised open. Two heartbeats later, his team sprinted inside just as he'd briefed them to do.

"It stinks like death in here," Ziva said when she reached him. She bent down and scooped him up, then held him to her cheek and pressed her face next to his. He nuzzled her back and then squirmed until she let him down.

"Two Veetanho came downstairs to look at the servers," he said. "I don't know how many more are in the building above. I don't think they'll be missed for a while; they seemed to be a troubleshooting team of some kind."

"Were? I assume they're dead."

"One is. The other… will be soon. Remember what I told you about my Houston contract?"

Ziva's eyebrows went up. "The paralytic. That's fitting, I guess."

"I thought so, too," Fssik said. "Especially since I tricked her into thinking her freeze ray weapon still worked on me. That's how I got close enough to strike."

"Clever Hunter."

"Thank you. I am rather, aren't I?"

Ziva laughed and shook her head, then looked up as one of her team called out to her.

"You go do the spy stuff, I'll guard the stairs," Fssik said. He rubbed against her legs one time before he leaped away.

* * *

Fssik had tucked himself into a deep, shadowy recess high on one of the server racks. It was a good spot. It afforded him a clear view of the stairs leading down to the basement and a partial view down three approaches through the forest of racks. So, as soon as Ziva started walking back toward him, he stood and stretched in anticipation of her news.

"We got it," she said, her voice soft, but elation clear in her tone. "Full schematics of their occupation of the city and what they're planning to do. There's too much data to analyze here, so we down-loaded everything we could."

"Time to go, then." Fssik arched his back in one more stretch and then leaped unerringly for her shoulder. Ziva braced herself for his sudden weight and then steadied him with one hand as he wound around the back of her neck.

"Yes, my Hunter. Let's get out of here and go home."

She stroked his fur in that delicious way of hers as she headed back toward the members of her team who were busy packing up their equipment. Within minutes, they'd stowed all their cords and slates and hacking tech into the sleek packs they wore on their backs. One of the team nodded to Ziva and murmured that they were ready.

"I'll get the door, as before," Fssik said. "It's close to noon, so there shouldn't be too much traffic out and about. Just head back to that same hole up. I'll close the door and be along shortly."

Ziva stroked him once more, leaned her cheek against him, then nodded. He returned her affection with a head rub, breathing in the way his scent mingled so naturally with hers, then he leaped down and padded past the bodies of his kills on his way to the door pad.

"Are we worried about them being found?" Ziva asked softly as she followed him, stepping carefully to avoid tracking through the blood.

"I want them found," Fssik said, with just a hint of a snarl in his tone. "Let the Veetanho fear."

Ziva didn't say anything more, but Fssik had the distinct feeling she didn't fully agree with his logic. Not that it mattered much. They had other things to worry about.

The team took up positions flanking the door and hidden by the server racks, as Fssik approached the keypad. He punched in the command, and searing daylight poured in as the door irised open. With a thought, Fssik snapped his daylight goggles into place and leaned out to look and listen and inhale.

As he expected, the street was empty and quiet, and the scorching sun rode high in the sky. He ducked back inside and pointed at the first team member lined up and ready.

"Go," he said, and she nodded and took off in a respectable sprint. She was fast, for a Human. He watched her dart across the open expanse of the street and dive into the sheltered area they'd used before.

"Next," he said, and another Human—this one male and not quite as fast—followed. One by one, they crossed the street and sought cover on the other side. Finally, only he and Ziva remained.

"I'll be right behind you," he said, leaning out to scent the air once more. "Go."

Ziva took off, moving with grace and speed. She had almost reached the far side of the road when Fssik heard a small *pop,* and Ziva stumbled forward and twisted as she slapped her hand to her left shoulder. Fssik watched in horror as she fell and hit the ground hard on her right side. Another *pop* echoed, and the dust flew up from the road where the projectile hit.

"Ziva!" Fssik cried. He launched himself through the door after her. She hunched her head and reached forward with her good hand, which was now streaked with blood from the wound in her shoulder. Fssik pulled his quintessence around him and ran toward her as she began to crawl forward on her belly. "Ziva's hit!" he called out, not caring if the enemy heard, as long as one of his people did. The man who had been the second person out the door hunched low and grabbed Ziva's outstretched hand, then pulled her quickly over the dusty ground into their hiding spot.

Fssik didn't remember crossing the street. He was just suddenly there, leaning on Ziva's chest. She held him in her lap with her good hand while the other Humans ripped open her sleeve to examine the wound.

"Through and through," the man said. "Looks like a dumb projectile. Smallish caliber, especially for a sniper."

"Do they know we're here?" Ziva asked, her words breathy with pain.

"Either that, or it was a target of opportunity. I've got nanites if you want them."

"Save them," Ziva said. "If we have to shoot our way out of here, we're going to need them. Just bandage me up, I'll be all right."

The male Healer—medic, as Fssik suddenly remembered Humans called their Healers—nodded, injected something into her shoulder, then wrapped it tightly in a bandage. "I gave you some antibiotics, just in case," he said. "This world's pretty uncharted; who knows what all is deadly here."

"Everything," Fssik put in. He shoved his head up under Ziva's chin and inhaled deeply the scent of her skin. "Are you well enough to move, my Human? We need to go."

"Yeah," she said. "Just need a hand up."

Fssik didn't want to leave her lap, but they were not exactly in a secure position, so he stepped away and let one of Ziva's team members help her to her feet.

"Fssik, need you to scout our route back to the tunnel," Ziva said once she was vertical, "and let us know if we're going to have a problem. The rest of you, stay low. Most of our route here was covered; let's use what we've got and move fast."

They did. Fssik pulled his quintessence around him and ran ahead, scenting the air and listening. The shot that had hit Ziva had come from above, and he hadn't been able to see the shooter in the glare of the noonday sun. Not that he'd been able to think about anything but her in that moment… and that was a potential problem. He'd worry about that once they were back on his ship and safely out of Khatash.

He followed roughly the same twists and turns they'd taken on the way in, deviating only to choose a path more suited for cover and concealment. They had reached the edge of the city, within a block of the tunnel's entrance, when he halted.

Something wafted on the breeze. It was dusty, metallic…

"Wait here," Fssik said, dropping his quintessence. "Be ready; I think they're waiting for us ahead."

The team had already drawn their weapons, and Ziva gave a quiet order for them to spread out in a defensive formation. Fssik didn't bother to see how they did it, he just re-cloaked himself and ran the rest of the way down the winding path they'd been following through the buildings of the old marketplace.

Sure enough, as he rounded the last corner before the wall with the tunnel exit, he saw the telltale tracks of at least two vehicles— probably more. He lifted his head and looked around, but the glare from the noonday sun made it difficult to pick out details in the distance, even with his goggles on. Just as he was about to retreat, something across the thoroughfare glinted in the light, pulling his attention that way. Fssik squinted and inhaled and listened.

There. It was so deep, he could barely hear it, but it was there: the throb of engines. More than one, and over that, the metallic *click* of a weapon being readied. The faint greasy hint of vehicle exhaust sealed it—they were walking into a trap.

Fssik turned and sprinted back to the group.

"No good," he said as he slipped into the shadowy space between market stalls where Ziva had secreted herself. "It's a trap. They've got the tunnel exit covered. I saw signs of two vehicles, maybe more."

"Is there another way out to the ship?" Ziva asked.

"Not that we can easily access from here," Fssik said. "We're going to have to go—"

Eeeeeeeeeeeeeeeeeeeeeeeeeeeeee… BOOM!

The ground heaved up and then somehow sideways as a solid wall of heated air hit them. It bowled Fssik over and threw him hard against the support pillar of the nearest market stall. His head impacted with a sickening *crack*, and he felt his vision go dark. A piercing ringing stabbed through his ears and into his brain, cutting off all other sound. The air smelled scorched.

"Ziva!?" Fssik cried out. He could barely hear his own voice. He shook his head and twisted his body to get his paws back under him. Pain wreathed every movement, but he shook his head again and shunted it away. *"Ziva!"*

"Fssik!" Her answering shout came from the left. It was a mere faded ghost of sound under the incessant ringing. He felt her arms come around him, and she lifted him up and cradled him next to her. Then he felt a nauseating sort of lurching back and forth. He blinked his eyes rapidly as his vision started to come back, and immediately regretted doing so. Ziva was running, carrying him close to her chest, and the bouncing view of the marketplace made his nausea roar to the forefront. He retched, spilling the remains of his earlier meal over Ziva's arm and side.

She didn't falter. She just kept moving, the pounding of her boots on the pavement reverberating up through her body and into his. Fssik's stomachs heaved again, but they had no more contents to spill. Slowly, gradually, the ringing in his ears faded, and he could make out Ziva's shouted calls to her team as they ran. She twisted and turned, at one point ducking low and hunching over him, but she never stopped, never slowed the jouncing, pounding run that hammered through him like torture.

He must have passed out. He opened eyes he didn't remember closing and looked up into Ziva's face. Fssik reached up with a paw and extended his foreclaw to trace the lines that creased her forehead and wreathed her eyes. Underneath his skin, he felt a lingering burn, like he'd walked across a hot shuttle pad or something.

"Hi," Ziva said softly, a smile curving her lips but doing nothing to dispel the worry creases.

"Hi," Fssik said. "Nanites?"

"Yes, the blast threw you pretty hard. You passed out, and I was worried about a concussion. Does it still hurt?"

"A little lingering burn; nothing terrible," he said. "Are we safe?"

"For the moment. Do you remember what happened?"

"I remember the blast."

"Yeah, the Rats found us. Probably the same group that shot me. Not a very large group, thank all the stars. They trailed us all the way through the city, but they stopped at the edge. They wouldn't follow us into the jungle."

"Smart of them," Fssik said. "I'm surprised you made it this long without me."

Ziva didn't move, but somehow, her face hardened, and her eyes grew sad.

"Oh," he said, "I see. Not everyone made it."

"Fssik, I don't know how you Hunters lived here. *Everything* is deadly."

"That is why we are who we are, my Human. How many did we lose?"

"Two. Drezin and McCreary. It happened when we stopped to treat you. They sat against a tree that had this flowering vine thing—" She broke off, and Fssik nodded.

"I am sorry," Fssik said. "Nyralor. Are they dead?"

"Yes. They went so fast, there was no way to save them. We ended up shooting them."

"That was the correct choice. There is no counter for Nyralor oil. Not even nanites would have worked."

Ziva nodded, then swallowed. Fssik pushed himself up to a sitting position, and she moved quickly to help him.

"How far into the jungle are we?"

"Maybe an hour's run? We stopped when we found a cave-like spot between two boulders. It looks like it would work for a hole-up site, but we didn't want to go in without you."

"Again, you are wise, my Human. Show me this cave-like spot."

As it turned out, the hole-up site was empty, though it had been used recently by some predator or another. Bones lay scattered about the long, narrow space that had been formed by a rockfall off the nearby mountain eons ago. Fssik scouted the entire space and then welcomed what remained of their team inside.

"No fires," he cautioned. "We'll draw too much attention that way."

"Right," Ziva said, and the male medic who'd treated her back in the city nodded.

It was tight with all the Humans, but, eventually, they got settled and built a cold camp. Most of the Humans huddled together in pairs, but Fssik and Ziva curled up a short distance away from the rest.

"Fssik, I'm worried…" she started, once the steady sounds of exhausted Human sleep began to softly echo through their tiny, shared space.

"Yes," Fssik said, rubbing his cheek hard against her hand as she stroked the length of his spine. "Me too. If they've found the tunnel, they've likely got my ship. I don't think we can go back there."

"So, is that it, then? Mission failure? If we can't get this data back to Land's End, what did we come here for?"

"I didn't say that. We might not be able to get out, but if we can get the data to the ship, we can broadcast *it* out. It's the same way Cahli broadcast her message five years ago—quintessentially encoded communication via her ship. She used her pinplants to send a message. Broadcasting all the data we found… well… that's a bit more difficult."

"But not impossible," Ziva said, and he felt her arms tighten around him as excitement threaded through her tone. "We already have quintessential radios on us."

"Yes, but those are short-range radios for communication within the team. They need line-of-sight and no more than a few kilometers' distance."

"Sure, but the ship's got a quintessential receiver, right? And you could send it a broadcast command through the radio?"

"Yes, but—"

"Listen, we went through the mountain to get to the city, and we're huddled up against the same mountain, right?"

"Yes, but on a different side—"

"What if we climbed to the top?"

Fssik felt his pupils widen in surprise.

"You're serious?"

"As a contract, my Hunter. Think about it. If we can get to the summit, we'd have line of sight with your ship. We can set one of the radios to data transmit, and you can use the other to order the ship to remote launch and travel back home to Dama and the others. That way, even if *we* don't make it out of here alive, the data does, and it wasn't all for nothing."

Fssik shivered, his entire body rippling under his fur. "This plan is insane. You know that, right?"

"Have you got a better idea?"

"No."

"Then I'll take insane. Over giving up? I'll take insane any time."

* * * * *

Chapter Ten

They slept the day away and started their climb the following night. It might have been easier on the Humans to travel under the sunlight, but there was never much sunlight at ground level anyway, and they weren't skilled enough to travel through the tree branches the way Hunters sometimes did.

Besides, after the night and day they'd had in the city, they'd needed the rest.

Fssik napped too, on and off. He didn't want to sleep too deeply in case some predator found them interesting. Several times he left the narrow, cramped shelter between the boulders and scent-marked the surrounding area. Some jungle predators would willingly take on a Hunter, but there were many more who would rather not.

When the deep green shadows began to stretch from west to east, Fssik returned to the shelter and woke Ziva and the rest of the team. Ziva explained in quiet tones what they were going to do, and the various Humans on the team nodded in agreement. Fssik saw hard determination in their faces, as well as the knowledge that they might not ever make it off this planet. He quietly said as much to Ziva, but the male medic overheard him.

"We knew that when we signed on, Hunter," the man said. "We all volunteered anyway. Let's just make sure it means something, right?"

Fssik slow blinked at the man. "I greet you, Human Healer," he said. "I would know your name."

"Paul Bisdorf, Hunter. And you're Fssik."

"I am. I am pleased you're on our team, Paul Bisdorf, Healer."

"You can call me Paul, Hunter."

"And you may call me by my name, as well."

"If you two are finished setting up your cross-species bromance, we can get going," Ziva said, her mouth twisted in a half-smile. Fssik slow blinked up at her, repeated the gesture to Paul, then headed out into the dawning night.

As in the tunnels, the mercs moved quickly and quietly. Not as quietly as he, but passably well for a species so generally clumsy and unwieldy as Humans. Fssik heard Ziva cautioning the others to follow his path exactly, and he took pains to remain on the ground as much as possible.

Even so, he had to climb into the trees several times to scout the way ahead. He caught the unmistakable smell of a male cheelin in rut, so he scampered back down and led the Humans in a wide circle around the source of the odor. Cheelin were fun to hunt, but not when there was work to be done... and definitely not with a chain of Humans in tow!

Between that detour and their overall slow pace through the jungle, it took the rest of the night for them to make the steep, treacherous climb up the slope of the peak that separated his ship from the city. For the most part, Fssik kept them on a path sheltered by the triple-canopy jungle, but every once in a while, as they climbed higher, he caught a glimpse of the stars burning whitely in the night sky and wondered if he'd ever fly among them again.

Not that he'd ever want to be anywhere else. Not as long as his Ziva was here. She was right; what they were doing was not a small thing. If they could get the intel they'd stolen back to Land's End,

Dama Tsan and everyone else could form a plan of attack and truly retake their home. What they were doing mattered.

If they could get the data out.

Fssik's thoughts continued to circle back as they climbed toward the peak. His head still throbbed a little from the blast the night before, and it got worse as they ascended. Slowly, the air turned thinner and colder, and the dense concealing canopy began to thin out, shrink, and eventually disappear.

The first hint of dawn lightened the eastern sky. They passed beyond the tree line and continued to climb amid the sharp-edged rocks and tumbled boulders that littered the slope to the summit. The horizon turned grey, then pink, then a blazing red as the sun climbed along with them. Fssik had to snap his goggles into place as he took his final steps up to the small, flat space at the summit.

"Here," he said, turning toward Ziva. "Welcome to the top of the world."

"You aren't kidding," she said, and her words sounded just as breathy and short of oxygen as his own. "Any idea what our elevation is?"

"About four thousand of your meters," Fssik said. "A little more. Look, if you turn east and look downslope, you can just see the break in the trees. That's our LZ."

"So, do we have line of sight? Because I can't see it."

"You can't see it because of the jungle canopy. The quintessential radios will be able to reach it, though."

"I'll take your word for it," Ziva said. She turned and motioned for her team to gather around. Fssik met Paul's eyes and slow blinked a hello. The medic inclined his head in acknowledgment of the greeting.

"All right team, listen up. This is our relay spot. Let's get an antenna rigged up and get the radios configured for data. I think we can set the rig up right over here by these boulders—"

Fssik tuned out Ziva's orders and wandered a little away from the group, his eyes on the cut in the trees where his ship was waiting. He'd hoped to see it directly, but the angle of the mountain slope from the summit to the LZ prevented that. He pushed down the frustration that rose within him and forced himself to try and think clearly. Maybe, while the Humans were setting up the radio relay, he could sneak down and take a look...

"Incoming! Take cover!"

Paul's shout reverberated off the rocky slope, and even in the thin air around them, Fssik could hear the urgency in his tone. He was about to turn and look when something else caught his attention—movement in the canopy below, not far from the LZ where his ship waited. Fssik heard the *pop, pop, pops* of the team returning fire behind him, and he watched in horror as a Veetanho atmospheric craft took off from the trees below them.

"They've got a bird in the air!" he shouted, but with the air so thin, he wasn't certain anyone heard him. So, he did the only thing he could think to do and sprinted back to Ziva.

She was with the rest of the team between several large boulders. In front of her, the female merc who had been the first to cross the road back in the city and another male who was not Paul worked feverishly to connect one of their quintessential radios to a portable antenna someone had brought. The other mercs, Ziva included, crouched with their backs to them. They all had weapons out and were searching the path they'd climbed.

Whizz... CRACK!

A *ping* off the boulder beside him sent a shower of sharp-edged rock flakes in all directions. Fssik flinched, then turned to look in the direction from which the shot had come.

"Be right back," he said softly to Ziva. "Keep your head down."

"Don't die," she told him as she stroked her trigger and fired a burst down the slope.

Fssik pulled his quintessence and bounded away from her, sprinting in the direction from which the shots had come. Before long, he found the shooters—a group of about twenty Veetanho, all carrying weapons with long-range optics, unless he missed his guess.

He didn't bother with pleasantries. He dropped his cloak and leaped, claws extended. He took the first Veetanho sniper by surprise and gouged out her eyes before slashing her throat open on a backswing with his left foot. He didn't recall drawing his knife, but he certainly held one. She died gaping, blood fountaining from the wound in her throat.

One of her fellows turned and began shooting wildly in Fssik's direction with one hand, while awkwardly holding something that looked like a freeze ray in the other. Fssik slashed the tendons at the back of her leg joints, causing her to fall heavily to the ground and her weapon to shoot wildly into the air. Fssik buried his foot-knife in the Veetanho's eye socket, past the satisfying *crunch* of bone, and finished her off.

He left his knife where it was and straightened, looking for his next target.

His next target was down, struggling under the weight of a smallish Lumar who used all four of her fists to beat the Veetanho's head to a pulp. Just beyond the Lumar, a Zuul ripped the throat out of a second Veetanho with enough precise savagery to make Fssik blink in admiration, and a creature with long, thick tentacles like tree trunks wrapped itself around a third Veetanho and appeared to be squeezing it to death.

There were still more Veetanho, so Fssik ran after one of those who continued to fire up the slope at his people. A scream ripped through the sky, followed by bursts of burning light, as the Veetanho fighter streaked by, strafing the rocky slope with her energy cannon. Fssik flinched, then leaped at his target, as the Veetanho raised her weapon to keep firing. He landed on her back and had a hard time getting his claws around to any vital organs. She dropped her weapon and ripped her knife from a sheath on her chest, then angled it back over her shoulder to try and stab him. Fssik let go and dropped to the ground, pulling his quintessence around him once more. He rolled and came up between her feet, then looked up and saw a gap in her body armor, right where the inside of her thigh met her torso. Quicker than a thought, he drew another one of his knives and drove it into this gap. The Veetanho screamed and crumpled, and he had to roll quickly to avoid being trapped under her body, as she bled out in a few beats of her dying heart.

The fighter came back around, this time unleashing its fire higher up the slope, where Ziva and her team were. Fssik looked around, desperate for a weapon. His gaze landed on the long, sniper-style energy weapon the Veetanho he'd just killed had been using. He didn't know if it would do any good against an atmo craft, but he had to do something! He couldn't stand by and watch the fighter strafe his Ziva over and over.

He grabbed the butt of the weapon and brought it awkwardly up, pointing it in the general direction of the sky. It was too big for him—long and unwieldy. He fired one bolt that veered off and went nowhere near the atmo craft that was turning for another attack run.

"Try this, Hunter."

Fssik turned just in time to see the smallish—female?—Lumar lift a stubby tube he hadn't noticed when he attacked. Behind her, another Lumar and a host of other creatures continued to fight off the rest of the Veetanho, who were still pressing their attack upslope.

The female Lumar placed the tube on top of a flat rock and fiddled with the base. Overhead, the Veet ship completed its turn and headed straight for them, nose down as it prepared to strafe. Fssik looked up at it and then back at the female Lumar as she covered her ears with her lower hands and steadied the tube with her upper ones. Then, incredibly, she slow blinked at him.

Thwoomp.

The tube spat fire, which arced up over him and impacted the Veetanho craft, just as she was starting her run. The ship disintegrated before his eyes, raining smoking, hot bits of metal and composite down on them. A ragged cheer drifted down the slope to him, seconds before he saw his Ziva leading her team in a counterattack down the slope.

"Don't kill anyone but the Veetanho!" Fssik shouted, putting as much air behind the call as he could. He didn't know who this Lumar and her compatriots were, and he didn't know what they were doing there, but he knew they'd been helpful, and he didn't want them turning their fury on his Ziva.

Carnage followed, as the Cavaliers' intel team and the motley crew of various beings overwhelmed the remaining Veetanho resistance. By the time the sun rode high in the sky, the grey rock of the mountain slope had turned dark red with Veetanho blood. Fssik finished off his last victim, then turned and saw Ziva facing the Zuul. Both held their weapons at the ready. Both stared at each other through narrowed eyes.

Fssik bounded over to place his body between Ziva and the creature that should in no way be present on his world. He was about to open his mouth when Ziva spoke.

"I am Ziva, Hunter companion to Fssik. I greet you, Zuul. Welcome to our negotiation."

The Zuul flicked her ears back, and her tail waved to the side. "Interesting phrasing, for a Human."

"Ziva's not exactly Human anymore," Fssik said. He sat down on a convenient hump of rock and began grooming the blood off his forepaw. "I am Fssik, Deo of Clan Tamir. She is mine."

"I greet you, Hunter," the Zuul said. "I don't entirely understand. Have you given this... not quite Human... your sigil?"

"Something like that," Fssik said. "It's a bit more personal now. How do you know of sigils?"

The Zuul reached inside the tattered neck of what remained of her clothing and pulled out a thin, metal chain. The noontime sunlight flashed off the metal charm, making Fssik blink and squint behind his goggles.

Then the bottom dropped out of his stomachs, and he found that, for just a moment, he couldn't speak.

He knew that sigil.

It belonged to Whispering Fear.

* * *

"**D**o you belong to the ship we found in the small clearing below?" the Zuul asked. One of her ears pointed at him, and the other swiveled.

"Yes," Fssik said. "We used an old tunnel to access the city, but we were cut off when it was time to return. We need my ship to get the intel we stole back to those who will use it, whether we're on board or not."

"Others?" Before he could answer, she snapped her jaw and shook her head sharply to the side. "No, tell me later. We'll escort you to your ship, for your safety." Without taking her eyes off him, she lifted a hand and extended two fingers. The smaller Lumar immediately came to her side, head swiveling from side to side.

For our safety? Who does this Zuul think she is? Fssik glanced at Ziva, who gave him a smile and a tiny shake of her head. Fssik let out a breath and nodded, then leaped to Ziva's shoulder, as their small group started to follow the Lumar down the slope. The Zuul fell into step beside Ziva, and Fssik arranged himself on her shoulders so he could murmur into his Human's ear on the side opposite their strange, sigiled guide.

"She is presumptuous," Fssik said, once he was settled.

"She and her group have survived the jungle for five years on their own, my Hunter," Ziva muttered back, turning her face away. "Surely, that earns them some consideration."

"That is true," he said. "I would not have believed such a feat possible. That's the whole reason we altered your DNA and that of the other companions. It's remarkable. I admire her—all of them."

"Then I should perhaps tell you, Hunter, that I can hear you very well." The Zuul did not turn her head. She kept her eyes focused on the path ahead, but her upright ears continued moving. "I am Aryo, and I have lived in this jungle far longer than five years."

Her jaw opened as though she would say more, but another figure appeared on the vague path ahead of them. Fssik let the conversation go and fixed his eyes and ears on the being. It was the larger of the two Lumar.

"Stop here," he said. "Basreen at ship. Kill Veetanho. Do not see. Danger."

"The Basreen is known to me," Fssik said, leaping down from Ziva's shoulder. "I asked her to help cover my ship."

The Zuul, Aryo, glanced at him, then back at the large Lumar. She nodded, the Lumar shrugged all his limbs, and Aryo motioned Fssik ahead.

"Lead the way, Deo," she said and inclined her head toward him. "We will guard your back."

Fssik glanced up at Ziva, who nodded and held up a hand to stop the other Humans as they caught up with her. Fssik slow blinked at her, then pulled his quintessence and bounded through the last line of trees into the clearing ahead.

Here and there around the perimeter of the field, Veetanho bodies lay slumped, not moving. Fssik paused next to one and examined its features. Its eyes were distended and clouded over, its mouth was encrusted with blood, and its tongue protruded—all hallmarks of the kind of nerve poisoning a Basreen sting could cause. Warmth coursed through him, and he looked up to try and find any sign of his little friend. When he found nothing, he dropped his field.

"I greet you, Basreen. I have returned to compliment you on your work here!"

She gave him no warning. The trees didn't even rustle before she shot out, wings extended, glided down, and landed in the short grass next to her kill.

"Many came," she said. "Too many, and a ship."

"We saw them," he said. "They will not bother you again."

"My thanks, Hunter."

"It is I who owe you thanks, Basreen. You have made many fine kills in this field this morning. Will your young prosper on their meat?"

"Too many clothes and armor. Meat will spoil."

"I and my friends can help you with that if you will allow us to approach my ship."

"Good trade, Hunter. My thanks again." She moved in a sinuous line, circling around where he stood, then shot off toward the tree line and vanished from his sight. Fssik slow blinked after her, then called out in the direction Ziva and the others waited.

"It is clear; she has gone back to her young. I have bargained with her. We must strip her kills of their clothes and armor, so she can feed her family before we go."

"Veetanho serve better purpose dead than alive," the smaller Lumar announced as they emerged into the clearing.

"They have yet to learn," Aryo replied, holding her hand above her head. Five other figures bled out of the jungle around them, and the work was completed in short order.

At Aryo's signal, the nameless additions melted back out of the clearing, and the Zuul turned her focus back to Fssik.

"How long have you been on Khatash?"

"Not long," Fssik said, his voice regretful, "but I promise you, as I promised the Basreen, we will return." He drew in a breath to speak again and then stopped. *No*, he realized. *No one may say what a dama might do. It will be better if I say nothing about Tsan.*

"I... you said others." Aryo's ears twisted back, then forward again. "Never mind that. I will not hold you, but... thank you, Deo. You bring hope where we looked for none."

"Thank you, Aryo, and your band. Without your assistance... well. We all owe you. I and all the others. And there are many. We have found ways to thrive. You will see when we return." He slow blinked at her and then gestured for Ziva to bring her team forward and load up. He saw the two Lumar gathering up the rumpled camouflage material the Veetanho had discarded when they uncovered his ship. The larger one inclined his head toward Fssik, then followed Ziva's instructions about where to stow it.

Moments later, Fssik let out a sigh of relief as he settled into his command seat and began toggling the ignition sequence for the ship.

"She's still there, watching our backs," Ziva said quietly as she pointed through the viewscreen. Fssik looked up and saw Aryo in the shadow of the tree line, her eyes fixed on them. As they watched, she raised one hand and straightened her tail behind her in a gesture of farewell.

"Remarkable," Fssik said. "I feel we will see her again."

"I hope we do," Ziva replied. Beneath them, the engines roared, and the watching Zuul disappeared under the canopy as Fssik lifted his ship into the air and turned for home.

* * * * *

Chapter Eleven

Fssik keyed in the "detach" command and watched as the freighter that had carried them home started to recede in the display. He waited the appropriate interval then engaged his in-system drive to turn his lithe little ship and set a course for Land's End. Then he arched his spine in a stretch.

"Hyperspace always takes the same amount of time, so why did this trip seem so long?"

"Because we have news and wounded, and many things depend on what we're bringing back," Ziva answered with a smile in her tone. He swiveled in his straps to look at her, and she reached out her arms in welcome. Fssik slow blinked, disengaged his straps, and pushed off his seat so he could float to her. She caught him with a minimum of fuss and cuddled him close, while he clipped his harness to her seat restraint. It wasn't strictly necessary; he could have held on, but it was easier this way, particularly in micro G. He spent the rest of the short trip in-system cuddled up with her, just as he'd spent most of their time in hyperspace.

Truth was, the trip to Khatash had unnerved him in more ways than one. Something itched under his skin whenever he thought about it. Maybe it had been the eerie emptiness of the city or the surprise of meeting Aryo and her friends in the jungle, but something tickled his instincts and made him feel as though things were not quite what they seemed.

He was out of time to contemplate his discomfort, for Land's End suddenly loomed large in the display, and he reluctantly wriggled out of Ziva's embrace and returned to his seat, so he could steer them through the arrival procedures.

A short while later, Fssik stood in the docking bay and watched as the intel team disembarked. Ziva stood nearby, tirelessly giving instructions and directions, even though he could hear the fatigue in her voice.

"My Hunter," she said suddenly, breaking him out of his reverie. "I am going to escort the team and data inside where we can analyze it. Can you take Cox and Brite to the Healers? I know we patched them up, but I'd still like Deo Esthik or Lara or someone to look at them."

"Of course," Fssik said. He shook his body as though the bone-weariness he felt could be discarded like drops of water from his fur. "Then I will meet you in your room, where you will rest."

"I will," Ziva said, letting her lips curl upward just a bit at his autocratic tone. "I promise."

"As do I." He leaned against her booted calf then turned to walk away, confident the two wounded, but ambulatory, members of the team would follow. Or that Ziva would direct them to do so. Or something.

"Your return is even more timely than I expected," Tsan said. She dropped her field, and he found she was already in step beside him. "Esthik knows your honored compatriots are on the way," she added, turning her head to slow blink at the Humans who followed. "Dama Tamir and I are grateful for what you have done, and we are glad you have returned." She kept one ear toward them as they

band," she added, her tail lashing behind her. "Would that I could go and find them."

"I did tell her we would return," Fssik said. "I promised. And I think we must. It's part of what you'll see in the intel report we gathered. It's clear to me Khatash has done to the Veetanho what we always feared it would do to our loved ones, and yet your sigiled Zuul survives. There's something in that thought Ziva would enjoy." He leaned into her touch and then shook himself from crown to tail.

"Regardless, we found the reports of a buildup of Veetanho forces are correct. They remain clustered in the city, but the bits of data we analyzed in transit suggest they're working on some kind of large-scale plan to expand outward. They're burrowers by nature. It seems that now that the galaxy has turned against them, the Veetanho are trying to go to ground in our home. I do not think we should let them."

"No, Deo of mine." A purr throbbed low in her voice. "I do not believe we will allow such a thing."

* * *

Tamir sat straight in her chair, the tension in her arms speaking to the effort it cost her. Her scent had changed since Tsan had last been home. Still hers, still her, but…

Later. Now was not the moment to welcome mourning. Now was the moment to plan justice long awaited. She leaped up to the table to put herself on Tamir's left and watched silently as their small group assembled.

They'd opened the first council to the entirety of Land's End, and while she trusted their clan and respected their opinions, this needed a more directed approach. Large groups could inform, and much was gained in such an approach. When decisions had to be made, a targeted council was best.

Tsan had several plans to propose for the council to debate, and she fully expected they would come out with something related but entirely different. Such was the power of an informed decision-making body.

She repeated that to herself more than once. A Dama makes many decisions on her own. A wise Dama knows there is no one path to a successful hunt, and that a faster decision is not necessarily a better one.

Except for when it was.

No. She twitched her fur into place, grateful Tamir contented herself with a knowing grunt rather than reaching out to stroke her. No, a fast decision was not the path here. They could not engage immediately.

The weight of the seasons between the Veetanho attack and this moment twisted her nerves into fire, but they had waited this long to come this far. Only a little longer, and blood would run before her in a flood.

In pairs and small groups, they arrived—Michelle and Yrra, who could obtain anything from anyone, given enough time and the proper credits. Freedom and Bridgwater, whose newly upgraded prosthetics appeared innocuous under his clothing. Fssik and Ziva, wearing their gear with the Cartwright's Cavaliers insignia. Will and Twilight, with a command of able mercenaries from Twilight's past. Pura, Hrava, Meredith and Aryss. Esthik on Alinore's shoulder, with Ward and Lara right behind them.

"Welcome," she said as they settled, "to the end of the Veetanho." She surveyed them, noting the shiver of anticipation that passed through swiveled ears, lashed tails, and twitched shoulders. "The intelligence received from Theela, and confirmed and built upon by Deo Fssik, Ziva, and their crew of Cavaliers, is good."

"The Veetanho have retreated to Khatash and are receiving little outworld support. They have moved in a great deal of ships, weapons, and likely troops, though numbers and species are unclear." Tamir tapped the controls embedded in the arm of her chair, and a screen rose in the center of the table. The Khatash system rotated slowly before them—gate, station, home planet, solar bodies. Tags representing ships appeared, coded orange.

"Unfortunately, there's also word of a weapon they are close to finishing. We can assume it's not targeted at Hunters specifically, given they do not believe enough of us remain to pose a threat." Tsan lifted a hand, claws bared, and flattened her ears. "That we don't know what it does provides both threat and urgency. We cannot underestimate their cleverness, but given their isolation, it remains unlikely they know of Land's End and our work here." She nodded at Ward, who lifted one of his longer tentacles in response.

"We cannot wait for further information on this weapon. As best we can tell, if we move fast enough, we can overcome them and it, though losses will…" Tamir trailed off, then took a deep breath and squared her shoulders. Tsan did not glance back at her, but she raised her ears and kept one focused on her Human compatriot's breathing.

That had not been hesitation, Tsan was suddenly sure.

"Losses will vary based on the details of what and who the Veetanho have accumulated in the system and what exactly this 'superweapon' they are so smug about does."

"And if it's ready," Esthik said, his tail curled high behind him.

"Yes."

"We are not alone either," Ziva said, placing her hands on the table in front of her, eyes fixed on the system map before her.

"Indeed, we are not," Tsan agreed. "Thanks to Ziva's and Fssik's work on Earth, we will be joined by Ziva's intelligence team and two CASPer units of Cartwright's Cavaliers. They stand ready for the ground assault they do so well."

Tamir toggled her controls, and a subsection of the display changed, adding Cavaliers in blue.

"I imagine there's more—you have been away more than you have been here, Dama," Alinore said, her head tilted to the side as she regarded Tsan. "We have heard some, but perhaps not all?"

"Correct," Tsan replied, with a slow blink for the former Human mercenary. "While all four of the Horsemen of Earth have little to spare, given their own conflicts, all have committed some. Asbaran Solutions has committed two companies to add to the ground assault and two further companies of their Lumar shock troops which, given their experience, will greatly expand our chances of success. The Golden Horde has a company of CASPers to drop onto Khatash to establish the beachheads they are so skilled with and two squadrons of bombers for air support."

"Horde bombers are good." Alinore nodded, fingers not quite tracing the display.

"SalSha, yes. I have heard much of their skill." Tsan twisted her ears back toward Tamir and continued as the other Dama's breath steadied. "The Winged Hussars are able to contribute two ships, which will give us coverage in the system and perhaps allow us to isolate the station and whatever the Veetanho have waiting there."

"That is…" Lara shook her head. "I wouldn't have expected all that, given all the…" She waved both hands in the air. "Everything they have going on."

"We have provided aid and very likely will again." Tsan regarded her compatriots as they studied the additions Tamir made to the screens.

"In addition, we will have two companies of Zuul, along with two larger ships to work with the Hussars. They will provide additional dropships, to ensure all the Humans can be dropped in a single run. For the ground assault, we have the majority of a large Lumar mercenary company, Thunder Fist, who stand ready to fight alongside us. The Veetanho have burrowed into our city, and it will take no little effort to root them out.

"Cavaliers and Asbaran to flank the city and march in, the Horde to establish fallbacks and attack points to move us forward, Zuul and Lumar to press along the fight…" Alinore hummed low in her throat, already anticipating the broad strokes of the plans Tsan had put together over conversations with Nigel, Tula, and Veska.

"This is a hell of a lot more than I expected," Twilight said, planting an elbow on the table. "And it still feels like a hell of a risk."

"This is not counting, of course, our own contingent on Land's End." Another group, larger than any one of the other groupings populated the corner of the display in purple. "We will be in the jungles and in the middle of the fighting for the city. And I have a great deal of hope there is one additional cohort we can rely on."

"Peacemakers?" Bridgwater asked as he drummed his fingers on the table.

"No." Tsan bit the word off. "Much is changing, where they are concerned. But... a connection. We still have friends there, whether they remain with the Guild or no."

"When will they... no, that's not the question." Alinore cut herself off, chewed on her lip, and shoved her hands through her short hair. "We'll know about that last group when we know. When do you propose we move?"

"We have a limited window, both in terms of what the Veetanho may be planning and the availability of our allies. I recommend..." Tsan curled her claws and spread them wide. "I propose we attack within the month."

"We have a number of ideas about how to make it work," Tamir said, her voice steadier. "Option the first..."

Something rattled in the Human dama's chest, and Tsan kept her narrowed eyes on the screen. If she looked at Tamir now, changing scent and the wrongness of her breath and all, she knew there would be confirmation of a fact she did not wish to hold now.

Better to plan where to deploy Horsemen, Zuul, Lumar, Hunters, Humans, and all the allies they had gathered. Better to consider the death they would bring, rather than the one that waited directly behind her, the one that would take Tamir all too soon.

* * *

The halls loomed taller than Khatash's canopy, and Tsan glanced at the pipes built through the ceiling more than a few times as she walked the long route to Tamir's quarters.

No enemy stalked above her, but her fur lifted down her spine regardless, and each step landed in perfect silence.

She twitched her ears and struggled for the calm that was so often second nature. It bled through her claws, insubstantial and impossible to hold.

You are not being hunted. You are not hunting.

Tsan told herself this every other stride.

In the last turn to Tamir, she stopped and curled her tail closely around her body. She leaned against the cool metal of the unadorned wall and stretched her claws wide.

You are not being hunted. You are not hunting. You go to pay respects to a dama.

Her fur rose in patches, faster than she could smooth it. Contained in her field, with no one walking near, she closed her eyes.

You go to say goodbye to a friend.

She had lost more friends than she cared to count, and it was a wound that did not heal. A Basreen bite, envenomed and unclosing, pulsing with loss. Each new one widened it, or deepened it, or simply pushed the venom further into her veins.

She was Dama. She would carry on until the limb rotted off around the wound and then she would go faster, for spite.

No. Tsan twitched her tail, retracted her claws, and stood on two legs. *You are not poisoned. You are not an ever-healing wound. Your people live, much in thanks to Tamir.*

She would greet her friend with joy. She would sit close beside her, and honor the life that would end comfortably, in old age, in a bed in her den. Would that they all could be so lucky.

Tsan took a moment to preen, then dropped her field and stepped around the corner, keeping an ear tilted for the others who would undoubtedly be coming. Tamir wanted to say goodbye, and none with power to travel the galaxy would fail to meet that wish.

The door slid open, and Esthik turned his head slightly, though he didn't move from his position, curled close to Tamir's side.

Seeing the Hunter of Hurts away from his equipment, a small ball against the frail form of their dama, stole the air from her lungs. She steadied herself and moved into the room, her slow blink a cover for the pause she'd taken.

"I expected you to arrive in your field," Tamir said, her tone breathier but still hers, despite everything. "To become visible only when you were about to land on my head."

"My apologies, Dama. I can leave and try again if you would like?" A purr throbbed under her voice, which hid the mewl she wanted to utter. *Joy*, she told herself, *she has earned that and more from me.*

"We have time enough for that," Tamir answered, with a rough sound more laugh than cough.

"No one is jumping on your head," Esthik said, and he placed a paw on Tamir's arm. He cleared his throat and flicked his ears in apology. "Though, of course, the damas may do as they like."

"A joke, my Deo. Entropy allow me a few more of those."

Tsan leaped as soon as she was close enough and landed on the bare edge of the bed, careful not to disturb Tamir with any excess motion.

"I am glad to see your face," she said with another slow blink. "Dama, I greet you."

"Dama, I greet you," Tamir replied with a slow blink of her own, "and I am very glad I cannot see my own face in this moment." She laughed again, coughed, then shifted to sit up a touch further. "Yes, I am comfortable. Yes, there is time. No, I will not change my mind."

"You would buy only minutes, not days. Better to choose." Tsan nodded, though her words were as much for herself and Esthik as for Tamir.

"It is a luxury few are afforded in this galaxy," she responded, some tension leaving her shoulders at Tsan's reply. "I have had a generous allotment of years."

Esthik stirred, his tail lashing, but he swallowed his protest before Tsan needed to intervene. He curled more tightly against the Human dama's side and muttered something both damas chose to ignore.

"You have used them well indeed, my Tamir." Tsan moved in precise steps across the length of the bed, along the opposite side of her Human from Esthik. She touched her head to Tamir's cheek and breathed for a long moment.

The tang of medicine, the cut smell of life winding down, but most of all, Tamir's unique smell. Human, female, elderly, spice, and warmth… Tsan closed her eyes and leaned harder before lifting her head again.

"I wish…" Tamir paused, a quick frown passing across her face. "Not for more time. To see it through, maybe."

"No." Tsan pressed her hand onto Tamir's shoulder. Not hard enough to bruise, but with enough pressure to make her point. "You have seen it through. You saved us. The rest is—what was it you said?" They smiled at each other, both knowing very well the strength of a Hunter's eidetic memory. "The rest is our weight to carry."

"That is true." Tamir tilted her head back toward Tsan, who met it with her own. Then she poked Esthik and smiled at his indignant expression. "Did you hear that?"

"I have said very much the same!" Esthik protested, his fur bristling in a huff before realization dawned. His ears twisted to the side, and he smoothed his fur before curling back up against her. "As you very well know. You have earned your rest, Dama."

"Indeed, I have, my little love. And I know what remains is in the best of hands."

"Speaking of," Tsan murmured, tilting her head back toward the door.

"Hi, Mommy," Ziva said, her voice soft and thick with unshed tears. She walked into the room at a measured pace, as if she were fighting to keep herself together—which, Tsan realized, she probably was. Weren't they all?

Fssik said nothing, asked no permission, paused for no objection, but simply leaped. He landed with admirable lightness.

"Dama," he said. "We greet you."

"Hi, Baby," Tamir said, reaching a hand toward her youngest child as her other hand moved to stroke a line down Fssik's spine in welcome. "I greet you both. Did you see your sisters? They were just here."

"I passed them," Ziva said, taking her mother's fingers in her own. "I will catch up with them later. I—I didn't bring Thaddeus because you said… and I didn't know if there would be…" *time.*

The word hung in the air, unsaid.

"I did say. We said goodbye during his last visit. Better he remember me that way than this husk of me who can't play with him as he would like. He's my youngest grandbaby, you know? I am very lucky to have so many. Human and Hunter alike."

"The day has been full of visitors," Esthik said, calmer with Fssik nearby. His ears still twisted, but he did not curl quite so tightly. "I think some, like Aryss, are still here."

The faintest of huffs answered, and Tsan slow blinked.

"A legacy worthy of you, Dama," she said, tail sweeping slowly behind her. "And beyond. You have overseen new iterations of two species into the galaxy. How many can say such a thing?"

"In the end, it doesn't matter," Tamir said, shifting her body slightly and gripping her daughter's hand. "That's not exactly right. It matters; of course, it does. I'm proud of my role in it, but the best is this—you. All of you." She sucked in a breath, the rattle audible in the small room. "This matters more."

"Of course, it does," Alinore said, and Tsan turned slightly toward the Humans entering the room. She hadn't registered the door opening, which should have bothered her. In any other circumstance, it would have, but, now, it simply meant Alinore, Lara, Ward, and Ref had arrived. Or returned. Tsan murmured her greetings and paid some small measure of attention to their words. Her hearing remained focused on the sounds of Tamir's chest, and it became difficult to make room for much else.

"You shouldn't…" Tamir swallowed, squeezed her eyes closed in frustration, then opened them to continue. "Spend all night here, waiting for what's coming. There's… planning."

"We've done all the planning that can be done." Tsan flicked an ear sharply. "All will change the moment we return to Khatashi space, regardless."

"No plan survives," Tamir murmured, her eyelids fluttering on their way up from a slow blink.

"So, we will watch." Aryss dropped her field but remained in the corner, her tail sweeping the ground behind her. "Until it is no longer needful."

"Comforting." Tamir rasped another laugh, and Esthik bumped her with his head before turning to regard Aryss, his ears soft.

Fssik made a low noise, and Ziva's lips quirked up in a Human smile. Warmth twined down Tsan's spine. Tsan had had no such opportunity to sit at her dama's bedside—Lirou had died in the jungle, as so many did, at the advanced age of twenty-five. Tsan had not been calm when word reached her, and the object of her contract had suffered for it. The additional blood and begging hadn't made her feel any better, but it had soothed her enough for an uneventful return to Khatash. Ziva was handling a similar situation with a great deal more composure.

She smoothed her fur and wrenched her mind back to the beings around her. There was no good way to lose a friend, nor a dama, but Tamir was right. Dying after a long life, well-lived, surrounded by those one loved… Tsan saw no such future for herself, but she was glad of it for her friend. There were many good ways to die—for clan, for principle, for taking one's enemy with one—it was the survivors who needed to carry the loss. How well it was, then, that everyone in this room was well acquainted with that weight.

"Do Hunters believe in an afterlife?" Ref asked, his voice a low rumble.

Aryss' ears flattened, but she didn't curl her lip. Tsan tipped her tail toward the younger Hunter in approval.

"We live, and then we do not," Tsan answered. "But there is much in the galaxy left to surprise us."

"Maybe…" Tamir's blinks edged longer, as though her eyelids became heavier with each movement. "One more surprise left for me."

Aryss sprang onto the bed, next to Esthik and close to Tamir. Her tail lashed, but her voice was calm.

"We carry your hunt forward," she said, ducking her head, her eyes steady on Tamir. "We speak your name in our dens."

Tsan thrummed in approval. Stalking Blade had not been quite as old a clan as Whispering Death, but it had been a strong clan for many generations. She had never heard their farewell to the dead or dying before but was glad to know it now.

"You are all…" Tamir lifted her free hand, but it didn't quite make it to Aryss. The Hunter leaned forward and pressed her cheek to the Human fingers, and the rumble in Tsan's chest deepened as the silence lengthened.

"Mom—" Ziva said, the sound more of a choked cry than a proper word.

"Precious—" Tamir managed, her eyes closed, eyelids no longer twitching as they tried to open, "—to me. Love."

Tamir's last words held none of her fierceness, but all her warmth, and the Hunters' combined purr thrummed through the space until their Human dama's breath eased to a stop.

* * * * *

Part Three

Chapter Twelve

This time around, Fssik made his insertion at sunrise.

Since the Veetanho invaders had discovered his previous LZ, Fssik had chosen to aim for a spot further from the city. It worked better for their mission parameters, too. If they were going to identify drop zones, staging areas, and maneuver routes, it was just as well they begin further out and work their way in.

The team was smaller this time, too. Cox and Brite were still recuperating, but Tiffany Reynolds and Paul Sparks were there with their signals and communications expertise—and their newly acquired experience with the wonders of Khatash. Paul Bisdorf was back, too, as the team medic, along with three new team members.

Fssik also had another mission. He had promised Dama Tsan that he would find Aryo and her band of survivors again. He would warn them about the incoming attack and invite them to join in, if they wanted.

They had certainly earned the right.

The third advantage to landing away from the city was that Fssik could ride the dawnline all the way down to the cool green darkness under the canopy. Satellite imagery confirmed his memory of a river snaking through the jungle, carving deep, vertical cliffs into the rock surface. That unnamed river would make the perfect ingress point.

"My Hunter, I hope you know what you're doing," Ziva muttered behind him, as he reconfigured his ship for atmospheric flight and dove down into the narrow cut in the terrain.

"Don't I always, my Human?" Fssik asked, using his bank to dissipate some of the incredible velocity he'd gained while penetrating the planetary envelope.

Ziva didn't answer verbally, but Fssik heard her snort, and he grinned Human-style in response. The truth was this kind of flying was fun. Their last insertion had whetted his appetite and made him miss it even more. He banked back in the opposite direction, keeping the nose of his ship down below the level of the terrain to keep from highlighting himself against the brightening dawn sky.

Truth be told, the river wasn't particularly hard to fly. While the water below rushed fast and hard, cutting deeply into the rock with every drop, the course it took curved and meandered in lazy arcs, so Fssik found it easy to manage his energy states and power settings. They soared above the rapids, hugging the upwind side of the canyon, as the trees crowded closer and closer on the rim of the chasm above.

"This feels wrong," Ziva said as the canopy began to close over them, aided by the great clinging vines that stretched across the span ahead.

"We've got several hundred meters of altitude above the water," Fssik pointed out, "and another hundred to go before we impact any vegetation. We're fine. I've done this a million times."

"A million?"

"A couple." He glanced over his shoulder and Human-grinned at her again, then turned his attention back to the business of not crashing into the green-coated cliff walls ahead.

As the overarching canopy thickened, Fssik snapped his goggles away from his face and dialed up the ship's visual and near-IR sensors. The display brightened, and he cut the power back to slow their velocity even more. Not for the first time, he thanked all that was good under the stars that he'd invested in upgraded atmospheric flight and hover capabilities for his ship.

He picked his way toward his chosen landing zone—a wide cliff ledge that jutted out from the wall of the canyon on the upwind side. The canyon widened at that spot, but his ledge was far enough down that it remained mostly invisible from the sky. The approach was tricky, though. The river's course made one of its rare ninety-degree turns just before the ledge appeared, so he'd have to start his descent/deceleration well before that point... blind.

Fssik waited until his navigation told him he was within a half-kilometer of the point, then cut his power back to idle. He kept his nose level, letting the descent gradually develop into a steady downward trajectory. The cliff wall loomed ahead, giving the impression that there was no way out short of impacting the rock. Behind him, Fssik heard Ziva suck in a breath, but she said nothing, and her trust in his skills and knowledge filled his chest with pride.

He held his heading for a second more, then he pushed his throttle forward a touch, the tiniest of increases, until he felt the shudder through the frame of the ship. As soon as he felt it, he banked the craft over and let his nose come up. His speed decreased even more as the ship cruised around the turn, the rock of the cliff blurring as they passed. Fssik rolled out and saw his ledge there before him, green and inviting... and exactly where it was supposed to be in his display.

Pleasure rippled under his fur as he poured on the power and pulled his nose up, causing the ship to carve a steady line down to the springy, vegetation-covered surface. He touched down lightly on the ship's main landing struts and cut the power, slowly letting his nose drop down to rest on the nose strut.

"Wow," Ziva said behind him. "That was… wow."

"Thank you, my lovely one," Fssik said, warmth spreading through him at her admiration. "I told you, I'm the best pilot you know. Now, shall we get our team and get moving?"

As before, Ziva and the Humans unloaded their gear while Fssik shut down and secured his ship. He probably didn't need to pull out the concealment netting he'd used on their last mission, but he figured he had it, so he might as well.

Besides, this was Khatash. No precaution was ever wasted here.

"There is one downside to landing on a cliff face midway down a canyon wall," Ziva pointed out, as the team gathered with their packs and gear near the nose of the aircraft. "We gotta climb out of here and then we have to cross the chasm. Any ideas?"

"Generally speaking," Fssik said, "we've found it's better to go up than down in the jungle if you have the choice. If we climb up, those vines are large and stable enough to cross. I can scale the cliff easily. Can you?"

"Maybe," Sparks said. "Especially if you can sink some pitons for us and set up a belay on your way up. Do you know how to do that?"

"I will if you tell me," Fssik said, with a slow blink.

"Are you sure? It's tricky work and usually takes practice to remember how to do it."

"Hunters remember everything," Ziva said. "Show him once, Sparks, and he'll know it as well as you do."

While she might have been exaggerating slightly, Fssik's eidetic memory did help him learn the process in a matter of minutes. Before the sun broke over the eastern lip of the canyon, he'd scaled the cliff and set up the belay, and his Humans were well on their way to the top.

Crossing the vines proved to be a bit of a challenge. Like most vegetation on Khatash, the clinging vines bristled with defenses. Their thick, thorny main trunks projected out over the chasm, braiding over and under each other as they fought for more sunlight.

"The skin is slippery," Fssik warned, "and studded with thorns, as you see. The sap is toxic, so try not to break off any branches. I don't *think* it will kill you, but it will give you a painful rash on any unprotected skin."

"This planet…" Reynolds muttered. Fssik grinned Human-style in her direction.

"Watch your footing and use handholds," Ziva added. "The way the vines twist around each other can be tricky. We'll go slowly. Lead on, my Hunter."

Fssik slow blinked at her. Then, just because he could, he leaped up onto the nearest branch of the clinging vine bundle and ran across, darting from trunk to trunk, crossing as if he were chasing prey through a flat meadow. On the other side, he found a convenient spot on a tree branch and sat down to wash his face and wait for his Humans to pick their laborious way across.

"Show off," Ziva said, as she unclipped from the climbing harness they'd used to secure themselves to each other for the crossing.

"You know this about me," he said, standing up and stretching his spine. "You shouldn't sound so surprised. And you got across very well; I was expecting you to take longer."

She let out a laugh and rolled her head around on her shoulders, then she began removing the harness and stowing it in her pack. One by one, the other members of the team hopped down from the vine bridge and began to do the same. They took a moment to grab water and a snack, then headed out to start doing the work they'd come back to Khatash to do.

They moved west and south, keeping approximately the same distance from the city, hiking in a sweeping arc around the populated area. They rarely saw the sun as they kept their paths under the canopy of the jungle and only stopped to identify natural clearings and terrain features that could make likely drop zones for CASPer deployment.

As they went, something began to bother Fssik. It started as a tiny wonder, like an itch behind his ears that he couldn't quite scratch, but as they hiked on, moving deeper and deeper into the undergrowth, the wonder grew to worry, and he finally he mentioned it to Ziva.

"We haven't seen Aryo or any of her beings yet," he murmured while pressing his head against her hand. They'd stopped to make camp and rest near one of the millions of streams that crisscrossed the jungle floor. "I told her we'd return, and I imagine she's been looking for us. I wonder why they haven't reached out. This concerns me."

"I'm sure it's nothing," Ziva said, running her fingers over the top of his skull and down along the curve of his neck. "We're pretty far away from the mountain where we encountered them before.

They're probably down in that sector. It sounded like that was where they usually operate."

Fssik said nothing, but he pressed his body closer to her ribs and pulled her comforting scent to him. She may be *Homo venatores* now, but there were still things his Hunter-Human didn't understand. Aryo would have been looking for them. They weren't so far away that she couldn't have made contact by now if she'd wanted to.

Or been able to.

Something was wrong. He knew it but he couldn't do anything about it.

And that made him angry.

* * *

No trek through the jungle was ever quick, and this mission was no exception.

The team was far more worried about stealth than speed, so they took their time, hiking up and down over uneven terrain under the thick canopy where almost no light penetrated to ground level. Fssik tried to teach them to move as a Hunter would, through the first level of tree branches, but only Ziva had any success at leaping from branch to branch, and even she struggled when loaded down with her gear.

So, they kept to ground level, which was slow and often dangerous. Their third night in, Fssik found the scent trail of a broody cheelin mother and at least one, possibly two, babies. Any Hunter would see the sense in avoiding that situation if one were alone, never mind if one were trailing a team of loud, clumsy, but oh-so-necessary Humans behind them.

He needed to talk to the team, so Fssik leaped up to the lowest branch overhead and waited for the rest of them to catch up.

"We need to swing further to the west," he said without preamble. "The terrain is more difficult, but we don't have a choice."

"Why not?" Sparks asked, breathing heavily. As their chief communicator, he carried one of the most massive loads, so Fssik did not think his sweat and gasping unreasonable.

"There are cheelin up ahead. A mother and at least one calf, maybe more. We have to deviate."

Ziva looked around at the tired faces of the team and then nodded slowly. "All right," she said, "but let's take a quick break here first. Refill water, grab a snack, change socks… whatever we need to do. Is this spot safe?"

"For the moment," Fssik said, "but we should be moving soon."

"Okay. Ten minutes, everyone."

True to her word, Ziva had the team up and moving before long, and Fssik pointed them toward the setting moon. The rolling ground gradually took on a steady uphill slant as they walked, pushing their way out until Fssik deemed it safe to turn back south.

They came to a clear spot at the top of a hill and looked up to see the moon just touching the western horizon. To the east, a thin line of gray heralded the coming day, and Fssik felt a sudden instinctive urge to get under cover, to hide from the daylight that lurked beyond the eastern horizon. He turned his face away and looked up at his person.

"Should we camp here?" Ziva asked. "Not here in the open, but down in the tree line perhaps? It's too bad this hill is so far from the city. It meets our needs for a DZ exactly—"

BOOM!

The sound was distant and hollow, like a bomb exploding kilometers away. Fssik spun back to the east—the direction from which the reverberating echo had come. At first, nothing more occurred, save the startled rising of thousands of the jungle's flying species. Fssik twitched his ears and inhaled deeply, reaching out with all his senses to try and find out what had happened.

BOOM!

Another explosion, still distant, still from the east. Then another and another.

A faint whiff of something—not fire, not electricity, but something in between—teased his nose. A rumbling started beneath his feet. Initially, he could barely feel it, but as each moment passed, it swelled in intensity, until his ears caught the crashing roar of something—or several somethings—very large, moving very quickly.

"Ziva," he said, his voice intense. "We need to move."

"What?" she asked. "Because of those sounds? Were they explosions?"

"Yes. Maybe. I don't know. They sounded far away, but I think those cheelin are stampeding, and there is something on the wind…" He trailed off and lifted his nose again. The scent intensified—scorching, singing heat and withering death.

"Excuse me, Deo, Ziva? You might want to look at this." Tiffany Reynolds tapped Ziva lightly on the shoulder and pointed to the east. Ziva gathered Fssik into her arms, stood, and turned in that direction. Fssik squinted. The rising sun made it difficult, but he could just barely make out the canopy wilting in a rolling wave that spread toward them.

"Shit!" Sparks said, grabbing his pack and looking at a slate attached to it by a lanyard. "The radiation detection just went haywire! Whatever that is, it's hot as fuck!"

"We need to move! Everyone, get your gear! We go west, fast!"

Fssik jumped out of Ziva's arms and sprinted into the tree line. He leaped up into the low-hanging branches and began racing ahead to scout the best—the clearest, fastest—path for them to take. For once, fortune smiled on him. He found a game trail that followed a stream that flowed near the western edge of the hill.

"This way!" he shouted, knowing Ziva, at least, would hear him. Seconds later, she appeared, running full out with the rest of the team on her heels. Fssik saw her look up, her eyes unerringly seeking his. She gave him a single nod, and he sprang forward again, leaping from branch to branch along the trail, scouting ahead as far as he could, while keeping his Ziva in sight.

The terrain sloped down from the hill and then began to climb upward again as the trail inexorably turned south. Fssik followed it, knowing that pushing further west toward steeper and steeper climbs would just slow his Humans down. He wasn't intimately familiar with this stream, but he knew that, generally speaking, the terrain sloped down to the south for a stretch before opening up to the west again.

Not that he had time to puzzle it out, exactly. Every time they topped a rise, Fssik bounded to the top layer of the canopy and looked behind them. Every time, the slow-moving ripple of destruction loomed closer.

The third time he did this, Fssik realized the cheelin stampede they'd initially heard had never materialized. The big animals were deadly, but they weren't particularly fast, even in a flat out run. He looked back in the direction they'd come and saw… nothing. Smoking, scorched earth covered in a nauseating orange slick of something that shimmered in the dawning light. Just ahead of the devastation, the jungle withered, trees slumping and wilting as they dissolved to the ground. That same hot, electrical scent stained the air, and it was getting stronger as the ripple of death moved toward them.

Fssik ducked back under the topmost layer of the canopy and raced down the branches of the tree. In his haste, he didn't step as carefully as he should have, would have, under any other circumstances. Pain lanced up through his back left foot as his padded toes grazed a vine coated in a natural toxin. He hissed out a breath and pushed on, racing forward to get back ahead of Ziva and her stumbling, tiring team of Humans.

"Keep going!" he shouted as he caught up with the last of them. "The radiation is still moving outward this way!"

He heard Elizabeth Archuleta gasp and cry out as she caught a foot on something and went down hard, landing with a sickening *crunch* on her knee. Paul Bisdorf, the team's medic stopped, doubled back, and reached out under her arms to lever her back up to standing. They lurched forward, just as Fssik heard the sickening sound of timber falling behind them.

"Ziva!" he called ahead. He didn't want to call her back, but he couldn't do anything to help alone.

"Fssik, go!" Paul called out, waving him forward with his free hand. "We're right behind you!"

"Ziva can—"

"No! Just go! We'll be all right, or we won't, but without you and her, the mission fails! Go!"

Something twisted inside Fssik, and the hot, electrical scent intensified as the darkness beneath the canopy suddenly began to fade. Behind the two lagging team members, a tree wavered, then crashed to the ground. It slumped as it hit, then melted over the smaller trees and stumps it impacted on the way down. Everywhere the tree-sludge touched, the sickness spread, until a wall of stark, sickening, orange light began to peek through the jungle behind them.

"Go!" Paul shouted once more, and Fssik turned and bolted up his current branch and leaped to another beyond. Maybe if he could get to Ziva in time... maybe... .

A strangled cry sounded behind him. He turned to look and let out a scream as the brightness scoured his retinas for an instant before his day-goggles could snap into place.

Without you and her, the mission fails.

Fssik hunched his face away from the burning, decaying light and dove forward, desperate to get under cover. Grief clawed through him, shredding his mind as he pushed on, away from that orange light and the way it dissolved everything it touched.

Lost somewhere in the sound of his blood pounding in his ears, Fssik thought he heard Ziva screaming.

He didn't know how long he ran. He moved blindly, guided by feel and scent and Ziva's quintessence signature blazing in his mind. Slowly, bit by bit, his vision started to return. His eyes still felt like searing coals in his head, but he could make out the shapes of the trees around him and the path below. He realized they'd left the stream behind and were once again climbing.

Fssik sucked a breath into lungs which were burning from the effort and bunched his body to leap across another gap, from branch to branch, as he'd done thousands of times in his life. This time, though, just as he pushed off, something small and sleek came hurtling down from the upper level of the canopy. Something sharp scraped across his right shoulder. He twisted in midair to wind around whatever it was that was attacking.

He felt something pull at his harness, and he reached up with his left front paw and swatted at it as the ground rushed up to meet him. With less dexterity than he should have had, Fssik hit the ground in a roll that made his right front leg go numb but had him up on his feet and ready to fight back within less than a heartbeat. Once more, he grabbed at the stinging intruder tangled in the shoulder strap of his harness and found a long, sleekly muscled tube of a body wrapped there.

"Basreen!" he said, grabbing the deadly, semi-intelligent animal and ripping it away from his vest. "Not a good time to attack. Nor a good target!"

"Mother!" the Basreen said, desperately twisting its body around his wrist as it spread its wings. "Mother hurt. Hunter help."

Chaos and Entropy. This Basreen was just a hatchling! Her—he could tell she was female by the coloration developing on her wings—body was barely the length of his foreleg. If this young one's mother was hurt, she wouldn't survive long in the jungle alone. And with that rolling orange light of destruction behind them...

"Show me," Fssik said, making the decision before he could think too much about it. "Quickly."

"Up," the Basreen kita said, and Fssik leaped back up into the trees. She guided him higher and higher, until they reached the top layer of the canopy. Fssik swallowed the fear that pressed into him, snapped his goggles shut over his eyes, and turned to look behind them.

The orange light continued to roll along behind them, but its progress had slowed. It filled the valley like a noxious cloud, lapping at the rising terrain all around. Everywhere it touched, everything died.

"Hunter!" the little one screeched, and Fssik recalled himself to his task. He may not have been big enough to save Elizabeth and Paul, but maybe he could save this baby's mother.

"Show me," he said again and followed her urging to a nest tucked in the joint of two branches in the top layer of the canopy. Inside the nest, a Basreen mother lay curled around a clutch of eggs. The outside of her body was covered in black-singed red burns, and Fssik swallowed hard against sympathy for the pain she must be feeling.

"Basreen," Fssik said. "I greet you. I am Fssik, a Hunter. Your young one has found me and asked me to help you. The orange light that kills all is coming. We must go now, quickly."

"Eggs," the Basreen said, lifting her head and hissing. Her tone was tight with pain and fatigue. "Will not leave them."

"I will bring them," he said, reaching down and opening one of the many pouches he carried on his harness. This one was for projectile ammunition, but it was empty. "We can put them in here, and you can ride with your kita on my harness, but we have to go *now*."

"Hurts," the Basreen said.

"Mother, come!" her child wailed. She lifted her head in the kita's direction, and Fssik could see that her eyes, too, had been burned to a blackened ruin.

"Your young one found me. Let me help you. I'm going to lift your eggs and put them in my pouch, Basreen, then I will carry you as well. But we must do it now."

"Yes," the Basreen said, laying her head down again. Once more, Fssik heard trees falling, and the bone-melting scent of death teased his nose. His muscles burned with fatigue, but he was a Hunter. Maybe he couldn't save the Human members of his team, but he was going to save this mother and her children, come entropy itself.

Which wasn't far from the truth.

Another tree fell behind him as he slipped the last egg into his pouch. Their shells were completely hard, and he could feel the frantic movement of the young ones within. They would hatch soon, likely in his pouch. He only hoped they would survive long enough for their mother to feed them and not turn on each other in the desperate throes of hunger.

One problem at a time, he thought, using one of Ziva's favorite sayings. He closed the flap on his pouch and then lifted the Basreen out of her nest, using the greatest care. She still shuddered in pain with every movement, but he got her safely curled around his shoulders next to her first-hatched kita. Behind them, another tree fell, and it slammed into the base of the one he stood on, sending a reverberation through the trunk as the orange light sickness began to spread.

"Hang on, Basreeni!" Fssik said and leaped, blindly, up the slope and away from the light. His claws grazed a nearby branch, and he threw his body toward it. His feet touched the rough bark just in time to push off and leap again… and then again.

He'd lost the path a long time ago, but Ziva's presence called to him like a beacon in his mind. He could *feel* her with his quintessence, a blazing haven of love and safety. She was out there… up there, higher on the steep slope.

So, with the Basreen family in tow, that was where he would go.

* * * * *

Chapter Thirteen

For the first time in too many seasons, Tsan returned to her home system. She'd traveled to nearly every part of the known galaxy in the time since Khatash had been lost to her, and she'd found new homes for herself and her people. She'd even found more people to make her own.

And yet, hours away if all went according to plan, was the home of her birth. The den where her kits had been born. The jungle where she'd learned to hunt. The members of her first family who were still left to her. Somewhere.

Death lay thick between her and reclaiming that home, and the tip of her tail twitched at the thought. Aryss paced nearby, her tail as wide as a gnarra bush. Pura and Criuch muttered together in the far corner of the room. Grown now, Pura and her siblings had last seen Khatash as den-bound kits.

Tsan's tail lashed. It would not be only the enemy who would die, and not all of her allies would fall to the Veetanho. She tilted her ears toward the longer side of the command center, where Ref and Tula leaned over the various sensor reports.

"Doesn't look like the rats have moved anything closer to the gate since Fssik and Ziva's crew ran intelligence." Ref snorted, his mouth turning down as though that lack of immediate attack had insulted him.

"Veetanho think safe here. Far system. Little traffic even before." Tula ran two sets of fingers over a display and made an elaborate Lumar shrug. "Watch gate, protect planet."

275

"It's not theirs to protect," Aryss spat, her direction shifting to cross paths with her companion. Meredith reached out but made no effort to halt her partner's motion. Wise. Aryss made brief contact and continued her path around the semi-circle of the command center.

"They're leaving the station open," A'nief said, looking at the readings from his seat near the pilot. Tsan had taken care to note Zuul tones and moods—they did not use their tails and ears exactly as Hunters did, but it was close enough that she had learned much in little time—and he remained calm. "Inviting an attack."

"A little obvious for a Veetanho ploy, isn't it?" Meredith asked.

"Depends on who they think they're tempting." A'nief had been a warrior for as long as Ref had been alive, and he talked more than his chosen pilot, Tagar. Tsan approved of the old Zuul fighter and had grudgingly admitted to herself that Tagar was a perfectly competent pilot. If she couldn't fly, and Fssik were otherwise occupied, Tagar would do.

"You mean they understand a Hunter came home and wreaked havoc. They expect a small, desperate force, one that would be tempted to take the high ground." Tsan spoke for the first time since they'd exited the gate into the system. Pura and Criuch twisted away from their conversation to watch her, and Aryss slowed her pacing.

"Veetanho smart." Tula looked up and bared her teeth in Tsan's favorite smile. "And Veetanho stupid."

"In this matter," Tsan replied, her voice roughened with a rumble from deep in her chest, "how would they ever expect to see a force such as this coming?"

"A small force would be best served to take the station, even assuming it is a tempting morsel in a snapping cage." A'nief twisted an ear backward, his tail half-lifting. Tsan had deemed that 'considering,' and so far, that had held true. "If the Hussars pull away as we planned and light up on their trajectory toward the station, the Veetanho will believe their trap set."

"That should pull enough eyes to drop the CASPers." Ref grunted and crossed his arms with a nod. He was satisfied, Tsan thought.

So far, they were still following the loose plan they'd agreed on before entering hyperspace.

Each arm knew each other's goals and had full autonomy in reaching their own directives as the situation shifted. Plans had been made and remade, and contingencies had been imagined. Once they engaged the Veetanho, all would shift again.

No plan survived contact with an enemy, and certainly not with the former masterminds of the galaxy.

They ran as dark as they could, accelerating or falling from the emergence area in as many directions as possible to muddle their numbers. The Veetanho thought they had no true threat to their power, to their ability to recover and quietly rebuild on the outskirts of the galaxy.

Tsan and her allies had been careful to do nothing that would alter that belief, not before the time came to prove how wrong they were. Her claws curved in readiness, and she stilled her breathing until they were sheathed again.

"We should start to receive the drop zones Fssik, Ziva, and the Cavs marked as we get a little closer. The dropships will be able to adjust their approaches in plenty of time." Meredith's voice, always steady, picked up a deeper note. An attempt to soothe, Tsan realized as Aryss shifted her path again to bring her to her Venatore's side.

"I still want to take the north side of the city," Aryss muttered, her tail beginning to smooth down to its normal size.

Closer to Stalking Blade's den. Tsan empathized enough to say nothing aloud, though she flicked an ear at the younger Hunter. Criuch leaped from his conversation with Pura to touch his head to his sister's, and Aryss ceased the low thrum of a growl that had been building from her center.

"We will see how Fssik has marked the drop zones, and, between them, Asbaran Solutions and Cartwright's Cavaliers will... how did they say it?" A'nief asked.

"Call dibs," Ref answered promptly, glancing up from the display.

"We take part of the city best for us." Tula thumped her chest. "Lumar, Hunters, Venatores, Humans, and Zuul. All Thunder Fist. All Hunters."

"Allies," Tsan murmured, pleasure rising against the anticipation of the hunt. She had engaged beings with such strengths for a reason. A single hunt she could plan with ease. The best way to deploy some few of her clan? Also well within her experience.

A full-scale invasion of a planetary system to take back her home? No. Trusted others were charged with planning those details. She had brought them together, brought them here.

And she was only getting started.

* * *

Fssik stumbled forward and leaped again. He stretched his leaden body, fighting the burn in every muscle and fiber, and reached for the far branch.

He missed.

His outstretched claws gouged ten gashes in the wood of the branch, but it wasn't enough. He heard the Basreen kita let out a tiny scream and felt her wrap more tightly around his neck as they fell. Her mother didn't move—was she unconscious? Dead? Fssik didn't know, but he reached up to grab her tubular form and hold it tightly to himself as he desperately turned, flattening his body out as much as possible, so when he landed, he would at least protect her and her fragile young.

"Fssik!"

He hit hard, his back legs collapsing under the impact with a *snap*. He let out a gasp of pain. He blinked away the sudden spots of brightness just in time to see Ziva throw herself down beside him, her beautiful face streaked with tears and creased with pain.

"Fssik! Oh, my Hunter! I thought—"

"Alive," Fssik managed to croak as she gathered him into her arms and pulled him in close to the warm, safe scent of her. "Elizabeth and Paul... I couldn't... I..."

"I know," Ziva said, her voice soaked with tears. He felt her stand slowly. "None of us could. We turned back, but they were already gone, and I thought you—"

"*Hssst!* My legs! And Ziva—"

He stopped as a shudder went through Ziva, and he felt the tiny head of the Basreen kita lift from somewhere around his collarbone. She let out a hiss of warning and coiled her body as if to strike.

"No, kita, no!" Fssik's cry came out as a sob of pain and desperation. Basreen venom was deadly, like everything else from the jungle. He reached with his other hand to try and contain the tiny predator, knowing she was only acting out of her own overwhelming fear. "Ziva! Drop me!"

For the second time in as many minutes, Fssik hit the ground hard enough to drive the wind from his lungs. The pain in his back legs exploded through him, and he again lost his vision in the overwhelming brightness of agony.

"Kita, please! Ziva is mine," Fssik whimpered as he reached up to contain the little one's fury. "She will help us; you cannot hurt her. Please, little one. Listen to me!"

"She's—" It was Ziva's voice, drawing near.

"Ziva, stay back, she's fast! Little one! Do you understand me? I'm hurt, and Ziva and her Humans can help your mother and siblings."

"Hurt?" the little Basreen asked. Her hissing faded, and he felt her coiling back down around his body. He exhaled, and it sounded like a whimper.

"Yes, little one. I got hurt when I fell. But Ziva can help if you let her. You must promise. She won't hurt you or your family. She will only help."

"I will, little one," Ziva said. Fssik blinked. He could just barely see her bending close—but not too close. The light flickered oddly on her face, and for a moment, he wondered if he'd damaged the visual centers in his brain.

"Help. Mother. Eggs." The Basreen kita continued to coil around Fssik's spine and forearms. He fought the urge to curl into a ball around the pain in his back legs and held himself still. "Help Hunter. Yes."

"Ziva…" he whispered. He saw her bend toward him again and felt her soft hands in his fur. "Eggs in my ammo pouch…"

Blackness pulled at the edge of his vision.

"I've got them, my love. I've got you all."

* * *

Fssik opened his eyes and saw that same weird, flickering light. He blinked several times, then turned his head and realized what he was seeing was light from a mostly-shielded fire.

"Back with us, my Hunter?"

He turned his head the other way, toward her voice, and slow blinked up at the partner of his life. "It appears that way. What did you do? I feel fantastic."

"Hunter-specific nanites. New formula I got from Ward before we left," Ziva said, smiling back at him in both the Hunter and Human ways. "He thought they might be useful."

Fssik stretched his spine and all four of his legs. Sure enough, the sickening pain and numbness had lessened to a dull ache. He extended each of his claws one by one, retracted them, then pulled his body back into a ball and flipped himself up onto his feet.

"Whoa, easy there, killer," Ziva said reaching out a steadying hand that he did not need. "Even with the nanites, you did a number on yourself getting back to us. Take a minute."

"Do we have a minute?" he asked, looking pointedly at her.

Her smiling face fell, and he instantly regretted the question, necessary though it had been.

"One or two," she said, rolling her neck around on her shoulders. "We've climbed high enough that the radiation cloud has stopped. It appears to be settling to the valley floor. We've got time to take stock and make a new plan."

"How are the rest of the team?"

"Not great," Ziva said with a grimace. "It hurt to lose Elizabeth and Paul. And after them… well, we dropped our packs and anything else that was slowing us down, so we don't have much in the way of supplies. Just what was in our pouches or pockets."

"We can hunt," Fssik said. "At least, I can, and the Basreen kita if she's up for it. Where is she?"

"With her mother and siblings by the fire. The eggs hatched. One of the hatchlings didn't make it, and one of the others isn't looking good. But we gave nonspec nanites to the mom and she seems to be healing pretty well. I didn't know Basreen nursed their young."

"They do. It is part of why we honor them. Basreeni are legendarily good mothers."

"Is that why you saved them?" Ziva asked quietly.

"Yes. And… because I could."

"Fssik, what happened to Paul and Elizabeth was not your fault."

"I know," he said, pushing down the throat-clenching anger and sadness that rose with the thought. "I could not save them, but I could save the Basreeni, so I did."

Ziva nodded and reached out a hand to stroke the top of his head with her fingertips. Fssik leaned into her touch and closed his eyes, soaking up the love they shared. Just for a moment. Just to strengthen himself.

"Right," he said, opening his eyes. "Let us make that plan."

Ziva smiled at him in response and opened her arms in invitation. He leaped into her embrace, feeling a quick spurt of joy at the renewed strength in his muscles, and let her carry him over to the fire to talk with the others.

From what the team had been able to discern, the killing orange light was actually some kind of radioactive defoliant weapon. Tiffany mentioned that she'd seen something like it used on a much smaller scale on another job elsewhere in the galaxy. Somehow, the Veetanho had modified it and weaponized it against the jungle that had fought them so well during every step of their occupation. The good news was that the radioactivity of the weapon had a very short half-life. The cleared ground would be safe in another day or two. The bad news was that it severely interfered with their plans.

"We have to get word to the fleet," Ziva said. "They need to know that the situation on the ground has changed. If they're expecting to drop troops into jungle, and it's all cleared—"

"Not to mention the damage that weapon could do," Sparks said, nodding and looking up from where he was busily fiddling with a hand-held comm set. "They need to be prepared."

"I've been thinking about that," Ziva said. "And I think… I'd have to do some observation and triangulation… but I think they fired the weapon from the mountains to the south of the city. The same peak we were on before unless I miss my guess. From the last glimpse I had of the valley, the damage looked like it was almost a cone spreading out from there."

"That would make sense," Fssik said. "The city backs right up to those mountains, as you saw. So, if their goal was to destroy the jungle, they wouldn't need its radius directly south of the city. They could have dropped from orbit, I suppose."

"No." Ziva shook her head. "Not if we're right about them trying to colonize Khatash. If they're trying to rebuild here, it makes sense that they wouldn't do anything that might be perceived as breaking interstellar law. They won't violate the ten kilometer rule."

"But they used a hot weapon!" Tiffany protested. "Nukes are against the law, too!"

"It wasn't a nuclear blast, per se," Ziva pointed out. "If it was, we never would have been able to run from it. No, what they used was a defoliant. A radioactive one, sure, but a defoliant that has a short enough half-life that they could argue it's not a nuke. It's pretty ingenious if you think about it."

"The Veetanho have always been cunning," Fssik said, his deep anger and hatred threading through his words. "But that won't save them."

"It might," Ziva said, her voice tired. "Especially if we can't warn the fleet about what they're facing. Fssik, is your ship…" She trailed off as he met her eyes, then looked away. "No," she said gently, reaching out and stroking his fur for comfort. "I suppose it was too close, wasn't it?"

"Yes," Fssik said. "I doubt there's anything left of it."

"I'm sorry," she said.

"It was a ship. We lost friends today. Let us focus on how to avenge them."

She stroked down his spine again, but she nodded and let it go.

"All right, so how do we get a message to our people?"

"What if we use the weapon?"

The voice belonged to Jeff Paquet, one of the team members who didn't talk much but had been with them on their previous mission. Paquet, who used the nickname "Pocket," was a hacker and comm technician of the first order, Fssik remembered. He sat up straighter under Ziva's caresses, his ears flipping forward in interest.

"What do you mean?"

"Remember when we were here before? How we set up the comm relay to bounce to your ship? If Ziva's right, and that weapon was up there, I'm betting it's got communications components. We already know how to hack Veetanho tech, thanks to our earlier mission. If we get up there, maybe we can disable it and use the components as a kind of... I don't know... giant antenna for our quintessentially encoded message?"

"But without my ship," Fssik said, "what good is sending a message? It will never make it to Land's End in time."

"The fleet won't *be* at Land's End!" Ziva said, snapping her fingers. "By that point, they'll be in-system! We can broadcast to them directly!"

Fssik felt a tremor under his fur, and he raised his eyes to his beloved Human's face. "There will likely be plenty of Veetanho up there guarding their weapon," he said, his voice a rumbling purr of anticipation.

"Isn't that a terrible shame for them?" Ziva answered, and her savage grin matched the sudden fierce joy that sang through him.

* * * * *

Chapter Fourteen

For the rest of his life, Fssik would remember the journey back to the southern peak as the most trying experience he'd ever had.

After what they'd been through, every single member of the team—including the Basreen and her two surviving young—expressed the same glee Fssik felt at the prospect of destroying the Veetanho weapon that had caused such devastation. But while their spirits were savagely willing, their bodies were woefully weakened. All the Humans nursed injuries, some worse than others. Ziva limped from a fall she'd taken during the desperate flight to escape the cloud of destruction. Fssik had healed after his nanite treatment, but he keenly felt how much he'd stretched his stamina reserves, and he tired more easily than he should have. The Basreen mother was healing slowly, nurtured by Fssik and Ziva, even as she nursed her two young ones.

They had no food, no water, and no means of patching up their wounds. Worse, they carried no weapons besides the smallest of their backups and only minimal ammunition.

What they did have, was rage.

It was rage that carried them forward, step by torturous step, south and east, curving back around to the tallest peak beside the city. The top of the world, as Fssik had called it once before. The mountain they seemed destined never to escape.

It took them too many nights to make the trek. Fssik didn't bother counting. It seemed forever, but eventually, sunset found them crouched on the shoulder of the slope, sheltered by an ancient fall of boulders below the summit, listening and watching as a Veetanho flyer approached the flat area approximately a kilometer away.

"You have to stay here," Fssik said to Ziva. "We don't have the weapons to assault them in a traditional sense. I can get in and do what is needed, as I did in the city on our previous mission."

"I don't like it," Ziva said and sighed. Fssik slow blinked.

"But your body language says you agree with me."

"I do." Ziva nodded. "And if… if something happens to you—"

"Nothing will happen to me, my Human. I am a Hunter. This is what I *do*."

"I don't like sending you in without anyone to back you up," she said. "Isn't that why you have a companion in the first place?"

"I back Hunter up."

Fssik and Ziva turned to look at the Basreen mother, who winged down from the uneven rock ceiling of their hiding place and landed on Fssik's shoulders.

"I deadly too. I back Hunter up, come here if problems. Get Humans." She shuffled her wings together and coiled her body around Fssik's in something that felt very much like anticipation.

Ziva gave them both a long look. "Will the Veetanho see you, Basreen?"

The Basreen let out a chirping kind of laugh. "Only if I want see."

"Okay," she said softly. "I guess. I hate that it can't be me... but okay. You're both children of this jungle. I trust you both to keep each other alive."

Fssik stepped carefully forward, balancing the Basreen's weight, as he rubbed his head under Ziva's hands.

"I will come back to you," he promised.

Ziva pressed her lips together and nodded, her eyes sharp and bright with unshed tears. He slow blinked at her one more time and then turned to leap out of their small shelter into the soft darkness of the rising night.

Fssik ran most of the rest of the way to the summit before he stopped and pulled his quintessence around him like a cloak. The Basreen mother didn't react, except to unwind herself from him and disappear into the deep shadow of a nearby boulder.

"Good hunting, Hunter," he heard her raspy voice whisper on the night breeze. "May you have as many kills as me."

Fssik smiled in both styles.

"Good hunting to you, Basreen," he murmured, knowing she had excellent hearing. "May you do your best to keep up with me."

With a sense of laughter and fierce, savage joy, he stalked up toward the structure the Veetanho had built on the summit. He could see the weapon mounted on top of a scaffolded tower. It looked like a standard artillery piece, but it had an overlong barrel and a large fluid tank attached where the breach should have been. The flyer sat between him and the tower, its large aft door open. As he watched, two Veetanho emerged from the building at the base of the tower and headed for the flyer. Together, they grabbed a crate of something from the cargo bay and then they turned and began hauling it back toward the building.

Careless, he thought as he padded up to the ship, *to leave the cargo door open. Careless or arrogant. Not that it matters. They're not going to live long enough to regret it either way.* He slipped inside and made his way through the small cargo bay to the flyer's cockpit.

The Veetanho ship wasn't nearly as nice as his had been. The interior was dingy, and it looked as if it hadn't been thoroughly cleaned in a while. From what he could tell by looking through the displays—more carelessness that they hadn't fully shut down—the ship was severely underpowered, with engines that had been governed to less-than-optimal performance. Disdain rippled through him, making his fur rise between his shoulder blades. Why do something like that to a perfectly good atmospheric shuttle? Sure, it would save fuel, but not enough to justify hamstringing the entire drive train!

The scuffing sound of footsteps behind him recalled him to his present objective, and he turned and saw the crew returning. He quickly punched in a series of navigational database commands, then pulled back behind one of the two pilot stations in the ship. And he waited.

"That's it," one of the Veetanho said, and Fssik felt the *thunk* of the cargo door closing reverberate through the airframe. "Let's get back to the city. I hate being out this far."

"You saw how they cut back the jungle," the other Veetanho answered, her voice higher pitched than the first. "And anyway, there've never been any trees up here. We're perfectly safe."

The first Veetanho snorted. "Nowhere on this entropy-cursed planet is perfectly safe, Sheloo. You know that. I hate this place. I wish we could go home. Hey! What was that for?"

"Because you sound like a whiny brat. You heard General Deero. This is our home now. It's what we've got. So, shut your mouth and let's do the job."

The first Veetanho opened her mouth to fire back a response that, judging by her wrinkled expression, would explain her disdain for her peer's suggestion, but by then, Fssik was on her.

He struck from within his cloak, knives in hand, moving like water as he reached out to slice the tendons in both of her lower legs. She stumbled forward, her arms reaching out as she fell into her crewmate. Fssik continued to flow. He leaped up along the back of the pilot seat, then flipped in midair and severed her windpipe and main throat artery before she could let out more than a squeak.

"What in entropy?" the other one asked, shoving the not-quite-dead body off her and stumbling backward. Unfortunately for her, she had nowhere to go since the cockpit seats were right there. The moment of disorientation cost her dearly, for Fssik wasn't done. He landed on the instrument console behind her, with a knife in each hand. He drove the blades in through her back, penetrating the tough layers of fur and hide, and pierced her lungs just below the shoulder blades in a pinpoint strike he'd been studying and practicing for years.

Veetanho anatomy didn't have many vulnerabilities, but there were some, and Hunters knew them all.

The second Veetanho made a strange sort of gasping sound, then she, too, slumped to the flyer's deck.

Fssik dropped his cloak, powered down the flyer, and cleaned his knives on the Veetanho's uniform. Then he exited through the back and headed toward the building.

It turned out that it didn't take many Veetanho to crew the enormous defoliant weapon. One by one, he stalked them, delivering quick, silent deaths that any training molly would find acceptable. There was a time and a place to play with violence—this wasn't it. He moved quickly and silently as he slashed throats and stabbed through eyes and ears.

When he'd dispatched his seventh or eighth victim, the Basreen made herself known.

"Good hunting, Hunter," she said, and he looked up just in time to watch her wing down from the corner of the wall near the ceiling. "Many good kills."

"You too," he said, for he'd seen evidence of her work on the way in—Veetanho bodies lying twisted in the frozen throes of agony as Basreen nerve poison did its damage. "Is that all of them?"

"Yes. No more hearts beat. Only yours and mine."

"You can hear my heart beating? That's how you know where I am when I'm cloaked!"

The Basreen rustled her wings in what Fssik was coming to realize was a form of laughter. "Secret."

"I will only tell Ziva, I promise."

"Good promise. Go get them?"

"Yes," he said. "I don't have a clue how to disable the weapon without them."

"Yes. Burn it down."

"Well, something like that," he said with a grin. "Come, Basreen. Let's go find our friends."

* * *

A llied Fleet, this is Recon One transmitting in the blind. Be advised, enemy has developed and deployed a radioactive defoliant weapon that has eliminated the jungle surrounding the city in a 5km ring. All drop zones are exposed. I repeat, all drop zones are now completely exposed. Recon One reports two KIA but has possession of the defoliant weapon. Will destroy. Request further orders.

Fssik sat cradled in Ziva's arms as the message scrolled across the improvised display. Sparks and Pocket had cobbled together a rudimentary comm terminal from the weapon control components they'd ripped out. Between that and their improvised antenna from the scaffolding that held the weapon, they were pretty sure this would work.

Mostly.

"That's it," Sparks said. "How long do you want to wait for a reply?"

"How long is it going to take to destroy the scaffolding and the weapon?"

"Honestly, not terribly long," Tiffany said. "It's really not that different from your standard automated artillery. Looks like they just modified it to shoot frangible shells filled with that nasty hot goop. Thank all the stars above the tank for that stuff was empty when we got here."

"Yeah," Ziva said, and Fssik felt a tremor of disgust and fear shudder through her. "All right. Let's start breaking shit, and then—" She cut off as the terminal flickered, and new words began to scroll across the display.

Message received. Will adjust accordingly. Continue with neutralization plans, then proceed to the following coordinates no later than attached time.

A quick burst of data manifested as a string of characters that Fssik couldn't decode. Pocket apparently could, though, because he began frantically inputting them into the data slate he had appropriated from the facility.

"I've got it," he said after a moment. "It's—"

"Wait!" Fssik said, pointing at the display as it began to scroll again. "There's more."

Hold on. We're coming.

* * * * *

Chapter Fifteen

It took another three nights to get to the coordinates the message specified. They'd scavenged what they could carry from the Veetanho outpost, but there hadn't been much that was useful. Lots of ammunition, but no food, and only a few emergency flex packs of water. Nothing really in the way of first aid gear, and no nanites to replace the team's spent stash.

The trek wasn't easy. They proceeded almost due south, along the spine of the mountain range to which the peak belonged. Though they dropped down below the summit to be on the far side of the city, vegetation was scarce and scrawny at this elevation, and Fssik hated the neck-itchiness of being exposed.

But there was no moon, so that was a piece of luck. Fssik found himself looking up at the icy stars glittering in the sky and wondering—hoping, really—that his clan and his allies were up there. Were close.

Hold on, the message had said. *We're coming.*

So, he, Ziva, Sparks, Tiffany, Pocket, the Basreen mother, and her two daughters pushed on. Before the end of the first night, the Basreeni had hunted enough of the small ground sprinters that each Human had one to eat. Fssik hunted his own.

"Remove the tail at the base and save it," he advised Ziva and the others when they stopped to camp as first light began to paint the rocks around them rosy. "Their venom makes an excellent poison. It's non-lethal, except in huge doses, but very painful, so don't touch

293

the stinger at the tip. Then you just remove the head, split the breastbone, and crack them open. The largest muscles run along the spine and down into each of the six legs."

"You eat these raw?" Pocket asked, and Fssik slow blinked at the barely disguised distaste in his voice.

"I do. You might enjoy cooking yours. There's plenty of fat in the meat, despite how active the sprinters are. If you roast it over our fire for a few minutes, I think you'll find it's quite good. Don't forget the organs!"

The next two days passed in a similar fashion. They hiked from sunset to sunrise, following the trail on Pocket's pilfered data slate. The Basreeni and Fssik hunted as they went, though the sprinters and other prey became increasingly scarce. Despite everyone's best attempts, their strength began to wane. Even Fssik found himself stumbling over the uneven ground as the nights wore on. He wanted nothing more than to curl up and cuddle in Ziva's arms, but she was exhausted enough without the additional burden of carrying his weight.

On the third night, disaster struck again. Heavy clouds had gathered during the day while they slept, and shortly after they started out that evening, the skies opened, and rain pelted down in torrents. Within minutes, Fssik felt his fur plastered to his body. The extra weight of the water dragged at him as he leaped from boulder to boulder along their nonexistent trail. The ground quickly became saturated, and more than once, his Humans lost their precarious bipedal footing and fell down a slope or onto a rocky pile.

The Basreeni quickly sought refuge inside the Humans' collars, but the rains hit so hard, even that was only dubious shelter.

At least they'll stay warm… ish, pressed next to Human skin like that.

Fssik recognized the jealousy in his thoughts and pushed it away. Ziva couldn't carry him right now; she could barely keep herself upright.

The rains continued through the night, slowing their progress to a crawl. The mud began to accumulate on the slopes, making them nearly impossible to climb. Fortunately, their path had brought them down back below the tree line, so they had *something* to grab onto for assistance... most of the time. Fssik's feet became coated with layer upon layer of sticky mud.

Then the wind started.

At first, Fssik hoped the wind would dissipate the clouds and give them some relief, but the downpour didn't abate. Instead, the water started pelting them from the side, carried by the fury of the wind as it whipped through the mountain passes. Thunder cracked overhead, shuddering through Fssik's bones, and blinding light ripped across the sky.

For a moment, panic seized him by the throat. Had the Veetanho found them and fired their weapon again?

No. Don't be stupid, he berated himself, sucking in a deep breath and willing his pounding heartbeat to decelerate. *You destroyed it. You stuffed the charges down the barrel yourself. That weapon will never fire again. Stop acting like a scared kit on your first contract. You're a Deo of your clan. They need you. Get your shit together, as Ziva would say.*

Fssik had never been sure what, exactly, one accomplished by collecting fecal matter in a single place. Other than hygiene, perhaps. That was always a worthy goal.

Between his self-administered pep talk and his slightly distracting thoughts about the weirdness of Human idioms, Fssik brought his sudden flash of panic back under control. The thunderstorm continued to rage overhead, with ragged bolts of searing white—*not deadly orange*—light flashing simultaneously with the deafening concussion of thunder.

"I can't see a damn thing out here!" Sparks cursed. "I'm going to fall on my ass! We need to hole up and let the storm pass."

"We'll miss our target time if we wait," Ziva shouted back. "We've got to keep going. Here, let me lead. I can see better in the dark than you. Fssik will bring up the rear and keep us together."

"I wish we still had the climbing ropes," Tiffany said. "I'm terrified I'm going to veer off and get lost. I can't see my hand in front of my face."

"Basreen!" Fssik said, as an idea struck him. "Help me gather some Mera vines."

The mother Basreen poked her head up out of Pocket's collar. "Mera vines hurt. Thorny."

"They'll cause a rash on Human skin, but better that than having them break ankles in the dark and the mud," Fssik said. He slogged forward to the nearest tree and started to climb. Sure enough, in the mid-level branches, he found some of the ubiquitous vines, with their short, hair-like thorns. Despite the sharpness of his knives, it took him a few minutes to cut through the tough vine, but eventually, he had gathered a respectable length. The Basreen mother and her children helped him gather the vine into a coil beneath the tree, and Ziva came over to help him lift it.

"Use gloves if you have them," he warned. "A Mera rash won't injure you permanently, but it will itch and burn like an allergic reaction."

"Got it," she said. "Khatash doesn't have any safe vines?"

"These *are* the safe vines," he said, as the lightning illuminated her pale, wet face and slicked hair for a second. Thunder cracked overhead, and he felt the booming in his chest. The sound of her sardonic chuckle floated toward him under the ringing in his ears from the concussive sound.

"Of course," she said. "Let's go."

The Humans who had gloves used them, and the others pulled sleeves down over their hands or wrapped rags around their fingers. They used the vine as a sort of handrail-rope—something to help them stay together in the darkness. It would have been better if they could have tied it around themselves, but it was too short for that, and no one wanted to risk the rash on a larger expanse of skin.

With the vine, they moved even slower in the darkness. The howling storm continued to pummel them, driving Ziva to her knees several times as the mud thickened and became slicker. Pocket tried to keep the data slate out of the rain as much as possible, so he didn't check it that often, but when they did look at it, its message was not encouraging. They were barely making progress toward their goal.

Fssik began to feel the weight of despair settle into his stomachs. He fought it down and pushed on because he didn't know what else to do, but in his mind, the certainty built.

They weren't going to make it.

They had crested one rise and started down the other side when Ziva let out a yell of warning. Thanks to his night vision, Fssik wasn't holding on to the Mera vine, so he didn't feel what happened. He heard Ziva's cry and saw Sparks' head disappear. He raced to the top of the slope and looked down at what had suddenly become a sheer cliff.

"Ziva!" he called out.

"I'm here! Be careful, my Hunter! The entire slope gave way under us!"

"Are you hurt?"

There was a long pause, and he didn't wait for her answer. Dread and love tangled inside him and flashed through his nerves to push back the soaking cold that enveloped him. He leaped forward, stepping as lightly as he knew how, darting from an outcropping to the side of the cliff to a protruding root to a tumbled rock as he zig-zagged to the base of the hill.

"I'm all right," Ziva said, her voice breathless. "Wrenched my knees, hit my head, but I'll be okay. Find the others!"

"I'm here!" Sparks called out nearby. Fssik blinked in his direction, then darted over and found the Human pushing himself up to a seated position. "I'm okay, I think. I hit and rolled. Are you all right, little friend?"

The Basreen poked her head out of his collar and shook herself, then she emerged fully and spread her wings, as if checking their function.

"I well," she said. "Find others. Find Mother." She let out a terrifying screech that hovered just on the edge of Fssik's audible range. To his great relief, two answering screeches came back.

Slowly, one by one, they located the members of their group. All were living, all were hurt. As the rain pounded down, Fssik and Pocket helped them gather under the dubious and incomplete shelter of a couple of trees that listed in the storm's fury.

"We can't keep going," Ziva said, her voice soaked with exhaustion. "We've got to stop and wait out the storm."

"But—" Fssik started.

"I know," she said, "but we physically can't, my Hunter. Maybe once the storm abates, we can try to send another message—"

"There is no need," Tsan said as she stepped out of the darkness toward them. "We are already here."

* * *

The rain still pelted down, and the wind still flung it sideways into them, but the fierce, bright joy that burned in Fssik's mind overtook the sodden discomfort and seared away the grinding despair.

"Dama!" he said, unable to keep the incredulity out of his voice.

"Deo, I greet you. You look as if you've had some trouble."

"Some, Dama," Ziva said, her tone a reflection of the relief that churned within Fssik. "We're hurt, and I fear—"

"Do not trouble yourself," Tsan said. "I do not come alone. Deo Fssik will accompany me to our camp—it isn't far—and we will return with others to help you. As I said, brave ones, you've made it. We're here."

And so, Fssik found himself moving in a dreamlike state, following the dama through the thickening foliage, down the slope to a sheltered clearing, where a ship sat at the center of a bustling, growing camp. Beings moved to and fro in light from various sources, and it took Fssik a long moment to identify them. Whether from fatigue or relief or whatever, his brain seemed slow to act, slow to perceive.

Perhaps he, too, had reached his limit.

"Tula and some of hers will return with us," Tsan said as she returned to his side and rubbed against him. Though the rain still pelted down, the canopy above was thicker, and he stood in a mostly sheltered spot. She felt warm and smelled like home.

"Tula?" Fssik said, blinking rapidly as he tried to make his brain focus.

"I, Tula of Thunder Fist. I greet you, Deo."

Fssik looked up, up higher, and up higher still until he saw the face of a female Lumar looking solemnly down at him.

"I greet you, Lumar—Tula. My apologies, I—"

"Deo Fssik's companion is at risk, along with his team. We must move quickly to bring them in, Tula."

"Lead me," she said and bent to gather Fssik in her lower arms. At first, he stiffened. Her arms and hands felt both like and completely unlike Ziva's familiar embrace. For just a second, he considered leaping down and insisting that he walk but then he suddenly felt the leaden weight of exhaustion in his body, and he knew she was being kind.

"This way," Tsan said, and started back down the trail.

Tula transferred him to her upper set of arms, and Fssik eventually climbed up onto her shoulder as she stepped—surprisingly quietly, for one so large and bulky—out after Tsan.

"Is this comfortable for you?" Fssik asked, feeling awkward.

"Yes."

"Thank you for carrying me."

"Hunters and Thunder Fist allies. Allies help. You hurt?"

"Not me, but members of my team are. There was a mudslide, and before that, the Veetanho surprised us with their radioactive weapon. We lost two people."

"My condolences."

"Thank you, Tula."

"Welcome, Deo."

Lumar moved fast, with great strength. It didn't take long for them to return to where Ziva and the rest of the team huddled together for warmth against the torrent. Tsan introduced everyone, and in typical Dama fashion, directed each of the Lumar to lift one of the battered Humans and carry them back.

"Which is yours?" Tula asked, and when Fssik pointed out Ziva's shivering form, his new Lumar friend picked her up and held her close in her upper arms.

"Fssik," Ziva murmured. He couldn't move fast enough to get onto her chest. Her skin was so cold and clammy, her lips blue as her body fought to keep her vital organs warm.

"I'm here, my love," he said, moving down and curling up on her chest, with his head up under her chin. "Tula's a friend. She's going to carry us back to their camp where we can get warm. You did it, Ziva. You got us back to our allies."

"Team… effort…" Ziva said, her eyes drifting closed. Tula jostled them, drawing a sound of protest from Ziva.

"No sleep," the Lumar said. "Sleep bad in cold. Stay awake. Almost there."

"Stay with me, my Human," Fssik pled. He could feel the clammy coldness of Ziva's skin. Tula was right, he couldn't let Ziva sleep and slip into hypothermia. Even though the air held its usual warmth, being wet through was always a risk.

"Not… Human…" Ziva murmured. "Venator."

"My companion," Fssik corrected himself. "My dear one. Don't you dare fucking leave me, my Ziva. Not now."

"Never," she whispered, and her lips quirked in a smile when she heard the all-too-Human curse from his lips.

As before, Fssik marveled at the speed with which the Lumar moved through the undergrowth. He lost track of the other members of the team and trusted that his dama would see them safely to the camp as he focused only on his Ziva.

He'd resorted to ever-so-gently pressing into her skin with his claws to keep her awake when they broke into the circle of light that surrounded the camp.

"Zuul ship," Tula said, heading directly to where it sat near the edge of the clearing. "Medic on board. Warm there. Food, too."

"Thank you, Tula," Fssik said, meaning it with every fiber of his being.

"Welcome, Deo."

"Tula? Who do you have here?" The voice was unfamiliar, but Fssik soon caught sight of the speaker—a male Zuul, wearing a uniform with a distinctive device on the chest.

"Hunter Deo and Companion. Ziva Alcuin. Hypothermic and injured ankle."

"Bring them in," he said. "I greet you, Deo. My name is Ace'to. I'm a medic."

"I greet you, Medic Ace'to," Fssik said. "Please help my person."

"That's what I do. Right through here, Tula. Lay them on the table there."

Fssik hadn't spent a lot of time around Zuul, and certainly Aryo had never let him get as close as Ace'to did. The medic stepped up to help Tula lay Ziva's limp form on his table and then immediately bustled about, finding heating blankets and beginning his checks and tests of her condition. Fssik hustled out of the way when Ace'to asked Tula to help remove Ziva's wet clothing so she could finally get warm, then he cuddled close to the side of her face, stroking her with his cheekbones as they worked to heal her.

Other Zuul and Lumar moved around him, and Fssik saw the other members of his team being brought in, but they stayed on the periphery of his attention. He was here, now, with his Ziva, and if by warming her and rumbling his purr he could help her battle against the cold and the wet and the exhaustion… well, that was what he would do.

Not yet, he whispered in his mind, addressing his old friend death. *You cannot take her yet. I need her to live, to thrive. She cannot die while I yet live.*

"I greet you, Medic. How are your patients?"

Fssik didn't know how much later it was when Tsan's voice filled the small sickbay of the Zuul shuttle. He looked up and met her eyes and returned the slow blink she gave him.

"Dama," Ace'to said calmly. "They'll all live. They need rest and warmth, and I had to set Pocket's arm, but they will all live."

"You have my gratitude, Healer," Tsan said, and Fssik wondered if Ace'to understood the subtle compliment in the change of title.

"We are allies, Dama. This is what I do. I must tell you, though, I will not release any of them for another night or so. They need rest more than anything else." He walked around Ziva's bed as he spoke, adjusting the blanket he'd draped over her now safely sleeping form.

"A wise dama does not argue with a Healer unless she must. My need is not so great. Our forces are in place as planned, but the Hussars must take the orbital station before anything else can proceed. I have no doubt they will, but we will not be ready to move for another ninenight or so."

"Jim?" Ziva asked, stirring slightly and proving she wasn't asleep after all.

"Yes, Damita," Tsan said, slow blinking. "Your lover has provided his promised forces and is on his ship as we speak. But you must rest, so your Healer does not murder you before you can see him again."

"Or so I do not," Fssik said, rubbing against Ziva's ear. She let out a breathy laugh, then let her head fall to the side, her breath almost instantly becoming soft and even.

"That ought to do it," Ace'to growled in satisfaction. He stood on the far side of Ziva's bed, looking up from the site of her intravenous drip. "I knew she was fighting sleep, so I gave her a mild sedative. She'll be out for the rest of the day."

"Clever Healer," Tsan said, approval in her tone. Fssik, too, found himself slow blinking in appreciation. At least until Ace'to's dark eyes fell squarely on him.

"You're next, Deo," the Healer said, with an edge of promise in his tone. "Unless you settle down and get. Some. Rest."

Fssik looked at Tsan, who merely slow blinked at him, then shook his head.

"Keep your needles over there, Healer," he said. "I will do as you require… and thank you."

"Sleep well, Deo," Tsan said. "You're safe here with us."

* * *

Tsan sat and curled her tail close around her, the scratchy fabric of the Zuuls' emergency tent remarkably dry underneath.

"Zuul have lived on many planets," A'nief had said, his jaw dropped in a Zuul smile. "We have experienced jungles before."

None quite like Khatash's, but their shelter did the minimum to protect them from creeping mud and soaking water as they spoke, which was a remarkable feat in and of itself, given the weather.

Not unlike their chances in the fight ahead—it would be remarkable, but not impossible, for them to win decisively. The Veetanho had not yet rooted into all of Khatash; their forces remained burrowed in the city.

This new ability to eradicate the jungle from a distance changed more than a few things, however. Tsan and her allies could take nothing for granted about where the Veetanho were or weren't. The combat drop of the various Horsemen would no longer have the cover of the jungle, nor would it have the dangers. This dropping into an unprotected, open area was something mercenary companies had quite a bit of experience with. The ones who did that sort of thing and survived, at any rate.

Their allies were en route, or currently above them getting into place. They didn't have overwhelming numbers or firepower, but they had—

Her thoughts snapped to a halt, and her nose twitched. Faintly, weaving through the deep loam of the jungle and the bright mineral smell of rain, came a Hunter scent that was unfamiliar to her.

Impossible.

She'd met each of the few that were left from Khatash, one way or another, and all that had been born since. This...

Her ears swiveled and her pupils widened, but beyond that faint trail...

"Assembled beings," a roughened voice announced from somewhere to the left of the tent in the line of draping vines, "you are in my jungle."

Fur lifted down Tsan's back, and she turned with forced slowness and padded to the tent's entrance.

"Hunter," she said, holding her hands at her sides, with claws sheathed. "We are in our jungle, and we greet you." Questions she couldn't yet ask crowded in her chest, and she lashed her tail once before continuing. "I am Tsan, Dama of Clan Tamir. We return to take back our home."

"Dama?" The voice skewed upward, nearly the yowl of a kit, but the words that followed were again in that stone-scraped tone, deep and bitter. "No *dama* would have survived, not from what I've heard. How do you come here?"

Tsan stepped into the rain, eyes slit against the force of it. She didn't reach to pull down her goggles. Let the other Hunter see her. Let the other Hunter know.

"Some survived. I was off planet when the Veetanho came. So were others. We could not come sooner, as there was too much to do. But if we had known…"

"Known what?" A flicker of movement between the vines pulled Tsan's gaze, but the other Hunter did not drop her field. "That I was here? That one Hunter survived because she had no pinplants and didn't know what had happened? You would have come for me?" A shiver of sound—a laugh more like a rattle of bones—threaded through the words.

"We would have found a way."

"I had work to do here." Movement again, the other Hunter coming closer. Tsan did not tense, but she flattened her ears briefly in warning. "Veetanho to kill."

"We did much the same, Hunter." Tsan's voice was biting, but she softened it for the next words. "We prepared. We are immune to the Veetanho's freeze ray now, and we have had kits. Many, many kits."

"Why would you lie to me?" The voice broke, closer again, followed by the rasp of bones on bones. "*How* are you here?"

"Aryss," Tsan said, only a hair louder. "Fssik. Pura. Criuch." She continued to name each of the Hunters who had come on her ship, and they responded to her immediately, stepping into the storm without their fields. "Perhaps you couldn't scent them in the rain, Hunter, but we are many now. Not as many as before, but soon… soon there will be more. We will return to our home, as we have returned to you, and take up new homes across the galaxy."

The Hunter appeared, her shape fuzzy in a way Tsan couldn't decipher for a moment. She bounded forward, her body cutting through the rain. Her tail was pierced through with bones, as were her ears, which explained the odd outline. Tsan kept her own body loose, offering no overt threat or tension at the other Hunter's approach.

"How?" she asked again, and the desperation of it hit Tsan in the midsection as the Hunter stopped a short distance in front of her.

"With allies." Tsan curled her tail in invitation, her ears pricked forward. "Come inside, and we'll tell you all, and hear of your—"

The Hunter's scent carried clearly through the rain at this distance. She smelled of jungle, rage, sadness…

Aryo.

Tsan spread her claws wide, and her pupils narrowed to the smallest of slits. She wrested control of herself, the effort leaving her winded. Not Aryo's blood, nothing that spoke of violence. Just... Aryo.

"Hunter," she said, showing her fingerpads with claws sheathed, noting the other Hunter had stiffened but not leaped away. "You know one of my clan."

"I know of no Clan Tamir," she replied, head tilted, one ear twisted back.

"Whispering Fear. I was Dama of Whispering Fear."

"Ah." A strangled sound, laugh and yowl twisted together, surrounded that word. The other Hunters had moved closer, though all held their silence. "That clan I know."

"Where is she?"

"I..." The Hunter drooped, her tail sliding back into the mud. "I have not seen her or several of my... the others since the Veetanho bled the jungle."

One more loss is not the end. The words were hers, though they came only faintly in her mind, garbled through a thunderous ringing in her skull. *So many have been lost. So many to be avenged. Aryo is one more.*

The scream built in her throat, but she swallowed it, kept her claws sheathed, and held her ears still. The ringing continued, but she could ignore that too. Soon there would be violence. Soon there would be vengeance. Soon she could stop to mourn. Not yet. Not now.

"Hunter," Tsan said, her voice smooth as ever, as though nothing clattered in endless waves inside her head. "We have a battle ahead of us to take back our home. Will you be a part of it?"

"Dama," the Hunter replied, sorrow joining the weight of her scent. "Welcome to our negotiation."

* * *

"The Basreeni aircraft are still in their hangars," the Hunter said, tapping her claws on A'nief's small folding table.

"More air support would be nice." Ref hummed in his throat, considering. "The SalSha are very good, but there's only so many of them. How likely is it the jets can still fly?"

"I don't know that the Veetanho have done any maintenance," the Hunter replied, her shrug indifferent. "Nor if they sabotaged them."

"That would be a waste of effort," A'nief interjected, flicking one ear in dismissal. "They didn't bother to destroy them because they didn't believe anyone was coming to use them, but they wouldn't throw away a resource."

"Not when they could strip them for parts."

"Or sell them down the way when the time is right. There are enough races who could fit inside and put them to use with minimal retrofitting." Fssik's shrug matched the Hunter's, though his tail was still behind him.

"Aryss."

"Dama?"

"You flew a Basreeni at one time, did you not?"

"I did." She glanced at her brother. "Pura has trained to repair machinery. She has not worked on a Basreeni specifically, but…"

"Between the two of you, you should be able to get in and make a judgement if it's worth further effort." Tsan nodded and touched her tail to Aryss' in approval. "If they are flyable, do not take to the air until we have confirmed contact with the SalSha."

"We will give them no false targets," Aryss agreed, with a slow blink. "If it's possible, we'll call for more pilots. How many do you think we can field?"

"At least five with Basreen experience," Tsan replied after a moment. "Fssik, had you marked any of the younger Hunters to be skilled pilots?"

Kits trained in all avenues of Hunter life as soon as they were old enough. They were not equally skilled in everything, but the aim of the last five years had been to have enough Hunters for two things, and two things only—the survival of their species and the retaking of Khatash. Training had therefore been critical, and Tsan had paid attention. She also valued her Deo's opinion.

"Yes, Dama." Fssik's ears swiveled, and his head dipped ever so slightly. "Justice is excellent, as is Luna." He paused and listed a handful more, one ear tilted to the side.

"Serviceable by your estimation is likely quite good by any other's," Tsan said, her tail waving approval of his standards. "Please tell them to standby in case Aryss and Pura find the Basreeni to be airworthy."

"Thunder Fist deploy small group if need backup," Tula said, tapping both left hands on the table. "Let know how many Veetanho around hangar."

"Excellent, Tula, thank you." Aryss inclined her head to the Lumar, who grinned back at her.

"Good plan." Tula lifted one of her right hands and tilted it in a question. "Time short. What else?"

"Hold a moment," the Hunter said, darting out of the tent without another word.

Tula turned her gaze to Tsan, who answered with a small shrug. They had prepared all they could ahead of the signal from the Cavaliers, indicating they were in position. Things would happen very fast from there, but now there was little else they could do.

"I didn't believe you," the Hunter said, reappearing a handful of moments later, "when you said all the allies were equal partners. Zia had much to say about how Lumar are treated by other races."

"You signaled someone." Tsan didn't need to question; she spoke the words as a statement.

"I have lost contact with nearly half of the sigiled beings who have fought with me for five years." The Hunter lifted her head proudly, shaking the bones pierced through her tail. "The rest await my word."

"You did not trust us?" Tsan had yet to decide if she were amused or insulted, so kept her voice neutral.

"I needed to know what chance they'd have. If we were to fail, the addition of five beings would not make a difference, but holding them in reserve means some fight will continue, even beyond us."

"And now?"

"You listen to your allies. They are free to question, which means they are also free to present better options. It took me a long while in the jungle to learn the same." The Hunter spread her arms wide. "I am very, very good at hunting. Others are better at war. Like Zia." She glanced sidelong at Tula. "She is a Lumar disposed of by the Veetanho, who has dedicated herself to revenge."

"Hm. Good." Tula folded her lower arms. "Veetanho like waste Lumar lives. Better to do to them."

"The thing about sowing is... eventually it comes time to reap." Ref chuckled, and several of the Venatores echoed it. Tsan didn't know the metaphor—humans loved such things—but she appreciated the tone as he continued. "For hundreds of years, the Veet have been out there doing what they wanted to who they wanted. Now, that's coming back to bite them in their furry, ratty asses like they can't imagine."

"I don't think they'll like this harvest much." Ziva's smile was slow and as deadly as the rest of her. Tsan slow blinked her approval before speaking.

"Then let us begin."

* * * * *

Chapter Sixteen

"*H*ot drop a go. On mark.*"

The message from Cartwright came with the correct codes and a countdown. A'nief confirmed his receipt of a similar message. The Cavaliers had been able to provide three companies of CASPers, but were short on dropships, and the Zuul had had less heavy armor troops, but plenty of pilots and transportation. Tsan had considered it a match perfectly made, and no one had argued too strenuously.

At sundown, it would begin in earnest. Before the execution of a contract, she felt nothing but calm—she planned, she waited, she acted. Occasionally, a surprise happened, and she adapted.

This, however planned it all was, required moving pieces so large and beyond her control, it was not calm she felt. Then again, she had never had a personal stake in those contracts; she had never cared one way or another about the life of the target, beyond the value of the contract.

"Thunder Fist take lead," Tula said as she and Arkak stepped away from each other. Arkak bellowed something the translators didn't catch, and the rest of the company roared in response. Zia and the Hunter exchanged glances, and the two Lumar who had arrived after the Hunter's signal moved in with Thunder Fist.

"Insho'Ze, in position," A'nief announced, and the Zuul marched into place.

Tsan didn't declare anything. The Hunters and their companions moved, placing themselves between the forces for ease of movement. Their goal was the council building, where they had the best chance of finding the largest number of Veetanho.

When the countdown ended, A'nief simply said, "Now," and everyone surged forward.

Ref, the unattached Humans, and several of the Zuul remained in their perches to lay down covering fire as needed. Tsan and the Hunter had done their best to make their positions as safe as possible, and the rest would be luck.

Luck certainly seemed with them as they ran down the mountain. The streaks of light above, visible even through the rain and lighter canopies, showed the arrival of the Cartwright Cavaliers and Golden Horde.

There was no immediate answering gunfire. No huge explosions from the city.

Surely the Veetanho weren't completely unprepared?

Around Tsan were the noises of the jungle, spiking and fading away in ragged patterns as they moved through it. Her ears strained for the sounds of combat, but either they were too far away, or it had yet to begin in earnest.

The Hunters who had taken invisible point reported no traps and no troops lying in wait.

They reached the base of the mountain. A much younger Tsan would have slow blinked at the ease of it, but now, her fur lifted in patches, and her skin jumped at what wasn't there.

The Veetanho were not fools. She and her allies had moved in stealth as much as possible, but there was no hiding all the ships coming through the gate. No hiding orbital insertion at these numbers. No missing the number of CASPers streaking through the sky.

Her ears swiveled, but there was nothing.

Fssik dropped his field at the first designated meeting point and stepped onto the path long enough to shake his head once before disappearing again. No traps. No enemy contact. No allies there yet. They couldn't charge into what was meant to be a war zone, so they'd planned to pause here, confer with the boots on the ground, and then move forward as needed. Only so far, it didn't seem to be much of a war zone...

Have they all taken poison to avoid us? Tsan wondered, not entirely sure if she meant it as sarcasm or not.

The Hunters and their companions faded into the jungle to secure their perimeter, and the Lumar and Zuul took up their positions. Tsan flexed her claws, longing to dig them into the tall tree nearby, one of the last between them and the city. She could climb to the top and peer over the dead zone, and *see* what was happening...

It was a foolish urge, and she ignored it. Within minutes, there was a stir to her right, and a Human in a Cavaliers uniform strode into their small clearing, with one visible Hunter accompanying him.

"Didn't lose anyone in the drop, and we're working on clearing a path to the target. Doesn't seem..." He stopped, head tilted slightly, hand half-raised. "There they are. Resistance in the southwest sector, getting hot fast. We'll do our best to keep the corridor clear."

Tsan pictured the map, traced the highlight Cartwright had suggested in her head, and nodded.

"We'll aim for the council chamber from here."

"Might have more air fight soon." Arkak said, already moving before the Human could ask any follow up questions. Tsan noted Tula's attention, and the Cavalier's confused expression.

"The Veetanho did not destroy the Basreeni fighters to the northwest of the city. We sent a small force to see if they're still usable and will confirm with the SalSha if they are."

"Got it, will pass that on. Air support should be kicking in any…" He lifted a hand, and as if on cue, something large exploded. "Now."

"We have allies in the city," the Hunter said, appearing at Tsan's side. "We tried to warn them, but…"

"The SalSha aren't going for the soft targets. They should have plenty of warning to get out, if the rats leave them anywhere to go."

"We are all in danger until this is done." Tsan shook her head, tail lashing. "There is little else we can do but continue."

"Only way out is through," the Cavalier said, cheerfully.

"Then let us go through," Tsan replied, and the Hunter spat to the side as her ears moved in agreement.

* * *

Fssik ran beside Ziva, reveling in the feel of his body now that it had been restored to full strength and fitness. Ace'to had been an exacting taskmaster of a Healer, enforcing his will upon his patients by means of medication, if necessary, but one could hardly argue with the results. Though he still occasionally woke gasping from nightmares where glowing orange light reached out to grab him, for the most part, Fssik was as good as new.

As were Ziva and the rest of the team. They ran beside the formation of Zuul warriors and Thunder Fist Lumar, weapons at the ready, eyes resolute. Come what may, they were in this, and it was time to finish it.

Only no one seemed to have told the Veetanho.

They encountered no resistance until after they made contact with a scout from the Cavaliers. He'd reported only light contact, as well, but had promised to keep their corridor clear. So far, Jim's people seemed to be living up to that promise because Fssik, Tsan, and the others continued unhindered, striking straight for the heart of the city and the old council chambers, where the Veetanho had built their HQ.

A thrumming roar of rockets ahead echoed through the foliage, and the various members of the strike force raised their weapons. Fssik pulled his quintessence around him, and Ziva took aim, while the Zuul and Lumar commander called a halt.

Trees crashed, and a CASPer crashed down in their path. A hatch in the front cracked open.

"Kill aliens!" a voice from within shouted. Ziva laughed.

"Get paid!" she shouted back. A Human head emerged as the hatch opened all the way, exposing a man wearing a broad grin.

"Figured that was a quick way to let you know not to shoot or stab me," the Asbaran Solutions driver said. "I greet you, Hunters, Lumar, Zuul... and people. Quite the diverse force you've got here."

"We are allies," Tsan said, her voice guarded. "You have news?"

"Yep! You're coming to the defoliated area. Best we can tell, the background radiation's well below danger levels, but I wouldn't go rolling around in the dirt if you can help it. My unit's got a klick-wide path cleared all the way through the damage to the edge of the city, and Proud Fist is holding a beachhead for you on the other side. You'll want to keep your heads down, though, the Veet got some of their aircraft up, and the SalSha are giving 'em hell, but they don't have 'em locked down quite yet."

"What is happening in the city?" the jungle Hunter, whom Fssik could still barely believe was real, asked.

"Don't know. Not my department. I'm off to shoot some more rats. Good hunting!"

With that, he disappeared back into his CASPer, which flexed at the knees then blasted back up through the last line of trees, leaving a wide hole where it had been.

"Asbaran was to drop on the outskirts and push in from the flanks," Tsan said. "The fact that they've made it this far should be very good news. It means they're grinding the Veetanho between them and the Cavaliers."

"Should be," the Jungle Dama, as Fssik had begun to call her in his mind, said. "I hear concern in your voice, Dama."

"'When a contract is too easy, check to see who's being hunted,'" Tsan said with the air of someone repeating an old saying. "My fur won't quite settle."

"You think this is a trap," Ziva said, nodding. It wasn't a question.

"It's possible."

"It's likely, given the wily rats," Ref said. "But then, that begs the question, what are we gonna do about it? Like the other guy said, it seems to me the only way out of this is through."

"Y-yes," Tsan said, her eyes narrowing. "We have allies, and we are strong. I cannot see another way. We will push on as planned, and when the rats spring their trap, we will just have to turn it back on them. They cannot know what we are bringing to the fight."

Let's hope they don't, Fssik thought. He exchanged a quick look with Ziva, but the formations started moving again, and the two of them had to hustle to keep up.

* * *

The dirt was orange.

When he first stepped onto it, fear rippled through him, raising his fur, making him hesitate. But all around him, Zuul, Lumar, Humans, and even his beloved Ziva ran ahead. Their boots kicked up small puffs of orange dust that made his breath stutter in his lungs, but nothing happened. No sickly glowing light, no melting flesh and vegetation. Nothing.

Just orange dirt.

Fssik snarled against his fear and shoved it back, then jumped forward, bracing for the touch of his feet on the discolored dirt.

He felt nothing. No burn, no pain. It was just dirt.

Rage misted red in his sight, and he shook his head to clear it. *They will pay,* he promised himself. *For making me fear, for taking my home, for killing my clan… for all of it. The Veetanho have much to answer for, and I'm here to ask ALL my questions!*

Pure fury got him through the worst of his instinctive panic response. He fantasized about ripping through Veetanho skin and fur and making them drink their own poisonous orange nightmare weapon. By the time the force was halfway across the blasted ring that encircled the city, he was calm and thinking clearly again.

"You okay?" Ziva asked him as they paused beside a hillock coated in orange powder.

"I will be," he said, with a snarl. She closed her mouth with a snap and nodded at him, her own eyes haunted. She reached out a hand, and he just had time to rub his head under her fingers before they were up and moving again, crossing the Veetanho-made desert at a run, heading for the buildings beginning to come into view up ahead.

A cheer rose from the ranks of the Lumar at the front of their force as they crossed from the blasted area into the cool green and grey of the city. A building—Fssik thought it had been a warehouse, once—stood with its large doors wide open, and additional Lumar looked out from the upper story windows, where they manned what looked like Lumar-scale crew-served MACs.

"Proud Fist welcomes Thunder Fist and our Allies!" someone shouted, and more cheers went up all around. Not joy—or yes, they were joyous cheers, but it was the kind of dark, savage joy that Fssik felt at the prospect of more Veetanho under his claws. He found himself grinning savagely.

Proud Fist, it turned out, was a kind of sister-company with Thunder Fist. Many of the Lumar knew each other, and Fssik watched as their allies filled their brief rest with back-slapping and four-hand clasps of greeting.

"I greet you, Deo, Damita." Ace'to approached as Fssik was drinking water while they prepared to head out again. "How are you both doing?"

"We're well, Healer," Ziva answered for both, as Fssik lowered his container. "Ready to push on."

"Good," Ace'to said. "I wanted to check on you. I just spoke with Dama Tsan, Tula, and A'nief. When we leave here, we'll be pushing deeper into the market, and they expect resistance to increase."

"Increase from zero?" Fssik said. Despite his best efforts, the discontent in his tone betrayed some of his frustration. Ace'to dropped his jaw in a Zuulish grin.

"That's what they say. I'll be along, but if there are wounded, my job is to get them to the Horde redoubt we'll be passing through. So, I wanted to come and say good luck and wish you both good hunting, since I probably won't get to say it later."

"Thank you, Healer."

"And good hunting to you, too," Fssik added. "If anyone can keep ours alive…"

"Coshke guide me that I might be the one," Ace'to said, nodding his great, triangular head. Then he dropped his jaw in another grin and turned to walk away, just as the call sounded for them to get up and move out.

To maneuver through the warren of streets and the remains of the old market toward the center of the city, their strike force broke into smaller units. They'd stay in contact, visually and via quintessential comms, but they'd move and fight as independent echelons. That being said, they only had one objective—get the Hunters to the Veetanho HQ and decapitate the enemy.

Literally.

Fssik and Ziva were grouped together with Ref, Tsan, and the other Hunters. They moved out, flanked by Zuul and Lumar squads, as they darted from building to building and began to strike toward the center of the city.

Mindful of their earlier experience, Fssik kept an eye on the roof-tops and upper story windows. So, he wasn't looking ahead when an explosion shook the ground and rained debris on them.

"Contact front!" someone shouted, and the Zuul on his immediate left began to fire her weapon. Fssik pulled his quintessence and saw that Ziva had taken cover and was firing back. Another Zuul crouched with her, working in concert to fire whenever his person had to stop and reload.

"Come, Deo," Tsan's voice breezed past him, though he couldn't see her. "Let's go play." The deep satisfaction in her tone promised the most delightful kind of violence, and he shivered in anticipation as he followed. They didn't need concealment, but he and Tsan—and he was pretty sure Criuch, too—darted from one covered position to the next as they moved up and around to approach the enemy from the rear.

He didn't bother to drop his cloak. Fssik simply went to work with knives and claws. They'd happened upon a sizeable patrol of about twenty Veetanho and about fifty of their Lumar slaves. Fssik tried to target primarily the "rats," as Ref was fond of calling them, but he didn't shy away from hamstringing a pair of the big male brawlers when they got in his way. Joy and battle-rage tangled in him as he stalked his prey, cutting them down even while his own people were firing back at them. Blood fountained over his claws as he ripped out a throat, then leaped free to stab a neighboring "rat" through the eyes.

A red haze enveloped his vision, but he didn't care. He didn't need his eyes anyway. He moved by scent and by sound, striking, slashing, stabbing, never stopping, moving relentlessly until someone very far away shouted his name.

"Deo! DEO! FSSIK, stop!"

He blinked suddenly and dropped his cloak. A Human lay on her back under his claws, her hands raised beside her face, terror in her eyes.

"Fssik, stop!" Dama Tsan shouted again, pushing herself into his line of view. "She is one of ours!"

Fssik shook his head, and the red haze receded even further. "I—I apologize," he said. His voice came out as a croak. He abruptly realized he'd been yowling a battle cry as he killed. *Oh, entropy, no!* "Did—did I hurt you?"

The woman shook her head. With his stomachs sinking, he stepped off her and realized that she wore the uniform of the Golden Horde.

"Dama," he gasped. "Did I—"

"No, my Deo," Tsan said, her voice pitched to soothe. "You stopped in time. You have slain many of the enemy but harmed none of our own."

He swallowed hard and turned to face the young Asian woman, who was in the process of getting back up to her feet.

"I greet you, Human Mercenary of the Golden Horde. I am Fssik, Deo of Clan Tamir, and I am in your debt. Please forgive me, I lost myself in the killing."

"It happens that way sometimes," she said. She stuck out a hand "I'm Naran Enkh. It's nice to meet you, Deo, Dama. No hard feelings." She looked around, the glass of her goggles glinting as they caught the starlight. "Looks like we're about done here. Between your people up ahead and my scout platoon—not to mention Deo Berserky McBerserk there, I don't think there's anyone left alive to cause any problems. Why don't you two get your people, and I'll have my scouts let you in."

"Let us in where?" Fssik asked. Disorientation still filled his mind. She turned and flashed a wide Human grin at him.

"Into your fallback position, of course," she said. "Courtesy of the Golden Horde!"

They did as she suggested. Tsan used her quintessential radio to call the strike force forward, and Naran ordered her scouts to form up on the outsides of their formation and escort them in.

As they crossed the perimeter, a shock of recognition rippled through Fssik.

"This is the old market!" Tsan noted.

"Centrally located, easily defensible, with the narrow alleys that can be blocked off and upper story windows for our sniper teams— Hello!" Naran said, waving up at one of the darkened recesses. A glint of light from a scope was her only answer, but it was enough to make her chuckle. "We figured this was the perfect spot to stage you for your final push toward the Veetanho HQ. We've even got a field hospital set up."

"Any trouble getting established?" Ref asked.

"Not really," Naran said, her tone indicating some disappointment. "I would have thought the rats would have had more than a few patrols out, but that's about the worst of it. I got so bored, I went out looking for you guys—and found you!"

Fssik was about to reply and apologize again, but at that exact moment, the sky lit up so brightly that he flinched and snapped his day goggles back into place over his eyes. A deep rumbling sound thrummed through the ground beneath his feet and up into his chest, and for one terrifying heartbeat, he thought the orange cloud of radiation was back.

But no. The general brightness resolved itself into the exhaust trail of an exoatmospheric ship taking off and streaking across the sky.

"Ha!" Naran said, her face lighting up. "This oughta be fun. Carney! Get that comm set over here!"

Another Human, wearing light scout armor, ran up, carrying a powerful comm set on his back. Naran grabbed the slate he handed her and punched in a few codes. A holograph of a Human woman wearing the black of the Winged Hussars appeared.

"This is Horde Redoubt One, I've got a medium-sized exo/atmo departing from city center," Naran said. "Think you can do something about that?"

"City center, you say," the Hussar said, looking at something that wasn't shown in the holograph. "Oh, hello! Yes, got them on lock. Standby, Horde Redoubt One. Maybe you'll get to see the light show."

"Oh, goody," Naran said as the holograph disappeared. Fssik had time to draw in three breaths as he watched the Veetanho ship tracking across the bowl of the heavens. Just when it was about to disappear over the far horizon, he caught sight of a flash, and the little ship—now indistinguishable from a star—went supernova in front of their eyes.

"Nice shooting, Hussars!" Naran said. "How's that station battle coming?"

"Mopping up now, Horde." The holograph reappeared. "We are currently providing 100% topcover over the city. Whenever the Hunters are ready to strike, we'll have their backs."

"We are ready," Tsan said, eagerness vibrating in every line of her body. The holograph nodded and touched two fingers to her eyebrows. "Then I wish you good hunting," she said and disappeared again. Before Tsan could say anything else, a two-ship of SalSha craft streaked overhead.

Ziva turned to look at Fssik.

"Looks like it's time," she said.

"Finally," he said, flexing his claws.

"Yes," Tsan said. "It is finally time. Thank you for holding this fallback for us. Let us hope we do not need it. Hunters… we go. Now."

* * * * *

Chapter Seventeen

The city—*her* city—had changed in the time she'd been gone. She'd known it would, and yet… Even in an eyeblink of observation as they ran, as explosions and gunfire filled the air around them, even then, each change was a sharp rap against her nose.

The food stand Tahl loved so much when she'd been newly out of the den, gone.

Fip's corner of weapons, shiny toys to browse and buy, now a small building smelling of burnt fur.

Night Wind's city den, now something with flashing lights and too many signs.

Each unexpected building, stark in the night, snagged at her, each an attempt to pull her attention from the matter ahead. She narrowed her eyes, focused her breath, and ran.

At the end of the next turn, the council chamber rose ahead of her. A long, low building, formed around its large circular meeting space, the chamber was made of pale green stone and carved with the many sigils of the many clans. A flash of fire ran down her limbs, and her pace nearly faltered.

The Damas did not meet overly frequently; clans governed themselves and only rarely did matters rise to a level that required a council. More often, the chamber served as a neutral meeting location for trade agreements, to share news, or for clever Damas to send the younglings of their clans to run errands and meet potential mates.

She'd spent nearly as much time in this building as her city den. With her own dama. With her damita. With Cahli...

Remember the dead later, she told herself as they approached the large doors of the main entrance. There were smaller side entrances, as there were in clan dens, but they were not particularly hard to find. Any Veetanho worth its reputation would have found them all over the last five years and closed them in or set traps in case any desperate survivors made their way home.

They didn't have time to find and dismantle any barriers, and none of their allies could fit in any such place anyway.

The Hunters vanished into their fields, and the non-invisible members of their party hugged the sides of the streets. The deep night brightened periodically as battles spread throughout the city, though their chosen path remained clear.

Exceptional work from the Horsemen or more oddness from the Veetanho? Surely her enemy knew they were coming and planned to protect their headquarters?

"Blow the doors," she said, falling back to match her pace with Arkak's. They had planned to have Ziva and Meredith take point at the doors, trusting that their enhanced reflexes would protect them while they covered the Hunters' unseen entrance.

"Messy from distance," Arkak answered, but he was already smiling.

"Better them than us," Ziva said, her breathing as steady as any Hunter's or Lumar's.

They all faded to the edges of the streets and took advantage of the limited cover of the low-slung buildings. Zia dropped to one knee and aimed a gun she hadn't had when she'd strode out of the jungle.

Even the *thwoom* of its firing couldn't drown out the sounds of pure joy coming from the other female Lumar. Two more *thwooms* followed, and the doors finally collapsed inward.

They paused, but there was no answering fire.

Tsan stood in a once familiar street, in the comfortable dark, in the middle of her home, and her skin *crawled*. The edge of her nose tingled, searching for scents she couldn't possibly find over the burnt air of recent explosions.

"No." The jungle Hunter didn't drop her field, didn't reach out to touch Tsan, but her voice was close in Tsan's ear. "Not you."

Tsan twitched, the motion would not betray her as long as she remained cloaked in quintessence. The Hunter had anticipated her, as she so often did to other Hunters.

"One of us must go in. You are still vulnerable to their freezing weapon. Criuch is—"

"On his way," the younger Hunter interjected, his field rippling. "Thank you, Dama."

Tsan would not argue. The argument rose in the back of her throat like bile, but she did not let it free. Her people were not reliant on her survival for the continuance of the species. They'd forced Esthik to stay behind, so a measure of leadership would continue uninterrupted, regardless of what happened on Khatash. She could charge into the council chamber and determine what ploy the Veetanho thought to use to lull them. She should—

"It's always easier to do than it is to wait," the Hunter said, something like amusement in her broken voice. "That I remember better than anything from the days I had a clan."

"You have a clan now, Hunter," Tsan replied, refusing to sigh. "And we wait, we watch, we find a way."

"I'm glad to know you take your own words to heart." The feel of the Hunter's quintessence field faded, and Tsan allowed herself a small chuckle. The moments dragged by, and only muffled sounds of conflict broke the silence of their corner of the street.

Zuul, Lumar, Humans, Hunters—all held still.

"It's clear." Criuch's voice over comms was not hesitant, exactly, but there was a question in his tone. *"I mean that literally. No one is in here."*

Impossible. Or, rather, improbable. Every bit of information they had indicated the Veetanho had taken over the Council for their headquarters. Surely, they hadn't all attempted to flee in that ill-advised ship launch?

"We should clear the space," A'nief said. "See what they left behind."

Tsan clenched her hands and pressed her claws into her palms, grasping for something that wasn't there. Anxiety and rage lifted her fur, and her skin jumped as itchy nerves fired randomly. She sent her agreement over the comms and only waited to hear orders given to the various groups before bounding forward.

She paused at the recently enlarged doorway and craned her neck around the wreckage to see what Criuch had seen. The male Hunter hadn't dropped his field, so she couldn't be sure where he was, but she imagined he'd taken one of the high perches to better cover their entrance and keep an eye on the upper seats.

Paying only minimal attention to the movement of the rest of their group as they moved into the building, Tsan stalked across the open floor of the main space. The Veetanho had taken out the columns and seating areas the clans had used for all of recorded history.

Her feet slowed without conscious direction as she crossed the area Whispering Fear had claimed for countless generations.

"What's this?" Fssik demanded from the corner across the room that led down a corridor to old records.

"A sensor," Ziva answered, her low voice carrying in the purposeful acoustics of the chamber. "Look, there's one—"

Tsan would never know where the other one was. As the last of their company moved into the chamber, disciplined and covering every corner, the attack came from the only place it could.

Below.

* * *

One moment, the floor was whole and solid under her feet. The next, she was leaping ahead of movement she hadn't yet consciously processed.

Movement everywhere. Screams. She dug her claws into a small perch, ears swiveling.

"Dama!" Criuch's voice was near enough to cut through the chaos, but she couldn't turn her head, couldn't tear her eyes away from the scene resolving underneath her perch.

Below her, remaining chunks of the floor disintegrated, leaving only patches of stable ground. From the space beneath—tunnels that had not existed during her time in Khatash—seething movement resolved itself into…

Tortantulas. Countless numbers. No Flatar, no visible lines or formations, only… madness. Tsan spared a thought for Esthik, who would have to push himself through yet another catastrophic loss. He would live. She held on to the warmth that gave her and tensed to fling herself down into the madness. Was this the sort of chaos Xiyo and Spalee had told her about on Planet 8190?

They would have liked to see this fight, Tsan thought, flexing her claws. What a feast they could have had.

"Thunder Fist!" Arkak's bellow rose above the screaming. "Path to door!"

"Insho'Ze!" A'nief somehow matched the volume, despite his smaller chest. "Cover Thunder Fist!"

"Dama!" Criuch again, but Tsan couldn't answer. The Tortantula were crawling over each other, under each other. Even her sharp eyes couldn't identify which legs belonged to which body. They were smaller than Xiyo, but far more than double her size.

Regardless, when one enterprising individual, faster than its peers, began scurrying up the wall toward her—could it sense her, like Xiyo had? She had not spent an inordinate amount of time amongst Tortantulas, but surely such a thing would have been noted by some Hunter. She set the analytical corner of her mind to work on the problem, while the rest of her leaped clear of her ledge.

She landed on the closest Tortantula's body and dug both sets of claws on her left side into the resistant flesh. Then she spun, kicking with her rear right claws and dragging her right hand through as many of the Tortantula's eyes as she could before it threw itself back from the wall.

Tortantula and Hunter spun above the mass of bodies that filled what had once been the Council Chambers for the Damas of Khatash.

The Damas were no longer. Only her. She would not die here without taking every Tortantula with her.

Tsan flung herself free of the Tortantula, pulled out two knives as she twisted in mid-air, and fell upon the next ten-legged body with knife and claw. To the next and the next. Tortantula were hard to cut, but their eyes were vulnerable. She raced from eyes to the thinner connective tissue of leg joints, the world blurring around her. Everything was legs, movement. An acidic scent that burned the back of her throat.

Something sizzled past her nose into the Tortantula above her, and she blinked, recalling where she was. Recalling, more importantly, who she was with.

"The door!" Criuch, she thought. He'd tried calling her before. She needed to kill the Tortantula. No, that wasn't right. The Tortantula were a trap. They were beings the Veetanho had disposed of to stop Tsan and her allies. To protect their soft underbellies under the massed bodies of those they enslaved. The Veetanho chose to burrow away from danger and sacrifice others to build their power, and Tsan needed to end that, once and for all.

She would not, could not, die here, atop an endless pile of slain Tortantulas.

She had hunting yet to do.

She dragged her knife free of the dying Tortantula under her and shoved off, leaping from one to the next, aiming higher for a chance to get clear enough to get her bearings. Tsan twisted and sprang, her path erratic to avoid the stabbing limbs and the shots of her friends.

Every option is deadly, she thought, with something like a laugh. *At least, I can ensure one of my allies won't kill me by accident.* She dropped her field and flung herself to the side.

"DAMA!" It was Ziva who spotted her first, Ziva who crouched in the doorframe, back to back with a Zuul, firing rapidly at writhing shadows outside the building.

A trap. The entire city, a trap.

As Nigel might say... *Fuck.*

She ran from Tortantula to Tortantula and took in the room as she moved.

Zuul and Lumar, dead and strewn underfoot.

Ref, pinioned underneath a fallen Tortantula, unmoving.

Sunny will never forgive us.

Meredith, bleeding from a handful of different wounds, leaned against the wall and fired with her one good arm.

Criuch, tail shortened, one arm hanging by little more than a strip of muscle, screaming defiance at the horde of Tortantula climbing over each other to close in on him.

A'nief and Arkak took shot after shot to clear a path for Criuch, but there were so many. Too many.

No.

The word dropped with calm finality into her thoughts.

"Tula!" she called, and the Lumar answered with a volley of fire that led Tsan across the chamber, keeping any Tortantula from successfully reaching up for her.

She felt a flicker of movement at her side, and only the brush of quintessence kept her from lashing out, as the jungle Hunter appeared next to her. They raced together, stabbing where they could and digging claws in deeply to better launch for the next many-legged body that served as a floor.

She needed to get out of this death trap, find the Veetanho, and end the threat.

But she could not—*would* not—leave another Hunter behind, not if there was a chance to save him. Death coated her tongue and covered her fur like her quintessence field. There were too many bodies beneath them, and not one of them Veetanho.

No.

She and the Hunter launched over the building mass of Tortantula between them and Criuch. The Hunter snapped around and dove underneath A'nief and Arkak's line of fire, tearing out the relatively vulnerable undersides of as many attackers as she could.

Tsan bowled into Criuch, rolled them both to their feet, and propelled them away.

"Dama," Criuch gasped, "My legs…"

Tsan was likely exacerbating his injury, but the alternative was worse. Criuch clung to her with his one working limb, and she dropped her knife to secure him as they moved. Tortantulas pressed in on all sides, and with Criuch out of his field, there was only so much she could do.

Only way out is through, she repeated to herself, licking ichor off her lips. Tortantulas tasted like old fire and the bitter burnt remnants of gnarra seeds. Quintessence twitched around her, and she snarled as they moved. Only the steady fire of her people kept her clear, then the Hunter and Fssik fell in around her.

The remaining Lumar had formed a blockade around the door, though there weren't enough of them to hold indefinitely. As Tsan approached, she saw the remaining Zuul had done much the same on the outside of the door.

More Tortantulas. And smaller forms, lower to the ground, and even faster. *Goka?*

"Empty night," she breathed, squeezing between two of the Lumar and easing Criuch against the wall.

The city had brightened while she'd been lashing out in the pit of Tortantula. Not dawn…

The fight they'd been expecting had come, the Veetanho had managed an ambush.

"How many?" she asked, not expecting an answer.

"Too many," Tula replied, dropping back.

Comms were a mess. Static interfered, and only half sentences came through.

"West quadrant under heavy—"

"Fallback sec—"

"Air support to coord—"

"Evacuate, evacuate, overrun at—"

Tsan breathed herself to stillness and unholstered her gun. They would not all die here. Perhaps Ziva and Fssik could—

"Tsan."

She froze. The voice, unlike all the rest, cut through the static with bell struck clarity.

"Jessica?"

"Tsan, we're coming, and hell's riding with us." A pause, something muffled, and then the Peace… no, the Venatore's voice again, perfectly clear. *"Anyone with you have a personal beacon?"*

"Ziva!"

Tula ran to take Ziva's position, and Ziva came closer as Jessica did something to include her in the transmission.

"IDENT if you will, Ziva. Things are about to move fast."

No sooner had the words landed, than the sky outside exploded into light.

"CASPers," Ziva said, her voice catching.

Tsan bolted to the entrance, ears flattening against the din.

The CASPers—so many of them they blotted out the stars—plummeted to ground, shooting all the while. The Zuul immediately broke formation, half moving back inside to layer with the Lumar and hold the line inside, the other half maintaining some measure of clear space as the approaching mass of Tortantula and Goka pivoted to face this new threat.

"Air is friendly, repeat, air is friendly." Tsan recognized Naran's voice, and the tip of her tail twitched. This wasn't over.

"MinSha reinforcements at south southwest quadrant," another voice cut in.

"MinSha reinforcements at north ten."

"CASPers on site, east twenty."

Reports flooded in. Whatever had been interfering with comms had been disrupted.

One of the CASPers dropped between the Zuul and the now-breaking multitude in the streets ahead.

"Ziva Alcuin?" The Human voice was male, though the mechanical armor showed nothing of the being within. "Dama Tsan?"

Ziva and Tsan stepped forward, with Fssik an eyeblink behind.

"We rode in with, uh, the MinSha. I'm Bjorn Tovesson III, Commander of Bjorn's Berserkers." He saluted, and the motion was natural, even in the over-sized equipment. "We're here courtesy of Theela Financial."

Tsan blinked, her tail high behind her.

"Jessica Francis commands and wants you to know we're contracted for the taking and holding of Khatash to the service of the

Hunters and their Allies." He cleared his throat and turned his back fully to the battle still happening behind him.

The CASPer crouched, and a seam opened, revealing a normal-sized human. The commander tossed a small folio down to them. Ziva caught it before immediately dropping to a squat to open it at Fssik and Tsan's level.

For the sigil which I still wear, now and forever.

* * * * *

Chapter Eighteen

Fssik hauled in breath after breath, willing his fight response to slow, his body to steady. All around them, CASPers and MinSha landed and began slaughtering the attacking Tortantulas and Goka. As he watched, they pushed them back, herding them into smaller and smaller enclaves away from where he stood beside his Ziva.

"Thunder Fist! Form with CASPers!" Arkak's shout penetrated Fssik's thoughts, and he turned to see A'nief following suit with her surviving Zuul warriors. They continued to push outward, clearing a path from the council chambers back to the Horde redoubt in the market.

The market was a mess. The Veetanho had laid their trap well, and several of the buildings Naran's troops had incorporated into their defenses had apparently also had their floors disintegrate under the enemy forces boiling upward. Fssik heard the sharp retort of MAC rounds as they approached and saw even more CASPers and MinSha pushing into the buildings to rescue the snipers and spotters trapped there.

Tsan led them to the center of the defenses, where Naran held her command, and Ace'to and the other medics labored to save the quickly mounting numbers of wounded, including Criuch and Meredith. A while later—Fssik couldn't have said exactly how long—Jessica and Azho landed and joined them there, along with the Berserkers' commander, Tovesson.

"Reports are positive," Jessica said by way of greeting, as she reached out to give Ziva a quick, hard hug. A MinSha warrior, wearing the insignia of a general, followed closely behind her. "Our forces have corralled most of the enemy in the northeast corner of the city, with a larger grouping over on the west side. They're trapped there on the beach, so while they're fighting hard, we've got them. Same in the northeast. There's nowhere for them to go."

"Are they mercenaries?" Ziva asked.

"The Goka are," Tovesson said. "We've already had some groups surrender according to merc convention when their situation became untenable. My people will take custody of them until they can put up their parole. The Torts, though, they're mostly feral if I had to guess. Although we did find a group of males, which is interesting. They've surrendered as well. They were part of the group in the northeast. We're holding them in an old warehouse."

"Did you get the Veetanho?" Naran asked, looking at Tsan.

"No," Tsan said, and Fssik caught the way her fur rippled with rage as she spoke. He felt the same way. "It was part of the trap. The council chambers were empty."

"They've got to be close," Ziva said quietly. "There's nowhere for them to go."

"Veetanho are burrowers," the MinSha general said. Fssik didn't recognize him, but Jessica and Azho nodded as he continued. "Burrowers would go to ground. Apparently, there are tunnels under this city, yes? Check there."

Next to him, Tsan stiffened, her ears perking up.

"I know where they are," she said, and the edge of violence in her tone made Fssik's skin quiver in delight.

* * *

Tsan called the Hunters back to their position. Aryss, already annoyed by their failed mission, fretted over Meredith's wounds and yowled over Ref's body.

Of the ninety-nine Hunters that had returned to Khatash, only eighteen remained in any fit state for what needed to happen next.

It would have to do.

"There are two hidden entrances to Whispering Fear's city den," Tsan said, claws dug into her harness as she kept herself from pacing.

The sky had begun to lighten from approaching dawn this time—rather than orbital insertions and fiery explosions—but they could not afford to let the Veetanho have any more time.

"I don't believe the Veetanho would have been able to find the one from here, given that it's gone undiscovered by other Hunters for generations, and it does not exist on any map or record." She considered the gathered beings and twitched her ears, tail waving in a semi-amused admission. "I do not believe such a thing was supposed to exist, but not all of my ancestresses were as concerned with the well-being of Hunters as we are these days."

"Zuul and Venatores would fit on all fours, perhaps, but we cannot keep you hidden if the way from here is compromised."

"We'll prepare to set up a perimeter on your signal," Jessica said, pressing her hands on her thighs. "Not close enough to give it away, but we'll be able to move in fast if you need us."

"I trust in your judgement," Tsan replied, inclining her head toward the former Peacemaker. Jessica had proven herself every bit as valuable an ally as Tsan could ever have hoped for. The reason Azho and his companion had left the guild though… even her thoughts shuddered away from it. Minerva and more of its kind were out there, moving against them. If anything Peepo had said could be believed, if all the information Sunshine had carried were true, there were many more punishing fights ahead of them on a far bigger scale than the retaking of one planet.

Her thoughts touched on the matter and spun away again. One barrier at a time. Alone, the Hunters would not have gotten so far, and the same was true for the wars-to-come that crowded close. Allies, credits, and an unkillable rage would see them through.

"I wish I could go with you," Ziva said softly to Fssik. Tsan affected not to notice, her eyes on Aryss scolding Meredith into returning to the fallback position. Other companions said their goodbyes, and Tsan strode to the edge of the semi-circle they'd created for their discussion.

Whispering Fear's city den was one of the oldest in Khatash and one of the largest. It had a public facing entrance that was not meant to be hard to find and a large underground chamber with enough space for many Veetanho. It had served as a training and storage facility for the clan, and, though smaller than the council chambers that had become a pit of Tortantulas that had attempted to eat them, it was more than enough for a burrowing creature to feel secure. If the Veetanho weren't here, the best next place to find them was her home. It had once fit some hundred Hunters and was more secure than the smoking council chambers behind her.

Her claws stretched from their sheaths, and she slid them back, tail lashing.

One by one, the Hunters gathered around her. She ensured they knew the alternate path to the den in case the path from the chambers was blocked, and then she nodded. In a flicker of movement, the group disappeared.

"You ever get used to that?" Tovesson asked softly.

"It's better if you don't," Jessica replied, her tone dry.

Azho chuckled briefly, somewhere to Tsan's left.

Stone and Tortantula bodies hid the way to the concealed entrance, so they moved through their city with less weight than shadows. Tsan kept her eyes ahead, though her ears swiveled for anything unexpected. She would not be distracted by the wreckage or the bodies. What was done was done, and if all went as it must, they would mourn and recover and rebuild when the time came.

She could have made the trip from the council chambers to her old city den asleep and blindfolded, and the familiarity of it was nearly enough to cause her to drop her guard and look around, as though it were any other day of her long ago past.

She hissed a breath through her teeth and did not slow until she reached the entrance to her den. It was ringed with Nyralor flowers, still healthily blooming years after anyone had groomed them. There was no hint of discoloration to indicate anyone had touched them in a long while. Tsan climbed the decorative rock nearby. She examined it closely, then placed two sets of fingerpads in the appropriate depressions.

A small rectangle of flowers lifted away from the wall, and she warbled the signal. Azho warbled back from the entrance after he'd counted each of their company going by, and she jumped down to join him inside.

The flower door sank closed behind her.

Though she knew it wouldn't smell like it should—how could it, five years untouched—she took a deep breath anyway.

A sound burst out of her, and several Hunters dropped their fields.

"Dama?" Pura asked, her voice uncertain for the first time in seasons.

"Wait here," she said, or meant to, as she leaped over the space where her compatriots had gathered. Her feet must have touched the floor again, but she didn't note it or the streaks of disturbed dust.

A figure lay in a heap at the junction where the corridor turned deeper toward the den or continued back to the council chambers. Too big for a Hunter. Too big for a Veetanho.

But that one breath had told her everything she needed to know.

"*Aryo!*"

The figure stirred, and a small whimper answered her.

"I have nanites." Fssik pressed close against her, which made her realize she had frozen, dropped her field, and outstretched a hand to the body that had been lost to her twice over.

"I—"

"Ziva wouldn't let me leave her side without loading me up. They aren't specific to Zuul, but they should do enough."

His matter-of-fact tone recalled her to herself, and she closed the distance between her and her oldest surviving friend.

"Aryo," she said again, stroking the line between her Zuul's eyes. It seemed to be the only place not burned and blistered.

"Dama." The word was mumbled, slurred, but one of Aryo's eyes flickered open. "Coshke... brought... dead?"

"No, my Aryo, my love. I'm not dead. You're not dead." A thrill stabbed from the base of her spine to the end of her tail. Aryo was alive! All her dead could not return to her—Cahli, her kits, endless others—but here, now, one she had lost not once, but twice, was returned to her.

Fssik moved at her side, injecting Aryo, and Tsan lowered her head until her nose touched Aryo's.

"You are a child of Zuul, and you have no fear," she murmured. "You live. I will return to you."

Aryo's other eye opened, and both focused briefly on Tsan. "Coshke... wills," she said, and she began to push herself up.

"Aryo, rest." Tsan's voice shook underneath her, and she sat up to steady herself. "We will return for you."

"Here." Pura, ears deferentially to the side, came closer with a pile of cushions and blankets in her arms. "The small room was just there, I grabbed—"

Tsan lifted a hand and stroked Pura's dark-furred face. She whispered her thanks, and Fssik, Pura, and Tsan took the seconds required to make Aryo more comfortable.

"These are like the wounds I took from the Veetanho weapon," Fssik said, his tone steady. Tsan forced herself back from Aryo and touched his cheek.

"The Hunter said Aryo was in the jungle near the city when the bomb hit. She must have run in to survive. How she made it here, undetected…" Tsan shook her head. "It is a story we will hear when this is done."

"Hunters," Fssik said, head held high. "We go."

* * *

Some hundred Veetanho had gathered in the large underground room that had once been entirely hers, busily checking screens, speaking on their commlinks, and moving around to talk to each other.

She leaped for the closest one and landed on the back of her shoulders.

"No negotiation for you, little mouse," she said, raking her claws across the Veetanho's throat. Not enough to kill her immediately, because what fun was that? She slid down the Veetanho with all her claws embedded, making sure to rip each connective tendon that would allow her enemy to fight back.

Seeing one of their number erupt in blood and begin to sag to the ground, the next closest Veetanho had the presence of mind to scream one all-important word.

"DEPIK!"

A string of curses and a mad scramble to action answered her, and the largest of the Veetanho, sitting on the highest ledge that would fit her, smiled and reached into her vest.

"Stupid—"

Another Veetanho fell, then another. The shouting reached a new pitch, though the Hunters continued to move in silence. The large Veetanho pressed the control in her vest again and again, her motion becoming frantic.

Tsan allowed her field to flicker as she streaked from one part of the broad, open space to another, hiding her path to the one who thought herself in charge.

"Foolish little mouse. Five years, and you didn't make a new plan?"

"Bring in the—"

Tsan had no interest in finding out who or what the Veetanho were about to call in. She tore out enough of the creature's throat to sever her vocal cords, then disemboweled her for good measure.

* * *

The red mist was back, but this time, Fssik kept his head. He looked through the battle rage and the blood that splashed over his face and grinned, Human-style, showing all his teeth, as he bounded from the falling body of one Veetanho to the next.

Finally, his mind rejoiced as he drove his blade repeatedly into the vulnerable ear hole of a screaming Veetanho. *Finally, for my clan, for my Ziva, for Elizabeth and Paul! For my home, for my ship, for my species, for my allies, for Ref, for Criuch, for me!*

His victim kept screaming and scrabbled at him with small hands. One held an energy pistol, but she couldn't shoot him without putting a bolt in her own skull, so she battered him ineffectively. Another time, it might have hurt. But rage and killing joy had hardened his mind and hardened his body, and he rode her shrieking, dying corpse all the way to the floor before leaping free.

He landed upon another victim without even trying. He went to work on her eyes, while whispering into the soft, wide discs of her ears how much he'd been waiting to meet her, to open up her skull, to pull out whatever he found inside.

This one fell too, and Fssik found himself in a position to leap onto one of the central seating pillars in the room. As there were no other potential victims in his immediate vicinity, he decided to look around.

He didn't see Tsan, but the knot of Veetanho around the area where their leadership had huddled continued to fall, one by one. In the opposite curve of the room, Fssik caught a flicker of Pura's dark fur as she darted in and out of her quintessence field and severed the spine of another Veetanho just above the creature's pelvis. The screams startled Pura's next victim, who hesitated long enough that Fssik could see the exact moment Pura's knife entered her sternum.

Below him, Azho spun and fought with all four feet like a cyclone of pain. He had a small energy pistol in his hand and fired it while he stabbed deep into the throat of a Veetanho with the long knife in his back right foot. Azho was a big male, but he was *fast*, and, apparently, he had decided not to bother with quintessence. Fssik opened his mouth in a grin at his friend's performance.

Throughout the room, chaos reigned. The screams and yowled laughter echoed through the vaulted space as the Veetanho cried out and fought and tried to escape, but every time one came close to the doors, it died, deprived of eyes or guts or, once, an entire head. Aryss, he presumed, and possibly the Jungle Dama.

Fssik gathered his body, preparing to leap back into the fray, when something he never would have expected happened.

Across the room, Tsan suddenly dropped her field and leaped onto a ledge in the wall.

"Hunters! Stop!"

* * * * *

Chapter Nineteen

Tsan dropped the pieces of the freezing weapon to the ground with utter disdain. She'd taken the button from the lead Veetanho's still-warm corpse and deactivated it, so the jungle Hunter could fight, but she wouldn't leave it whole even after it was made harmless.

Unlike its creators, it had no other purpose to serve.

"What do you mean with these gestures," she asked, tilting her head and regarding the closer Veetanho, who'd been waving and crying from her knees for the last series of breaths.

"We surrender, we surrender, please, this wasn't our fault... we didn't mean... we didn't *do*—"

"You ask this of us? That we spare you, after what you have done?"

"We didn't know!" the smaller Veetanho gasped, nose twitching. "We were just following orders. We didn't know you would... Depik would... we just thought you'd work for us. We didn't mean for all this to happen!"

"A poor excuse, as you sit in my home, in my city, on my planet that you took." Tsan's eyes narrowed. The trembling of the Veetanho was genuine as far as she could tell, but how long would the fear last?

"What can we offer?" The Veetanho glanced around, and, when she realized she was one of six survivors, she shook harder. "We'll do anything!"

"Anything!" others chorused, all frozen in place.

"Anything?" Tsan asked, a purr under her voice.

They spoke over each other in their agreement, then the others fell silent and let the first one speak.

"Anything," she confirmed, nodding until her ears flapped.

"Welcome," Tsan replied, "to our negotiation."

Pura made a noise deep in her throat, but Tsan did not take her eyes off her target.

"The truth is this, Veetanho, you will die on this planet never seeing another sky. The manner, however, is within your choosing."

"Depik... ah, Hunter... I... we—"

"You will die now, screaming, or you will wear our sigil around your neck. You will never take it off. Never betray us."

"Yes." She stepped forward, eagerly. Far too eagerly.

Azho moved as well, but Tsan lifted a hand, halting them both, and slow blinked.

"It is not that simple, little enemy. My Wrogul allies will change your brains. You will believe to your smallest cell that you exist only to serve me and my interests. You will be more enslaved than any being your kind has yoked to the Guild." Her tail waved softly behind her. "You will have no thought other than what will help Hunters. All your wisdom, all your cunning, they survive only to aid my allies and me. Do you understand?"

"I... that—"

"Terrible, I agree. My people nearly ended to avoid such a fate. But, consider this. You will live a long life. A comfortable life. You will die old, and blind, and having served well, knowing you spent the rest of your life, from this moment to the end, atoning for all you have done."

"We—" The eagerness had died. Tsan smiled to see it.

"No!" The survivor in the back broke for the door, only to come up short.

Aryo stood there, upright, *alive*, a gun aimed unwaveringly at the scurrying Veetanho.

Warmth sang through Tsan, then she turned her gaze toward Fssik. Fssik leaped without hesitation, dragging his claws across the attempted escapee's face. He raked through her eyes, licked the tips of his claws, and dismantled her in seconds.

"Yes!" The remaining five Veetanho chorused, eager again.

"Then I claim you as my own, little enemies. You will add your strength to ours for all the fights to come. All here witness it. You are mine."

* * * * *

Chapter Twenty

A Few Weeks Later in Houston

Fssik stretched, reaching his spine and limbs out to their full length, spreading his fingers and toes, and extending each of his claws. Then he retracted them and cuddled in close to the warmth of Ziva at his back. She lay tangled in the sheets of Jim Cartwright's bed, though the man wasn't there.

If he had been, Fssik would not be in the bed. That would have been awkward.

Ziva and Jim's reunion earlier had been emotional. Like all of them, Ziva had sustained minor injuries when the Veetanho sprang their final trap, and the Tortantula and Goka had come boiling up out of the ground. She hadn't sought medical attention on the surface because there were others in much more dire need. He swallowed hard at the thought of Criuch and Ref's lifeless body. But once it was over, Jim had come through the city to find her and had brought her and Fssik back to his ship where he thought they would be safe. Then he'd avoided her for the entire trip back to Earth.

Until last night.

"Good morning." Ziva's voice sounded sleepy, but satisfied, as she, too, stretched, and then curled around him.

"I don't think it's morning," Fssik said, rolling over to face his companion. "The sun has been high in the sky for hours."

"You know what I mean. Did you sleep well now that we're off the ship, my Hunter?"

353

"Like the dead, but unlike since I woke up again. You?"

"Same... after." Fssik felt a tendril of joy at the deep happiness he saw in Ziva's smug, satiated smile.

"Hmm, yes. You both seemed quite enthusiastic to be reunited."

"Enthusiastic. That's a good word for it. We talked, too."

"Good. I hope it was a good talk."

"I think it was," she said, nuzzling down into the fur between his ears. Fssik reached up with his claws sheathed and patted her face. She kissed him and then paused.

"I feel good and content," she said, "but what about you, my Hunter?"

Fssik let out a gusty sigh. He should have known he couldn't hide his inner turmoil from her for long.

"Are you worried about me and Jim?"

"No," Fssik said. "No, he was genuinely affected to see you. I think you two are healthier than you have been in a long time if I'm being honest. No, for once, my Human, you are not the source of my discontent."

"Then what is it? Ref? Criuch?"

"No. Ref is gone, and I mourn, but that is the way of things. Criuch will be well again, though it will take time and therapy. No, my Human, what worries me is Tsan."

"Tsan? Why?"

Fssik drew in a deep breath and considered exactly how to articulate what was bothering him. *Fuck it*, he decided, borrowing his favorite of Ziva's expressions. *I'll just say it.*

"Why did she stop us? Why did she save them? Adopt them, even? To give them her Sigil, the same Sigil Aryo wore so faithfully for so many years. The same Sigil that caused Theela Financial to purchase our salvation! They should have all died! Shredded under our claws and discarded like rotten meat! Why are they still breathing, and *why did she preserve them?*"

Ziva pressed her lips together and pushed herself up into a seated position. Then she gathered him close, held him to her chest, and leaned her head down to rub against his cheek.

"I declined my mother's request to become Dama because I don't think like one, my love," she said after a moment. Fssik shifted in her arms. He *knew* that already! She cuddled him tighter and held him still while she went on. "Dama Tsan, on the other hand, absolutely does. To understand her actions, my Hunter, you've got to look at her motivations. Everything Tsan does, every choice she makes, *everything* is driven by one goal—the survival of her clan, her species. Tsan will see to it that the Hunters will *never* again be trapped between slavery and death. Because of her, there will always be other options for our kind."

"But—"

"No, listen. By putting her sigil on the surviving Veetanho, she's made slaves of some of the greatest strategic minds in the galaxy. You heard her, she's going to have Ward *change* them. They won't be able to be anything but slaves, made so by their own devotion, their own need for connection and love. And thanks to those changes, they'll eventually breed more slaves who will be bound to the Hunters of their own will, thanks to their genetic makeup. It's terrifying and awful, but kinda amazing, too. Because as soon as Ward is finished with them, those Veetanho and their offspring will do *anything* to protect their Hunters… out of devotion."

Fssik lay still in her arms as he turned this perspective over in his mind. *Ziva was right,* he realized. *If Tsan could bind the brilliance of these Veetanho to the Hunters forever—*

"Do you feel like a slave?" he asked. "Because Ward increased your devotion to me?"

"No, my Hunter," Ziva said. "I was already devoted to you. I chose you just as much as you chose me, and I've never regretted it, not for an instant." She gathered him in even closer and scooted back down to lie curled around his body. Fssik pressed into her as well, breathing in the scent of her, her strength, the sound of her heartbeat—

Oh.

Well, hello there, little one. Fssik slow blinked as he felt the tiniest stirring against his quintessence field. *Your mother will be very excited to meet you.*

* * * * *

About Kacey Ezell

Kacey Ezell is an active duty USAF instructor pilot with 3000+ hours in the UH-1N Huey and Mi-171 helicopters. When not teaching young pilots to beat the air into submission, she writes sci-fi/fantasy/horror/noir/alternate history fiction. She is a two-time Dragon Award Finalist for Best Alternate History. She's contributed to multiple Baen anthologies and has twice been selected for inclusion in the Year's Best Military and Adventure Science Fiction compilation. In 2018, her story "Family Over Blood" won the Year's Best Military and Adventure Science Fiction Readers' Choice Award. In addition to writing for Baen Books and Blackstone Publishing, she has published several novels and short stories with independent publisher Chris Kennedy Publishing. She is married with two daughters. You can find out more and join her mailing list at www.kaceyezell.net.

* * * * *

About Marisa Wolf

Marisa Wolf was born in New England, and raised on Boston sports teams, Star Wars, Star Trek, and the longest books in the library (usually fantasy). Over the years she majored in English in part to get credits for reading (this...only partly worked), taught middle school, was headbutted by an alligator, built a career in education, earned a black belt in Tae Kwon Do, and finally decided to finish all those half-started stories in her head.

She's currently based in Texas, but has moved into an RV with her husband and their two ridiculous rescue dogs, and it's anyone's guess where in the country she is at any given moment. Learn more at www.marisawolf.net.

* * * * *

For More Information:

For a suggested reading order guide to the Four Horsemen Universe, go to:

https://chriskennedypublishing.com/the-four-horsemen-books/4hu-suggested-reading-order/

* * * * *

For a listing of all the Four Horsemen books, go to:

https://chriskennedypublishing.com/the-four-horsemen-books/

* * * * *

Do you have what it takes to be a Merc?

Take your VOWs and join the Merc Guild on Facebook!

Meet us at: https://www.facebook.com/groups/536506813392912/

* * * * *

Did you like this book?
Please write a review!

* * * * *

The following is an
Excerpt from The Fall of Rho-Torkis:

The Fall of Rho-Torkis

Tim C. Taylor

Now Available from Theogony Books

eBook, Audio, and Paperback

Excerpt from "The Fall of Rho-Torkis:"

"Relax, Sybutu."

Osu didn't fall for the man steepling his fingers behind his desk. When a lieutenant colonel told you to relax, you knew your life had just taken a seriously wrong turn.

"So what if we're ruffling a few feathers?" said Malix. "We have a job to do, and you're going to make it happen. You will take five men with you and travel unobserved to a location in the capital where you will deliver a coded phrase to this contact."

He pushed across a photograph showing a human male dressed in smuggler chic. Even from the static image, the man oozed charm, but he revealed something else too: purple eyes. The man was a mutant.

"His name is Captain Tavistock Fitzwilliam, and he's a free trader of flexible legitimacy. Let's call him a smuggler for simplicity's sake. You deliver the message and then return here without incident, after which no one will speak of this again."

Osu kept his demeanor blank, but the questions were raging inside him. His officers in the 27th gave the appearance of having waved through the colonel's bizarre orders, but the squadron sergeant major would not let this drop easily. He'd be lodged in an ambush point close to the colonel's office where he'd be waiting to pounce on Osu and interrogate him. Vyborg would suspect him of conspiracy in this affront to proper conduct. His sappers as undercover spies? Osu would rather face a crusading army of newts than the sergeant major on the warpath.

"Make sure one of the men you pick is Hines Zy Pel."

Osu's mask must have slipped because Malix added, "If there is a problem, I expect you to speak."

"Is Zy Pel a Special Missions operative, sir?" There. He'd said it.

"You'll have to ask Colonel Lantosh. Even after they bumped up my rank, I still don't have clearance to see Zy Pel's full personnel record. Make of that what you will."

"But you must have put feelers out…"

Malix gave him a cold stare.

You're trying to decide whether to hang me from a whipping post or answer my question. Well, it was your decision to have me lead an undercover team, Colonel. Let's see whether you trust your own judgement.

The colonel seemed to decide on the latter option and softened half a degree. "There was a Hines Zy Pel who died in the Defense of Station 11. Or so the official records tell us. I have reason to think that our Hines Zy Pel is the same man."

"But…Station 11 was twelve years ago. According to the personnel record I've seen, my Zy Pel is in his mid-20s."

Malix put his hands up in surrender. "I know, I know. The other Hines Zy Pel was 42 when he was KIA."

"He's 54? Can't be the same man. Impossible."

"For you and I, Sybutu, that is true. But away from the core worlds, I've encountered mysteries that defy explanation. Don't discount the possibility. Keep an eye on him. For the moment, he is a vital asset, especially given the nature of what I have tasked you with. However, if you ever suspect him of an agenda that undermines his duty to the Legion, then I am ordering you to kill him before he realizes you suspect him."

Kill Zy Pel in cold blood? That wouldn't come easily.

"Acknowledge," the colonel demanded.

"Yes, sir. If Zy Pel appears to be turning, I will kill him."

"Do you remember Colonel Lantosh's words when she was arrested on Irisur?"

Talk about a sucker punch to the gut! Osu remembered everything about the incident when the Militia arrested the CO for standing up to the corruption endemic on that world.

It was Legion philosophy to respond to defeat or reversal with immediate counterattack. Lantosh and Malix's response had been the most un-Legion like possible.

"Yes, sir. She told us not to act. To let the skraggs take her without resistance. Without the Legion retaliating."

"No," snapped Malix. "She did *not*. She ordered us to let her go without retaliating *until the right moment*. This *is* the right moment, Sybutu. This message you will carry. You're doing this for the colonel."

Malix's words set loose a turmoil of emotions in Osu's breast that he didn't fully understand. He wept tears of rage, something he hadn't known was possible.

The colonel stood. "This is the moment when the Legion holds the line. Can I rely upon you, Sergeant?"

Osu saluted. "To the ends of the galaxy, sir. No matter what.

* * * * *

Get "The Fall of Rho-Torkis" now at:
https://www.amazon.com/dp/B08VRL8H27.

Find out more about Tim C. Taylor and "The Fall of Rho-Torkis" at:
https://chriskennedypublishing.com.

* * * * *

The following is an

Excerpt from Book One of Murphy's Lawless:

Shakes

Mike Massa

Now Available from Beyond Terra Press

eBook and Paperback

Excerpt from "Shakes:"

Harry shook his head and yawned, then looked at the instruments. Crap, they were very nearly on the surface! There was no time to be surprised; he needed to work the problem. The shortness of the landing checklist didn't make his situation any less dire.

"Ten seconds!" Volo said, unnecessarily warning both Terrans. "Prepare for manual deployment."

If Marco Rodriguez was anything like Harry, he was watching the altimeter with growing apprehension. An impatient SpinDog technician had carefully repeated the instructions to an audience he doubtless regarded as incapable of using tools more sophisticated than rocks and sharp sticks. In theory, each craft would use a flicker laser to sense the minimum height-over-ground required for deployment of the chute to guarantee a safe landing. If he didn't feel the automated systems deploy the capsule's drogue and parachute combination, he'd have less than two seconds to mechanically initiate that critical step. Harry placed both hands on the pebbly surface of the L-shaped lever and took a deep breath. He watched his displays intently, counting down internally.

In three, two, o—

He was interrupted by the audible *pop* of the drogue ribbon launching over his head. One of his screens flashed the corresponding message, as the drogue gave his capsule a single, hard jerk, pressing him heavily into his couch. After dramatically slowing the freefall to a speed the twin parachutes could withstand, the drogue detached. A second, mushier jerk announced the canopies' successful opening.

The capsule had barely steadied underneath the green and brown parachutes before the capsule crashed to a painful stop. The scant padding on the seat might have prevented any serious injury, but Harry still ached all over. But like the pain caused by a misaligned crotch strap during a regular jump, this was a good sort of pain to have. The parachute had worked, and the capsule was down. The

369

cone-shaped vehicle came to rest on its side, however. Getting out was going to require a bit of scrambling.

"Four, Five, this is Six," he said, trusting the hands-free microphone on his helmet while hanging sideways in his straps. "Sound off."

"Five on the ground. Mind the first step, it's a doozy," Rodriguez said jauntily.

"I've opened the hatch already, Lieutenant," Volo answered. "It's daylight, and we must cover the ships immediately."

"Copy," Harry said, releasing his chest strap. He fell heavily against one of the instrument panels, painfully bruising his arm. He suppressed a heartfelt curse.

"Popping the hatch."

He reached for the door lever, now inconveniently located over his head. After a pause, the capsule verified his intent, requiring a second yank before it obediently ejected the hatch outward with a percussive *bang*. Instantly, a cold wind filled his capsule, making him shiver. He poked his head outside and surveyed a bleak and rocky landscape which was partially obscured by the capsule's billowing parachute.

After donning a hooded parka from a storage cabinet underneath his feet, he withdrew his personal equipment and weapon. Then, with an athleticism he didn't feel, Harry used an inner handhold to swing outside. On either side of his aeroshell, the terrain rose several meters in elevation, forming a shallow canyon. His 'chute was tangled in some stunted gray-green trees that bordered the drop zone. Knee high, rust-colored spiky grass poked up in between the fist-sized stones covering much of the ground. The breeze smelled wet and musty, but the ground appeared dry. A football field distant, Harry could make out another capsule, and began trotting over. It was supposed to be dusk on R'Bak, but the overcast diffused the light. Out of reflex, he checked his wristwatch, which rode alongside a new gadget doubling as a short-range radio and compass. Both were still set to SpinDog station time, adopted during the mission prep. He supposed he could check with Volo. It didn't matter yet. Experience had taught the SEAL exactly what time it was.

The local hour is half past "your ass is in a sling." My team is untested and outnumbered, the local population is mostly hostile, the wildlife carnivorous, and, in two years, the local star is going to approach its binary twin, boiling the oceans and scorching the land. Oh, and your extract off-planet depends entirely on mission success, so don't screw up.

Welcome to R'Bak.

* * * * *

Get "Shakes" now at: https://www.amazon.com/dp/B0861F23KH.

Find out more about "Murphy's Lawless" at:
https://chriskennedypublishing.com.

* * * * *

The following is an

Excerpt from Book One of the Singularity War:

Warrior: Integration

David Hallquist

Available from Theogony Books

eBook, Paperback, and Audio

Excerpt from "Warrior: Integration:"

I leap into the pit. As I fall in the low gravity, I run my hands and feet along the rock walls, pushing from one side to another, slowing my descent. I hit the pool below and go under.

I swim up through the greenish chemicals and breach the surface. I can see a human head silhouetted against the circle of light above. Time to go. I slide out of the pool quickly. The pool explodes behind me. Grenade, most likely. The tall geyser of steam and spray collapses as I glide into the darkness of the caves ahead.

They are shooting to kill now.

I glide deeper into the rough tunnels. Light grows dimmer. Soon, I can barely see the rock walls around me. I look back. I can see the light from the tunnel reflected upon the pool. They have not come down yet. They're cautious; they won't just rush in. I turn around a bend in the tunnel, and light is lost to absolute darkness.

The darkness means little to me anymore. I can hear them talking as their voices echo off the rock. They are going to send remotes down first. They have also decided to kill me rather than capture me. They figure the docs can study whatever they scrape off the rock walls. That makes my choices simple. I figured I'd have to take out this team anyway.

The remotes are on the way. I can hear the faint whine of micro-turbines. They will be using the sensors on the remotes and their armor, counting on the darkness blinding me. Their sensors against my monster. I wonder which will win.

Everything becomes a kind of gray, blurry haze as my eyes adapt to the deep darkness. I can see the tunnel from sound echoes as I glide down the dark paths. I'm also aware of the remotes spreading out in a search pattern in the tunnel complex.

I'll never outrun them. I need to hide, but I glow in infra-red. One of the remotes is closing, fast.

I back up against a rock wall, and force the monster to hide me. It's hard; it wants to fight, but I need to hide first. I feel the numbing cold return as my temperature drops, hiding my heat. I feel the monster come alive, feel it spread through my body and erupt out of my skin. Fibers spread over my skin, covering me completely in fibrous camouflage. They harden, fusing me to the wall, leaving me unable to move. I can't see, and I can barely breathe. If the remotes find me here, I'm dead.

The remote screams by. I can't see through the fibers, but it sounds like an LB-24, basically a silver cigar equipped with a small laser.

I can hear the remote hover nearby. Can it see me? It pauses and then circles the area. Somehow, the fibers hide me. It can't see me, but it knows something is wrong. It drops on the floor to deposit a sensor package and continues on. Likely it signaled the men upstairs about an anomaly. They'll come and check it out.

The instant I move, the camera will see me. So I wait. I listen to the sounds of the drones moving and water running in the caves. These caves are not as lifeless as I thought; a spider crawls across my face. I'm as still as stone.

Soon, the drones have completed their search pattern and dropped sensors all over the place. I can hear them through the rock, so now I have a mental map of the caves stretching out down here. I wait.

They send the recall, and the drones whine past on the way up. They lower ropes and rappel down the shaft. They pause by the pool, scanning the tunnels and blasting sensor pulses of sound, and likely radar and other scans as well. I wait.

They move carefully down the tunnels. I can feel their every movement through the rock, hear their every word. These men know what they are doing: staying in pairs, staying in constant communication, and checking corners carefully. I wait.

One pair comes up next to me. They pause. One of them has bad breath. I can feel the tension; they know something is wrong. They could shoot me any instant. I wait.

"Let's make sure." I hear a deep voice and a switch clicks.

Heat and fire fill the tunnel. I can see red light through the fibers. Roaring fire sucks all the air away, and the fibers seal my nose before I inhale flame. The fibers protect me from the liquid flame that covers everything. I can feel the heat slowly begin to burn through.

It's time.

* * * * *

Get "Warrior: Integration" now at:
https://www.amazon.com/dp/B0875SPH86

Find out more about David Hallquist and "Warrior: Integration" at:
https://chriskennedypublishing.com/

* * * * *

Made in the USA
Monee, IL
21 December 2021